Whatever Happened to Emmeline?

Whatever Happened to Emmeline?

Nicole Schubert

Earnest Parc Press

Whatever Happened to Emmeline?/Nicole Schubert.--1st ed.

ISBN paperback: 979-8-9873441-1-8
ISBN eBook: 979-8-9873441-2-5

For my lovely friends Deirdre Arthur Malafronte and
Jessica Cohen Herbert

CONTENTS

CONTENTS

CONTENTS

CONTENTS

Panic in the Coffin

There it was again, in Clara's dream—the woods, pines, grey skies—suddenly surrounding her. And the dampness. It was always damp, the air thick with the smell of wet pine needles carpeting the dark, rich earth, new growth pushing upward, towards the light. A moment of beauty until she felt the fear grip her stomach as it always did. She continued walking anyways, slowly, barefoot, gently, the moss tickling, waking, cradling the soles of her feet, the damp needles comforting in spite of the inevitable. It was inevitable— the fate of that moment, repeating itself, always repeating in every dream, as much as she didn't want it to.

The clearing came into view—the rain drizzling on her long hair. She never looked down to see her hair, but she felt it, damp, clinging to her shoulders, her white cotton nightgown hugging her body, fresh, cold drops running down her face as she stepped into the small clearing.

As much as Clara wanted to, she couldn't look away, run away, her feet were immobile. But she forced herself to take in what lay before her—the two simple gravestones and the rain drizzling down on top of them.

Clara wanted to turn but it was impossible. Fear gripped her again. She spotted the house, through the trees somehow—not really seeing it but assuming it was there and that it was an old craftsman in style. Or was it just a knowing that it existed in the distance without her actually seeing the house? It wasn't clear. But it made Clara's heart race.

And there was the rat—always the rat, coming from behind the trunk of the sturdy pine that guarded the graves—scampering over to the headstone, the one at the right, the one with the wood casket peeking up through the dirt at the corner. The rat disappeared down into the casket.

Then, there was the scream, her scream— *Was it her scream?*—filling her ears like a vortex. And BAM. WHOOSH—

She was in. In the coffin. Damp. Water dripping. Heart pounding. Blood-rush roaring. The rat running up along the skeleton—feet, thighs, ribs then up to the nest coddled by the hand, as if Clara could feel the sensation on her skin—tiny, quick, padded paws scampering up, up to the bones of the hand, her hand—as if the rat were scampering up her own body, even though she knew it was the skeleton. Again that knowing. But was she the skeleton? Clara?

Then, Clara felt the rat jump from the hand into the nest, where the baby mice waited next to the broken pinky finger jutting out at a strange angle, just like Clara's crooked pinky in real life.

Clara wanted to scream in the dream. And be free. Free. *Please someone help me escape this prison.*

Which is when Clara awoke with a start, a quiet gasp. Her eyes opened. She saw her own hands on the pillow in front of her as she lay on her side. They rested on the white, perfectly ironed, cotton pillow cover, 500 thread count, sateen finish, from her favorite shop on Walton Street in London—her pinky finger jutting out at a strange angle just like the skeleton in the dream, like it always had since she was born. She was born with that crooked pinky.

Clara quickly looked away from her hand and the crooked finger to calm herself and get her bearings. She looked out the window —through the beautiful, old, willow-green window frame she'd painted just last month, past the cheerful lemon-yellow tulle curtains Greta had sewn for her—out to the tree with the shimmering bright-green leaves just outside, grey sky, morning, drizzle, the next house over, a gorgeous, old brownstone like theirs, with a laundry line and playhouse in their backyard. In Brooklyn. She loved Brooklyn. *Remember, you love it here*, Clara told herself, trying to get away from the dream—to the now.

Be here, be now, Clara repeated in her head as Seamus rolled effortlessly towards her and sleepily wrapped his strong, lightly tanned arm around her. He felt warm, loving, spooning, cozy. God, how Clara loved him. They fit so perfectly together. *He is perfect*, Clara thought and told herself, *And you are safe*.

"You okay?" Seamus asked, gently kissing her neck. Clara felt Seamus's strength, his confidence, his protection, and let herself melt into it, wishing this endless inner turmoil away, focusing on the golden hairs covering his sun-kissed forearm, blending seamlessly into her light, creamy-brown skin, two varied shades, similar but different, no stain of her inner pain visible.

Plus, looking at their arms together gave Clara something else in the now. And she did everything to stay focused. On the physical, the present, their skin, their bodies—slowly allowing herself to escape into the moment. It did always work. And that certainty was a relief, thought Clara. Also, she knew Seamus wouldn't ask her about the dream. For that she was grateful. They'd been over it too many times—her being trapped in the coffin. That's all she ever told him, no details. She didn't see the point, and it was enough for Seamus, enough for him to understand that she needed comforting.

Seamus kissed Clara's shoulder, turned her towards him, his lips knowing. Clara closed her eyes and let Seamus embrace her. Was she ready? *Probably not*, she thought, but being with Seamus would take her away from the dream. And it was all she wanted: to love and be one with her love, to feel him next to her, melting together. And Clara promised herself, like she did every time, that she would continue trying until they succeeded.

And slowly, she got there—to that place of letting go, turning off her mind completely at last to focus only on the sensations in her body, on the man embracing her, on the present moment. Clara felt the fear and anxiety fall away, replaced by a surge of warmth as Seamus pulled her closer, lips exploring, kissing her with intention, his beautiful confidence, playfulness enveloping her, touching her soul and body, drawing out her own beauty. This was the reason she had loved Seamus from the start—that deep, unexplainable, poetic connection, as if eternal and unfathomable. And Clara knew Seamus felt it too. He loved her, and she knew it as truth.

But as Clara let herself go, the inevitable began to happen, again—her other unexplainable, inescapable truth. She felt her lungs tighten, her upper airway squeeze. Belabored breathing. *No air.* Struggling. Gasping. Unable to speak—*no air, no air, can't breathe!*

"Oh, shoot," Seamus cried, realizing, scrambling for Clara's inhaler in the nightstand. She grabbed it from him, pressed it down, drawing in the cool droplets, and finally getting air. A relief, but with it came the pain, desperation and tears that gave her away, revealing her true emotions. Clara didn't want to reveal them. There was already enough revealing between her and Seamus. And it always brought the sorrow amidst the love. And Clara wished with all her heart that this wouldn't happen ever again, and every time.

"Don't think about it," Seamus comforted, "I love you—that's all that matters," his warm smile reassuring.

Clara nodded, forcing herself to appear comforted. "I'm going to see Goldberg today," she told him as she sat up and took another breath with the inhaler.

"You really think that's helping?" Seamus asked, delicately.

"At least it's something," Clara replied, even though she didn't think her analysis sessions with Dr. Goldberg were helping at all.

"And *something* is what we need," Seamus added playfully, deftly abandoning his doubt and replacing it with humor, smiling as if everything were perfectly fine. He kissed Clara's forehead and went into the bathroom.

Clara leaned back against the headboard. Everything was not perfect, and they both knew it, even though it definitely had been. Before. But now, their life seemed to be a constant throbbing ache, and as Clara leaned back, she saw Seamus's truth through the crack in the bathroom door—the new, gorgeous brushed-iron track lights highlighting him as he leaned forward on the sink, heavy, head hanging down, shaking, almost weeping but not quite getting there, not getting the relief that would come with tears. And the truth that Clara saw through the door was that Seamus was entirely defeated.

Which just made everything worse, Clara's heart clutching with sorrow.

Cracks in the Morning Show

Clara sat at the kitchen island, still in her cotton nightgown, covered by an elegant sage-green robe—the picture of refined class and beauty, with just a hint of artist. She sipped coffee and jumped back and forth between perusing social media—her favorite escape —and stealthily checking on her business partner, Greta—the one who had made the tulle curtains for her, to help cheer her up. Greta had also taken the reigns to their dress label, Frock, last summer, so that Clara could take a hiatus. Still, it was hard for Clara to stay hands-off even though Greta let her dabble in fabrics and ideas whenever she wanted to.

Clara and Greta met at NYU ten years prior—Clara studying art and design and Greta business and fashion. That's where they started Frock—from their dorms, for fun—before it took off. Greta sewed dresses for herself and friends regularly, and when Clara, on a whim, designed a few fun fabrics for Greta's creations, the magic happened. And before they knew it, their simple-but-whimsically patterned dresses and skirts were in boutiques throughout the city. By the time Clara and Greta graduated, the dresses could be found in Paris and London, and a few years later, Frock became an international success.

Clara loved their little-but-not-so-little business, but she'd been unable to show up emotionally after her second miscarriage a year ago. She'd lost all motivation and any real ability to concentrate and be there professionally. Luckily, Greta was a business maven and was happy leading the charge while Clara recovered and tried again for another pregnancy. Greta encouraged Clara to continue to choose fabrics for the Frock dresses and skirts whenever possible, the key ingredient to the line's success. Having a good eye was Clara's natural gift as an artist—knowing what popped and what made a fabric playful, classical and gorgeous all at once.

Today, Clara was deciding between pears, pinecones, canoes and white-spotted red mushrooms. She liked them all and was happy Greta had found a fabulous designer to take her place—for now, while she was on this awful, extended hiatus. Clara picked the canoes and mushrooms and suggested adding something coniferous to the canoe print. *Perhaps pinecones somewhere in the design?* Clara texted Greta.

Which is when Seamus sauntered into the kitchen humming. Clara was relieved that he was happy again. It was good for both of them and inspired her to stay positive. Or at least try.

Seamus grabbed cereal from the cupboard and watched Clara. She liked how he paid such close attention to her every move and was always present. Clara glanced up quickly with a coy smirk before diving back into the photo dump her friend Kate had just posted that morning. It was from the backpacking trip through Europe they'd done together just after college. It was hard to look away from all the silly faces, especially Jake's—he was her ex, wearing a weird lobster hat from Sitges, Spain. Clara couldn't contain a laugh

"What's so funny?" Seamus asked, coming over, glancing over her shoulder to see what she was so amused by.

Clara quickly switched windows to hide her abandon, embarrassed. "Nothing. Just, Kate and Jake. From that trip to Greece. A million years ago," she told him and smiled up lovingly at his stubbly mug, scratching his chin, catching a flicker of jealousy, which he quickly hid. "Here, fine, I'll show you the photos," Clara conceded playfully, "just ignore my hair," as she switched back to the Europe trip photos on her screen.

"Oh, yeah, I saw that this morning," Seamus teased, grinning.

"It is morning."

"Look at that hair! Frizz! Fro! Retro! What were you in Earth, Wind and Fire or something? Oh, wait, that's before your time." Clara smirked up at him, playing along with his jest. "And mine too," Seamus added, "way before my time," then he went back to the counter to grab a bowl and spoon for his cereal as if completely unfazed by the photos of Clara with her ex.

Seamus followed both Kate and Jake on social media too, even though Clara had dated Jake. But as Seamus always said, he trusted Clara, and Clara knew Seamus could trust her. She'd never cheat on him. Also, Jake was so long ago, long before Seamus. And Clara's feelings for Jake hadn't even come close to how deeply she loved Seamus. Her feelings for Jake were light, fleeting, whereas her love for Seamus was heavy, dense, textured. It touched her soul—then, now, and maybe always.

Besides, Clara figured a little jealousy never hurt anyone. She even admittedly relished in Seamus's cute, protective, possessiveness. It made her feel beautiful and wanted. It was part of Seamus's magnetism and their attraction—their back and forth.

"I was young," Clara replied to his chiding of the photos, playfully flirting.

He flirted back, "And you always will be much younger than..."

"You!" Clara cried out as Seamus simultaneously bellowed with amusement, "...me!" Seamus was fifteen years older than Clara. He was forty-five, and Clara would turn thirty in August—four months from now. They were forty and twenty-five when they met. The age difference wasn't an issue at all now. And it never had been.

They laughed together at their favorite self-deprecating joke, and Seamus sat down on the newly painted country-red barstool next to Clara to eat his granola with goji berries and raw goat milk. Clara loved that Seamus was so healthy and fit, and she admired his arms again for a moment and his whole being—the perfect blend of hot and nerdy gaming entrepreneur. Then, she went back to her friends' photos, amused and finally relaxed.

Which encouraged Seamus. He needed her to be in a good place for what he was about to say. "So, I've been thinking," Seamus ventured in, testing the waters, looking for Clara's reaction.

"Uh, oh," Clara teased. She could tell he was about to lay something big on her. He had that look on his face like when he presented a new idea to an investor—charming, confident, but not too confident, leaving room for input, making sure the door stayed open if the investor wasn't onboard, friendly, diplomatic.

"Now, let this sink in before you say anything," Seamus tested further, "Okay?" pausing playfully, hoping she'd be patient.

Clara toyed with him, "Oh, this should be good. Go on."

Seamus chuckled. He'd just have to go for it. "Okay. What if we spent the summer at the lake house?"

Clara paused. "*Your* house?" she laughed. This was surprising. And odd. Seamus never talked about the lake house, the Dunne family house where he grew up. In fact, he hadn't been there in years. And it was boarded up.

"Yeah. You'd love it," Seamus insisted. "It's beautiful. Quiet. You could relax."

Clara studied him. "The house you haven't been to since you were eighteen?" This was so unexpected. What was he doing?

"Derek, opened it up last week," Seamus continued, as if it were no big deal when it clearly was a huge deal.

"The house where no one's lived for thirty years?!" Clara exclaimed, unable to contain her shock any longer.

"He said it's fine," Seamus defended. "We could stay there. And you could fix it up. You'd love fixing it up. Flowers. Fresh paint. Your thing."

"Why are you doing this?" Clara asked, even though she was starting to see exactly what he was doing—he was trying to fix *her*—and she didn't want to be fixed.

"Because it's close," Seamus replied. "You could have a vacation, and I can still come in to work." He shrugged and smiled, again trying to be nonchalant. "I could drive or hop on a quick commuter. A couple hours each way. Win win."

"You don't even like it there—*too small, nosey people*. And your brother. You should sell it."

Pain flashed across Seamus's face. But he hid it well, taking another bite of cereal. Still, Clara saw. And she knew: That house caused Seamus nothing but sorrow. And she couldn't fathom why he and his brother kept it or why he would want them to go there. Were they really still holding onto their parents' death that tightly?

"I'm sorry," Clara apologized. "I know it's special."

"Which is why this'd be good," Seamus persisted. "Spend time there with a new perspective. And—" He stopped, afraid to go on.

Clara felt it. "And me," she said, the squeezing ache clutching her heart again, a different ache—spurned by worry that something was wrong with her. That she wasn't good enough to be a mother and that's why fate was keeping it from her. And now he was making it her fault. Anger was right behind the sorrow. "Just say it," Clara insisted. "Maybe it'll fix me."

"Clara, we need to change something," Seamus pleaded. "Whatever we're doing isn't working."

"I need to not feel pressure!" Clara shouted and stood up, grabbing her mug. She threw it in the sink with a loud crack. "Oh, no," she gasped, sure she'd just broken the beautiful ceramic piece. It had been her grandmother Selma's. She picked it up carefully and examined it. "It's fine," Clara uttered in relief and rinsed out the flowered teacup gently, then put it on the side in the dish rack. "My gran's," Clara told Seamus, barely audibly, "I miss her. Dearest Gran Selma."

Seamus got up and took Clara in his arms and held her tight. "Please, at least consider it, the lake house, for a couple of months, for the summer," he said. "Or we can go now and fix it up before summer. You can help me ease in. Redecorate. Plant things. And there's a guesthouse. And one of those great old porches with a swing. You can turn the guesthouse into a studio. Get back into photography. Drawing! Maybe you can try some new fabric prints again."

Clara pulled away. Angry. "What do you think I've been doing here?" she demanded, so frustrated, the pain rearing its head—because Seamus nailed it, the elephant in the room: Clara hadn't been doing any design at all for a very long time even though she tried to, pretended to, and they both knew it.

They stared. Frustration filled the space between them. They'd been here a million times.

Seamus backed down. "Maybe *I* could use the change," he admitted, defeated, and went back to the kitchen island and his cereal.

This was too much for Clara. It was one thing to deal with her own despair, but she couldn't even think about his. *Especially now,* she thought, *Why is he doing this now? When I need him to be the strong one!*

Clara shook her head, feeling the anger rise again. She grabbed her laptop and wound her way through the house—modern design, arcade games, gaming posters. A pleasant mix of youth and style.

Halfway down the hallway, Clara passed the nursery and stopped. A hot searing pain rose from her stomach, through her heart, to her throat, like a vice with a lock. And she couldn't get herself to pass the doorway. Her feet were like lead, too heavy to lift, just like in her dream. But they allowed her to turn towards the nursery as her instinct called her to do so. Or maybe, the nursery itself was calling her, pulling her closer as if there was no escape.

She went in, staring, her heart racing as she took in the perfectly decorated room—everything she'd always dreamed of and imagined in a nursery. It was almost the same as her room as a little girl—a white antique dresser, soft green rug covering most of the beautifully stained hardwood floor. She held back tears as her eyes scanned the whimsical wall art that her parents had sent the previous month, early March, before it happened again—Beatrix Potter characters, painted on thick cardboard cutouts. They were timeless. They were from her favorite books as a child. Mrs. Tiggy-Winkle, Jemima Puddle-Duck, Tom Kitten, Squirrel Nutkin, Peter Rabbit and Flopsy, Mopsy and Cotton-tail. Clara and her mom had seen the art in a little shop in London when her dad was at the embassy there—up until last year.

London had also been Clara's favorite of her dad's stations in the foreign service. She loved the English traditions—charm, romance, classical decor, the tea, the cucumber sandwiches, the pomp, the manners—and even the countryside. It had sparked her imagination, and she'd designed a line of dress fabrics inspired by it.

That was last year, before the despair and her inability to create set in. She'd made one fabulous dress print with country stone walls covered in pink fairy foxgloves. Another with metal dairy-milk cans and black-and-white cows. She designed a fabric dotted with a variety of pub signs. Another had old, red, British phone booths, and one was covered in tea cups. Clara had also designed a series of English garden fabrics with traditional blooms like pinks, hollyhocks, delphiniums, lavender, primroses, hydrangeas and foxgloves. And one dress fabric inspired by a trip north with beautiful, rustic Scottish Highland cattle.

But that was then and this was now, a year later, and Clara's eyes moved from the charming nursery art to the latest package from her parents sitting on the dresser, opened but not unpacked. They had sent a few onesies from Brussels, where Clara's father was currently stationed as embassy head. The onesies were still in the box of goodies that had arrived early the previous week—four days too late, four days after the inevitable, unbearable, unthinkably sad occurrence: her third miscarriage. Also in the box were her dad's Ugg house slippers. They seemed to have managed to sneak into the package as if by accident, but Clara knew their presence was no coincidence. Clara always co-opted those slippers whenever she was visiting her parents—they were just too soft and cozy to pass up, so surely, her parents had sent them along on purpose as a surprise. *So, sweet,* Clara thought, which made her heart ache more. Which made her feel so inadequate. Which made her feel the pain that her parents were surely feeling as well over this miscarriage. Which made her not want to talk to them about her own pain. Or lean on them for support. Even though she could use their support.

Clara missed her parents so much, but she never wanted to cause them more distress than needed, and if they understood how much she was grieving over this new loss, it surely would only increase their own. So, instead of going to visit her parents or doing anything to find comfort from them directly, Clara pulled the Uggs out of the box and slipped them on her bare feet—much more comforting than the moss on the forest floor in the dream, she thought. The slippers made her feel safe.

But as soon as Clara looked back up at her beloved Mrs. Tiggy-Winkle art above the beautiful light-pine crib that she and Seamus had so carefully chosen, Clara's stomach clenched in dread and fear. She looked at the tiny mattress tucked neatly in the beautiful sage-colored sheets they'd picked out because they hadn't wanted to know if their baby was a boy or girl, even though, once again, they'd made it far enough to find out—before the inevitable.

"Maybe we can get someone to come and clear out the nursery," Clara yelled out to Seamus, which prompted tears, and she clutched the rail of the crib and leaned on it for a moment.

The pain gripped Seamus too as he sat at the kitchen island. "Please, can we wait—just a little longer?" he asked, voice quivering.

Clara squeezed the railing as tightly as possible as the pain in his voice traveled to her—through the kitchen, down the hall, into the room and straight through her back, past her spine—and there, it cut like a knife into her own wound in her heart. She nodded to herself, shut down her feelings with every ounce of strength she had, released her grip on the crib and went out, slowly closing the nursery door, then disappearing down the hall, clomping along in her father's oversized Ugg slippers. The heaviness of her silence and inability to reply to her beloved Seamus permeating the whole house and space between them.

Clara stopped at the door to their bedroom, realizing she hadn't even looked back at him when she came out of the nursery door— which just made everything worse. Was it really coming to this?

Would they be able to come back to normal a third time after such a tragic loss of another baby?

Clara couldn't think about it now. She just couldn't do it. She needed to recover on her own first before thinking about him and entered their bedroom and locked herself in the bathroom where she could stay until Seamus left for work. She knew he wouldn't come in. He had that meeting with the venture capital people he was wooing for his latest gaming app.

And Clara knew he wouldn't come back there to see her before he left, because if he did, both of them might crumble.

3 |

What If I Can't Have a Baby?

After Seamus left for his meeting, Clara finally was able to shed some of her sorrow, at least for the moment, and found her way into her element—watering and trimming her many potted plants in the bay window in the kitchen nook. She was so happy Seamus had insisted she include her window design in the remodel. That was before the last miscarriage and after the second. The remodel had been an excellent escape during that time. It had allowed her to heal. And now, she was relieved it was done so that she could appreciate all the details and lose herself in the moment.

Clara gently and caringly trimmed the white hydrangeas. She had a way with nurturing plants that soothed her. It was like a meditation. Her mind could go blank, focusing on the growth in her hands and tending to it. She disappeared into the moment, picking the few fallen leaves and old growth in the cyclamen pots, then pressing down on the soft earth of her favorite, the African violet. *So pretty,* she thought. Then, she sat back on her heels for a moment to itch her nose with the back of her potting glove.

As always, the stunning beauty outside the window caught her eye. She'd done a happy, more-vibrant look around the patio for the spring last week as a distraction. The plants were young but already starting to bustle with pink and purple hydrangeas, ready to engulf the window and spill onto the top—that was the plan—along with ivy, white anemones, lavender wisteria and soft-pink dogwood. She'd seen something similar at their favorite brunch spot, Court Street Tavern, last summer and had been inspired. And now, it brought her so much joy. And peace. And hopefully, there wouldn't be a frost. It was getting to be mid April after all, so they should be fine. Which is what she was thinking—

—when the doorbell rang and in burst Clara's friend Erin, a wonderful goofball and happy mom of three, the latest of the brood, Henry, in a Baby Bjorn on her chest. Clara and Erin had met at a pregnancy yoga class two years earlier when Clara had made it to five months with her first pregnancy. Erin had helped her through that first miscarriage, and the next, and had invited her and Seamus into their little family as it grew.

Surprisingly, that welcome had quelled some of Clara's fears. At first. And it gave both her and Seamus hope to see Erin and her husband, Joe, waddle through building a family with a ton of joy, humor, imperfections and some grace and style to boot.

"Tada!" Erin exclaimed as she rushed over, holding up her phone for Clara to see her screen. "Confirmation with *the* best new massage therapist in town: Heister, at Chill. And he's hot. We both have appointments this afternoon." But Erin's joy disappeared when she saw Clara's face looking up with a sad, forced smile. Erin frowned.

"It happened again," Clara managed.

Erin knew exactly what Clara meant. It meant Clara had had another asthma attack during sex. "With Seamus?" Erin asked. "When you were...?"

Clara nodded and stood up, taking off her potting gloves.

"Well, then, lucky for you I came over here to make sure you get to that shrink of yours," Erin said with a grin.

Clara groaned. "Which is probably a waste of time. Coffee?" she asked and walked over to the counter to pour a cup for herself from the French press. "No, wait, you're not doing coffee still," Clara remembered. "Henry's got you on track with the healthy boob milk, right?"

Erin laughed. "Exactly. He's got good taste."

Clara poured thick cream into her coffee, a lot of it. "And, yeah, I'm not holding my breath," Clara said. "Terrible asthma pun—but yes, head-shrink time." She grinned, eye-brows raised, amused at her own joke as she took a sip of the warm, soothing coffee.

"Hey, be happy you can go to Goldberger, digger, dream-maker. If I'd had three miscarriages, you'd be wiping me off the floor, not giving me an inhaler and an overpaid ear."

Clara smiled at her friend, but then, the tears came, and Erin gave Clara a much-needed hug, careful not to squeeze cooing Henry between them. "And, just so you know," Erin told her, "Seamus not only sent me here to take you to the overpaid shrink, which *he* thinks is a huge waste of time. Because *he* doesn't want you driving there on your own. And *he* is concerned. Which is *the* absolute sweetest and hottest thing. So count your lucky stars. He also wants me to convince you to go to the summer lake house."

Clara groaned and pulled away from the hug to look her friend in the eye.

Erin smirked. "I know, he's over-involved," she continued, "but one day, when you have five kids, you will be very happy about that."

Clara laughed. She loved her friend Erin. "Easy for you to say."

"It is easy for me to say," Erin agreed with another grin on her face.

"Meanwhile, I'll be living in a one-horse town, bored and lonely." Clara sipped her coffee and leaned back on the kitchen counter.

"It's two months!" Erin proclaimed. "Or a bit more. If you like. An hour or two away. Or so. Why won't you give yourself this? I'll come visit. You can come to Montauk and babysit if you're bored. Little baby weekday trips when Seamus's at work. You'll get through."

Clara stopped. It was too emotional. Her eyes welled up. "I don't even know anymore."

"Oh, honey." Erin moved in for another hug.

"I'm so afraid I won't be able to have a baby," Clara cried.

Henry squealed between them and the hug. "You do know that miscarriages are a good sign, right?" Erin assured her. "Remember? It means that you can get pregnant!"

"Can you please stop saying that?" Clara insisted, pulling back, wiping her eyes and looking at her well-meaning friend.

Erin continued anyway. She wasn't going to let this opportunity for hopeful, positive encouragement slip by. "It means that your body is fine," Erin insisted. "You just need to find a way to calm your spirit."

4

Blood on the Dress

Clara's heart pounded, nerves racing as she sat across from her psychiatrist, Dr. Maxine Goldberg, reminding herself that she was simply there to calm her spirit. *Just relax,* Clara told herself as she looked at Dr. Goldberg's warm, brown eyes deftly hidden behind black-rimmed glasses. *She's so, calm,* Clara thought. *Why is she always so calm? And why is she just sitting there waiting for me to talk? I don't want to talk any more!*

Dr. Goldberg liked having the thicker frames corralling her eyes. They made her feel like she was exuding an air of professionalism even when a client's story struck a chord and she couldn't help but get emotional. Clara's story was like that sometimes—Clara's grief each time she lost a child—but Dr. Goldberg always managed to hide her own feelings.

Which is why Clara endlessly wondered if Dr. Goldberg had any feelings at all. There had been a couple of times when she had seemed vulnerable, but mostly, she kept the focus of each session on Clara, which, if Clara was honest, always felt so abrasive. Why couldn't Dr. Goldberg be more human? Have a real reaction? It was as if Clara were hitting badminton birdies and, instead of getting in there herself to hit them back, Dr. Goldberg was using a mirrored shield that mechanically blasted the badminton birdies back at Clara, the red-rubber end giving her little bruises of her own reality.

And today, Clara was already overwhelmed by that reality, which is why they were sitting there staring at each other. It was her first visit back since her miscarriage three weeks ago. They'd just gotten through Clara's pained description of the events, including the asthma attack, and Seamus's suggestion that they go to the lake house for the summer, and now, Dr. Goldberg seemed to be waiting for more and Clara didn't know what to say, which is why her heart was pounding so loud—panic consuming her as she worried that there was no solution to her distress, especially if she was supposed to come up with it on her own. *If only Dr. Goldberg would lift the mirror!* Clara thought.

Which is when they heard a scream and a bang from the next room, the waiting room, and saw Erin rush by, singing, "Sorrry," and yelling, "Jack, no!" Erin disappeared from view and then, a moment later, peeked back through the door joining the two rooms with a smile. "Sorry," Erin repeated and shut the door.

Clara laughed. The interruption was a relief in any case and shook up the standstill. Dr. Goldberg seemed to agree, chuckling warmly. At least Dr. Goldberg had a sense of humor behind that emotional brick wall, Clara thought. She also managed to keep their sessions friendly, which is what kept Clara coming back at all and gave her hope that maybe Dr. Goldberg could help her. Clara didn't know anything personal about Dr. Goldberg except from the diplomas on the walls and a few family photos on her desk, so she didn't have much to go on. The diplomas were from Yale and Columbia, and one of the photos told Clara that Dr. Goldberg was married and had a daughter that looked about ten years old. Clara didn't know when the photo was taken so she couldn't be sure about the daughter's age, but she did know from the photo that the Goldbergs had gone on a tropical vacation once where the three of them bought touristy flower-and-palm-tree-patterned outfits. Clara guessed that Dr. Goldberg was somewhere in her forties or fifties and assumed that Dr. Goldberg had waited to get married and have her daughter until after she had earned her medical degree. Dr. Goldberg just seemed so practical and her diplomas had her maiden name on them, which was Cohen, so Clara's assumptions made sense. Plus, Dr. Goldberg's husband looked just like her: conservative in his button-down shirt in another of the photos, so he probably would've wanted to wait until graduating before getting married too. Clara guessed they'd met at med school or something. There was also a photo of two teenage girls on Dr. Goldberg's desk that looked like it was from the 80s or 90s. Clara wondered if it was Dr. Goldberg with a friend or sister. Or maybe, it was her nieces, and Clara was wrong about the time period.

"So, you're considering this move," Dr. Goldberg launched back in, breaking the silence and Clara's musings, much to Clara's relief, and getting on with their session after Jack's outburst and Erin's ever-comical-and-loveable parenting.

"Temporary visit. For the summer. Yes," Clara replied.

"So you can relax for a few months," Dr. Goldberg said with that assuring-analyst nod that Clara always found so stereotypical and annoying even though it *was* better than the badminton birdies coming back at her.

"If you call two months of being alone and doing nothing relaxing," Clara volleyed back.

"I think it sounds good," Dr. Goldberg told Clara. "There'd be plenty to do fixing up the place. Now, how about the asthma?"

This question made Clara uncomfortable, but she nodded, resigned to the fact that it was best to put everything on the table here. "Yeah, it happened again," she said.

"With Seamus?" Dr. Goldberg asked.

"Yes," Clara replied.

"And only with Seamus," Dr. Goldberg pressed.

"Yes, I already told you that," Clara said, unable to hide her annoyance at having to repeat this fact again.

"Alright, then," Dr. Goldberg said, changing her angle, "since this asthma is relatively new, we're going to see if we can't figure out where it's coming from."

"It's not that new," Clara reminded Dr. Goldberg. They'd been over this painful tidbit before many times as well.

"You said you started getting asthma when you met Seamus," Dr. Goldberg continued.

"When I moved in with him," Clara clarified.

"Well, that's relatively new, given that it was two years ago. Right?"

"Look, I have asthma because of the pollen," Clara snapped. "It's summer, and it's horrible in our neighborhood." Dr. Goldberg shot Clara a look, and Clara backed down, knowing she'd only snapped because she really didn't want to talk about this or anything. *I don't want to be here!* she cried in her head.

Dr. Goldberg continued, "Alright, now, what we're going to do may seem a tad unconventional compared with what we've been doing until this session, but I've been using the technique for many years, and it's proven to be quite helpful in discovering instances which we choose not to remember, whatever the reason may be."

This sounded awful to Clara. The last thing she needed now was more discomfort and emotion, but she agreed, "Okay." She just wanted this to be over with.

"Now, first, I'd like you to close your eyes and relax," Dr. Goldberg began.

"Oh, no," Clara said, instantly realizing what Dr. Goldberg was up to. "I am not going to be hypnotized," she said. Dr. Goldberg had briefly mentioned hypnosis in their initial get-acquainted meeting. She'd explained to Clara that hypnosis was a tool she used sometimes, but it was one among many tools and Clara hadn't really thought more about it since that meeting.

"Is there a reason why not?" Dr. Goldberg inquired. "Why you don't want to try it? Or is there something you're afraid of?"

Clara grimaced. She knew where this was going too—if she started answering Dr. Goldberg's questions, they'd just talk about her fears over and over and get nowhere, like they'd been doing for the nine months or so since she'd been seeing Dr. Goldberg. Her alternative would be to try something new.

"You never know," Dr. Goldberg assured Clara, "this asthma may be showing you something that you don't want to look at. And we haven't actually explored it yet more deeply since we've mainly focused on the grief."

Blah, blah, yes, yes, I know this, thought Clara.

"I think it's a good launching point at this time," Dr. Goldberg continued. "A new angle."

Clara nodded—the irritation bubbling up again even though she knew she was better off playing her part in the analysis than resisting. It was just so painful when she let her guard down. But these miscarriages and asthma were coming out of nowhere and she didn't know why, and at this point, she was willing to try anything, even if she didn't believe in it. "Fine, tell me what to do," Clara said.

"There you go," Dr. Goldberg chimed and smiled. "Good choice."

Clara exhaled, nodding in agreement, surrendering defeat to her awful fate.

"Okay, let's start with closing your eyes and breathing in and out through your nose like we've done before," Dr. Goldberg began, "focusing on the air as it enters, travels through and then leaves your body."

Clara closed her eyes and let Dr. Goldberg draw her into a place of relaxation, breathing in and out through her nose, paying attention to her breath, letting go of each part of her body, slowly, as she imagined the oxygen traveling through her entire being.

Finally, Clara got to a point of relaxation from head to toe, and Dr. Goldberg leaned back in her high-backed chair with her notebook and started, "Now, on this journey, I want you to remember that we're looking for an answer to a simple question: When did this asthma begin and why, okay?"

Clara nodded.

"Excellent," Dr. Goldberg continued with her calm, steady, assuring voice. "Now, first, I'd like you to imagine a place that makes you feel comfortable, at ease, and safe—Clara's safe place. Just like what we've done with meditation."

Clara took a few moments and several more deep breaths before, slowly, an image appeared in her mind. She was sitting on a boulder overlooking a pine-tree-filled valley and a crystal-blue lake. She nodded so Dr. Goldberg knew she was there at her peaceful spot, prompting Dr. Goldberg to continue: "Alright, Clara, now, we're going to go back a year—to a year ago today. What do you remember?"

Clara imagined herself at a desk creating fabric illustrations for Frock, seeing the whole scene as if watching a movie. "I'm working," Clara said. "Wait. But no..." Clara saw herself putting down her pen, grabbing "Anna Karenina" and walking out to a garden with a glass of iced tea. "That's more than a year ago. Before I met Seamus. Before I stopped reading those books," she told Dr. Goldberg with a smirk. She and Dr. Goldberg had spent several sessions discussing how Clara loved romance novels about big loves that withstood time and that Clara was an absurdly romantic idealist.

"Could that be the cause of the asthma?" Dr. Goldberg asked. "Ceasing to read books you love? Holding yourself back?"

Clara laughed, "I don't think so. It's just that I don't have the time. And now, I have Seamus. My own big love." Clara smiled—it was true, and she had no doubts about him.

Dr. Goldberg was pleased and tried to hide her amusement in her voice. "Alright then, how about if we go forward to when you met Seamus," she continued.

Clara imagined herself in a coffee shop, reading one of the diaries of Anais Nin, another romantic indulgence, and then spotting a younger Seamus ordering coffee.

"And?" Dr. Goldberg inquired.

"It's not when we met. It's before we met. When I first saw him at the coffee shop..." Clara imagined Seamus walking by and smiling. "I kept seeing him around," Clara told Dr. Goldberg, "and I just had a feeling." Clara remembered spotting Seamus through a crowd in the subway. He saw her too and smiled. "It was something, some kind of feeling, like he was just...comfortable," Clara added.

"Okay, very good," Dr. Goldberg encouraged. "Continue."

Next, Clara remembered a party at her friend Luna's in the Village. She saw herself getting stoned with Seamus and playing chess. "I see it—where we met. It was a coincidence. At Luna's, a mutual friend. I beat him at chess." Clara laughed. "Seamus said that's why he liked me. Said it was years since anyone had beaten him. And I'd never played before. So it was a strange coincidence." Clara remembered the moment fondly and then saw herself talking to Seamus on giant floor pillows later at the party.

"And why did you like *him*?" Dr. Goldberg asked.

"It felt like I'd come home," Clara said and exhaled with relief, as if she were there, feeling it all again.

"Excellent," encouraged Dr. Goldberg. "Now, let's try to go back to when the asthma started. Go slowly and tell me whatever you see."

Clara instantly saw herself having sex, as if from above, but it was blurry. "I'm with someone," she told Dr. Goldberg.

"Seamus?"

Clara tried to discern whom it was, and slowly, it became clear that she was with her ex, Jake, in a tent. "No, it's my ex," Clara told Dr. Goldberg. "We're in Italy, camping, just outside of Venice. It's hot and uncomfortable; I feel uneasy, on edge. But it's not him that's making me edgy. It's the heat. It's stuffy in the tent, but I'm getting air in my lungs, so this can't be the start of the asthma." Then, suddenly, Clara saw an image of herself at age five drawing a picture of a knight. "And now, it's me drawing my knight," Clara said, her voice suddenly sounding like a child. "And my dragon too."

"How old are you?" Dr. Goldberg asked, witnessing Clara's transition to childhood.

"Five. Mommy likes my knight. And my dragon. She says I'm a good drawer," Clara replied as her five-year-old self.

"Clara, honey, do you ever have trouble breathing?" Dr. Goldberg asked, softening her voice as she spoke.

"No," Clara replied with her five-year-old voice again, and suddenly, the knight turned angry and grew bigger. It came at five-year-old Clara in the vision. She screamed. Then, the angry knight ran past her to the dragon, who took flight and got away.

"Clara, are you okay?" Dr. Goldberg asked.

"The scary knight disappeared," she said, and then, Clara's vision turned to black—all black—and then, Clara heard someone jumping on a bed with squeaky springs, like a cot. The person was laughing so she knew it was a girl. And somehow, she also knew it was a teenage girl. Then, BAM, WHOOSH, Clara was the teenage girl, jumping. And Clara saw the girl's world through her eyes. The room became a blurry streak of colors. The bed was a daybed with a frame like a sofa, with armrests and a back. Then, suddenly, she fell and hit her forehead on the frame.

BAM, Clara snapped out of the moment and back into Dr. Goldberg's office, but everything was hazy—and her forehead hurt as if she'd actually hit it on the armrest of the daybed. Clara grabbed her forehead, damp with sweat. "Ow," Clara said out loud.

"What do you see, honey?" Dr. Goldberg asked gently.

"I don't know, I'm...," Clara replied and began to see a new image—a blurry image, fumbling, a blanket over her face—or was it her tee shirt? The fabric was blue and gauzy. And someone was on the other side of it. Then, WHOOSH, Clara was the girl again under the gauzy fabric, calling out, "It hurts; it hurts"—both in the scene and out loud in the room with Dr. Goldberg. The person on the other side of the thin fabric covered her mouth. Or maybe was kissing her. And stroking her face. Clara wasn't sure.

"Your head hurts?" Dr. Goldberg asked.

"Yes," Clara cried, then the person on the other side of the gauze spoke in a deep voice, telling her, "shh," and that she was okay, that her head was okay, comforting her, saying he was there to help, his face close, kissing her cheek through the cloth, getting on top of her. The girl started crying, afraid, and calling for him to stop, but no sound came out. She had no voice, like she was in a dream, helpless, thinking the words but not able to say them even though she wanted to, her heart racing. The girl felt shame, like this was her fault—the girl's fault, Clara thought, somehow knowing what was in the girl's head. And the girl was wondering, *Why do I have to do this? Why is it the only way?* Clara didn't understand what any of it meant.

Dr. Goldberg observed Clara's distress. Clara was sweating profusely as she recounted what she saw. Then, suddenly, a red spot began to form on Clara's forehead. It looked like blood. Dr. Goldberg felt uneasy as it grew. She'd never seen anything like this before and insisted with urgency, "Alright, Clara, I want you to come back and find your safe place."

Clara began to have trouble breathing.

"And breathe," Dr. Goldberg added.

Clara had a flash of blurriness, then again, she was the girl jumping on the bed.

"Did you find your safe place?" Dr. Goldberg asked.

Clara saw color streaks as she jumped, and then, everything became even more blurry. And then, she was falling, hitting her head again. And she couldn't breathe.

Dr. Goldberg saw Clara grab her head in distress.

"Ow," Clara cried.

"Clara, I want you to wake up now," Dr. Goldberg insisted and clapped, loudly. It didn't work. "Erin?" Dr. Goldberg called out to the waiting room. "Can you come in here? And bring Clara's inhaler!" Dr. Goldberg got up and kneeled in front of Clara, coming down to her level. She took Clara's shoulders, squeezing them firmly, trying to urge Clara back to the present as Clara gasped for air and Erin ran in and grabbed the inhaler out of Clara's bag.

"Clara!" Erin screamed when she saw Clara's face and forehead.

Clara's eyes shot wide open, filled with terror. She grabbed the inhaler from Erin, drawing in the cool drops and finally getting air. She breathed it in, letting it fill her lungs, feeling the relief.

"Are you okay?" Dr. Goldberg asked Clara, trying to hide her concern. "Do you remember what happened?"

Clara shook her head and took a moment. "No, yes, I do. I'm so thirsty." Erin hurried back into the waiting room and returned with a bottle of water. She gave it to Clara while staring at the blood on Clara's forehead, unsure, afraid to say anything, not wanting to make this worse or cause alarm.

Clara drank the water and started to feel better. Erin took her hand and smiled.

"You can tell us what you remember but only if you feel comfortable," Dr. Goldberg said.

Erin squeezed Clara's hand. Clara looked at Erin's smile. It gave her courage and she nodded. "It seemed violent," Clara began, glancing up at Dr. Goldberg. "Like someone was getting hurt. Her head was hurt, but there was more too because she was afraid and embarrassed about herself somehow—because I could feel her feelings— and that shame was worse and more painful to her than actually hitting her head."

Dr. Goldberg nodded, giving Clara assurance, even though the wound on Clara's forehead was making her so uncomfortable behind her thick-framed glasses. "Very good, Clara. Did someone hurt the girl?"

"I, I'm not sure. There was some kind of force, but maybe the sense of violence also came from inside her, like in her throat, like she wanted to scream and couldn't. Like her voice and ability to express herself were bound by some invisible rope. It's not clear. But she wasn't me. I know that. I'm glad she's not me. It makes me feel like I'll be okay. But the girl wasn't. Whoever she was. Do you think I'll be okay?" Clara looked at Dr. Goldberg, voice quivering, feeling quite desperate all of a sudden.

This caught Dr. Goldberg off-guard. "Uh, yes," she managed then pulled it together. "And excellent work," Dr. Goldberg comforted as she saw Clara clutching the skirt of her beautiful Frock dress covered with bees, sewn by Greta, fabric by Clara, and the blood smudging out from under her fingertips. Dr. Goldberg knew she shouldn't push Clara much further but asked another question in hopes of finding some grounding in reality: "And has anything like that ever happened to you?"

"No," Clara replied with certainty—because it never had. And saying it out loud gave Clara so much relief.

Dr. Goldberg watched Clara let go of her grip on the skirt of the bee dress and smooth it out. Dr. Goldberg felt relief too—that Clara was back.

Then, Clara noticed the blood. "Oh my god," she said.

"It's okay," Dr. Goldberg assured Clara. "Don't worry."

"But...," Erin interjected, distressed by the blood as well.

"Your body was sensing pain," Dr. Goldberg explained, "internal pain, and it created the wound. It's unusual but has been documented before. I'll admit I've never seen such a thing but..." Dr. Goldberg stopped and looked down to regroup, then continued. "It's a very good start. Think of it like a psychosomatic reaction that's here to show you something."

Clara's eyes filled with tears.

"No, no," Dr. Goldberg told Clara and handed her the tissues. "This is what we want but in small amounts. And this was a large amount. So, since this isn't about imminent danger—besides the asthma, which I believe we have begun to address here—you will begin to feel more free. And we will give you a break, and I suggest you find a way to take the summer off. Or however long you need. I'm here if you're ready again sooner, but you need to take your time. Okay?"

Clara nodded, wiping away the remaining tears.

"I don't know," said Erin. "I also smell alcohol. Were you drinking in here?" she asked. "This is getting pretty weird."

Clara shook her head. "No." And laughed—a nervous release. "Now you're getting weird," Clara teased Erin.

Dr. Goldberg nodded and wrote down Erin's comment about the alcohol.

"*She* doesn't think I'm getting weird," Erin pointed out about Dr. Goldberg.

Dr. Goldberg looked up in all seriousness. "Yes, this is a bit *weird*, Clara. Erin is right. We're not going to be in denial here, but the mind is powerful and it serves the individual. It seeks to heal. It won't hurt itself. I believe we should trust it. It serves your best interests, Clara, as we all do. We are all here for you and so is your internal compass, and this office is a safe place. Like your rock overlooking the valley. I believe your experience is shining light on a fear. A fear from an experience in your past that gets triggered when you get the asthma. And yes, it's a blessing that the girl you saw and her experience is not your hard reality. I would like, before you go, for us to discuss this a bit further and then for you to find a way to relax for a month or so, like I said. Up to you. The lake house or a trip abroad or to the coast or anything."

Clara nodded.

Erin exhaled. "Okay. I'm going back next door. Call me if you need me."

5

The Girl Behind the Veil

Dr. Goldberg thanked Erin with a warm smile as Erin headed back to the waiting room so she and Clara could finish out the session after Clara's hypnosis.

"You good?" Erin checked with Clara before closing the door behind her, feeling completely uncertain now about this whole freaky therapy experience.

"Yes, yes, thank you," Clara told Erin. "We're gonna get this over with so we can get to that massage." Clara wasn't certain either if continuing this session would help, but she really did want to hear what Dr. Goldberg had to say, hoping for more relief.

Erin laughed, "Fine," shaking her head as she saw Henry throwing blocks. "No!" Erin yelled and shut the door behind her, leaving her friend Clara to mine the depths of her psyche.

Clara looked at Dr. Goldberg apologetically. "I'm sorry. I feel so bad. Like this is all my fault. Like something's wrong with me."

"You're being human," Dr. Goldberg assured Clara. "You're experiencing something deep inside—emotions, your spirit, some kind of trauma—and it's manifesting itself in your body."

"But I never had trauma before. Before the miscarriages, my life was fine. Except the asthma. Which came shortly before the first miscarriage. But that's what's so weird. No trauma. So, what could possibly cause me so much stress?"

"That's why we're here, Clara," Dr. Goldberg said with a comforting smile. "To find the symbolic meaning. Something is pushing you to be afraid. And it is likely an irrational fear. We have those you know." She smiled again. "So, why don't we just go back for a minute to the bed that the teenage girl was jumping on, in your imagination, the symbolic bed frame, right after you felt like you hit your head."

"I don't want to go back," Clara said.

"Let me rephrase that. When you felt the *girl* hit her head. No need to go back into the deeper hypnosis. We'll just recap what happened in words and understand the feelings behind it. You mentioned a force or pressure from the other side of the blue gauze. Perhaps a man. Was that force hurting you?"

Clara thought about it for a moment. "No. The force...it was...someone trying to help, but the girl didn't want his help or need it, and she tried to say no but the person couldn't hear. And maybe it was because her voice didn't actually come out."

"Do you know who it was? On the other side of the gauze? An acquaintance of the girl? Or maybe it was someone *you* know?"

Clara shook her head. "No, I don't know who it was, but he seemed to love her. He was kissing her."

"So, a lover of some kind," Dr. Goldberg said.

Clara laughed. "Lover. That's such a funny word. My grandma used to say that—*Oh, is he your lover?* she'd tease me. I miss her so much, my Nana."

"Do you think something bad happened to your grandmother?" Dr. Goldberg asked.

Clara laughed again, exasperated. "No. I think you're reaching."

"Okay," Dr. Goldberg said. "We're just investigating. No need to get frustrated. Now, does the guy on the other side of the gauze *feel* like Seamus? Or your ex—Jake? From the tent?"

"No," Clara said.

"Okay, great. That is good news." Dr. Goldberg smiled, even though she was starting to feel uncertain again, wondering if maybe this vision Clara had had was more directly about Clara—some trauma she'd experienced in real life but was blocking out.

Clara nodded. "It'd definitely be worse if it was someone I knew."

"Yes, that is a relief. And maybe it's not important right now. And all you need to do here is try to say whatever comes. Okay?" Dr. Goldberg was doing her best to stay neutral and not show her suspicions.

Clara nodded.

"So, then, let's just have you finish up by telling me what the girl felt then. If there was anything in addition to not wanting the person to help her—like maybe she didn't want help from just him. Maybe she didn't want help from anyone. Or maybe only from someone specific."

Clara took a deep breath, ready for this to be over, remembering the feeling of being under the gauze with the guy on top of her. "The girl felt bound," Clara explained, "like in a dream when you can't run, like she couldn't make herself run or stop the person on the other side of the gauze."

"What was he doing?" Dr. Goldberg pressed.

"Uh...he was on top of her, but...he was helping her. It doesn't make sense. And the girl was thinking *no* but not saying anything, like she didn't want to hurt him, hurt his feelings."

"So, she had no voice."

"I guess, metaphorically," Clara agreed.

"And she felt trapped," Dr. Goldberg went on, "like she was suffocating because someone was trying to help her."

"Something like that," Clara said.

"So, have you ever felt like that?" Dr. Goldberg asked. "Maybe with Seamus?"

"No!" Clara insisted. "Sorry. Like I said, Seamus listens to me. I talk to him."

Dr. Goldberg stopped, took a deep breath to calm herself down. "Okay."

"I'm sorry," Clara told her.

"You're fine," Dr. Goldberg said, making a note.

Again with the friggin' notes, Clara thought, and she could see Dr. Goldberg getting frustrated now too and backing off. Clara didn't want that either so she tried to give more description. "But I've become more quiet around Seamus," Clara admitted. "Not talking. Since the miscarriages. For the past few weeks, I haven't been able to talk openly to Seamus and didn't even want to. Even though he just wants to help. And it feels like I want to help him too. It's too much for both of us. And it's hurting both of us."

"So the pain is suffocating."

Clara groaned.

"Okay, you're right. We've been over it. How about when you were younger? With your parents? Or even now, with your parents. Do you ever hesitate to express yourself with them?"

This hit a chord. Clara hadn't been able to talk to her parents openly since the last miscarriage, a year ago. "Yes," Clara replied.

"Yes?" Dr. Goldberg asked.

"I hold back with my parents," Clara clarified.

"How?"

Clara took a deep breath. "And then, we're done."

"Yes, and then, we're done," confirmed Dr. Goldberg.

"I held back talking to my parents about the miscarriage the last two times. I haven't talked about it with them at all. I told them I was fine."

"Because?"

"I didn't want to hurt them."

"Don't you think they can handle the news? And be there for you? As adults?"

Clara felt her heart squeezing. "I think it would hurt them too much. And I don't want to hurt them more."

"And how did that make you feel?"

"It hurts like a knife in my heart," Clara said firmly, as if it should be obvious, and looked at Dr. Goldberg. She really was done now.

"That's hard on you."

Clara groaned then nodded. "Yes."

"And other feelings?"

"Like the walls are closing in and I want to burst out and run through a field. Get fresh air. Like it's stale inside. But then, I'm afraid to go out."

"And when you were younger?"

"I thought we were done."

"Okay, then, we're done." Dr. Goldberg smiled and shut her notebook.

"I kept a lot of things from my dad," Clara blurted out. "When I was younger."

Dr. Goldberg stopped. "Okay." She reopened her notebook again.

"I wanted to be an artist. That was frowned upon. But my mom encouraged me."

"Did you ever talk about it with your dad after you became an artist?"

"No. We didn't talk about it ever, but in high school, I took a lot of art classes, and then, when I was an art major in college, I also took some business classes, and he could relate, so then, he came around and saw that me being an artist wasn't so bad."

"So then, you talked about it? Expressed your feelings?"

"No, but it was okay then that we didn't talk. Especially when Greta and I turned Frock into a business. He helped us with it. That made the discomfort between us disappear."

"But you didn't want your dad's help?"

Clara stopped, getting more exasperated. "No, I did," she said. "There was no weirdness with it. He was in his element, and he helped us make some connections and that was good." Clara shrugged because it was. "I mean, maybe this whole thing was just that initial irrational fear lingering. My dad's irrational fear. Maybe I took on his worry that I wouldn't be okay as an artist." And then, Clara snapped, "Or maybe this isn't working!"

"It could be irrational fear," agreed Dr. Goldberg with a smile, but she didn't look like she believed that entirely.

Why? Clara thought and exhaled. This was getting too frustrating.

"Okay," Dr. Goldberg said, clapping her hands together. "I think we are done for today. And for a while. You have done amazing, and my prescription for you right now is to go and take a holiday and relax for a month or so. And then, contact me and let me know how you're feeling. Okay? And when you're ready, you're ready. And maybe, this will be it. Maybe you just needed to shine a light on how you don't want people helping you when you can do it yourself or want to go through it yourself, and you feel badly saying no. Basic boundary setting. That's an easy fix."

Clara nodded and managed a smile, hoping Dr. Goldberg was right. "Thank you," she said. "I think that's something I can handle."

Dr. Goldberg gave Clara an uncharacteristic hug and squeezed her long and tight, hoping Clara really would be okay.

The hug helped, and Clara felt relief, surprisingly, like maybe this would be manageable after all.

6

Permission To Let Go

Clara continued to feel relief after her session with Dr. Goldberg, and it followed her through the day. She and Erin dropped Erin's kids at Erin's mom's and got their massages at Chill. Clara continued to feel relaxed and relieved even when she came home and had mint-chip ice cream and took a bath. But most of the relief Clara felt came from knowing that the distressing incident she had witnessed in her mind at Dr. Goldberg's wasn't a part of her own history or reality—that there had been no trauma in her own life causing the asthma and, therefore, it was something she could conquer. The trauma was something outside of herself, something she wasn't responsible for or wounded by or that she needed to be ashamed of, an exaggeration of a teenage fear possibly, and if she kept taking baby steps, the asthma would stop and, even more importantly, they would be able to have a baby—a happy, healthy baby—and build a family.

With this new perspective and hope, Clara had been open to hearing Dr. Goldberg in her office and when she had walked her and Erin to the elevator. They had made small talk about the general state of living in a world in turmoil with overbearing media and how that was an obvious possibility for Clara's stress too, just like it was for everyone else. Clara didn't think that was the cause of her stress but was willing to entertain it. She'd grown up talking about the world and seeing it through the lens of her dad's work in the foreign service. Her dad had always made her and her mom feel okay and safe, assuring Clara that the world would figure itself and its problems out. Humanity had a penchant for joy and survival, he always said—it made mistakes but always corrected itself. And Clara had always believed him and was grateful for his eternal optimism.

And now, knowing this trauma wasn't hers, Clara felt a twinge of freedom.

Dr. Goldberg hadn't seemed completely convinced that the asthma was the world's problem or her fear of hurting her parents with bad news, but Dr. Goldberg had given Clara permission to move beyond it and to at least be open to the idea of being free of worry for the summer, whether at the lake house in the small town upstate or in the city, whatever Clara decided.

But Clara had heard it loud and clear when Dr. Goldberg had nudged her at the elevator to go to the lake house specifically, probably for Erin to overhear. "It's always good to try something new, get a new perspective," Dr. Goldberg had said. And then she'd suggested that Clara think in short spaces of time, "For example, give yourself permission to relax and not worry about anything but yourself, Clara, for the next two months. And after two months, if you want to worry again, you can, whether you go away or stay here. No one is going to take that option away from you—the worry is always there, and if you want it, it's yours," Dr. Goldberg had teased. Dr. Goldberg didn't usually tease—she was such an old-school analyst, so Clara took this as a good sign, especially because it spoke to her. It spoke to her soul—laughter and wonder and joy were things she craved.

Which is exactly what she was thinking as she splashed cool water from the bathroom sink on her face, getting ready for bed, letting it wash away any fearful thoughts—like how she could be powerful enough to create a gash on her forehead out of her imagination.

Which is when Seamus came up behind her. She noticed his bare feet and Tin Tin boxers first. She'd given him the shorts last Christmas. Tin Tin was a Belgian comic-book character, and she'd found the boxers last fall when she was visiting her parents in Brussels. The boxers were so silly but with a fabulous cut and quality fabric, and Clara found it incredibly sexy when Seamus wore them—again, the perfect blend of hot, classy irony and playful—and just her style.

Clara stood up, water dripping down her face, and her eyes met Seamus's in the mirror as he gently pulled her long black hair behind her shoulders, admiring her beauty, the back of his fingers warm as he let them slide down the back of her arms.

Then, Clara's eyes moved to the cherry-colored wound on her forehead. It had gotten much worse since earlier at Dr. Goldberg's—it was bruising, swollen, blood swelling beneath the surface. Clara touched it lightly—"Ouch."

"Let me see," said Seamus.

Clara turned and let him look at the wound. He exaggerated his inspection. "If I remember correctly, you told me that you fell once, off your bike, and hit your head. When you were five...?"

Clara was charmed. "How do you do that?"

"What?" Seamus laughed.

"Remember everything."

"Maybe it's because I found something good to remember," Seamus replied and kissed the side of her head gently.

Clara felt her cheeks crimson, and she smiled up at him. "At least you're remembering reality and not being forced into mumbo-jumbo hypnotic-introspective symbolism crap."

"And that's exactly why I brought you this," Seamus said and disappeared quickly into the bedroom and reappeared with a vintage 35mm film camera in his hand—a Voigtländer. Clara's eyes widened. "To remember our summer by," he continued, "and for something for you to do—here in the city while I'm working. Not in the country." Seamus was clearly resigned to the fact that Clara didn't want to go to the lake house and that they'd be staying in Brooklyn all summer.

Clara took the camera. What a thoughtful gift. It was stunning and was exactly what she'd been looking for. It was also incredibly understanding of Seamus.

"And it's so you can spend the whole time ignoring yourself and focusing on other people, right?" he continued, teasing her, knowing her so well. "Just the way you like it."

Clara laughed, then lifted the camera and snapped a picture of him. She took the camera down. Their eyes met, and that feeling washed over her again—that they were eternally connected. "I want to try," Clara said softly. "I want to go to the lake house now and stay for the summer. I want to believe this can work. I want to do whatever it takes for us to be a family."

This took Seamus by surprise. His eyes widened with a mix of emotions barreling through—relief, love, hope—then fear, as he imagined the lake house before him. Suddenly, he felt the ground fall out from beneath his feet and the vault of sadness open in his heart. For a second. Just a second. Because then, he shut it again, quickly—he'd gotten good at that over the years—and the ground rose again. And he felt the warmth of the heated bathroom floor on his bare soles, and he felt Clara's love embracing him. *I'm bigger than this,* Seamus told himself and smiled and exhaled and nodded with a smirk and a little laugh, admitting, "I was secretly hoping you'd come around to the lake house. But I will miss this heated floor."

"I told you it'd be worth it," Clara teased.

"It's worth it. I love this floor. And the whole remodel. You're always right. And I love you. Thank you," Seamus said, and for a moment, he knew Clara would bolster him enough to get over his past.

And for a moment, he looked like a child, grateful for Clara's entire being and the power she had over him.

Clara loved it when he looked at her like that—like he was seeing her as a goddess. And for a moment, she felt forgiven. So strange. *For what? Why forgiven?* she wondered. *What have I done? Nothing,* she told herself, but nevertheless, there came the un-nameable pain. And the shame. The gnawing fear in her stomach. But it didn't make sense, so she tucked it away in her own vault like she always did. After all, she hadn't done anything wrong. And as soon as she found that strength, Seamus became a man again before her—there in the bathroom, and they came together as equals. And she knew Seamus was the answer to her life, whatever form it took, because they had so much love between them. And they'd built this home together, and it was solid. And now, maybe they could build a family too. Maybe it would just have to begin in his childhood home by the lake where somehow she knew the air would be full of truth and reality.

"I have another confession to make," Seamus told Clara playfully.

"Oh, yeah," she toyed back, "besides the fact that you and Goldberg and Erin are all clearly conspiring to get me to the lake so I can remodel the house there too? And put heated floors in your ancient family residence?"

"It was built in the early 70s," Seamus retorted. "Hardly ancient. But yes, I have something else to confess."

"Do tell," Clara said, playing along.

"Shake Shack," Seamus told her, trying not to crack a smile.

"That's your confession? Shake Shack?" Clara toyed back.

"Yeah, I really want it," he replied. "Now."

"You do?" she said.

"Yes, the bacon burger. And the fries," Seamus said, still managing a straight face but his twinkling eyes giving him away.

Clara laughed and nodded, playfully taking on a hoity attitude. "Well, I appreciate your honesty."

"I should also probably tell you then that I really like the strawberry shake better than the vanilla."

"No, that's not possible," Clara said, honestly surprised. "That means you've been lying to me. You always say the vanilla is fine."

"Yeah, I pretend," Seamus admitted. "So you feel okay getting vanilla. So that I never get a whole one myself. Of strawberry. I guess we could call it a compromise instead of a lie."

Clara laughed. "Oh, really?"

Seamus smirked.

"Well, no more secrets," Clara said. "And we'll get two shakes from now on—like right now—so everyone's happy. Beat you to the car. Loser has to drive," Clara challenged him and hoofed it out of the bathroom. They raced—throwing on sweats and hustling to the car.

Clara won, and Seamus drove them to Shake Shack where they sat in the car and stuffed their faces with burgers and fries and shakes, one strawberry and one vanilla.

7

Flowers Through the Cracks

Clara couldn't believe how free she felt as they drove out of the city and up the highway towards the lake house, backseat full of boxes and suitcases and duffel bags. She'd traveled this way with friends often on weekend getaways pre-Seamus but only once with Seamus, the time they drove up to Montreal for his comic convention.

But today, when they veered off towards the small lake town from the main highway, everything was new and exciting. Maybe everyone was right, Clara thought, maybe she desperately needed to try something new, see something new, get out of her self-made prison of doubt and sadness that she owned, at this point, all too well.

The odd thing was that Clara always loved to travel and knew it was a good reset for her—so why hadn't she been able to see that when Seamus suggested going to the lake house? *Because it's such a small town!* she thought, *Why would I want to be there? When we could go adventuring to far-off places?* Clara had, after all, been everywhere—traveled the globe, lived abroad in four countries as an expat thanks to her dad's job, gone to boarding school in Italy—until she landed at NYU and found home.

And now, she liked being in one place, having that base for a change, especially since her grandma had passed away. Going to the lake in Michigan to visit Nana had been home base for her whole life, and now, she felt proud that she and Seamus had built something together. Nana would've been proud of her too had she seen the remodel. Nana called it being "house proud" and made fun of herself for being house proud too. Nana had also told Clara to always take things slowly, be patient and wait for the openings of beauty and joy. Seamus *was* Clara's beauty and joy, Clara knew that, and she was so grateful that her grandmother had gotten to meet him before she passed. Clara was also grateful her Nana had approved of Seamus. "You're beautiful when you're with him," Nana told Clara. "You're you."

So, this sudden excitement about spending the summer in a podunk, upstate lake town was a surprise to Clara for two reasons. One, because she'd traveled so far and wide that going too small wouldn't normally sound exciting, and two, now, because she loved the city and her own home base and finally felt calm—except for the miscarriages.

Maybe she unconsciously thought it would be a reminder of the summers with her Nana—that it would be safe and inspiring. And now, looking at the trees pass by and her love in the seat next to her, Clara was open to the idea that maybe there would be more at this new destination at this new juncture in her life—maybe this would be a summer of discovery instead of misery. Maybe she would grow and learn more about herself—and Seamus. Maybe being in this new place would crack her open and more love could shine through—finally—and a baby could grow inside her and would be a blooming of love, their love.

Maybe change was possible and hope was returning, Clara decided because the more she thought about it, the more excitement she felt.

***

Seamus gripped the steering wheel more and more tightly as they approached the upstate New York town on the crystal-blue lake, nestled in pines, where he was born and raised. They passed the sign that read: POPULATION 1,800. "See, not as podunk as you thought," he said to Clara. "It's grown like a bean shoot."

Clara laughed at his silliness as their car approached Main Street, and she admired the pines, spruces, red cedars and other flora sprouting end-of-April leaves. She admired the blue sky and the lake and breathed it all in—*Heaven*, she thought and mused, "It's gorgeous. I can't believe we've never been here."

"And here's the corner store," Seamus pointed out. "Best popsicles ever."

Clara looked closely as they passed The Corner Market, a tiny mom-and-pop grocers with a freezer out front full of ice-cream. "And I'm finally gonna meet Derek," Clara added, sitting back. "It's so weird we've never met."

Seamus's jaw clenched, but he did his best to hide it and sound normal—"Just bad timing till now," he shrugged with a playful gaze.

Which is when Clara spotted a girl with long, curly red hair—probably around age twelve—on a bike, wind in her hair, laughing, joyous. The girl veered up ahead of their car as a sandy-blond boy, a similar age, raced up to her. They laughed and shouted back and forth to each other as Seamus and Clara's car approached.

Then, suddenly, the girl swerved in front of their car, and Seamus didn't stop. Clara screamed. Seamus swerved. "What?!" he shouted.

"Those kids!" Clara yelled back in panic, turning to look behind them out the rear window, seeing the kids still riding their bikes, still joyous.

"What kids?" Seamus said, slowing, looking in the rearview mirror.

"I thought you were gonna hit them, God," Clara said, voice shaky, and sat back.

"Hit who?" Seamus wondered, looking in his side mirrors. He didn't see anything and toyed with Clara, "Now, don't you go turning into a small-town drama queen, making stuff up and crying wolf because there's nothing better to do out here."

Clara gave him a smirky look.

Seamus grinned. "Actually I can think of something to do."

"Hey," Clara scolded playfully, "we're not supposed to be thinking about that, remember?"

Seamus grinned, and Clara was pleased, and they pulled off the main drag down a dirt road.

It was even more beautiful here, Clara thought. The quaint little town was quite charming, but this was beyond what she could have imagined. Pines and swaths of green grass with yellow and white wild flowers lined the way. *So peaceful*, Clara thought, and through the trees on the left, she caught glimpses of the crystal-blue lake. The road veered around the edges of the water, in and out of wooded areas, and they passed several houses, all set back from the unpaved street with long driveways, before arriving at Seamus's family lake house—a craftsman, not too far off the road, nestled in pines and other conifers, grass overgrown, paint chipping. It was obvious no one had lived there for years.

Seamus's hands clenched the steering wheel as he stopped before the driveway, car still running, like he was holding on for dear life. Clara looked out the front windshield, taking in the tall pines, and had a flash of déjà vu. She loved it when that happened. "Déjà vu!" Clara cheered.

"Really?" Seamus replied, voice croaking, laughing to cover his pain that seemed to be rearing its head all of a sudden. It was the first time in so long that he'd seen the house, and still, maybe it was too soon.

"Yeah, maybe it's a good sign, that déjà vu," Clara said as they parked in the driveway. The driveway itself was filled with flowers and grass sneaking up through the cracks in the old pavement. And in front of them, stood a shabby looking garage with chipped paint and a bent garage door that obviously wouldn't close fully. Clara guessed it was full of stuff and that no one had ever parked in there. She opened her passenger door and looked over at Seamus who hadn't moved. He'd put the car in park and turned off the ignition but was back clutching the steering wheel, just staring at the house like he was never going to get out.

Was it that bad? Clara wondered. *All the sadness that lived here?*

For Seamus, it was, and he was trying desperately to keep his emotions hidden, even though he was sure that his racing heart was giving him away. The house looked the same after all the years, which made all his old feelings rush in—the ground threatening to disappear again beneath him.

"You okay?" Clara asked.

"Yeah, yeah, it's just...," Seamus shook his head and opened his car door.

"Been a while?" she said, finishing his sentence.

"Yeah," Seamus agreed and managed a small smile. He didn't feel any better, but at least, Clara was trying to make light of his past, even if she didn't know the whole story. Seamus told himself, *C'mon, you got this,* like he always did. Like his dad would've said if he were still alive. Like his dad always said to him before the accident. And then, Seamus got out.

Clara followed and spotted an American robin sitting on the wood rail on the edge of the gorgeous porch. "Oh, look at that!" she exclaimed.

"American robin. You'll see a lot out here." Seamus nodded and took a deep breath. Then, they both walked to the front of the car and just stood there taking in the sight before them—admiring the beautiful old house standing proudly in front of the crystal-blue lake. The house definitely needed paint, Clara thought, but what a charming old porch and swing, and there was the guesthouse to the side by the woods that seemed to lead to the lake as well. An old gazebo—that also needed paint—stood about forty feet from the house on a grassy hill that needed mowing and replanting and sloped down to the water where there was a small pier and boathouse. "Dunne house," Seamus said, voice croaking again, revealing his feelings again—more revealing than he would've liked.

"It's truly stunning here," Clara whispered, trying to be sensitive but unable to hold back the unexpected joy she was feeling about being outside and feeling free for the first time in so long. "And I can see our family here," she whispered, imagining their children running on the grass, surprising even herself that she was able to utter these words.

And the words cut through Seamus's sorrow, as did Clara's joy—through the weight and history that was there for him, filling the air with its dense heartache, as if it were coming off the house to engulf them. But Clara's joy was setting them both free, and when Clara reached over and squeezed Seamus's hand, he nodded, "Yup, it is—stunning—I'll give that." And he tried to let his father's optimism push him forward. He shook off the sorrow and turned and swept Clara up into his arms.

"What are you doing?" Clara laughed as Seamus carried her like a new bride to the door.

"This place is going to be good for us, Clara Dunne, the Dunne house," he declared—with confidence and humor this time—and looked at Clara with love. "To new beginnings, my beloved," he said and kissed Clara and carried her through the threshold.

8 |

A New Day and a New Girl in the Yard

Clara slept soundly that first night in the lake house amidst fluffy pillows and her favorite down duvet, the one with the new white cotton cover that she'd brought along to keep her and Seamus warm in the big sleigh bed in the master bedroom of Seamus's childhood home—a total 80s throwback. The sun was just peaking past the trees when the phone rang, waking Clara from her calm slumber. She reached out for her mobile on the nightstand. But there was no nightstand on her side. *Where am I?* she thought and sat up, realizing—*no Seamus either.* Then, she saw the old olive-green landline phone ringing on the nightstand on Seamus's side of the bed. She scrambled over and grabbed the receiver attached by a cord to the phone. "Hello?"

"Shouldn't you be up by now?" Seamus's playful voice leapt out from the phone.

"I am up," Clara said, even though she wasn't. She swung her legs over to sit up. "Where are you? No wait, let me guess: work."

Seamus was at work in his huge, lofty executive office—playful but posh, posters of award-winning video games lining the walls and old but working Pacman and Fussball games below the posters. His feet were up on his desk, and he was squeezing a stress ball. "Jerry wanted to show me the Tworkman suit. And it's aMAAAZing."

"Of course, he did," Clara teased.

"Can't wait to show you," Seamus replied. "And I'm coming back soon, so you'd better get up and get moving!"

How'd he know? Clara wondered. *And how'd he get to the city so fast? He must've left early.* "I'll call you when I finish kitchen patrol, sergeant," Clara told him and hung up—so relieved that Seamus was happy. Finally, some of the heaviness lifting. *Maybe this'll work for him if he can go back and forth,* she thought. *Maybe he was right about that at least. As long as he doesn't get sick of the schlep.*

Clara stood up and looked around and took in the 80s details now that there was some daylight—the dark-brown armoire, burnt-orange curtains, silver-and-orange rug with angular shapes. Then, Clara's mind wandered to Seamus and the previous night. She blushed even though she was alone. There was no asthma last night. It was the perfect night together in the sleigh bed. Also, it was amazing. *Maybe this place will be lucky for us,* Clara thought, letting herself entertain the notion that maybe she could get pregnant here and carry it through. She'd had some spotting already since the last miscarriage. Maybe her body was ready again. *It's possible,* she told herself and went into the bathroom for a shower.

***

Half an hour later, Clara came out, towel-drying her long, curly, dark hair, her favorite sage-green robe draped loosely over her shoulders. She looked at her face in the standup mirror. What was it revealing today? She smirked and laughed at herself. "Love," she said out loud, "so get over the sappiness."

Then, Clara looked down at her belly, touching it gently, taking in a deep breath—no problem getting air, she thought and rubbed her fingers over her soft, smooth, brown skin and the two-inch white birthmark next to her bellybutton that looked like a "KAPOW!" sound-effect burst in a DC comic book. Clara wondered what the birthmark would look like if she reached the full forty weeks. *Maybe this place will be it, where we find out,* Clara thought then heard a noise downstairs—footsteps shuffling.

"Hello?" Clara yelled down and grabbed a cardigan to throw over her robe, slipped on her dad's Ugg slippers, clomped out and hurried downstairs where she found more 80s decor and their pile of suitcases and boxes waiting to be unpacked. "Hello?" Clara repeated. No reply. She noticed a note on the coffee table in Seamus's hand-writing: *Enjoy the mess. I'll be home soon to help. Love you, Seamus*

"Nice," Clara said and heard the back screen door in the kitchen open and slam shut. A teenage girl with curly red hair ran past the back sliding-glass door. "Hey," Clara called out.

The red-haired girl continued across the lawn and ran into the guesthouse at the back side of the yard.

"Hey! Wait," Clara shouted again and ran out the sliding-glass door, across the grass to the guesthouse. "Hello? Hellooo?" she called out then opened the door and peered in, sunlight illuminating the musty room. It was clearly more of an old work space than a guest room—a computer nerd's paradise, full of old computers, gadgets, drawings, flow charts and an old daybed with wooden side arms and a back that made it look like a sofa with a navy-and-green plaid cover, more of a couch than a bed. There was also a small hot-plate kitchen in the back. But the girl was gone.

Clara heard a laugh outside. She turned and saw the red-haired girl riding off on a bike. *How did she get out?* Clara wondered. *Must be a secret back door,* she assumed and wondered if the girl was the same girl as the one she'd seen on the bike when they arrived. This girl seemed older but had the same hair and laugh and light-hearted joy—and maybe some mischievousness too. *Maybe it's the sister of the girl on Main Street or something*, Clara thought. *Or maybe kids here just play more and all have red hair.*

Clara laughed it off and looked back into the guesthouse. She knew this had to be all Seamus's old stuff, unless there was someone else in the family that was into computers as much as he was. But that was doubtful. He hadn't mentioned it. And that's something he would have talked about. *And this could be a good thing*, she thought, because surely, she could convince him to clear it out with her. And the space would definitely make a great art and photography studio—another thing Seamus was right about. And that excited her. *But it sure as heck is gonna take a lot of work*, she thought. Then, she heard a CREAK and jumped. "And an exterminator," she said out loud.

9

White Daisies from Father Derek

Clara walked back across the lawn from the guesthouse, onto the back porch and through the sliding glass door, which was partially open. Had she left it open? Probably. She also heard something in the living room and noticed that the front door was ajar. "Hello?" Clara called out.

"Clara?" a deep, strong voice echoed from the living room.

Clara hesitated then entered, and there was Seamus's older brother, Derek, Father Derek, now a priest, smiling warmly, holding flowers—white daisies. His hair was black like hers—wavy, even though he was Irish, dark Irish—while hers was a blend of Italian and Cuban which could've come from either side of her family. Both of her parents were second generation Americans.

Derek was handsome in person, more so than in the one photo she'd seen of him. A flicker of charm flashed across his eyes, smile wrinkles showing. Clara noticed the worry lines on his forehead as well, showing his age, three years older than Seamus, so he was now about forty-eight, while Seamus still looked so young, as if Seamus had managed to keep his past at bay successfully while Derek had not been so lucky. Still, Derek was tall and seemed to exude a sort of magnetism in spite of doing his best to remain humble as a priest.

"Derek?" Clara asked and instinctively shut her cardigan to hide her chest.

"Clara?" Derek replied, again with jovial charm in his eyes.

But Clara saw a flash of pain too.

Then, suddenly, she heard creaking, like the creaking she'd heard moments earlier in the guesthouse. Then, jumping and springs, as if someone were on a trampoline—then BAM, BLACK, Clara saw all black. Then, BAM, a hit to her head. Then, FLASH—it was gone. "Ow!" she said and grabbed her forehead in pain.

"You okay?" Derek asked and touched her arm gently, kindly.

Clara heard another audio-flash of the creaking and then a guitar playing. "Fine, yes," she replied, doing her best to hide the strangeness. "I just—weird headaches lately. I keep getting them." She laughed, also trying to hide how much it hurt.

Derek let go of her arm and brought his hand down. "The heat'll do that," he said.

"Definitely," Clara agreed. "So nice to meet you finally."

They both laughed—strangers but not really, because Derek was Clara's brother-in-law after all. Still, it was awkward, so Clara did what she'd been taught growing up with parents in the diplomatic corps and went in for a cheek kiss, missing his cheek as he turned and kissing his ear, while he gave her an odd hug and pat on the back.

They both laughed again at their folly and pulled apart.

Clara heard kids laughing outside and saw the red-haired teenage girl and a sandy-haired teen boy run past.

"So, he finally got you out here," Derek said, smiling as if he hadn't noticed the kids.

It's probably normal to run through peoples' yards here, Clara thought and replied, "Actually, my doctor suggested coming out here. She thought it might shake things up a little for me to get out of the city. I'm sure Seamus filled you in."

"A little," Derek said and handed her the beautiful, happy flowers.

Clara's face lit up. They were beautiful and simple, just her style. And they made the awkwardness disappear. "Well, a little is all there is to this sad story," Clara added. "And these are beautiful. Let me grab a vase."

Clara entered the kitchen and scoured the pantry and cabinets for a vase.

"It's so nice to finally meet you too," Derek said from the other room. "I tried my darndest to get to the wedding."

"Santorini is a bit of a schlep," Clara admitted, finding an old vase under the sink with dried petals stuck to the glass. It must've been like that for decades, she thought.

"I'll have to make it up to you while you're here," Derek said.

"Seamus says you play guitar," Clara called out, turning on the water and rinsing the vase, scratching off the plastered-on leaves with her fingernails. "There's a bar at the docks with music I heard."

"Yup, it's the only thing to do in town," Derek told her. "Just say the word and we'll go. Anything for my favorite sister-in-law."

"Only sister-in-law," Clara shouted from the kitchen, trying to be heard over the running tap, finishing up cleaning the vase, filling it with water—which is when she suddenly felt stabbing pain on the scarring wound on her forehead. She stopped and grabbed her head. No blood. Then, the sharp pain eased up and went away. *What is going on?* she wondered, doing her best to shake it off. "Can I get you a drink?" she called out to Derek as she turned off the water.

"Oh, no. I just came to make sure everything is okay with the house," he replied. "I've gotta get back to the school."

Clara placed the flowers in the vase and came out and set them on the table. Derek was looking at the family photos on the mantel

—most were of cousins and grandparents, and there was one of their parents, Stella and Caleb Dunne, their wedding photo. Clara arranged the flowers. "These are wonderful," she said, "so bright," and watched Derek for a moment. He was lost in the photos. She cleared her throat quietly.

"Oh, sorry, sorry. So, do you...," he said, turning to her with an exaggerated smile, "think you're going to be okay here?"

"Definitely. I have a good feeling about this place," Clara admitted, then added with a playful whisper, "Although we're not supposed to talk about that."

This made Derek uncomfortable. "Any other plans?" he asked, picking up the photo of his grandparents.

"Yes, I'm gonna make that guesthouse into a studio," Clara told him. "Take photos. Draw."

"You're in the right place for art," Derek said, putting the framed photo back. "Amazing views. And subjects. Regular folk. Doing life. Even my kids. Fishing, dragging me boating."

"You sure you're a priest?" Clara teased.

"There's really only a few things priests can't do, and boating is not one of them," Derek joked.

Clara flashed to black—and suddenly, she was back in the hypnosis in Dr. Goldberg's office, a teenage girl jumping on a bed laughing.

"Clara? You okay?" Derek asked.

His voice brought her back to the present. "What? Yes, sorry," Clara replied. "Just a hot flash or something. I'm fine. Really. I should take a nap."

"Alright, well you know where to find me," Derek said with a warm smile. "Two miles that way." He pointed. "You'll see the monsters. Come visit."

"Monsters?"

"The pimple-faced ogres...teenagers, high schoolers," he joked, though he clearly adored them.

"Aha," Clara said, liking this brother of Seamus's. He was nothing like how Seamus had described him, which was that Derek was disciplined, boring and had a grey, somber attitude. Clara also had no idea why Seamus had been avoiding Derek. "Well, thank you for stopping by and for the flowers," she told him, as she and Derek stepped out the front door onto the beautiful, old porch. "I will definitely take you up on that visit amongst your monsters at the high school."

Derek laughed.

And a glint from a colorful glass mobile caught Clara's eye. It was hanging above the porch railing, seemingly out of place under the old, chipped paint.

"Wow," she said, gently touching one of the pieces hanging down.

"I can see you like it here at the old Dunne house," Derek ventured.

"Yes, it's gorgeous. Everything is gorgeous. This mobile is gorgeous. Where did it come from?"

"I planned to put it up when I opened up the house a few weeks ago, but I saved it till now," he told her. "I figured it'd brighten up the place a little to start. Our mother made it."

"It's wonderful," Clara said. "The green is beautiful. Thank you for that. And I'm going to start looking for a nice, old swing and rattan chairs and table as soon as I unpack. It'll make a wonderful spot for lemonade and mint juleps. You'll have to come by," she added with a smile.

"It's not exactly the South," he joked.

Which is when they spotted the neighbor lady coming out to water flowers on her porch and looking over at them.

"And beware the lookie-loo," Derek whispered mischievously. "People are watching because they have nothing else to do. It may be the same in the South. But don't worry too hard. They never really have any idea about what's actually going on."

"So, is that a good thing?" Clara played along.

"Sometimes," Derek teased. "Good for us with Mrs. Lee at least. She's not a very good snoop."

10

Derek's Story by the Boardwalk

Seamus and Clara sat eating messy fish and chips and drinking a local IPA at the lone lake-harbor brewery and gastropub overlooking the water. It was quite charming. *And nice that there's still sunlight,* Clara thought. She loved how it was beginning to stay light longer now that it was almost May. It made her excited about the summer to come. She knew she'd be down there by the lake often, watching people strolling happily along the wood-plank boardwalk like now, kids and dogs running and playing and jumping in the water even though it was already early evening.

Clara had been filling Seamus in on the details of her first day there, including the ideas she'd had for remodeling the porch and the visit from Derek. "He was fine," Clara told Seamus, "actually nice. And it made me so happy that we decided to come here and try it out. You were right. He offered to take me down here for music and for me to go visit him there at his school. If I need anything."

"Great," Seamus said, voice cracking, taking a bite of his burger, looking down at his plate while he chewed.

Weird, thought Clara, catching the tension at the mention of his brother. She wished it wasn't so because everything else so far on her first day had been perfect. "What is it with you and him?" Clara asked. "Why can't you just tell me?"

Seamus shrugged—and took another bite, not looking at her, still being evasive.

"Seamus?"

"Why do we have to talk about this now? Everything's fine."

"You know what I mean," Clara said. "I can see it in your face the second I say Derek's name. And I mean, your parents died. You were teenagers. I get that. I always have. It's tragic. But why don't you like *him*? It wasn't his fault. You know that."

"I never said that," Seamus defended. "That I don't like him."

"Maybe not, but I can see it," Clara insisted.

Seamus groaned. "Okay, look, the truth is I don't trust him. Okay? He couldn't handle it after they left. And he tried, but I wasn't capable of handling *him* falling apart. So, now, I just don't want to deal with it. Or go there. And it's not my business anymore. And it's not yours either. So, leave it alone."

"Died," Clara said, "your parents died. They didn't *leave*."

Seamus laughed off her comment, shaking his head as if she were being ridiculous. "We don't need to do this," he said and took a swig of beer, still not looking at her. This was strange. Seamus always got tense whenever his parents and Derek came up, but usually, he reigned it in. Now, it was as if he couldn't manage.

"Please," Clara said. "You can't just leave me hanging."

"Fine!" Seamus yelled. "He was grasping. For anything. Okay? And he hurt me. And I'm just done. I don't need to deal with it. So, can you just stop?"

"Thirty years later?"

"It doesn't matter!" Seamus shouted, slamming the counter. "He probably didn't even know it happened."

"What happened?"

"Nothing, Clara! You're pushing me!" His eyes flashed anger, and then, he signaled to the server for another beer.

Obviously, it wasn't nothing, Clara thought. In fact, it was probably the opposite. It probably was everything. Clara softened. "Can't you just tell me? I mean, why did we come up here otherwise? Clearly, you thought Derek was okay enough to bring me here."

"No, I said I don't want to talk about it. Why can't you respect that?" Seamus asked, shooting her another look of frustration.

"Fine," Clara said, slightly hurt. She took a bite of her burger and reminded herself that this wasn't about her. This was his stuff. And it would be best if she dropped it.

After all, they should both be grateful that Seamus didn't have guilt about their parents' death like Derek did. Seamus had told Clara the whole story once, early in their relationship when they were still getting to know each other. But he hadn't talked about it since. And now, Clara was starting to sense why. It had been a tragic car accident, and clearly, Seamus still couldn't handle it. It was like an open wound that she hadn't noticed until now. Caleb and Stella Dunne had been driving to another town to see Derek play at an away tournament for his high school baseball team. Seamus had stayed home. There had been an awful storm, and the accident happened just outside the parking lot to the baseball field when dark clouds dumped cold sleet and hail. Derek had made it to the hospital and held his mom's hand when she passed, and Seamus never saw his parents again. Derek blamed himself for the whole incident and made it his mission to take care of Seamus and make it up to him. Derek had told their aunt and uncle in New Jersey that he'd be Seamus's guardian—that he'd promised their mom on her deathbed that he'd take care of Seamus. And the two boys kept living in the Dunne lake house alone for the remainder of Derek's senior year and all of the next year until Seamus graduated.

All of that made sense to Clara, but she couldn't fathom what Derek had done to Seamus to make him so upset.

They ate in silence for a little while longer, Clara telling herself to let it go, watching a couple of kids jumping off the boardwalk into the water, doing cannonballs, trying to nonchalantly splash people strolling by.

"It was a relationship, okay?" Seamus finally admitted. "But there's nothing else to say. I'll do my best to be civil to Derek. I think we're fine here for all the reasons we've talked about. Okay? There you have it. Please drop it now."

"Thank you," Clara said.

Seamus nodded and continued to eat with his head down for a few minutes longer. She knew he was trying. "Seamus?" Clara said gently.

"Yeah?" he replied.

"I'm really happy to be here. With you."

Seamus finally looked up.

"I mean, right?" she grinned.

He laughed. "What?"

"I mean, I'm happy...assuming you're no longer in love with this sweetheart of yours," she teased.

He laughed again and nodded with his mischievous grin.

"And that you left her in the high-school-sweetheart dust," she added.

"I see what you're doing here," Seamus teased back. "And yes, I can assure you there was a lot of leaving in the dust."

Thank God he's dropping it, Clara thought and said, "That's what I thought," flirting, coy, sexy, "Ready? To go home?" she asked.

"Actually, I think we should go for a stroll first," he said, clearly messing with her now.

Clara smirked, toying back, "Yeah?" And she felt a surge of strength, suddenly feeling like a goddess, invincible, like their love and attraction could do anything.

Seamus took Clara's hand and led her to the boardwalk, where they strolled, close, veering around the cannon-ball-jumping kids, getting splashed anyway, running away, laughing, kissing, enjoying each other, in love, perfection—

—until they arrived home at the lake house, where their closeness and play turned into a romantic night again, in the sleigh bed with the giant master-bedroom windows open, crickets singing, passion, Clara losing herself, even when she felt her lungs tighten, struggling for air. She told herself it wasn't that bad and encouraged Seamus to continue. "Ignore it," she said, pushing herself, wanting this to happen so badly.

Seamus tried but couldn't help checking on Clara, his eyes opening, meeting hers, the asthma getting more intense. Clara smiled, hiding it as best as possible, but he couldn't continue. He stopped, rolling off onto the bed, frustrated. "I'm sorry," Seamus said, "it's me this time. I'm just, it's weird being here. I need more time."

"Of course," Clara said.

He turned away onto his side. Clara stared at Seamus's back, then spooned him from behind, not sure what to think. This was unexpected. And disappointing. Was it getting worse now? she wondered. The asthma? She'd always been the one having difficulties accepting it, but clearly, being back in this house was taking a toll on Seamus.

But again, she told herself to let it go. To focus on the now. To practice letting go of the worry, like Dr. Goldberg had given her permission to do. She had to take responsibility for her own joy, which seemed to be blooming here like she could never have imagined. And once again, the hope surged in Clara's heart, and she was certain that this summer was going to be the time for them to succeed as a family.

11

A Frazzled Girl and a Tempting New Friend Named Billy

Clara walked out of the guesthouse with her camera. She backed up and took a photo of the pines and maples against the sky. *Gorgeous,* she thought and looked around, taking in a deep breath and enjoying the beauty of the wispy trees and the relaxed mood.

Then, she spotted the red-haired teen girl walking down the street. The girl looked upset, like she'd been crying. Clara snapped a few photos of her and followed her through the lens until she spotted Mrs. Lee outside waving. Clara brought her camera down.

"Hi, Clara," the neighbor said, "I'm Mrs. Lee. Welcome to our neighborhood. If there's anything we can do, just give us a shout."

"Thank you," Clara said with a kind smile then quickly turned to go. She didn't want to get stuck talking to Mrs. Lee, but then realized maybe the lookie-loo neighbor could help. "Actually," Clara said, "do you happen to know who that red-haired girl is?"

"Red-haired girl?" Mrs. Lee asked. "No, I haven't seen any red-haired girl."

"The one who just walked by here? Who's really more of a teen than a girl? I mean, definitely a teen, maybe sixteen?" Clara started to lift up her camera to show Mrs. Lee but then remembered it was a film camera. She'd have to develop the negative before she could see how the photos came out.

"I didn't see any girl," Mrs. Lee replied, then yelled to her husband inside, "Dell?! Have you seen a strange red-haired girl around here?"

"No! It's okay, Mrs. Lee," Clara insisted, trying to stop her, not wanting to draw attention to herself or the girl who looked so upset. "I'll just find out myself."

"Well, if there's a new girl around here, I'll keep my eye out," Mrs. Lee assured Clara then felt her own forehead for a fever.

"Thank you," Clara said with another kind smile, "and nice to meet you," then started walking onto the road towards Main Street, hoping to get her bearings in town and see what she could find there. After a few moments of walking, Clara spotted the red-haired girl up ahead again. The girl was upset still and seemed to be angrily muttering to herself.

Clara decided to follow, keeping her distance so she wouldn't be spotted. The girl continued all the way to the general store with the ice cream freezer out front and a wooden bench, The Corner Market.

The store was attached to a weathered, two-story home that looked like a duplex. The red-haired teenage girl ran up the lawn and onto the big front porch leading to a stairwell. The whole building was badly in need of paint and renovation, even though it seemed to be lived in because there were tubs of flowers near the stairs. The girl ran around the side of the house, then after a moment, came hurrying back out and up the stairs to the front door and in.

Clara heard piano playing coming from the upstairs, a simple tune played badly. Then, an old woman appeared in an upper window. The woman stared out at nothing and seemed to listen or sense something.

Clara got a chill. Then, suddenly, she felt her lungs squeeze and started to have trouble breathing. She pulled out her inhaler and took a hit, the cool air reaching her lungs. This was strange. Why would she have trouble breathing now? She told herself not to worry. It was probably pollen that she wasn't used to, something causing an actual seasonal allergic reaction. "I'm fine," Clara told herself.

The eerie woman on the balcony seemed to hear Clara even though she'd spoken under her breath. The women turned her head as if curious to hear if there was more.

Clara felt her lungs tighten again. "Too weird," she whispered to herself and entered The Corner Market.

It was a typical small-town general store, with everything from groceries to hardware. The bells on the door jingled as Clara entered. She sucked in air and caught her breath easily this time, no need for the inhaler, even though there was cigarette smoke wafting up from behind the old cash register. It seemed to come from a ghostly-pale, heroin-thin guy with dark, curly hair, olive skin, a bit lighter than hers, in his early twenties, so also a bit younger, probably Irish, like the name on the front of the store—Flannery—but with something else mixed in. He was reading "Metamorphosis" and quickly glanced up at Clara after she stepped in, then went back to reading.

Clara strolled around the aisles then caught him peeking up at her a second time. He brought the book down revealing a mischievous-but-charming smile. "Can I help you?" he asked.

"No, thanks, I'm good," Clara replied, then continued to browse around, feeling him watching her. "Really, I'm just looking," she assured him.

"Yeah, I see that," the guy said, checking her out.

He was quite handsome, with striking black eyes and chiseled features. It made her uncomfortable, like maybe she shouldn't look.

"You're new here," he observed.

"Yup, just moved in down the street. The Dunne house," Clara told him, in case he knew the Dunnes. But the young guy just shrugged, his smile putting Clara at ease. She laughed, "Right, no one's lived there for almost thirty years."

"Oh, I did hear about that," the guy said. "Is it haunted?"

"No," Clara laughed again. "That's silly. But hey, you wouldn't happen to know who lives in the house next door would you? I mean, right here." She pointed to the two-story house with the balcony out front and the strange woman.

"That'd be my Gran and yours truly," he replied.

"Oh, wow, right. And what about the girl with the red hair?" Clara asked.

"Red hair?"

"Yeah, long," Clara explained. "About this tall, maybe fifteen or sixteen." She held her flattened palm to her nose to indicate the girl's estimated height. Clara was tall—five feet eleven—so the girl was likely about five-five.

"Probably one of Gran's piano students or helpers," the young guy said. "But I can't say I've ever seen her."

Strange, Clara thought, but everything seemed to be strange here.

"If you want, we can go find out," he added with a charming smile.

"No, she just looked upset, and I wanted to make sure she was okay."

"Maybe she didn't want to go to her piano lesson," he joked. "Those scales'll kill you every time."

Clara laughed. "Yeah, I know about that," she admitted, then imitated one of her childhood piano teachers, "Pronto! Andiamo! Aaaach."

"You Italian?" the guy asked.

Clara nodded. "On my dad's side. His parents came over here before he was born. And I lived there for a while. He's in the foreign service. I went to boarding school in Rome for second grade."

"By yourself?" the guy wondered, clearly intrigued.

"With my sister," she clarified. "Actually, it was a French Lycée, but we learned some Italian too."

"And you're... married?" he asked with a twinge of playful teasing as he noticed her ring.

"What is this? Twenty questions?" Clara teased back.

"Not much else to do around here," he said with a cute smile.

"Fair enough," Clara replied. "Yes, married."

"Aren't you a little young?" he teased.

"Twenty-nine," she told him.

"Wow. I mean. You look...twenty?"

"Old soul," Clara joked.

"No kidding," he said, eyes flashing, amused.

"Wait till you see my husband. Old. Forty-five," she laughed.

"Wow," he exclaimed.

"But it works," Clara told him with a mischievous smirk.

"Well, some people grow up fast," he quipped.

"What about you?" Clara asked and glanced at his book.

He hid it. "Not from here. Born here. Spent a lot of summers here..."

"And now, you're working here."

"Yeah, well, when you got nowhere else to go, that's what you do," he told her and kicked back against the backrest of his high stool, rolling a new cigarette, revealing track marks on his arm. "I studied philosophy. Not exactly useful. So, I quit that shit. Traveled. Came here. With a few bumps along the way."

"Well, if you feel like being useful maybe you can help me. I'm gonna need to stock up my art studio," she explained, looking around. "And do some renovations at the ghost house. Maybe you can order me a few items? Like a desk? And stuff to develop film?"

"Film? Like real film?" he exclaimed, even more intrigued now.

Clara laughed, "Yeah, for my camera," and lifted her vintage Voigtländer up for him to see and snapped a shot.

"Impressive," he said.

"Thank you," Clara agreed.

"Yeah, I could go online for you," he said. "Although, I'm sure you don't really need me for that."

"Great," Clara said. "No, I mean, yes, but it's more fun to work with someone. And it'll give you something to do," she teased.

"You like music?" the guy asked. "Cuz I could take you to hear some. Only thing to do around here. Besides skinny dipping. Or purchasing things online. Might be helpful. Or inspirational. For an artist." His eyes sparkled with flirtation.

Clara's stomach flipped. More flirtation, she thought, and now, it was coming from herself as well.

"I'm Billy, by the way," he said. "Twenty-six, younger man, Flannery, Billy Flannery. Irish. With a wee bit of the Balkan thrown in on my mom's side." Then, he put his smoke down and stood up and put out his hand to shake with a playful smirk on his face.

Clara gave him her hand. "Clara Aeillo," she introduced herself.

Billy took it, held it like he was going to kiss it. "Not Dunne?" he asked.

"Mrs. Dunne to you," Clara joked.

"Well, in that case, Mrs. Dunne...," Billy said and kissed her hand.

Clara laughed. Their eyes met. Yes, it was flirtatious but something inside her told her Billy would be safe, a safe friend—someone she could flirt with for fun. Hopefully. Maybe because he seemed to understood her boundaries. There was already a shorthand. And she was definitely better at setting boundaries with new friends than with old friends and family. She didn't have to worry that she'd hurt them. And perhaps, Billy was just what she needed right now. A grounding post that had nothing to do with her life. That was something Clara had always loved about traveling. She could meet people and be herself, go deep, honestly, revealing but with no judgments or caution. "Thank you, Signor Flannery," Clara said as she pulled her hand back from his lips. "And yes, I would love for you to help me order some supplies, *online*."

The Pale Blue Scarf

It was twilight, and Seamus had just returned from the city. He'd been gone for a few days, and Clara had spent the time working in the guesthouse, cleaning and sorting through some of the computer gear. She couldn't wait to show him what she'd accomplished. She led him across the lawn blindfolded so it would be a surprise.

"I'm glad you're enjoying this," Seamus told her.

"Shhh," Clara whispered, leading him up the two steps to the guesthouse. "Okay, one more step and you're in," she added and guided him through the door. She told him to wait there while she walked to the back and opened the door to the spacious walk-in closet. There was no second door back there, and Clara was still uncertain how the red-haired girl had gotten out so quickly the other morning. But she wasn't going to worry about that now. "Ready?" Clara asked Seamus and took off his blindfold. "Tada!"

Seamus stared at the space, wondering what he was looking at. "C'mon," Clara said and led him to the closet. It was still full of his old stuff—old computers, cords, notebooks, whiteboards, supplies. "You cleaned it out? Partially?" he asked, tactfully searching for what she could have possibly done.

"My future dark room!" she exclaimed. "I wiped off the million-year-old dust."

"Ah! Nice," he said. "And does that mean you'll be developing *film*?"

"Yeah, of course. After I get rid of all the junk," she teased.

"Junk? You're calling my prehistoric computers junk?"

"Yeah," she quipped.

"Hey, if it weren't for these computers, I wouldn't be a gaming king," he grinned and perused his *admirable* wares. "So glad the rain didn't get through here." He studied the leaky roof by the door.

"Definitely. We'll fix that," Clara told him. "And look, I washed the gross old blanket on the guest bed and will likely replace it too. I'm guessing no one ever actually was a guest in the guesthouse."

"Nope, we just used to invent things out here." His eyes lit up at one of the computers on the desk against the wall next to a type-writer in front of a big, ugly, orange, high-backed desk chair.

"You and Derek?" Clara asked.

Seamus laughed. "No, Derek wasn't a geek like me. He was the jock, believe it or not. Mr. Popularity. Mr. Quarterback. The girls loved him." He ran his hand over the top of the desktop monitor sitting atop a giant, off-white computer base. "No, it was just me and a friend. And my dad."

Clara lifted the camera to snap a picture of Seamus in his element. Through the lens, she spotted the red-haired teenage girl outside. "Hey, there she is!" Clara exclaimed and ran to the window. But then, the girl was gone. "I swear to god. There's this girl and these kids running around here all the time. I think she was even in the house the other morning."

"Well, they're just gonna have to get used to the fact that this place is no longer abandoned," Seamus quipped. "And I'm gonna have to get used to the fact that you like it here."

Clara heard laughter outside again, but when she looked, there was nothing. "I saw her in town too," Clara told him. "That same teenage girl that was in our house. I think she was crying, so I followed her, through the streets. Then, she ran into this big old house with this weird old lady standing on a balcony, staring off, and this awful music. Very country Dickens," Clara joked. "Or I guess that would be Yankee Gothic."

Seamus laughed, "Mrs. Flannery?"

"I don't know."

"Piano music?"

"Yes," Clara confirmed, "the lady that owns the shop, right? Or at least lives next to it."

"Wow, you really scoped things out," Seamus teased.

Clara smirked and lifted the camera to her eye again. Seamus stuck out his tongue. She started shooting. He playfully grabbed her arm and wrestled the camera away. Clara laughed and saw—a FLASH of the sandy-haired teen boy in the window. She ignored it. Seamus pressed her arm behind her and kissed her—playful, fun— she tried to get away. He didn't let her go and kissed her again. "Let's go inside," he whispered as his lips grazed her ear.

Clara whispered back, "How 'bout we pretend someone's outside and we're sneaking in here?"

"You mean, Mrs. Lee?" Seamus joked.

"Yeah, perfect. Lookie-loo Lee," Clara added, "she's gonna tell on us."

Seamus was amused and somehow much more relaxed than the other night after the dinner at the brewery. "How about we up the ante and sneak into the house? To the bedroom. Where it's not so dusty. And creepy."

"Hey, I dusted in here!" Clara defended playfully.

"And your nice, soft Egyptian-cotton pillowcases," he added.

Clara liked the idea, and Seamus pulled her out. On the way through the door, Clara grabbed a light-blue gauzy scarf hanging on the doorknob. She'd thrown it in the wash earlier and loved the colors—faded pale blue and a faint, greyish cornflower lavender. She loved how soft the fabric was and let Seamus lead her back across the yard to the house, grass cool on her bare feet. She felt excitement rise inside her. Seamus's hand was so firm as it clasped hers—heat, strength, comfort—and the moment felt like forever, like this was always meant to be. Her heart raced, and she let her body guide her for a change, not her mind, into the abyss of passion and love.

***

The moon rose slowly as Clara lay on her stomach, light-blue scarf woven through her fingers, watching Seamus sleep, moonlight coming in, illuminating his sandy-blond hair, wild, messy—the perfect moment. She felt pure joy being with him and next to him and was enjoying the whole sight. *Such a pretty pale blue*, she thought about the scarf, especially against his skin as he slept. Blue was a good color for Seamus, even when it was muted like this, faded from the sun. And she liked how the scarf went from the pale dessert blue to faint lavender-grey to almost white. Clara also was happy she'd finally put her new, beautiful French bedding on. It felt so crisp and fresh. It was pure white with tiny stitches of lemon yellow on the pillow shams and duvet.

As she took it all in, she felt magic there, in that moment, in that space—as if she'd conjured it up and it would bloom into something special. Because it was the perfect setting, a garden for love to grow. *So corny*, she thought and finally dozed off, free, at last, no worries— as the moon rose further, illuminating both their faces and leading Clara into a dream—*the* dream, again.

Clara stepped into the clearing, bare feet on the moss, dread in her stomach, the two gravestones before her. But this time, suddenly, she heard the creaky springs of the bed like in the hypnosis, the girl jumping. Suddenly, in the clearing, the deep-blue thin fabric came over her head, taught across her face, and she began falling into a hole, Alice in Wonderland, spinning over and over, hitting her head on the bed frame. The long, thin fabric was over her face, not a blanket. It was definitely a piece of fabric, like a shawl or a coffee-table runner, and it was starting to suffocate her with blurry turquoise and peacock-blue streaks of color.

There was someone on the other side of the fabric too. He was saying that it was okay, that she was okay, comforting, pressing on top of her, the cloth not letting her breathe or speak to tell him that she was okay, that she didn't need his help or for him to pressure her. But he couldn't hear, and the fabric pulled tighter across Clara's face—*can't breathe, can't breathe*. Was it a dream? Real? The person on the other side of the blue fabric definitely wasn't pulling the cloth tighter across her face, that was obvious. But then, who was pulling it? Was she doing it to herself—pulling the cloth tight? Suffocating herself? Like a slipknot that her body was pulling tighter? Was this her—the girl? Or was it Clara? Was the suffocating all her fault?

It got harder to breathe in the dream. Clara began to struggle to get out from behind the fabric, to breathe. Struggling, no air. Then, somehow, she saw Seamus's reflection in the window through the loosely woven threads of the peacock-blue fabric—even though they were in a clearing in the woods and there was no window.

Clara, deep in her dream, wondered if this was all really happening. Did she see Seamus in a window? Or was it the dream? And why wasn't he helping her breathe? Then, in the dream, Seamus started to walk away, leaving Clara at the gravestones suffocating behind the fabric.

"Seamus, wait!" Clara yelled from her nightmare and bolted upright and awake in reality on the sleigh bed under her crisp duvet.

Seamus jumped up from sleep and saw that Clara couldn't breathe—she was mid asthma attack. They both scrambled for the inhaler and couldn't find it. Clara heard someone crying outside, screaming—"No, leave me alone!" the voice shouted.

Is this real? Clara wondered, as the asthma got worse. She grabbed the phone and dialed 911, gasping for air, getting enough to respond to the request for her name. "Clara...Dunne," she managed just as Seamus found the inhaler. "Got it!" he yelled. Clara grabbed it from him and sucked in air—*Finally, relief. Real relief, not a dream*—cool, beautiful air, and she could breathe normally.

"Hello? Hello...?" the 911 operator's voice called out from the landline phone.

Seamus picked up the receiver off the ground. "Hi! Yes! Sorry!" he told the operator. "We found the inhaler. We're okay...Yes, thank you very much." Seamus hung up, angry with himself for letting this happen. "We have to be more careful," he insisted to Clara.

Clara nodded, shaken as well, but she couldn't hold back her joy about earlier. "At least it didn't happen earlier, you know." She smiled, feeling sexy, blushing—hoping Seamus could let it go. "I have a good feeling about tonight," she told him, gently, the thought bringing tears of relief to her eyes.

Seamus hugged her but couldn't shake the feelings. "I'm sorry. This place is just...I want it to work for us. But sometimes, it feels jinxed."

Clara snuggled closer to him. "It'll work for us. I know."

"I think you should see the doctor out here."

"Why?" Clara demanded. This seemed ridiculous, and all Clara's walls went up instantly.

"For the asthma. Just in case," he told her and stood up and put on his green-and-blue plaid pajama pants. Clara loved those pants almost as much as the Tin Tin boxers. "Where are you going?" she asked.

"Just to lock the doors," he replied, the tension still in his body.

This was ridiculous too, Clara thought. Now, he was getting paranoid. Clara knew she had to turn this around. "There is no way in hell I'm going to any small-town quack," she teased.

"A quack?!" he demanded, feigning shock. "Dude."

"Don't dude me," she quipped.

"Well, I know the local small-town quack—Dr. Eve Madison," Seamus toyed. "Harvard grad, Columbia med school, practiced in the city, and moved back here to raise her own family."

"People move back here?" Clara joked.

Seamus was amused.

"How about some chips and guac?" Clara chimed, jumping up. "I'm starved, and they had some great avocadoes at that corner grocers. And this local-made salsa. Could be good..." She gave him a mischievous smile and said, "Last one cuts the onions," and grabbed her robe and took off down the stairs.

"Careful!" Seamus yelled after her, not even trying to win the race, "just in case!"

Which made Clara smile. This was good. Seamus felt it too. They both knew—this might be it. This house might be lucky for them.

Even though Seamus also knew something was dreadfully wrong there. That he was being pulled backwards in time to all the old ghosts that he'd so deftly buried. The ones he had worked so hard to keep locked inside. And now, he'd have to work harder. For Clara. For himself. For their baby.

13

Crying in the Next Room

Clara followed the nurse down the hall of Dr. Eve Madison's office toward the examination room. It was now early June. They'd been at the lake house for just over a month, about six weeks, and Clara finally agreed to make the appointment with the obstetrician. She was happy to see the offices weren't in the dark ages. In fact, they'd been remodeled recently and were quite bright and happy, with high ceilings, modern décor, skylights and all.

Just before they got to Clara's examination room, Clara saw the red-haired teenage girl coming out of a bathroom down the hall. The girl looked pale and terrified and hurried into the examination room next to Clara's.

Once inside, the nurse weighed Clara and checked her blood pressure. Everything looked good. The nurse smiled, giving Clara a gown even though she was just there to meet the doctor. "Dr. Madison will be right in," the nurse told her and left.

Clara changed out of her summer dress, patterned with lemons, put on her gown and sat on the examination table. Which is when she heard voices through the wall—faint crying.

Clara slid off the table, the tile cold on her bare feet. She put her ear to the wall to listen and heard a man's voice say, "You're almost five months along, and I'm going to have to tell your parents." Clara assumed the voice belonged to another doctor at the Madison practice, even though she'd only seen Dr. Eve's name on the awning. Maybe he was new.

Then, Clara heard a girl's voice say, "Can't you help stop it?" Clara knew the voice had to belong to the scared red-haired girl.

"I'm sorry, that's not possible here," the man replied.

Clara felt a sharp pain in her head. She touched the scar on her forehead then heard a door slam from the next room. Clara began to sweat and heard crying—she felt her lungs begin to squeeze. She started having trouble breathing and grabbed her orange tote from under her clothes on the chair, pulling out her inhaler and taking a hit. As she felt the cool drops enter her lungs, she heard the door slam shut again in the next room and footsteps going down the hall towards the reception area. Clara peeked out the door of her examination room and saw the red-haired teenage girl leave just as Dr. Eve Madison was approaching.

Clara quickly shut the door and jumped back onto the table, just as Dr. Eve entered with a huge, gorgeous, warm smile and greeted her, "Hi. You must be Clara. I'm Dr. Madison." Dr. Madison seemed to be in her early 40s, elegant—*Not your average country-bumpkin doctor*, Clara thought.

"Hi, yes, Clara Aiello...Dunne, so nice to meet you," Clara replied and jutted her hand out for a shake.

Dr. Eve had a nice, firm grip and looked Clara in the eye as they shook hands. Dr. Eve must've noticed Clara's distress and asked, "Is there something wrong?"

"No, I just thought...I mean, I," Clara stammered, then admitted, "I heard the other doctor next door. I'm sorry. I couldn't help overhear. The girl seemed so upset."

"Other doctor?" Dr. Eve inquired, clearly surprised.

"The man," Clara explained.

"Maybe it was Geraldine. Her voice can get quite deep sometimes," Dr. Eve joked. "And she had a cold last week. But no, I'm joking. There are no other doctors here. It's just me."

"Geraldine is the red-haired girl?" Clara asked. "The teenager?"

"You sure you're okay?" Dr. Eve asked.

"Sure. Yes. I'm...humidity," Clara managed, laughing it off, trying to cover her confusion.

"Well, whoever was next door is nothing for you to worry about," Dr. Eve comforted with a warm doctor smile then perused Clara's chart. "So, this is a get-acquainted visit. Smart. Very smart. Severe asthma. And you're trying to get pregnant?"

Clara felt her heart begin to race but managed a smile. "Yes," she replied then felt tears rising—maybe because Dr. Eve felt so safe and comforting. Clara tried to hold them back but wasn't successful.

"Oh, honey," Dr. Eve said, "can I give you a hug?"

Clara nodded. "This must be a country thing," she joked, but the hug felt good and the tears flowed. Dr. Eve grabbed tissues for Clara. "We haven't had much luck," Clara admitted. "I just had a third miscarriage, end of March."

"Yeah, I see that here," Dr. Eve said, looking at the questionnaire Clara had filled out. "And you've had your hormones checked, blood panels..."

"Everything," Clara confirmed. "It's all fine. I'm healthy. Fertile. Him too. My husband, Seamus."

"You know, many more people have miscarriages than they talk about. And it's a good sign. It means you can get pregnant."

Clara laughed and shook her head. "That's what my friend Erin tells me constantly."

"Well, it's true," Dr. Eve assured her.

Clara let this sink in.

"And sometimes it takes a new environment," Dr. Eve continued. "A new headspace. And as I always say, the right baby is going to show up at the right time. Maybe your baby just wasn't ready."

Clara's tears rose again.

Dr. Eve squeezed her arm. "But that doesn't help till your baby is here, does it?"

Clara shook her head.

"I get that. You'll understand one day. I'm sorry. And you know what? I'm going to give you the number of an acupuncturist—in case you're up for something a little different. You're still trying, right?"

"Yes, yes, we are," Clara confirmed.

"And your period is back? I see you mentioned that here on the form."

"Yeah, I mean, a short one, spotting a month or so after the D&C. Mid April."

"Are you doing a temperature chart? For ovulation?"

"No, I think—actually, getting pregnant hasn't been the hard part," Clara admitted and forced a smile. Clara hadn't had a second period and knew there was a chance she was pregnant again—perhaps from that night last month with the moon shining so beautifully, before the asthma attack. Or maybe that first night in the house. But Clara didn't want to say anything to Dr. Eve. She didn't want Dr. Eve to do a blood test. She was too afraid to find out just yet if she was pregnant or not. She wasn't ready for more devastation.

"Well, it sounds like you know what's going on," Dr. Eve continued. "Maybe just have your OB in the city email over a copy of your chart there, the actual blood panels, etc. And we'll focus on Dr. Woo, the acupuncturist. She'll have you brewing Chinese tea concoctions and other things in no time. It'll give you something to do towards preparing your body and mind. It may not be very country doctor, but I did live in the city you know," Dr. Eve quipped, her eyes flashing with humor. Clara laughed, comforted by this. "And as for the asthma," Dr. Eve continued, "Geraldine will text you my number. You can call whenever you need anything. Dr. Woo may have a trick up her sleeve for that too. Whether you believe in alternative medicine or not, it can't hurt to try. I've seen it work miracles. Plus, personally, I always find it helpful to have some kind of practice, even if it's just making herbal Chinese tea every day."

Clara smiled, a sense of relief coming over her. "Thank you. I'm really glad we met."

"Me too," Dr. Eve said, pressing Clara's arm warmly one last time before heading out to her next patient.

***

On her way out of the doctor's office, Clara stopped at the front desk to talk to the receptionist. "Excuse me," she said, noticing that the woman's nametag read *Geraldine*. "Could you tell me the name of the red-haired girl who was in the room next to mine?"

The receptionist looked down at the schedule and shook her head. "That wasn't a red-head, dear. That was a platinum blonde, Mrs. Lane."

"Oh, wow," Clara laughed, hiding her shock. "I guess I should make an appointment with the ophthalmologist next. Thank you."

As Clara stepped out of the office, she passed a happy couple entering. The woman looked about eight-months pregnant. Clara's heart sank. Maybe she shouldn't have visited Dr. Eve after all. Maybe it was just a reminder that she wasn't meant to be a mother. Or maybe it was a reminder that she was losing her mind. Why had she heard and seen a girl that wasn't there?

14

Is That Emmeline?

Clara left Dr. Eve's office shaken. She couldn't get the red-haired teen girl out of her head now. She'd definitely heard her crying in the next room and seen her in the hallway. And Clara was certain that the man's voice in the next examining room wasn't Geraldine's. But why wasn't the red-haired teen on the doctor's schedule? Why hadn't the doctor or Geraldine known about her? And who was the doctor in the next room?

Am I losing my mind now too? Clara thought again. *No, no, I'm not. There has to be an explanation.* She stood up tall and continued down the pleasantly manicured walkway to the sidewalk. She couldn't go back to that place of confusion. Things were going her way here, and there was hope again, finally, that she might be pregnant too.

Clara thought about Seamus's quiet breath when he slept so peacefully next to her and the joy she saw in his eyes whenever he perused his old computers. It made her heart fill with love again, and she stepped out onto the street to walk home.

But then, she spotted the red-haired girl up ahead on a bike. Clara's heart began to race. She wanted to ignore the girl but couldn't. The girl seemed to be completely distressed now, weeping. And something drew Clara towards her, so she followed—picking up her pace as the girl rode into town. Clara felt her own anxiety build, sweat beads forming on her head—but she continued until the girl rode past The Corner Market and sped up, too fast to follow. Clara gave up and went into the market, bells ringing as she entered, her face pale.

Billy looked up from behind the old-school cash register on the counter, reading, smoke circling above his head.

"Hey, city slicker," Billy greeted her.

"Hey," Clara managed. "I came by to find out about the supplies and the chairs I ordered."

"You look like crap," Billy teased. "You look like me. And I know how that feels."

Clara felt her forehead—cold and damp. "Yeah, I feel a little weird," she admitted.

"What you need is some of Gran's fresh-squeezed orange juice," Billy told her. "Works every time. I could use some too. C'mon," he said and jumped up, locking the cash register and coming round, leading Clara out the front door and flipping the sign to say "Back in 10 minutes."

They walked out of the market onto the sidewalk, and Billy led Clara to his grandmother's place next door, the attached house with the balcony. There was a stairway going up the middle like an old apartment building, but it seemed to be a house with a unit upstairs and downstairs too. Clara could see Mrs. Flannery staring out the second-story window again as piano music wafted out.

"Reminds me of my cousin's apartment in Paris with these stairs," Clara told Billy as they started up, "narrow stairwell up to the premier étage."

"Fancy," Billy teased. "And I even know what you mean—rez-de-chausée is the ground floor there; premier étage is the first floor up."

"You speak French?" Clara asked.

"Oui, oui, and unlike here in the States, the French first floor is our second floor, not the one on the ground level." He smiled, and Clara was pleasantly amused, feeling slightly better as they entered the upstairs unit. "This is Gran's place," he told her. "Living room, kitchen, dining room, bedrooms back there, always something good cooking or baking, and her music studio is through that door." Billy pointed at a closed door that was directly off the dining room and led into the music studio. "I think at some point the building was two units and they converted it into one—Gran's home and a studio. Taking up the entire premiere étage, or second floor, if you prefer Americaine. And I'm down on the rez-de-chausée."

Clara took a moment to peruse the comfy apartment-like house. It was simple and had no art or decorations on the walls. But there was an Ella Fitzgerald and Oscar Peterson poster on the studio door, where the music wafted out.

"Piano lessons," Billy told Clara, "C'mon," and led her on towards the kitchen.

"Hmm," she mused and thought, *Seamus was right—piano.*

"Billy?" Mrs. Flannery called out from behind the closed studio door as they passed.

They stopped. "Yeah, it's me, Gran," Billy shouted through the door.

"You bringing me a visitor?" Gran called out.

"No, Gran! She's for me," Billy replied then whispered to Clara, "She may be old and blind, but she's still got a good sense of humor. C'mon."

Blind? thought Clara as they continued towards the kitchen. That explained the creepy staring off the balcony and why there was no art on the walls.

Suddenly, the music-studio door flew open and Mrs. Flannery stepped out. She was a short, feisty, blind-as-a-bat seventy-something year old, staring out at a wall with a look of surprise. "Is that Emmeline?" she demanded.

"No, Gran," Billy replied. "It's Clara. She's new here so don't scare her away just yet." Billy motioned exaggeratedly for Clara to keep walking into the kitchen.

Clara walked on.

"That *is* Emmeline," Mrs. Flannery insisted. "I'd recognize her step anywhere. Emmeline? Honey, I—"

"Gran! Her name is Clara," Billy corrected.

"But—"

"Hi, Mrs. Flannery," Clara said kindly and walked over to shake the inquisitive old woman's hand. "I hear you have the best orange juice in town. My name is Clara Aiello Dunne."

Mrs. Flannery smiled, squeezing Clara's hand, holding it a moment longer than is customary, as if to get a sense of Clara.

"She doesn't feel well," Billy told his grandmother and walked over to them to gently lead Mrs. Flannery back into the music studio. "So, we're getting some O.J."

"Nice to meet you too—sort of," Mrs. Flannery called back. "Next time, we'll talk."

"Yes, definitely," Clara called out and felt a wave of nausea as Billy shut the music-studio door and joined Clara in the kitchen. "Sorry about that," he said. "I guess Gran thinks you're someone who used to work for her or something."

"It's fine. She seems nice," Clara told him and felt her forehead. It was getting cold and clammy again.

Billy opened the fridge and poured them both a glass of fresh-squeezed orange juice, noticing that Clara had begun sweating and was having trouble breathing.

Clara was getting oddly light-headed too, and her lungs were constricting. *This is so strange. This never happens,* she thought. *Except with Seamus.*

Billy handed her the juice and kept his worry to himself. "I really hope she's not losing it," Billy joked. "I mean, not really, Gran's a tough cookie—as she likes to say."

Clara drank the juice, wheezing as she inhaled between sips, trying to maintain her composure. "Are you sure? Is she going to be okay?" Clara asked.

"Yeah, she just likes to act superstitious. But then again, who doesn't?" Billy laughed as Clara went for the inhaler in her bag.

"I really can't breathe in here," Clara said and sucked in the cool drops, the air reaching her lungs. "I have to get out of here. The walls are closing in." She headed to the front door of the flat.

Billy called after her, "Clara?"

Clara didn't stop and ran out and down the stairs, away from the house, quickly moving up the street. She had to get away. *Why? Why is this happening?* she thought, and the farther away she got from Mrs. Flannery's, the easier her breathing became. Her instinct was right to leave. But she didn't understand what was happening. More strangeness. More confusion. What was this place?

Billy caught up to Clara as she recovered. "I'm sorry," she told him.

"No, I'm sorry," Billy said. "And I'm going to make it up to you."

"You didn't do anything. I'm cursed with this asthma, and it makes no sense. There's no reason that I couldn't breathe in there. In fact, it only ever happens when I'm prone," she joked.

"And you're adorable," Billy told her, clearly amused and charmed by her.

"What does that mean?" Clara asked, taking in Billy's grin, realizing he was trying to distract her, which was a good move. She needed a distraction.

"C'mon," Billy said and grabbed Clara's hand, pulling her off towards the lake and the pier with the restaurants and boardwalk.

And Clara didn't resist. She didn't have it in her and needed a friend right now with no complications. And she needed to be able to breathe.

15

Escape and Temptation

Clara's lungs opened more and more the farther she and Billy got away from Mrs. Flannery's house and Main Street and the closer they got to the boardwalk—where Clara felt free again.

She liked that Billy had called her adorable. She needed that re-assurance right now, so she let Billy lead her on, letting go of all her worries, walking the docks, talking about Paris and Rome, telling stories about travel and talking about music, books and life and chasing gulls. They passed the playground. Clara told Billy about the kids splashing people with their cannon balls. And she felt elated somehow, which was just what she needed.

When they got to the little harbor, they entered a tiny lakeside bar right next to the brewery where Clara and Seamus had eaten when they first arrived. Billy and Clara were drawn in by the blues guitar on the jukebox, and Clara instantly fell in love with the locale—warm wooden beams, big old bar, stage for a band, checked table cloths. It had so much character, and she felt transported away from her stress. And Billy's cute smile was heaven as he pulled out a barstool for her. "What can I get you?" he asked.

Clara took a moment to peruse the beautiful bottles of alcohol arranged on the back bar—the different levels holding a variety of spirits, wine, a black-and-white photo of what was likely the owner with friends at the Grande Place in Brussels, a red model Chevy racecar, a Russian nesting doll, an old Persian samovar, a Yankees bobble head and other knick-knacks. It reminded Clara of traveling with her friends in Europe. Tenting with Kate and Jake. Swimming topless in Corfu. Riding the train and getting high on the scenery and edibles from Amsterdam. "I'm thinking ouzo, from Greece," Clara told Billy. "I haven't had ouzo in so long and this place reminds me of...not Greece, but being away."

"I know that," Billy said. "Ouzo. *And* being away."

Clara smirked and asked the bartender, "Do you happen to have ouzo here?"

"Oh, that's one we don't hear often," the bartender said. "But the owner had a bar in Crete for a while, so yes."

"Wonderful!" Clara exclaimed. "That's serendipitous, and we'll have two with ice and a splash of water." Clara turned to Billy who seemed equally free of burden.

When the ouzo came, the bartender added the ice and water in front of them so they could see the clear Greek spirit turn to white. "Gnarly," Billy said and tried his ouzo. "Love that licorice taste!" he exclaimed.

"Yup," Clara laughed, and the two sipped and continued talking, telling more travel-adventure stories until both of them were sufficiently buzzed.

"I kind of wish I could be on the road forever," Billy said. "But right now, that's not a thing for me."

"Well, this lake seems to be a good spot to rest for a while," Clara said, trying to be positive. "I mean, I get it. But I can tell you that eventually, well at least for me, it's possible to find a home too. Where you can just be. When you get older," she teased. "And grow up."

Billy was charmed again by Clara's mischievous grin. "Well, I will see what I can do," he joked, "about growing up. Scouts honor." He held up two fingers as if making a Boy Scout pledge.

"You weren't a scout!" Clara teased and bent one of his fingers up to make the proper three-finger scout pledge.

"Cub Scout? Yes, I was," he grinned, "but you're right—overly responsible, cheerful and helpful? Naw."

"Well, you seem cheerful and helpful to me. I mean, you did manage to get my paint and daybed cover. And construction supplies."

Billy laughed, loving the attention and her sense of humor.

"And you work!" she chimed but then remembered. "Oh, wait! Shoot! You forgot the sign!"

"What sign?" he asked.

"At the store. Back in 10 minutes. You said you'd be back in ten and that was two hours ago."

Billy laughed, "It's fine. Gran won't notice, and there's always Walmart. Thirty minutes away."

"No, I feel bad," Clara insisted. "Let's go back."

"Don't worry. No one will miss me," Billy grinned.

"It's right there. Five minutes. It'll make me feel better. It's so easy."

"Relax," Billy told Clara.

"This is relaxed," Clara insisted. "I like things to be ordered. And on schedule. And fair. It's not fair to your customers. They need to know that you're there for them. They like knowing that. It's a safety net that they can be sure about. Their sweet Corner Market. And I'm buzzed, so I'm telling you how controlling I am and how I like to fix things."

Billy laughed, charmed by her honesty. "The customers are all home eating dinner now, not at the market."

"But what if someone needs mustard?" Clara demanded.

"Mustard?"

"Yeah, like, you know, for their burgers. I'm guessing people out here eat meat?"

"Out here? In farmland? No man's land?"

"Yeah, and if they run out of mustard and you're not open, it ruins the whole experience. I mean, if they're waiting for multiple ten-minute chunks instead of going to Walmart, that is. Seriously, the burgers will get cold."

Billy was amused. He pulled a harmonica out of his jacket and played a few notes.

"What are you doing?" Clara asked.

"Trying to get you to calm down," Billy told her and walked over to the little bar stage and jumped up and played a blues song. Clara was surprised by how good he was and mesmerized by the way he swayed as he played. She applauded and whistled loudly with her fingers when he finished. He bowed and came back to their barstools beaming. "And?" he asked.

"And amazing," Clara said and high-fived him.

He ordered another round of ouzo to celebrate.

Which is when Clara noticed the bartender's watch and was reminded of the 10-minute sign. "But we have to go change the sign first," Clara insisted and jumped up.

"Why are you so worried about this?" Billy laughed.

"I don't know. I feel bad," she said playfully. "And I like to move when I'm buzzed. Give me the key." She held out her hand for the key.

"So, we should dance?" Billy toyed, standing up and taking her hand.

"Key!" she exclaimed.

"To the store?"

"Yes."

"You are something," Billy said and pulled the store key out of his pocket.

Clara swiped it from him. "It's called over-controlling and responsible," she told him and ran off—out the door of the blues bar, down the boardwalk, jumping up onto the old railroad ties lining the grass leading to the shortcut through the trees. She pushed herself to run faster—just like she had done when she ran track in high school, pumping her arms, feeling the muscles in her thighs getting hot and the air filling her lungs, her lungs that worked perfectly, and she felt so free.

When Clara got to the store, she saw Mrs. Flannery in the window as if staring out and felt bad about earlier. She'd been rude to the nice piano teacher and promised herself to go back and visit the next week. Then, she quickly changed the sign in the market window to "CLOSED" and ran back towards the lake.

Clara pushed herself again as she ran—the hit of endorphins filling her veins—and by the time she walked back into the blues bar, Clara felt as if she'd just ridden a rollercoaster. She definitely needed to do more physical activity. Play more. And worry less.

Billy was looking at the jukebox when she entered. She beamed as she handed him the key. "Wow," he said, "And thanks." Clara was glowing with sweat. She looked beautiful and free. "Better?" he asked.

"Much," Clara replied and headed back to her barstool and asked the bartender for a glass of water.

"Good. And you can finally relax now?" Billy teased, looking back at the songs on the jukebox, amused by Clara's need to be so responsible.

"Yes," Clara replied, downing the water.

"Any requests?" Billy called back to her.

"No, you pick," Clara said. "Or you could play some more."

"You liked that?" Billy asked.

"Yes," Clara replied. "And I can fully appreciate it. Now that I know your customers won't be waiting." Clara grinned and finished her drink, ordering two more.

Billy walked over to the bar and played another song on the harmonica from his barstool. Clara applauded when he finished. Her claps echoed. There were only a handful of other customers in the bar.

"There's a bit more action in here at night," Billy told her. "But barely."

"That was plenty of action for me," Clara laughed. "I'm old and boring now, remember?"

Billy sat back down on the barstool with a flirtatious smile and put his hand on Clara's leg. "Twenty-nine and old."

Clara looked into his eyes. "If I weren't in love with my husband, that might be a good idea," she said and pushed his hand off. "But I really love your company if you'll have me at a distance, like I said before. At the store. When we met."

"Whatever you say, gorgeous," Billy said with a smile and flagged down the bartender.

Clara laughed. The temptation to go there with Billy was real, but she knew she'd never act on it. But knowing the attraction existed made her feel powerful and beautiful and seen. Plus, they both had an adventurous streak, and she was enjoying getting back in touch with that part of herself right now.

The bartender came over with two more drinks, and Billy asked for the menu, which is when Clara noticed Derek pass by on the boardwalk—without his collar, looking much younger. "Oh, look. It's my brother-in-law."

Clara got up and watched Derek through the window as he walked away down the boardwalk carrying a guitar case. *Strange,* she mused then told Billy, "He's a priest," as she came back to the barstool. "I should be hanging out with him instead of you." She grinned flirtatiously.

Billy laughed, charmed, and they clinked glasses and drank. "My husband, Seamus, hates him," Clara told Billy. "My brother-in-law, Derek, that is."

"Hate? Why?" Billy asked. "That's a tough word."

"I mean, not hate, but there's a lot of tension between them."

"What happened?"

"Something about a relationship he says."

"Relationships'll do that," Billy concurred.

"And so will their parents dying," Clara supposed. "Which is what I think the real problem is somehow."

"Oof! Their parents died?"

"Yeah," she said.

"Well, that's heavy. Recently?"

"Thirty years ago. Hence the abandoned house that needs so much work."

"Oh, right, yeah, double oof. I mean, if that's still a thing. The pain that lingers," he mused, then looked down into his glass of ouzo as if he knew that pain all too well.

"They were just in high school," Clara told him, "when their parents died."

"Yeah, that's rough," Billy nodded again and downed a big gulp of ouzo.

"You okay?"

"Yeah, yeah, fine," he said. "What happened?"

Clara got the feeling Billy was rattled by something she'd said and wasn't actually interested in Seamus's story, but he definitely wanted to talk to her, needed to talk to her—needed the connection. And maybe it was worth whatever painful memory this was bringing up for him.

Clara hoped the memory wasn't related to her specifically and that Billy was okay with the boundary she'd set when she pushed his hand off her leg—the boundary that she was slightly, flirtatiously overstepping, because she felt herself being drawn further towards him. "Car accident," Clara said. "On a stormy night."

"Stormy night?" Billy laughed.

"It's not funny."

"C'mon, it's cliché," he said.

"Well, it's true."

"I believe you, go on."

So, Clara told Billy the whole story of how Seamus and Derek's parents died. And he listened. Intently. Watching her lips and her hair, mesmerized as she talked.

Clara told Billy how the accident happened when Seamus's older brother, Derek, the priest that they'd just seen walk by, was a senior in high school and playing a baseball tournament two hours away. And how their parents drove out to see him play and planned on spending the weekend by the Hudson to celebrate their anniversary. And how there was hail all of a sudden, and they got in a car accident near the baseball field. And Derek made it to the hospital but Seamus never saw his parents again because he was back at home.

And Clara told Billy that Derek has always blamed himself for the accident because it wouldn't have happened if his parents hadn't come to see him play. "And I'm still not sure why Seamus hates him," Clara concluded.

"Wow," Billy said, shaking his head, smirking, definitely more interested in Clara than the story.

Clara laughed. "Maybe it doesn't matter that Seamus hates him, and I should just let it go. He's trying. And he promised to be civil."

Billy asked Clara if she wanted another drink.

"I think we've had enough," Clara mused. "But how about some food?"

"Fair enough," Billy said and flagged the bartender down and ordered. "We'll have the schawarma and hummus and feta plate. And another round. Thank you," he added as he handed the bartender back the menu.

"You got it," the bartender replied.

"Another round?!" Clara exclaimed.

"You got a problem with that?" Billy teased.

Clara shook her head no. She liked how Billy knew exactly what she wanted—pita and hummus and feta. Maybe it was a travel thing—even though he did order more drinks just now and she was way over her limit.

"Good," he teased again.

"It's perfect," Clara chimed and took a sip of the ouzo still sitting in front of her and brought the conversation back to Seamus. "So, yeah, I really just want to help them—Seamus and his brother. With this tension."

"Now, that is a terrible idea," Billy said, "helping."

"No, it's not," Clara laughed.

"You can't help them. They have to do it themselves. Recovery 101. My territory."

Clara studied Billy. There was something so magnetic and charming about him. "Maybe I'm the one who needs help," Clara said and downed the rest of her glass. "Why is it that I'm so drawn to you?" she asked.

"Drawn to me?"

"Yes. It's not good. Or maybe it is."

"Why are you so worried?" Billy replied.

"I'm not."

"No, right, of course not. You did say that wasn't a thing."

"Yeah, no, not a thing. And if it were a thing, it'd be a thing no one would act on," she teased.

"But I am guessing you will act on helping Seamus and the priest. Even though you shouldn't. Right?"

Clara laughed. "Maybe. And maybe I like you because you see me."

"I do see you," Billy agreed. "Does your husband not?"

Clara was amused, enjoying the attention. "I'm sorry," she flirted, "but he does. My husband sees me, Clara Aiello, everything that I am. And we play. Like children. And make stuff together. His games. He makes games, you know. And I help. It's fun. Our home in Brooklyn is wonderful..." She stopped because Billy was watching her, entranced. "Stop," she said.

"Why?" he smirked mischievously.

"Because that is not a thing," she repeated, taking another drink of ouzo, eyeing him playfully.

"Fine, none of *that*," he said and winked.

Clara shook her head.

"So, what's the problem with Romeo then?" he asked.

"There's nothing wrong with him," Clara insisted.

"So, what's the issue? You did bring it up you know. I mean, with regards to the priest." He grinned, clearly trying another tactic.

"Hmm," Clara mused and took a moment to think about it. "Well, he does hold back sometimes. And it's not that bad. But I feel it more here. And sometimes it's like...he closes. But I know it has nothing to do with me. It's his issue. But what if that's the problem? With Derek? How can I make him not close?"

"Well, I'm definitely not closed," Billy declared.

"Why?" Clara asked in all earnestness.

Billy shook his head—he wasn't going to go there. Luckily for him, the food arrived. "Mmm," Billy said, deflecting as he dipped pita bread in the hummus.

Clara waited. She wasn't going to let him off the hook so fast.

"I really don't want to talk about me," Billy told her and playfully fought her pita for hummus-dipping space.

"Please, it's not fair otherwise," she said.

"You really want to know? Why I'm so...open?"

"Yes! Yes, I do," she said and snuck in a hummus dip.

Billy gestured for her to lean in close and whispered. "Because I want to reach God," he said then leaned back and laughed at her surprise, "that's why I stay open." Then, he went back to the hummus, smiling knowingly.

Clara laughed, not sure what to make of this.

"I'm sure you do too," Billy added. "You want to reach God. And your husband as well. Everyone wants to reach God."

What a strange answer, Clara thought. And intimate somehow. Maybe too much so.

"Maybe he sees God in you," Billy teased Clara. "Seamus. Which is why he's only closed sometimes. And open others."

"What?" Clara laughed.

"And God cuts through the pain."

"I have no idea what you're talking about," Clara told him and took another pita, dipping it in the hummus, enjoying the bite. It really was good, and she followed it with a sip of ouzo.

"I'm open because I have a lot of pain," Billy finally admitted.

"What?" she laughed.

"And I need a lot of God to fix it," he added. "Fix. Get it? Bad pun." He took another pita and put some feta on it. "Maybe I have more pain than your husband. And you. And so, I let more God in. And that's why you like me."

"Are you saying you're God?" Clara teased.

Billy laughed. "No, I'm saying I just desperately need help."

Clara could tell he was being honest now.

"But you can call me God if you'd like," he joked.

"You're insane," Clara laughed.

"Well, I do everything to let God in. And sometimes, he's there."

"Why?" Clara wondered.

"Because when I do this." He gestured to the track marks on his arm. "I see her too, with God."

"Her?" Clara asked, getting chills. He was suddenly so earnest.

"My mom," Billy said, voice cracking, his eyes pained, having to look down. Then cracking a smile, "I just need a mom."

Clara punched him playfully. "Great," she said, "because that is not me. To you. A mom, I mean. I think you got Gran for that."

"I do, and I love my Gran," Billy said. "And how about that song? It's getting too quiet and serious in here." He jumped up and went over to the jukebox. "Sometimes there's God in here too," he said and pounded on the jukebox with his fist.

Clara laughed. So strange, she thought. She knew he was hiding a lot of pain but she decided to drop it. "In the jukebox?" she asked and went over. "God's in the jukebox?"

"Yeah," Billy confirmed.

"Weird," she teased. "You are weird."

"I'll take it," he said as she perused the songs.

"How about The Weight?" she suggested.

"Old school, huh?" he said and bumped her playfully with his hip.

"Yeah, I'm old remember?"

"Big twenty-nine."

"Actually, I heard Dead and Friends do it at Madison Square Garden not too long ago. With Maggie Rogers and John Mayer."

"Oh, cool," he said.

"It was."

"This one's the original. The Band. That okay?" he asked.

"Sure," Clara said, and Billy put on the song.

Clara liked when people brought back old-school music and made it their own, which is what she'd liked so much about the live version she'd heard.

"Aretha covered it too," Billy told her. "And so did Weezer. Travis. Staples Singers. Supremes. Joan Osborne..."

"Joan Osborne?" Clara laughed as The Band's original recording started to play. And she felt the magic of that old song too. And it made her think about Derek down there at the boardwalk with his guitar. She peeked out the window again, wondering what he was doing without his priest garb. *Was that allowed?* she mused. She had no idea but decided in that moment with a head full of ouzo that she was going to visit Derek the next day and connect with him and get to know him. Maybe that'd help Seamus. *Forget what Billy said. You have to help people. What else is there?* she thought. *God?*

"Earth to Clara," Billy said.

Clara turned from the window and saw Billy grinning at her. Such a charming smile. And Clara knew that she and Billy were deeply connected somehow. And that he was good for her. He grounded her, in spite of his familiar pain. And maybe he would ground her enough to help her heal her own family. And maybe their friendship would heal both of them too.

16

A Visit with the Priest

After hanging out with Billy at the blues bar, and maybe because she drank too much ouzo and was so inspired by her new friend and fun evening, Clara found the courage to call Derek when she got home later that night and tell him that she wanted to get to know him better and that she wanted to take him up on his offer to visit at the high school where he taught.

But that was yesterday when Clara was ouzo-brave, and now that her head was clear, she was a bit nervous about seeing Derek later that day and was debating about which dress to wear for the visit. She even went back up to the bedroom twice to change in between sipping her coffee and getting her friend-media fix on. The WiFi connection was sketchy out there at the lake house, but Seamus had finally ordered Skylink after six weeks of being there and the guy was coming out in a few days. Clara could live with it till then. In fact, it was kind of nice to not be so easily connected.

The dresses in question were the happy lemons and the seed-head dandelion with seeds blowing off. Clara liked the happiness and brightness of the lemon yellow but ultimately chose the dandelion dress because it was whimsically joyful and hopeful. And she was hoping for a nice visit with Derek. Plus, the dress was mostly white with faint brown for the seeds, and Derek had chosen the white flowers for her, so it was fitting—a brother-and-sister-in-law color theme. It just felt right, so Clara went with it and headed over to the high school at noon—a nice short walk.

Derek had a free period just after lunch and suggested they take a stroll. He liked to get out as much as possible, he told her. And he seemed quite happy to see her when she arrived, which was such a relief to Clara. It was also a relief that their conversation was easy and that they had such a comfortable connection right off the bat. Clara hoped the ease would continue as they walked.

Clara had told Derek on the phone that she had "a lot" of free time and could use some local friends now that they'd been there almost two months. It would definitely help her stay positive so that she didn't drive herself crazy. She alluded to not wanting to feel lonely, and as they stepped out of the school onto the street for their stroll, Clara told Derek, "I really appreciate this. And your offer to talk when I needed it."

"Sometimes being alone with yourself can get pretty frightening," Derek joked without hesitation. Maybe it ran in the family, Clara thought. "If I didn't have the school and priesthood, I'd have made myself crazy a long time ago," he added.

Clara laughed, relieved about the humor and knowing there was some truth there. "Yeah, I guess I never realized how much I like being around people," Clara said and smiled, any hesitation of her own floating away.

"Then, I'm glad you came to visit me," Derek declared with a warm smile and led her on a small trail along the street.

It was a beautiful day with bright blue skies and huge fluffy clouds. They walked for a moment in silence, taking it all in before Clara started the conversation back up, "It really is beautiful out here. And so quiet. It gives you room to let all the bullshit fall away. I mean, sorry, bull-crud, stress fall away." Clara tried to cover up her bad-language faux pas and shrugged.

Derek was amused. "You can come walk with me again as your penance for cursing."

They both laughed, and for the first time, their eyes met. Clara saw something kind in Derek's gaze. There was that twinge of pain and longing too, but a kind of joy surged past. Clearly, Derek had a solid sense of humor and maybe some kind of compassion. He probably made a good priest, she thought.

"But yeah, I get it too," Derek said. "I mean, not the city stress you guys have in New York, but when you're out here, it's nice not to hear the incessant chatter of those little, or not so little, hooligans I spend my days with. I'm joking. I like those high schoolers. They're amusing. And so intense. All at once." He smiled at Clara. Genuine again. "Maybe you understand. You're not as far away from that age as I am," he teased her.

Clara laughed, "Gee, thanks. Maybe that's why I keep noticing this red-haired girl by the house. She's like fifteen or sixteen. Pale. Freckled. Serious. Any chance you know her? Or she goes to your school? I think maybe she and her friends were hanging out in the house or something."

"Hard to say. Red hair is quite ubiquitous around here. And the rest? Every teen ever," he quipped. "But I've never seen any kids skulking around the house to be honest."

"Maybe she just moved here or something," Clara continued. "She's really anxious. Although, I have seen her laughing too. And maybe I've seen her sister. And a boy, her friend. But yesterday, at the doctor..." Clara stopped, wondering if she could trust Derek with this information.

"Yes?" he asked with a kind smile.

Which made Clara feel safe again, so she went for it, hoping he could tell her what to do. "I heard her in the next room. And she's pregnant. And terrified. I want to help her," Clara told him.

Derek paused, trying to determine how much of this story was real and how much was Clara's overreaction to typical teen behavior.

"I'm serious," Clara said. "What do you think I should do?"

"Well, any girl that age would be scared," Derek stated calmly. "Next time you see her, talk to her. See how you can help."

This seemed like good advice. "That's a good idea," Clara agreed. "Thanks."

"My pleasure," Derek told her and went in for a fist bump, which she found hilarious. He was so confident—with an ease, like he was comfortable in himself, in his body, and comfortable helping others.

This made Clara feel relieved that she'd decided to come out to visit him. And even that they'd moved out to the lake house for the summer. Her intuition—with that little nudge from Dr. Goldberg —had led her here, and she was grateful. "Hey, maybe you can stop round for dinner some time," Clara ventured. "When Seamus's back. Next week?"

"I would love nothing more," Derek declared with a smile.

But there it was again, Clara thought, when she mentioned Seamus—that weird pain.

"You let me know when it's right," he added. "Don't want to overstep my welcome."

Yup, she thought, *he's still sensitive too, just like Seamus*. But the opening was there, and Clara felt joy in her heart. And hope. And a deep connection suddenly, through her body. And then, she heard a guitar strumming, playing "The Weight," and a man singing. She looked around—where was it coming from? But obviously, there was nothing. They were next to a small country road and a field.

Derek turned to see what Clara was looking at.

She laughed it off, "Bear?"

Derek's eyes sparkled, and she felt that strange, deep soul connection again, like what she'd felt with Billy, different from Seamus, but also unexplainable.

Maybe it was friendship.

Maybe God, Clara joked to herself.

But whatever it was, it made Clara feel like she'd stepped out of her self-imposed prison of grief from the miscarriages and that she was flying. And it continued as she and Derek strolled down the country road and through the fields and back and chatted about nothing important.

Then, Clara took that good feeling home with her to the lake house, where she made dinner, watched a stupid romcom on Netflix and checked in with Seamus who was spending the night in the city again—not a worry in sight.

17

Desperate Yelling in the Woods

Clara was thrilled to finally have wrangled Seamus into the guesthouse to actually clear out some of his stuff. It was late June. They'd been there almost two months now, and she'd already painted the outside of the guesthouse and replaced some of the old, rotted wood in the walls. Now, it was time for the inside.

Seamus had stayed in the city for several nights and was excited to see Clara, while she was excited to report back to him all the happenings of the past days.

She'd already told him about the visit to Dr. Madison on the phone several nights earlier. "It went great," Clara had said. "You were right, she's not in the dark ages, modern office in fact, and she recommended an acupuncturist." Seamus had laughed at that, and then, they'd gone on to talk about his day and the new game they were getting ready to release.

But Clara had waited until now to talk about the red-haired girl and Derek because she'd wanted to see Seamus's reactions—wanted to see his eyes, especially about Derek. Which she was nervous about.

So, she started in with the details of the girl at the doctor's office first and then told Seamus about her walk with Derek—all while pointing at each of Seamus's old computers and other items, waiting for his response each time as to whether or not he wanted to keep the item. Clara would point, and Seamus would shake his head *yes* or *no*.

"So, this girl is pregnant?" Seamus asked after she recounted the stories, picking up an old floppy disk and reading the description written in Sharpie.

"Something like that. I mean, it sounded like she was," Clara replied, but she didn't tell him that the receptionist at Dr. Madison's office hadn't seen a girl on the schedule or that the doctor's voice sounded like a man's voice through the wall. That part seemed a little crazy, and Clara wanted to find out more before bringing it up.

"And you told Derek? About the girl?" Seamus continued, dropping the floppy disk into a box of "things to keep" that was growing fuller by the minute.

"Yeah," Clara replied, "he said I shouldn't worry about it. That the girl was probably just scared, like anyone would be at that age. But I don't know, she was so upset."

"Whelp, Derek always knows best," Seamus quipped with a twinge of sarcasm. "At least he said not to worry."

Clara stopped pointing and made an exasperated—*Really?*—face at Seamus.

"Ten bucks says he's got a crush on you," Seamus replied to her look, picking up a random remote control and clicking it on and off. "Trash," he said and threw it in the box marked "bye, bye."

"He doesn't have a crush on me," Clara insisted, not sure if Seamus was being serious or not. "That sounds crazy."

Seamus looked at her, like—*Are you kidding?*

"Alright, maybe a little one," Clara agreed. "Maybe we can invite him over for dinner."

"You'd better watch it or he might try to convert you," Seamus teased.

"Ahhh!" Clara groaned. "You are so frustrating. Fine. We'll talk about him another time." Then, she pointed to another computer, and Seamus shook his head *no*. "C'mon, we gotta get rid of something," Clara insisted.

"But I love them all," Seamus cried playfully.

"We've been here almost two months!" Clara exclaimed. "I want to get started on my work."

But Seamus didn't hear her, distracted by one of the computers. He booted it up and typed in a password. It opened, and he quickly entered a command to bring up a game. "Here, this'll take your mind off that girl. And Derek," Seamus told Clara, pulling over the ugly, bright-orange desk chair with the high back so that she could sit in front of the old device. She plopped down, and Seamus started the game that seemed to be from the late 80s or early 90s: a treasure hunt with a dragon. "My first game," he told Clara. "At the time, not easy to beat."

Clara took the mouse. "But it's so cute," she said and found the start and began to play. She advanced through the mazes quickly.

Seamus was surprised. And a little confused. "Wow. You've played before," he said.

"Beginner's luck," Clara replied with a cute smirk as she deftly finished the game.

"Just like the chess thing," Seamus said. "How are you doing this?"

Clara tilted her head back with a coy smirk, and he kissed her forehead.

"Ouch," she said and rubbed her scar, going back to replay the game.

"Again?" he asked. "You're playing again?"

"Yeah, and then, I want to see the next level," Clara told him and began breezing through.

"You just like to win," he teased her.

"I do," Clara declared.

Seamus watched for a while as she aced the first level again and then the second and began the third. "Great, I'll take this as my escape cue," he said and kissed the top of her head and started out.

"No, wait, we have more work to do in here," Clara called after him, without looking up, fully into the next level of the game.

"Just let me know when you're ready. The last levels take a bit of problem solving, so go get 'em, kiddo," Seamus teased and left, relieved to go kick back with a beer and watch the game instead of clearing out his beloved old computers and valuable junk.

Clara kept going, playing the dragon game, completely hooked —until the sun went down, and it got pretty dark out and Seamus was long gone. He was right, Clara thought—the game got more complicated, and she liked that. She was in her element and could see how this storyline inspired Seamus for some of his later games, which he sold successfully all over the world.

Clara enjoyed working with Seamus on his projects—brainstorming, testing games, consulting on style and design, helping with characters and thinking through bugs in the apps. Seamus incorporated many of the strategies they talked about. Even though she was more of a creative, with Seamus, Clara had somehow found this logical, engineering-type part of her brain. She was glad, because in effect, engineering and writing software were creative too. That was something she and Seamus really connected on—building and creating together—and Seamus even brought her in on brainstorming sessions with the professional developers and coders. Once, Clara actually found the problem code and felt so absurdly proud.

Crazy! she thought. It was like a random hidden talent that she'd always had and didn't know about.

Plus, this connection with Seamus was another thing she loved about being with him. They were like children playing in the gaming industry. And it was sexy—watching him work—with all that confidence. That was something he had that no one else even came close to and probably why she never worried when she was attracted to someone else. She assumed Seamus felt the same about her. But was she right? Clara wondered.

She must be, she thought, because seeing this game now just solidified it.

Which is what she was thinking when she heard something outside—rustling, footsteps—and then, she saw the red-haired girl jet past the open door. Clara laughed at the girl's intensity and ignored her, going back to the game until she heard yelling in the woods in the direction of the lake. It sounded angry. And then desperate.

Clara grabbed her phone and called Seamus.

"You ready for me?" he laughed when he answered. "Cuz I'm not coming back out there. You're going to have to come in here to get me."

"No! Did you hear that?" Clara whispered in all earnestness.

"All I hear is you hooked on my game," Seamus teased.

"The yelling!" she insisted.

"Byyyyee," he quipped.

"No! No," Clara shouted, standing up and going to the doorway of the guesthouse where she could see Seamus through the sliding glass doors to the house.

Seamus waved from the couch where he was sitting, TV on, half working and eating a pizza. "What is it, my little gamer girl?" he teased.

"That yelling," Clara insisted, gesturing to the woods leading to the lake, annoyed that he was being so dismissive.

"What yelling?" Seamus asked.

Clara held the phone out in the direction of the noise to capture it for him. "There," she said pointing at her phone.

Seamus got up and walked to the sliding glass door watching her, not opening it or coming out, which was even more annoying. "I hear your voice from the back," Seamus said into the phone. "And that's all I hear. And I'd like to hear it in my ear, right here on the couch, while I watch the game, like cute, sexy whispers."

Clara whisper-yelled, "It's that girl I keep seeing! She's fighting with someone. Maybe it's the father."

"Oh for chrissakes, Clara. It's none of our business," Seamus scoffed.

Clara watched him shake his head and go back to the couch, grabbing a slice of pizza and taking a bite.

"Well, I'm going to see what's happening," Clara announced into the phone and hung up.

The yelling got worse. "I really don't care what you think!" the girl shouted. Then, Clara heard struggling and muffled screams and ran out of the guesthouse.

Suddenly, it was quiet. Then, there was more crying from the woods.

Clara followed the sounds, running into the trees, the voices continuing. It was dark.

Then, she heard the girl yell, "I don't care! I don't want this baby!" There was struggling—a scream, then a thud. Clara ran towards the sound, looking around—seeing nothing. She continued on tentatively, calling out, "Hello...? Are you okay...?"

"Clara!"—a man's voice behind her shouted.

Clara screamed and jumped, terrified—until she saw it was Seamus. She roared in frustration then yelled at him, "Oh my god."

"What are you doing?" Seamus scoffed, clearly irritated.

"That girl is not okay," Clara insisted. "They had a fight. Someone fell."

"Maybe you heard it when I fell over that dead body back there," Seamus joked.

"I'm serious!" Clara shouted. "Stop being so smug. We have to tell the police."

"We're in the woods," Seamus said. "It's a small town. People fight. You hear it. They make up. Let it be. And if you see that girl again, you ask her if she needs help."

Seamus's eyes flashed something she'd never seen—sternness, as if he were reprimanding her. It made her feel small and defensive. "What if she's in trouble now?" Clara managed.

"There's no one here, Clara," Seamus insisted then softened when he saw her forlorn look. "Look, you're wasting your time. And my time. And Mrs. Lee's time," he teased, "because you know Mrs. Lee won't let this go." And he cracked a small smile.

But Clara couldn't go there. "Why don't you believe me?" she cried.

"Because you're tired and looking for a distraction. I can't do this," Seamus insisted and turned to go.

"Right. Because you're too busy with work. Which is why I didn't want to come to this stupid house in the first place!" Clara snipped.

Seamus stopped. "That's not the issue," he snapped back.

"Of course it is," she said. "But it's fine. I'll just get my new friend Billy to help. He has plenty of time to waste. Just like me. Took me to that old bar a couple days ago. At the pier. Cute. Fun..."

Seamus was taken aback. "In the day?" he asked, his eyes looking shocked and hurt.

Suddenly, Clara heard a flash of the girl jumping on the bed with the springs. Then, she saw a flash of angry eyes in the window. She hid it and taunted further, "We'll waste some time at the police station, me and Billy."

"Who's Billy?!" Seamus shouted.

He looked so angry now. And wounded. Clara stopped pushing, realizing she'd gone too far. "No one," she told him, backing down. "He's the kid from the corner store. Mrs. Flannery's grandson. I'm sorry. I'm tired. You're right."

"He took you to the bar?! For music?" Seamus pressed.

"On the jukebox. It's nothing," Clara insisted. "He's struggling. He just needs a friend. And I just said that because this is so frustrating for me. That you can't hear me."

Seamus looked down, trying to hide his emotions—pain, anger—trying to regroup.

Clara saw it all and reached out, touched his shoulder gently. "I shouldn't have said it. I'll ask Derek. He knows these kids. He can go with me to the police. And if it's nothing, I'll drop it."

Seamus nodded, pulling it together, forcing a smile. "Derek sounds like a good idea. He knows the kids around here."

Clara wasn't sure if Seamus meant it or not but decided that she couldn't just leave the girl alone out there—somehow Clara felt her pain even though it didn't make sense. Clara knew the girl felt all alone, exactly how she'd felt for the past two years after the miscarriages, full of confusion and trying to connect and find her center and not succeeding until now. Now, Clara had it. She was grounded and centered, and she knew that helping this girl would only solidify that.

As Clara and Seamus walked back to the house through the woods, Clara called Derek, and he agreed to meet her at the police station. Finally, Clara was asking for help, and she knew in her heart that that meant she was about to find some kind of answer. But what the question was she had no idea.

18

Sounds Like the Girl Who Disappeared

Clara and Derek waited as Officer Peters searched the database on his computer at the police station. Clara had just described the girl that she kept seeing about town—red hair, about fifteen or sixteen, blue dress, probably pregnant—and Officer Peters was trying to find a connection to someone in the community. Clara also explained that she'd just heard the girl desperately crying in the woods. That there was a fight. And that she was worried now for the girl's safety.

"The last time someone fit that description was thirty years ago," Officer Peters said. "That McGuire girl who went missing. Remember that?"

Derek nodded solemnly, tensing.

"Yeah, that was too bad," Officer Peters continued. "Sweet girl. Just never turned up. Me and my uncle worked that case, hence me remembering your description and finding her file again here." Officer Peters smiled warmly, reassuring Clara and trying to lighten the mood. "Maybe she's got a new name and is living in Kentucky on a farm. And as for your girl in the woods tonight, it's on record now, so if we hear of someone missing or in trouble or needing help, we'll know where to start."

"Thank you," said Clara.

"The pleasure is mine," Office Peters replied. "Sorry I can't do more to help. And nice to meet you, Clara. I'm happy to see some Dunnes back in that house." Officer Peters smiled at Clara and then at Derek with a nod and a smirk. "Father."

"We'll see you Sunday," Derek teased. Clearly, they had some kind of inside joke.

"That you will," Officer Peters laughed. "Hopefully not at confession."

"Oh, we always have fun at confession," Derek said. "You keep me entertained, my man."

Officer Peters and Derek shook hands, and Clara and Derek left, stepping out into the warm summer night air, crickets singing, stars shining bright against the dark sky.

"You feel better now?" Derek asked.

"Not completely, but at least we tried," Clara told him.

"That's all you can do sometimes," he said. "Shall we?" He gestured in the direction of the Dunne lake house.

"Sure," she replied, and they started to walk. "But at the fork, you can go straight home," Clara told him. "I'm sure you're exhausted, and I really appreciate you coming out so late."

"It's not that late," he quipped.

"Seriously, you don't have to...."

Derek cut her off. "No, I will walk you all the way," he insisted.

Which was oddly comforting to Clara, and she agreed, and they walked in silence to the Dunne house. Derek seemed comfortable not talking, just happy to be out looking at the sky, watching for creatures amongst the trees, spotting two giant great horned owls swooping across the road. "Wow!" he said with wonder.

"Yeah," Clara replied, but she wasn't really present. All she could think about was the girl and how she could help her, wondering how she could approach her next time.

When they reached the house, Seamus was in living room. The curtains were open so they could see him through the front window. Derek stopped at the edge of the driveway. "I'd better go," he told Clara. "There's been enough emotion tonight."

Clara took a deep breath. "Thank you. I appreciate this."

"My pleasure," Derek replied.

"So, um, I'm just curious, but did you know that McGuire girl who disappeared?" Clara asked.

Derek nodded. "She went to school with us. One day she was there, the next day gone. No one knew what happened. My guess is she couldn't stand it here anymore and just got out."

"So, Seamus knew her too?"

"Yup, same year in school," Derek said. "But I wouldn't bring it up. It was really hard on that whole class."

"Yeah, I can imagine," Clara mused.

"Alright, missy," Derek chimed. "You go in there and get some sleep."

Clara smiled, giving him a thankful hug and going in. She entered hesitantly.

Seamus was still working on the couch, TV blaring. "How'd it go?" he asked, finishing up typing something on his laptop.

"They didn't know who she was. You were right," Clara replied and threw her bag down and flopped down on the couch. "Maybe I am losing my mind."

"You're not losing your mind. You're putting too much pressure on yourself," Seamus said, finally closing his file.

Clara nodded and felt tears of frustration welling.

"Come here," Seamus said and put his laptop on the coffee table and slid over next to her. She let him comfort her. "I'm so glad you're not mad at me," she said.

"You did the right thing. Now, if someone's in trouble, they have the information. Right?" He waited, then she gave him a half-ass nod. "And I'm behind you no matter what the neighbors say," Seamus teased. "No matter how many times Mrs. Lee called to ask where you went alone tonight."

"She called?" Clara asked, too tired and missing the joke.

"No, but she did walk by numerous times, which is why I left the curtains open. To get her going." This made Clara laugh, finally, which is when Seamus pulled a little calendar out of his shirt pocket. "What I want to know about is this," he said.

"Where'd you get that?!" Clara cried, trying to grab it out of his hand.

He lifted it up above his head quickly so she couldn't get to it and waved it around playfully. "Doesn't this little thing tell us that any day now we could know if we're... pregnant?" He lifted his eyebrows like Graucho Marx.

His stupid favorite, Graucho Marx, Clara thought as she lunged up and swiped the calendar away from him. "Give me that," she said. "What're you doing snooping through my stuff?!"

"It was right out in the open on the nightstand," he defended.

"You mean like out in the open inside the night stand kind of out in the open?" Clara teased.

"I can't stand it anymore. I want to know!" he shouted playfully.

Clara grinned. "Well, you're not supposed to even be thinking about it. I don't know who's crazier, you or me," she added and stood up and grabbed her bag and headed into the kitchen. "I'm thinking mint-chip ice cream with peanut butter and chocolate sauce," she suggested.

"And there's some pizza in the fridge too," he called after her.

"Excellent," Clara said, feeling a bit of excitement and fear, but the good kind of fear. She was late with her period, if that last one really was a period, and—*Maybe tomorrow, I'll check*, she thought. Her heart pounded—she still had a good feeling about this and the ice cream sounded so yummy.

As long as she wasn't disappointed again, she thought. The spotting could've been a nothing-burger. But it was time to find out. That's what this house was about: taking risks and shining a light on the truth, uncomfortable or not.

19

The Girl in the Bathroom

Clara wound her way from the kitchen to the downstairs guest bathroom while talking on the phone to Erin and carrying an EPT box.

"Yes, on my way," Clara told Erin grabbing her crotch for a second, bending over. "I sufficiently have to pee. Crap, crap." She stopped until the pee went back in—"Okay," she said and continued walking. "Though I think a tiny bit came out."

Erin made pee sounds.

"Stop!' Clara demanded playfully.

Erin laughed as Clara entered the small bathroom and admired the cute, sheer, lime-green curtains she'd put up the week before. There was nothing outside the bathroom windows, so they didn't really need curtains. There was just a big tree out there, and the window covering was more for decoration, which looked great in contrast to the old, dark-wood panels lining the window and the freestanding vanity with the white ceramic basin. The cabinet, basin and fabric were just a few of the items she'd ordered through Billy. That was working out well.

"Just tell me about Eliza. She slept with John?!" Clara continued as she opened the pregnancy test box.

"That's what I said!" Erin yelled, enjoying their gossip moment thoroughly.

Clara pulled out the magic pregnancy-detecting wand and sat down on the toilet.

"She's a slut! But not really," Erin continued jokingly, as Clara started to pee, letting some of it out before sticking the EPT stick in there under the stream and counting to eight. "I think they like each other actually," Erin added. "And I like them too. So, you know, it's okay to make fun of her."

Clara pulled the stick out, quickly wiped the urine off her hand with toilet paper and finished peeing. Then, she wiped and stood up. "That's good," Clara said and washed off her hand with soap in the sink. "But still, I can't believe that," Clara said, enjoying the gossip as much as Erin. She leaned against the vanity, afraid to look at the EPT-wand window, heart racing. Would there be two lines or just one?

Honking blared through the phone.

"Where are you?" Clara asked.

"Driving to the friggin' daycare," Erin told her. "The city misses you. But I'm guessing you don't miss the city. And yeah, to each her own. Did you do it?"

"Yeah, just a second more," Clara said, not looking at the wand, nervous. "And..."

"Honey, you're fertile as shit. I'm putting a hundred bucks on it that it's a yes."

"Well, if it is, I know exactly when it..." Clara looked at the little window and saw the two little red lines. In shock. She stopped. The test was positive. She was pregnant. She covered her mouth in happy disbelief.

"And?" Erin asked.

Clara screamed quietly and laughed joyfully, jumping up and down just a little.

Erin cheered. "Oh my god, hooray! You did it!"

"No, no wait. I have to stay calm, remember?" Clara said, still staring at the two lines, heart racing, feeling the pressure, the hope, the fear, everything—*Please, please, please let it be okay*, Clara thought. "I'd better just..."

Suddenly, the bathroom door slammed shut. Everything went black. Clara saw black. Then, light again. Normal. And there was the red-haired girl by the toilet against the window, holding a pregnancy test, crying. "This can't be happening," the girl said.

Then, everything went black again, and Clara heard the girl crying and the weird jumping on the bed and laughter. Then, BAM, Clara woke up sitting on the floor outside the guest bathroom in the hall, her back to the wall outside the open bathroom door—her phone in the middle of the bathroom floor, Erin's muffled yelling blasting out, "Clara? Clara?! What's going on?! Clara?"

Clara was shaking. What had just happened? *What happened?!* she cried in her head. "I'm coming," she told Erin, voice shaking as she crawled cautiously toward the phone, carefully testing each hand, each knee on the floor to make sure it was really there and wouldn't collapse beneath her.

She crawled over the old, beautiful wood plank separating the hall from the tile of the bathroom, the dark wood that she loved. She tried to focus on that and the beautiful white-and-willow-green hexagon mosaic tiles in the bathroom—they weren't 80s style and she wasn't replacing them, she reminded herself.

When she was close enough, Clara reached her arm in quickly and grabbed the phone, then sat back on the hardwood floor in the hallway and pushed herself away from the bathroom, hands shaking. "Hello?" she said to Erin.

"What the hell just happened?" demanded Erin.

Clara felt a sharp pain on her forehead—the scar. It hurt. She touched it—wet.

"Clara?" Erin cried.

Clara brought her hand down and looked. There was bright-red blood on the tips of her fingers. "I don't know I, I...just...," she managed.

"And what was so funny?" Erin insisted firmly.

"Funny?" Clara asked.

"You were laughing," Erin told her. "You sure you're alright?"

"No. I, I..." Clara looked around the hall confused, from left to right, trying to get her bearings.

"Clara?!" Erin shouted.

"I think I just saw a ghost," Clara replied, barely audible. "The red-haired girl I keep seeing. She was in the bathroom. Pregnant. She took the test. She was terrified."

20

Dr. Goldberg's Report

Clara's heart raced. She squeezed Seamus's hand in her lap so hard his fingers turned red. He didn't flinch, and she was grateful. She was so scared—was she losing it now too? Was the baby going to be okay? Were they going to be okay? What if she wasn't fit to be a mother?

Dr. Goldberg flipped to the next page in the report from the lab. Dr. Goldberg was old school and liked actual paper. Somehow that was comforting to Clara. Dr. Goldberg was consistent. She had habits. Clara's parents were like that. Clara was like that, but somehow, that was one of the things that had slipped away, that she hadn't been able to get back on track with, like with work. She'd been so confident and then these miscarriages happened. And now, this. *God, please let me be okay*, Clara thought, even though she wasn't sure if she believed in God. Though she probably did. Because of Seamus and the weird knowing. That was the thing that kept her going. She knew they would have a baby or were doomed to keep trying. She knew, somehow, that was their fate. And if there was fate in her reality, it had to be the hand of some higher being. And perhaps, there was love in that.

She hoped there was love in that.

Finally, Dr. Goldberg spoke, telling them what she saw in the report, "Nothing. Neurosurgeon's tests. Physically, you are fine."

Clara exhaled and laughed. Finally, she could stop holding her breath. Seamus's hand somehow hadn't fallen asleep, and he managed to squeeze Clara's hand back—both so relieved.

"And the OB says you're seven weeks along with a strong heartbeat."

"Yes," Clara said and smiled at Seamus.

"Also, excellent news. But I'd like to talk a little more about what happened in the bathroom," Dr. Goldberg continued. "I think it would help to go back to what we had been working on before. See if we can find a connection to the asthma."

"But this is totally different," Clara insisted.

"Maybe it seems so on the outside," Dr. Goldberg went on, "but there is probably some connection inside to this girl. Inside of you. And your mind wants you to know what that is. And we can keep it slow. And see. Or we wait."

Clara exhaled. "I don't want to wait," she said. "I'm pregnant. I feel so good about it. I love being at the lake house. Everything but this. Again. Like there's something wrong with me."

"There's nothing wrong with you," Dr. Goldberg insisted firmly.

"Agreed," said Seamus.

"In fact, you are clearly very empathetic," Dr. Goldberg continued. "It's likely about boundaries. And we can address that now or whatever is going on. Okay?" Clara nodded. "Seamus, would you mind waiting outside?" Dr. Goldberg asked kindly.

Clara felt frightened all of a sudden at the thought of Seamus leaving, but she hid it well and nodded to him, trying to make him feel confident in her. He kissed her and left, heading out into the waiting room. "I'll be out here. Or maybe, I'll just go for a little stroll," he said.

Clara smiled warmly and nodded, but as soon as Seamus shut the door to Dr. Goldberg's office, she began to cry. "I'm sorry," Clara said.

"No, no, you're fine," Dr. Goldberg comforted, handing Clara a tissue. "Everything is fine. Normal."

"I wasn't imagining it," Clara insisted, defensive of her story. "I was there. It was the same girl. In the bathroom. The girl that I keep seeing. She was afraid because she's pregnant."

"Do you think you are strong enough right now to try to find out who she is and what she wants to tell you?" Dr. Goldberg asked and looked at Clara in all earnestness, squeezing the lab report and her notepad a little tighter than usual.

Clara felt fear rising, and it showed on her face.

"Or not, Clara," Dr. Goldberg retreated, releasing her grip on the lab report. "We do not have to do hypnosis again. You have to be comfortable. That's all that matters."

Clara took a deep breath in. And blew it out. And looked down at her hands, contemplating what she wanted to do. She could tell that Dr. Goldberg was a bit on edge, which made Clara worried that maybe Dr. Goldberg was out of her league with this hypnosis experiment. But she also trusted Dr. Goldberg and knew she was her best option to get past this invisible trauma. Doubting Dr. Goldberg was just Clara's own fear rearing its head, she told herself. And Dr. Goldberg was a solid analyst. She had a track record. And Clara needed to deal with this problem now, at the start of her pregnancy, when her emotions would have less impact. She had to do it for her baby. She was responsible for this baby, and she knew that embracing this truth was the only way out.

Clara nodded. "Yes, I want to do the hypnosis now," she told Dr. Goldberg. "Now is the time to walk through this. Get through the dark forest so we can all be free."

Dr. Goldberg was pleased. She was also a bit nervous after the last hypnosis with the wound to the forehead, but she had consulted colleagues, and it seemed she and Clara were on a good path of discovery. As usual, Dr. Goldberg hid her doubts well, and Clara let herself be confidently guided into the hypnosis, eyes closed, until she was relaxed. "You're in your safe, peaceful place?" Dr. Goldberg asked, leaning back in her high-backed chair and bringing up her writing pad to take notes.

"Yes, I am here," Clara replied—imagining herself sitting on her boulder overlooking the pine-tree-filled valley and the crystal-blue lake.

"Alright, now, today, we are going to find out who this girl is and what she wants to tell you," Dr. Goldberg began. "What your heart wants to tell you, Clara. And we're going to start now. Are you ready?"

"Yes," Clara replied.

"Okay, let's begin by going back several months, to late last October," Dr. Goldberg started in. "When you found out you were pregnant the last time."

Clara saw herself hugging Seamus tight, both feeling so much joy. "We are happy, nervous but happy," Clara described.

"Now, back to the first miscarriage," Dr. Goldberg continued.

Clara saw herself devastated, Seamus comforting her. "He loves me so much. And I feel so guilty," Clara told Dr. Goldberg.

This surprised Dr. Goldberg. "Guilty? Why guilty?" she wondered.

Clara became flushed and anxious. "I don't know. I don't know why. He loves me so much. And I hurt him."

"How did you hurt him?" Dr. Goldberg asked.

"I want his baby. I love him so much," Clara insisted, her voice sounding distressed.

"How did you hurt Seamus?" Dr. Goldberg repeated.

"He's afraid I'll leave him. I need to show him I love him!" Clara felt desperate, and suddenly, there was a FLASH of light and she was in a boathouse. Then, BAM, another flash of light, and she was underwater, sunlight striations streaming down. She swam up to the surface, laughing, happy, and there was a dark-haired teen boy, laughing too. He had black hair, like hers, but his skin was white. His dark eyes were charming and made her feel desired and loved and like everything was okay in that moment. Like everything was okay in her body. And she was feeling her body and not stuck in her head. It felt so easy.

Who was that boy? she wondered out loud.

Then, there was another flash of light, and she was riding bikes with the dark-haired boy. They wove back and forth with each other. Then, FLASH, more light, and they were walking through a little path in the woods, a mossy path. She could see a lake and docks filled with boats. They approached the docks, and there were two musicians playing the blues on a bench—a guitarist and a harmonica player. She and the dark-haired boy stood off to the side on the grass, away from the crowd, and he discretely pulled out a flask hidden under his T-shirt, held in place against his waist by the elastic band of his swim shorts. He snuck it to her, careful so no adults could see.

She took a swig. It burned. But then, her head and arms filled with warmth, the warmth of the alcohol. She relaxed, laughed, took another swig. The boy followed, and they watched the musicians play. His arm touched hers—warm skin on hers, more warmth flowing through her body. She was happy that he had cut off the sleeves of his T-shirt so she could feel him closely. Her head felt blurry, but her heart felt happy and present.

Then, suddenly, another flash of light, and she was jumping on the bed, waving a long, cotton streamer of fabric around, a trim of extra fabric perhaps, from a dress. A blur of colors filled her vision, and she heard the boy laughing and a guitar playing "The Weight." The boy sang and so did she, "Take a load off Fanny...."—she felt so happy and described what she saw and experienced to Dr. Goldberg.

Then, in the vision as the girl, Clara mis-stepped, fell and, BAM, hit her head on the side of the bed. "Ow," Clara said and grabbed her forehead. Blood trickled down.

Dr. Goldberg gasped silently, trying not to let her fear and shock be sensed by Clara. "Clara?" Dr. Goldberg asked as calmly as possible.

Clara saw a flash of light, and then, there was the sandy-haired teen boy looking through the window at her as she held her forehead—his eyes were hurt and sad. *Seamus's eyes*, Clara realized. His eyes made her feel closed in, like she was suffocating, perhaps from the weight of their pain, like some kind of heartbreak was taking her down. She began to whimper, uncomfortable, turning her head side to side, like—*This can't be true.* "It's not true," Clara whispered under her breath.

Dr. Goldberg got up and hesitantly touched Clara's arm. Clara recoiled, crying softly, like a hurt animal, too afraid to move or try—*In a state of learned helplessness,* Dr. Goldberg thought. "Clara, what's happening?" she asked in a gentle whisper, the fear showing in her eyes, luckily hidden behind the black frames. Plus, Clara's eyes were closed and couldn't see her.

Then, Clara started rocking back and forth like a frightened, traumatized child.

"Clara? Clara! You are in my office," Dr. Goldberg said firmly and clapped twice in front of Clara's face.

Clara came back to the room and saw the blood on her hand and on the skirt of her cute lemon Frock dress that she loved. "Oh my god. Again. What's happening?"

Dr. Goldberg hid her concern and grabbed a tissue for the blood. "It's okay. You're going to be okay," Dr. Goldberg said and pressed the wound to stop the bleeding. "Sometimes when we remember a painful injury, just like a painful moment, we conjure up the same physical symptoms as we would emotional symptoms. Remember? From last time? Our minds and hearts are powerful regulators. And healers if we choose." She lifted the gauze. "See! Better already," Dr. Goldberg confirmed. "Do you feel alright?"

"I'm afraid I'm losing my mind," Clara cried and tears overwhelmed her. "I've never injured my head like that."

Dr. Goldberg sat down on the brown leather couch next to Clara and held her. "You're not losing your mind," Dr. Goldberg said. "You're deeply tuned in to this memory. And it is probably a metaphorical injury that's manifesting as an actual wound."

"But it's not mine," Clara insisted. "That's what's so frightening and confusing. It's her's. The girl's memory. But it's as if I am her. Seeing things from her point of view. Feeling what she's feeling. Laughing. Jumping. Pain. In my head. And..." Clara touched her belly.

"An abortion?" Dr. Goldberg wondered.

"I don't know. I've never had one," Clara told her.

"The D&C? With the miscarriage? One of the miscarriages? You said those were painful," Dr. Goldberg continued.

"No, no, it's like an ache, not sharp like the D&C. And the girl was scared. And in the window, there were Seamus's eyes. Like I told you. Right? You heard me. And he was so sad. Hurt." Clara's forehead wound began to throb. She grabbed it. "I don't want to lose my baby."

"Maybe this redhead is a part of you that hasn't let go of the miscarriages yet. Or you blame yourself for the miscarriages and not being able to control them. Or you blame the baby that left and didn't arrive to create a family. Maybe the red-haired girl is the part of you that's still grieving. And it's easier if it feels like it's someone else's grief, even an imaginary friend."

Clara looked at Dr. Goldberg's caring eyes and wished with all her heart that any of these scenarios were true so that she could just deal with it and be done. But she didn't feel like any of this was reality. Her reality. It wasn't her reality.

Dr. Goldberg sensed Clara's apprehension. "Or maybe it's Seamus's grief," she suggested. "And hence his eyes. Grief about the miscarriages. Or losing his parents so young. Does he still have a lot of grief?"

Clara nodded. "He does. But he tries not to show it. Maybe he blames me."

"I think it's complicated, and you should not take that on," Dr. Goldberg insisted firmly. "I think Seamus believes in you as a mother. But he also has some anger about his parents being gone. A feeling of abandonment. He doesn't know where to put that pain and, likely, it slips out sometimes."

"Yes, that's true," Clara confirmed.

"And who was the dark-haired boy?" Dr. Goldberg asked.

"I don't know," Clara told her.

"Maybe he symbolizes part of your loss. Or Seamus's loss. Maybe that's where Seamus's anger is directed—at his loss of control. Since he's looking for someone or something to blame. Blame and anger are always easier emotions than the sadness around loss."

Clara nodded. This made sense.

"But just to be sure—Seamus isn't grieving most of the time, is he?" Dr. Goldberg asked Clara. "I mean, he doesn't seem depressed, right?"

"No, but he is more agitated at the lake house," Clara told her.

"That's understandable. And healthy, in fact." Dr. Goldberg smiled. "And now, you. Your job is to let these feelings of yours out, wherever they're coming from. Ideally, it wouldn't happen now, while you're pregnant, but you need to experience your deep emotions," Dr. Goldberg insisted as gently as possible.

"And if they are her feelings? The girl's?" Clara asked.

Dr. Goldberg paused to contemplate this before finally answering, testing the waters, "This is out of my scope of experience, but I've done some research on regression. Going back before birth. Some people say they experience other lives. Past lives. The stories sound similar to yours."

"I don't understand," Clara said.

"Neither do I. Honestly. They are talking about reincarnation," Dr. Goldberg explained. "In the research."

"What?" Clara scoffed. This sounded absurd. Ridiculous.

"I, personally, see it as going to a deeper consciousness. The girl is your deeper self, appearing with red hair, like in a dream, to give you distance from the emotions," Dr. Goldberg continued. "And today, you walked through a new door, all on your own, and it's going to help this new life—to arrive safely. You should be proud." Dr. Goldberg smiled and put her hand on Clara's, which was still on her belly.

Clara nodded, even though the reincarnation mention still sounded incredibly off.

"So, stay alert," Dr. Goldberg continued. "See what happens. And if you see something strange at that house or in the town, observe it and know it's simply part of your very active unconscious.

Stay around people. And call me. And have fun. That's you're assignment. You're on the right path. Pregnant. Loving it. Healthy. Acknowledge your inner life now too. And ask it to come back another time if it gets too uncomfortable."

21

Booze, Lies and Unraveling

Seamus was on the phone in front of Dr. Goldberg's office building when Clara came out of the session. He looked animated and intense like he always did when he was working. Luckily, he also always left his work mode behind when he was done. He smiled at Clara and finished his call as she approached and hugged her tightly. Clara melted into him and let herself feel his strength. There was so much relief there. They stood like that for a few minutes, Seamus giving her little kisses on her hair, not commenting at all about the wound on her forehead or the blood on her favorite dress.

"You, okay?" he asked, pulling back.

She noticed he smelled like whiskey. Which was weird. "Where'd you go?" she asked, surprised.

"Just out here," he told her.

"You smell like you've been drinking."

"Oh, yeah, actually, a couple blocks down. I grabbed a sandwich. You hungry?"

"No, no," she replied. "Sorry, yeah, I was just surprised. You never drink during the day. Or do you?" She tried to sound playful, not sure what he was up to.

Seamus laughed. "Not really. But today, yeah, *that* was happening. You're putting me through it," he teased.

His words stung, but Clara laughed anyway. "Well, yeah. *That* is happening. But the thing with Goldberg was fine. In the office just now. And I'm fine." Clara smiled, reassuring him, not wanting to talk about the details. "And I guess we're going to be okay. Goldberg thinks so at least. She says I just have to go through the feelings." She shrugged.

"Excellent," Seamus replied and pulled her close again, studying her eyes as if he didn't quite believe her.

"What?" Clara demanded.

"I don't know," he said with a grin, glancing at the wound on her forehead. "But great then," he chimed and let her go, turning up the charm. "Park?"

This was so strange, Clara thought. He seemed off, but also not. What did it mean?

"A little ice cream?" he added, giving her his best Groucho Marx eyebrows for a laugh.

Which finally assuaged her fears. She kissed Seamus on the cheek and slid her hand into his, squeezing it tightly as they walked up 7th Avenue. She told herself that she was just being paranoid about the whiskey breath. Seamus was fine.

When they got to the park, they got ice cream and sat near the pond looking at the ducks, passing the ice cream back and forth, watching kids play. Clara felt calm again. It was perfect, especially with Seamus's arm around her shoulders, and because they'd popped into a store and he'd bought her a simple white cotton dress so that she could toss the bloody one. She was so happy and felt safe.

Clara took a lick of the ice cream. Not only did they both fit together physically but she and Seamus were both ice cream lickers not biters, so the ice cream looked as if they were making a beautiful clay pot, spinning and sexy—*Like that scene in "Ghost" with Patrick Swayze and Demi Moore,* Clara thought, *with the steamy Righteous Brothers song, but funny because it's just mint-chip ice cream.* She handed Seamus the cone for his turn.

"I love you, Clara Dunne," Seamus told Clara as he took it. "And I love our little bean." He rubbed Clara's belly. "And I will keep both of you happy and safe. If you let me."

Then, his phone rang.

Clara saw the screen: Dr. Goldberg. She instantly felt panic in her stomach. Why was Dr. Goldberg calling him? she wondered.

"I've gotta take this," he said and handed her the ice cream.

"What? Why?" This was too weird.

"I don't know what she wants. Let me see," Seamus insisted and got up to answer, stepping away from the bench.

"Why is she calling you and not me?" Clara demanded, following Seamus up off the bench.

He ignored her. "Hi. Yeah. I just wanted to check in," Seamus told Dr. Goldberg. "Thanks for returning my call." He turned his back on Clara.

This was too much. Clara rushed him and grabbed his phone away and hit speaker, furious. *There!*—she mouthed.

"Of course. How can I help you?" Dr. Goldberg's friendly voice came through the phone.

"I wanted to get your opinion," Seamus continued, annoyed as Clara held the phone out so both of them could hear, "about us staying at the lake house. Do you think it's the right thing to do?"

"I know you think she's unstable...," Dr. Goldberg began.

"What?!' Clara shouted, cutting Dr. Goldberg off. "Why did you lie to me?" Clara demanded of Seamus. "You called her!"

Seamus tried to wave Clara away.

"Why are you talking about me behind my back?!" Clara yelled.

Seamus grabbed the phone from Clara. "Clara's listening," he told Dr. Goldberg. "I'm sorry. She just...is here with me and put the phone on speaker."

Dr. Goldberg heard the tension in his voice and how upset Clara was. "Fair enough," Dr. Goldberg said calmly. "No need for anyone to get upset. We have nothing to hide. Right, Seamus?"

Seamus paused, angry, looking at Clara, jaw clenching, then agreed. "Right," he said curtly.

"...but I think it's fine that you would worry about this sudden instability Clara is feeling," Dr. Goldberg deftly continued, managing the high emotions on the other end of the phone. "Things are changing, which is what you both wanted. And Clara needs some extra attention right now and time. And she needs to know that you trust her. That is very important, Seamus. Clara needs to know that you trust that this unstable period will pass. Okay? You can trust her and her ability to heal."

Clara saw Seamus's tension grow. This hit a chord for him somehow. The wall came up. He turned away again. Clara could see he was hurting *and* that he was trying, which reminded her that this was about him now. It wasn't just her here, and she had to respect his space. She stood back and gave him that space, eating the ice cream, watching the ducks, while also watching him, still listening—as Dr. Goldberg continued, "Seamus?"

"Yes," he replied.

"You lost your parents, Seamus. But Clara is not going anywhere."

"Right," he managed, and Clara felt his wall get higher.

"Just enjoy your time together," Dr. Goldberg advised. "She loves you. You both want the same things. You're both in this together. And enjoying that, right? And I think that partnership is what's going to help this baby arrive safely."

Seamus nodded. His shoulders relaxed a bit.

"Seamus?" Dr. Goldberg's voice rang out.

"Yes, yes, I'm here," he replied. "And you're right. Thank you, Dr. Goldberg, from both of us. We'll keep you posted. This was just what I needed. Focus on the joy." He hung up and stood there for a moment, body tense, trying to regroup.

He turned to Clara.

Clara saw how upset he was and felt badly that she hadn't trusted him when he was the one needing desperately to trust her. "I'm sorry I did that," Clara told him, "following you, not giving you privacy. Like you did for me."

Seamus nodded. "This hasn't been easy for either of us."

Clara shook her head. "No, it hasn't." She instinctively touched her belly. "We're in this together," she told him. "And *I* do have to work on trust as well."

"We both do," he said "And luckily, Goldberg's good like that, telling it like it is. I hope at least." He softened.

Clara saw the opening and cracked a smile. "Or maybe it's all just a crock of shit," she joked.

Seamus laughed, "Yes, maybe it's just a crock 'o shit," eyes smiling now, their eyes meeting. "More ice cream?" he asked playfully, taking the cone from her. Fixing the drips. "This one's about had it."

"Sure," she replied.

"I think we need more of this, that's one thing that's certain, ice cream," he said and went over to the stand and stood in line for another cone.

Clara watched Seamus from afar and thought about how perfectly balanced his physique was and how she was so glad to be having a baby with him, even if there was suddenly all this tension and anger rising. Hers was a primal feeling, from that deep instinctual place. There was never a doubt in her mind about having a child with Seamus. And she hoped this pregnancy, this baby, was it, the one that would live to bring them joy.

Clara walked over to Seamus in line. He gave her a side hug and kissed her head—forgiveness filling the space.

He grabbed her bum. She laughed and leaned into him, hugging him, looking up at him, feeling something inside his hoodie jacket. "What's that?" she asked, laughing and pulling out a flask.

"A promo gift, like a tester to see if we want to use it to advertise," he defended.

Clara was suspicious.

"I'm serious," he insisted.

She opened it. Alcohol wafted out. It was the whiskey she'd smelled earlier on his breath. She took a tiny sip. "Whiskey sour?" she laughed.

"Something like that."

She nodded and gave it back to him, unsure what to make of it.

"I couldn't finish the drink at the bar with the sandwich," he explained. "I wanted to be there when you came out. Okay? Relax. This is our time to relax."

Clara knew Seamus was right and had to just let this all go. He was everything she wanted, and if he was having a hard time like she was, it'd pass. She knew that. Seamus was a rock. He always bounced back, even if he was a weary rock at the moment. It was nothing time couldn't fix.

22

The Girl and a Boy in the Boathouse

After the session with Dr. Goldberg and the afternoon with Seamus in Central Park, the joy kicked in for Clara at their beautiful summer lake house. It was late July, and she suddenly felt like she had permission to be herself—or maybe it was more like her old self. Or maybe it was a new self—a hybrid between her pre-Seamus-pre-trying-to-have-a-baby self and her current hopeful-this-might-be-it-in-a-small-town self.

From the hypnosis, Clara had discovered that she had been holding onto the grief from the miscarriages, and it was manifesting in these strange visions of a girl. Her prescription was to enjoy herself and her time with Seamus. That said, after a few days at the lake house, she'd gone off for a month to Montauk with Erin and the kids while Seamus worked day and night in the city on the release of his latest game. Clara had gone back to the city as well for his flashy game-launch party at the Georgia Room in The Freehand Hotel, which was quite fabulous—the perfect city fix to launch her further into her pregnancy with big, positive emotion and energy.

When Clara got back to the lake again, she decided that they needed to take advantage of the beautiful house and their fabulous friends and do some summer hosting before fall came around. First, Clara took a few weeks to do a slew of renovations, and then, she threw several dinner parties with Erin, Joe and their kids—baby Henry, ten-year-old Sophie and six-year-old Jack. Those evenings went perfectly, and after another few weeks, Clara dared to host a BBQ by the lake with Erin, Joe and the kids plus Greta and boyfriend Hank, a few other city friends, like Luna and Bass from Frock, and Derek.

Clara also invited Billy, but he only showed up briefly. He'd been helping her with the renovations since she'd been back from Montauk. He'd ordered everything for the remodel and rolled up his sleeves to do most of the handy work himself. He was quite good at it and seemed to get lost in the woodwork especially, taking pride in making it look stunning, just the way Clara liked it. He always instinctually knew how she imagined each new feature to the house. And as long as it was just the two of them, Billy was right there and an amazing friend. He loved to make Clara happy and always brightened when she said, "It's exactly how I saw it. How did you know? Perfect! Thank you, Billy!"

But Billy always disappeared when Seamus or anyone else came around. That had been the pattern since their night at the blues bar.

And it was no different as they kicked off the lakeside BBQ party, which was well underway by midafternoon on this stunning August day.

The Dunne's property behind the house and over the little grassy hill, butted up to the lake. Billy helped Clara set up a canvas tent cover the week before, and he resealed the wooden gazebo where Clara laid out a fabulous spread and where guests could eat and get shade.

It was hot and muggy that afternoon, so people were moseying in and out between the cool gazebo, the tent, swimming in the lake and playing croquet. Billy helped set up that morning and stayed until Seamus joined the party and Erin and her family arrived. Then, as Clara welcomed her guests, Billy disappeared. Her heart felt sad, but she understood. She and Billy had a strong connection that was good for both of them, but he wasn't part of this social circle of hers. Sometimes friends didn't mix or were better one on one. That's just how it was. She knew that.

And Clara let it go and went to join the kids in the lake.

By late afternoon, Seamus had dusted off the old BBQ, gotten the coals going and was happy to be grilling. Erin sipped sangria with Henry in the front pack, both she and Seamus watching Erin's kids, Sophie and Jack, swim in the lake. Joe and Derek were jumping off the little boat-loading pier, and Clara was also in the lake, treading water and cheering them on. "Do it, do it, do it! It's not cold, at all," Clara shouted.

Which is when Erin decided to suss out how things were really going from Seamus's point of view, because Clara seemed great. Erin hadn't had a moment alone with Seamus in person since the episode in the bathroom, so the timing was perfect. "You are doing amazing," Erin launched in with her most encouraging and cheerful voice. "As Clara's best friend, I say that with confidence. She loves you, Seamus. The ghost thing is weird, but hey, she'll be five months along in just a few weeks—right? September? And with a strong heartbeat and no complications—you're off to a good start, Dad."

Seamus smiled. He clearly was profoundly happy. Which is when Seamus saw Derek cannonball into the water right next to Clara, obviously trying to splash her. Clara laughed, and all Seamus could see was tension between them. A flash of jealousy shot across his face. It didn't get lost on Erin, and she hoped this wasn't a new problem brewing.

"Alright! Bring those plates," Seamus shouted to everyone. "Burgers, dogs and sirloin await!"

The swimmers came up to the gazebo for the feast. Everyone stood around eating the delicious BBQ in bathing suits. Luckily, thanks to the heat, they dried quickly.

Clara wore a cute red-and-white gingham bikini, her belly starting to stick out a bit. She felt proud and beautiful and was enjoying the fact that Seamus was happy and even telling stories about the lake and him and Derek as kids. "Yeah, we swam across to the island a lot," Seamus said, completely animated. "We even camped in the woods. Right over there. And raced across in the water. Derek beat me every time. The master of the crawl." Clara laughed and smiled at Derek. Seamus rubbed her belly. "Maybe if this one had been around, I would've had more luck."

As Seamus moved his hand over Clara's brown skin, you could see the white KAPOW!-burst birthmark next to her bellybutton. Derek paled when he saw it. Seamus noticed Derek's reaction. "Yeah, right?" Seamus responded, calling out the birthmark. "Clara, tell 'em what your birthmark looks like when you're full."

"Like now? Full of baby?" she joked and pushed her stomach out further. "It looks like a walrus."

Derek choked on his sirloin when he heard her say "walrus" and started to cough.

"Imagine, when you get bigger," Seamus teased Clara.

Derek kept coughing.

"You okay, bro?" Seamus asked him.

Greta handed Derek a beer.

"I am. I am," Derek replied through the coughs, taking a sip from the bottle then giving Seamus a thumbs up. "It's just uncanny. You know how to find 'em, my brother. Well-rounded, no pun intended, whip smart without being nerdy, athletic and even funny."

"Them?" Clara asked. "Who's them?"

"You!" Derek teased. "You. And overly sensitive too," he added, teasing both of them now, forcing a smile, hiding his shock at the birthmark.

Clara turned to Seamus and kissed him—so proud in that moment to be with this beautiful man, neither of them noticing Derek's continued discomfort.

***

By evening, the adults at the party were sufficiently tipsy and Erin's kids, Sophie and Jack, were sufficiently punch-drunk and tired as they sat around the fire-pit bonfire roasting marshmallows and listening to Seamus ramble on with funny and spooky stories. "The best things usually happened when we camped over on the island," Seamus recounted with an animated grin. "I was always scared, and Derek milked it, usually by praying, like to keep away the evil spirits." He looked over at Derek and laughed, taking the piss out of both of them, enjoying the irony that he was now a priest. This was a great release. "And this one time," Seamus continued, "well, every time, I was very scared. And Derek was praying: Deliver them from evil, now and at the hour of our death... Which just spooked the heck out of me so much more. And he knew it."

Derek nodded and chuckled, remembering. And Clara was so happy that the brothers were connecting. Finally. They needed it so badly. Maybe they'd get some closure and heal their past yet.

"And this one night," Seamus went on, lowering his voice for effect, "I was asleep and had to pee so badly, and I was so scared that I didn't want to get out of the sleeping bag. But I couldn't hold it in, so I had to get out, and as soon as I started to...clank, clank. Clank, clank again and—" He jumped up to scare the kids. "Rahhhhh!"

Everyone screamed, and Seamus laughed so hard. "It was the ranger on a bike," Seamus explained.

"A bike?!" Erin demanded.

"Yup, pretty funny, huh? He was checking some of the official campsites out there, I guess." Seamus shrugged and shared a look with Derek, both remembering the moment fondly.

"But are there ghosts here?" Erin's daughter, Sophie, asked.

"No, no ghosts here. Just over there," Seamus told Sophie, pointing into the woods, followed by Graucho Marx eyebrows for effect.

"It seems spooky to me," Sophie continued. "Did anyone ever die here?"

There was silence.

"No, no one died here, exactly," Seamus replied, as the memory of his parents' accident transcended down on the group. Seamus tried to maintain a smile for the kids. "But there are definitely ghosts everywhere. RAH!" He lunged at Sophie and Jack, who screamed, and everyone laughed, relieved that Seamus was keeping it light.

But Derek couldn't get there. It was too heavy for him. He shook his head and stood up.

"No, you cannot run away," Seamus told Derek. "We need some music. Where's that guitar?"

"I'll get it," Clara said. She was standing next to the card table covered in graham crackers and chocolate, and she was eating a S'more, mouth full. She'd seen the guitar in the boathouse earlier and strolled down, enjoying the cold grass on her bare feet.

As soon as Clara entered, she spotted the guitar behind an old tarp. "Yup, right where I remembered it," she said out loud to herself and picked up the guitar and immediately got a chill—as if there were a sudden breeze. Then, Clara heard a boy and girl laughing and saw the red-haired girl, a teenager, run by, giggling, playfully running away from the dark-haired boy who had a look of love and mischief on his face. Clara closed her eyes and told herself, "It's okay," then told the baby in her belly, "We're okay. I haven't done anything wrong. I am observing. To help her, the red-haired girl. With her grief. It's not me." Clara rubbed her belly under her white-cotton cover-up and reiterated firmly, "We are okay," then grabbed the guitar and ran back to the bonfire. She hadn't seen the girl in a while and wasn't going to let her barge back into their lives now. She quickly let it go.

Derek was sitting again in the beautiful, newly stained Acacia-wood Adirondack chair with bright-green pillows. Clara handed him the guitar and sat down next to Seamus.

"What should I play?" asked Derek.

"What's that song you love so much?" Seamus asked Clara. "The song we heard at Madison Square Garden? Old, like me? Well, older than me. Or maybe not?"

"The Weight," Clara laughed. "It must be. It's old." Then, she turned to Derek. "Do you know that one?"

"Sure, I do," Derek confirmed and started to play.

"That's it!" cheered Seamus.

"I know that one!" Luna chimed in.

"The Dead covered it and the Staple Singers," Greta added.

"That's who we heard!" Clara exclaimed. "Dead and Friends with Maggie Rogers. And John Mayer."

"It's The Band!" insisted Greta's boyfriend, Hank.

"Hank's really into these old tunes," Greta teased.

"Because they're good," defended Hank.

They all laughed and sang along to Derek's version of "The Weight," and Clara was mesmerized by how good Derek played it. On the chorus, Derek sang to Clara directly. "For you," he interjected then went back to the lyrics.

Seamus called Derek out on his flirtation. "Hey!" he teased. "Don't you dare be better than me with this creative thing. I mean, you got me with the camping in the woods, but I gotta keep some level of decorum here and keep Clara thinking I'm the one, the superhero, Superdad, just for her." He laughed.

Which made Clara so happy, and she grabbed Seamus's arm and snuggled her head against him as she continued to enjoy the music.

Which is when, BAM, Clara suddenly saw a flash of light and was transported to her blurry vision from Dr. Goldberg's office, jumping on a bed, laughing, blended purple and blue colors, head buzzing. It was as if she was in that crazy spot, but she could hear Derek playing and singing "The Weight" clear as day, no other voices, as if Derek were in the room with the bed in the vision too.

And then, Clara was back at the bonfire, heart racing, as if the rug had been pulled out from under her. *I'm back*, she thought and blurted out, "I'm okay," with a jolt.

"What?" Seamus asked, unaware of the weird episode Clara had just experienced.

"I love you," Clara told Seamus and pulled his arms tightly around her, trying to make sure her racing heart stayed hidden. Seamus kissed Clara's head, and she tried her best to relax and just enjoy the music and her friends, but this time, she couldn't quite get there.

It'd been weeks, a month and a half at least, since she'd seen the red-haired girl—since the girl appeared in the bathroom, since the second hypnosis in Dr. Goldberg's office—and now, all Clara could think was, *Is she back? Why? Why now, when everything's been going perfectly? Why won't she let it be perfect?*

And Clara felt a flash of anger for the first time. Why was this girl ruining everything? Why was she still here? And who the heck was she?

23

Big Secrets Always Emerge
from the Shadows

After the girl appeared at the backyard BBQ party, Clara decided to set out on a mission of discovery. She had to find out who this girl was. And she had to find out more about Seamus and Derek's past. There was something hiding beneath the surface, and she was going to find out what it was.

She began that very night by trying to find some photos of Seamus and Derek as kids. She waited until all the leftover stuff was in the fridge after the party and the gazebo was mostly cleaned up and everyone had left in their rideshares to nearby hotels, too buzzed to drive back to the city.

Seamus was plopped down on the couch, surfing the TV. He'd drunk quite a bit more than usual again that day and was pretty plastered. But Clara let it go, hoping it was just because of the fun party. Everyone drank a lot, and it had helped ease the tension between Seamus and Derek, a catalyst perhaps, which was a blessing. And right now, Seamus being drunk was an advantage too, because it meant he wouldn't interrupt her snooping for photos or anything that would give her a clue about the Dunnes' past.

She started in Seamus's childhood room, and it only took a moment for her to find his high school yearbooks. They were on the shelf above his desk, neatly arranged—freshman, sophomore and junior years, but not senior year, the year after their parents died.

But Clara was thrilled with what *was* there, because this was it—she finally was going to see Seamus and Derek as kids. First, she opened junior year—where she found lots of funny early-90s haircuts on the kids.

"What're you doing?" Seamus called to her from the couch downstairs, as if he somehow sensed the sudden quiet and the fact that Clara had stopped wiping down the kitchen counter.

"Nothing!" Clara shouted back to him as she continued perusing photos of pep rallies and then the theater group and a performance of "The King and I."

"Doesn't look like nothing," Seamus said, appearing in the doorway.

Clara screamed and jumped. "Jeez!" she cried. "What are you doing?" And went back to the photos. "This is so great. Why have you never showed me these?"

Seamus sat down next to Clara on his old brown-and-red-striped bedspread, hardly thrilled. Clara grinned at him, then started turning pages quickly, in anticipation. It was obvious she was looking for the brothers' class photos.

"Derek was a senior that year," Seamus said.

"Right," Clara replied. "And you were a junior. Because you skipped, how many? Two years, right?"

"Mmm, hmm," Seamus confirmed as Clara found Derek's senior-year photo. He looked quite handsome, even with the funny, long-ish, cool-guy, jock-ish hair.

"He looks so happy!" Clara exclaimed.

"Yeah, I guess he was," Seamus said.

Clara looked closely at Derek's eyes. They looked so familiar. Suddenly, she saw a light flash. She was running in the woods, turning. Behind her was the dark-haired boy. He had Derek's eyes. Then, FLASH again, and she was back looking at the photo of Derek in the yearbook. Clara pretended nothing happened, heart racing. "Yeah, he really looks so happy," she repeated.

A shadow filled the room. They both stared at Derek in the yearbook, both knowing the photo was taken before the accident. Clara contemplated the change in Derek's eyes from then to now. Seamus nodded. "Yup," he said. "Better times."

And Clara saw another FLASH—and she was back in the boathouse with the dark-haired boy drinking from a flask. Another FLASH. And Clara was back to reality in Seamus's room—sadness still filling every nook and cranny, weighing them down.

"He couldn't face it," Seamus managed about Derek. "He just, as soon as we buried them...it was too much." His jaw clenched.

Clara let him be. She was just happy he was talking about it. He never did, and it probably was the alcohol. But it had to be healing, however it came out, and she was grateful.

"Yeah, Derek was all about us," Seamus continued, "and being the man. And keeping us together. Family first. But he couldn't control me forever." Seamus said and turned the pages looking for another photo of Derek. "Or himself," he added. "He couldn't control himself. And he couldn't hold his emotions in. Or see how they affected other people." Clara saw anger rise in Seamus's eyes. "Maybe that's why he's a priest. Which is ridiculous."

It didn't seem that ridiculous to Clara anymore given what had happened.

Seamus found Derek's photo as an all-star football player and showed her.

"Wow," she said.

And then, he showed her another photo of Derek in a blue tux with a date at the homecoming dance. "Homecoming king? What?!" Clara exclaimed, and they both cracked up. "I think we should make him Little Bean's godfather," Clara said.

"I'm not there yet," Seamus replied, clearly not thrilled with the idea. "But I'll think about it."

"Good," Clara said and grabbed the next yearbook. "Freshman year? How about you? Let's start from the beginning."

Seamus grabbed the book from her. "No, let's look at senior year instead. When I had at least hit puberty."

"There is no senior year," Clara told him.

Seamus went over to a drawer in his desk and pulled it out with a smirk. He must've hid it, Clara thought. It was the year without his parents, but he hadn't thrown it away. That was a good sign.

"Excellent," Clara said, smiling coyly, flirting, trying to make it light as she took the yearbook from him and found his senior photo. Clara gasped, doing a little happy dance. "You're so cute!" she exclaimed.

Seamus laughed. "Little-guy cute," he said, making fun of himself. "That's what happens when you skip two grades."

Clara was charmed again by his self-deprecating humor, which seemed to offer a bit of courage. "Isn't this fun?" she teased. "I'm having fun!"

"Fine, fine, it's okay. And a little fun," he admitted and showed her his science club photo. "This was my second video game."

"Wow. You look...little," Clara teased.

"No shit. That's what *I* said!" he toyed back.

"That must've been strange," Clara observed, "especially if the girls were always older." Clara was teasing, but another shadow crossed his face.

He hid it well. "Mmhmm," he said and joked about himself. "Painful. So painful."

"Yeah, I guess being a nerdy brain isn't all it's cracked up to be."

Seamus thought that was funny, and Clara knew she'd hit the nail on the head. "Yeah," he said. "It's definitely not good to be a nerd in high school, but when you grow up, you get to be the cool guy. And get all the hot girls."

"Exactly!" Clara exclaimed and put her hand on sophomore year, looking at Seamus with funny puppy dog eyes. "Please. Just one photo of you."

Seamus wasn't thrilled but took his tenth-grade yearbook and quickly turned to the juniors and Derek, still with his jock-ish dark hair and a funny smirk.

Clara heard a flash of guitar playing.

Then, Seamus turned to his own sophomore photo. Clara squealed with joy and tried to grab the book.

He slammed it shut. "I said, no," he insisted, suddenly angry, serious, spooking her.

He got up.

"Wait! What happened?" Clara asked.

Seamus didn't answer. He grabbed all four yearbooks and locked them in the armoire, taking the key and shoving it in his jeans pocket. Clara's heart raced. Seamus leaned his head on the armoire door, closing his eyes, clearly in so much pain. "I'm sorry. Again," he told her.

"Okaaay," Clara replied, uncertain, heart still racing. And suddenly, she heard the guitar again. "Did you hear that?" she asked.

"No, but maybe it's those kids in the woods again," Seamus scoffed sarcastically, then backpedaled. "I'm sorry. Maybe it's really some kids," he added trying to sound genuine.

Which is when Clara saw three kids run through the yard, lit by moonlight. "Yeah," Clara said to Seamus, pretending she hadn't seen them. "By the way, thanks for inviting everyone out here today. It made me feel better."

"That's because you did all the planning, and I'm so wise," Seamus teased.

"And old," Clara teased back.

"Old," he agreed playfully and gave Clara a hand up and kissed her—better again.

And Clara heard the guitar strumming "The Weight" from outside the window.

24

The Kids in the Room Upstairs

Clara let the incident with the yearbooks and Seamus's strange, angry outburst go. This was what Dr. Goldberg had said might happen. They needed to shine a light on the trauma, feel the sadness and get past it. Then, and only then, would it disappear. And the more Seamus experienced his own feelings of loss, the more Clara could move on too. That made sense to her, and she had turned her focus back on herself and what *was* working—namely, fixing up the house and getting creative.

The ghost girl had appeared off and on since the party, but Clara had simply acknowledged her and asked her to leave in a friendly voice every time. It seemed to work. And now, as Clara walked across the backyard grass in bare feet and saw the girl sitting at the base of the giant maple tree, furiously writing in a small book, she looked at the girl and whispered, "Thank you and good-bye," and continued on, humming while carrying a pitcher of lemonade and sandwiches on a tray that she'd found at a local thrift shop. It was a super find, both the tray and the thrift store full of unsuspecting antiques and emptied closets.

Now that Clara had fixed up the yard for the party and the basics in the dining room for entertaining, she had found the inspiration to finish the guesthouse, finally putting the finishing touches on the structure. Then, she'd officially turn it into a darkroom to start developing the photos she'd been taking all summer.

Billy had agreed to help again. She was paying him now too, and they both loved to hang out, so it was a win, win, win. Clara had told Billy that she was sorry he'd missed the S'mores at the party but left it at that. She wanted him to know he was welcome without overstepping his boundary or taking down her own.

"Okay...," Clara sang to Billy as she stepped through the open guesthouse door, "you can take a break now. Lemonade and tuna sandwiches!" She set the tray on the little card table she'd covered with a yellow-and-pink paisley cloth—bright and cheerful.

Billy was painting the ceiling he'd patched two days earlier.

"Thank you, madame slave driver," he teased.

"I wish I could help," she said, rubbing her belly playfully. "Thank you."

"No, these fumes are no good. You might start seeing ghosts again," he joked and his eyes sparkled.

Clara glanced outside at the red-haired girl sitting at the base of the giant tree trunk and stopped, wondering if she should say anything. She poured a glass of lemonade for Billy and clenched it tightly as she looked back in the yard. The girl was still furiously writing her little notebook. Clara turned and handed Billy the cold drink, her eyes suddenly solemn. "I see her all the time again," Clara admitted. "Ever since the party. So, two weeks now. I just ignore her. She's outside writing in her diary or something at this very moment." Clara's heart was pounding, unsure if she was revealing too much even though she felt safe with Billy.

"Time for a little country bar escape?" he teased playfully.

Clara shook her head *no* and handed him a sandwich with a cute ladybug-print napkin that she'd also found at the thrift shop. Billy's hand was shaking, and she noticed he was sweating. "You okay?" she asked, concerned.

"Fine. Yeah," Billy told her.

But Clara knew he wasn't fine. There was that pain in his eyes again, like at the bar and like Derek's. "So why did you do it again?" Clara asked Billy, knowing he was back in bed with his demons looking for God and maybe his mom. "When you have other solutions. Right? You said..."

"Relief," Billy interjected. "From the pain. It never leaves. And like I said: God is there. And sometimes so is she."

He was so matter of fact that Clara didn't know what to say. "I'll go get you some orange juice," she managed.

"No, no, I'm good with lemonade," Billy replied and looked back up at the ceiling, ready to dive back into the work.

"You're helping me. I want to help you," Clara told him and touched his hand warmly. His eyes looked pained. Again, she heard the guitar—and saw similar eyes in her mind—pained but charming, black eyes, like Derek's. And Billy's.

Clara ignored it and walked out of the guesthouse and across the yard and went inside the house through the sliding-glass doors on the back porch for the orange juice, passing the staircase on the way to the kitchen.

Suddenly, she saw the red-haired girl, sandy-haired boy, and dark-haired boy all together, running into Derek's old childhood room upstairs. Startled, her heart started racing. *Where did they come from?* she wondered. She had a straight view from the bottom of the stairs to Derek's door. Clara heard the guitar, her heart pounding faster, and started cautiously up the stairs. *Are there three ghosts now?* she wondered. *Or maybe two of them are actual kids—with the balls to come in here while I'm home*. Clara laughed at the insanity then slowly cracked Derek's old bedroom door and peeked in: nothing. Her heart pounded harder, louder, like a drum. She could hear it—blood rushing and beating in her ears.

Then, Clara heard crying downstairs. She slowly went down. It was coming from the downstairs bathroom, the one with the nice, dark wood and gauzy green curtains where she'd gotten the positive pregnancy test and seen the girl—the ghost with the terror in her eyes.

Clara peered around the corner. The guest bathroom door was ajar, and there was the red-haired girl, standing and looking in the mirror. Clara inched closer, terrified but determined, when suddenly, the girl yelled at herself in the mirror, "This is all your fault!" It was so loud that Clara stopped, cupping her ears, hands shaking. The girl whispered angrily to herself in the mirror, "The baby's going to ruin everything. You are not going to have this baby. I won't let you."

Clara gasped, terrified, shaking, and took a step back. Was the red-haired girl talking to her? Threatening her? Was she going to hurt Clara's baby? *No, no, no!* Clara screamed in her head.

Then, the girl began scratching at her own face, clawing down, drawing blood. Clara got a light FLASH. Her head began stinging. The girl turned and glared at Clara and said in a seething whisper, "I hate you."

Clara screamed and started backing up, trying to get away, afraid to turn her back on the girl, reaching, stumbling—

—as Billy ran in to help her. Clara grabbed him, clutching onto his shirt for dear life. "She wants to kill me," Clara whispered desperately. "And my baby. Look." Clara turned toward the bathroom and saw the girl there, still glaring. Clara pointed for Billy to see.

"C'mon, we're going to my gran," Billy told her.

"You don't see her?" Clara cried, looking into Billy's face and realizing he didn't see the girl.

"No," he said. "I don't see her. But I understand."

And Clara crumbled and sobbed, wondering how this would ever end.

***

Billy led Clara up the stairs to his grandma's home and music studio. He opened the front door and let Clara go in ahead while he stayed in the doorjamb and yelled, "Gran?! It's me."

"Hi, Billy," Mrs. Flannery replied from somewhere behind the closed music-studio door.

"I brought a friend that could use a good ear and tea!" he called out, then turned to Clara and whispered, "I gotta run. Just go on in." He kissed her cheek quickly, his skin clammy and damp, then bolted out and down the stairs.

"Wait! Billy!" Clara yelled after him and ran out into the stairwell. But Billy didn't listen, disappearing up the street.

"Ain't nuthin' you can do about him, dear," Mrs. Flannery said, coming out of the music studio, looking eerie as if staring out into the living room area with the light shining over her shoulder from the studio behind her. "But you can come in and do yourself a favor," she told Clara with a warm smile and stepped all the way into the room, letting the studio door shut behind her.

"I just want to help him," Clara said, coming back into the house.

"Oh, honey, don't worry," Mrs. Flannery comforted, walking towards Clara, starting to reach out.

"He wanted to go hear music," Clara cried, feeling desperate now and guilty. "I should've gone."

The old feisty woman came closer, following Clara's voice. "Like I said—ain't nothing you can do. That kind of pain can only be healed on a spiritual level."

"What kind of pain?" Clara asked.

"We all got pain," Mrs. Flannery said, reaching Clara, finding her hands, taking them. "And we all gotta find our own way to deal with it. Billy lost his mama. Aneurism. He was eight, poor baby. My boy, my son, Rowan, couldn't take it. Left him with me to raise."

Clara took this in. "So, he lost both parents. In a sense. I mean, I'm sorry. Is Rowan okay now?"

"Stop makin' it yours to fix. Come have some tea," Mrs. Flannery said, ignoring the question about her son—Billy's father, Rowan. "Fix your own thing."

Clara followed Mrs. Flannery back into the music studio. "Billy brought me a lovely and extra-practical English tea kettle from London," Mrs. Flannery told Clara. "It's the best. I was just cooking water when you arrived. My usual time between students. I have English Breakfast and Earl Grey, if you'd like some." Mrs. Flannery stopped to listen to Clara's response, turning her ear with a small, warm smile. It was a kind gesture. Clara felt that Mrs. Flannery cared—a gentle soul with a bit of humor like Billy. And even Seamus. "If you'd like another type of tea, you'll have to run down to the store. My niece is in the shop, Noelle," Mrs. Flannery said.

"Earl Grey is perfect," Clara told her.

"Wonderful," Mrs. Flannery chimed, pleased with her choice, then continued on to the table where the tea kettle sat, water boiling. Clara followed. Mrs. Flannery turned off the kettle and stopped, frozen.

Clara stopped too. "What? What is it?" Clara wondered.

"Emmeline?" Mrs. Flannery asked, hesitant but also hopeful and full of surprise.

"No, it's just me, Clara," Clara told her, letting out a small laugh of worry and confusion.

"There's no one else with you?" Mrs. Flannery wondered.

"No," Clara replied.

"Strange," Mrs. Flannery said, taking this in. "Your step has the exact same cadence as hers. And I never miss a step." She deftly opened a tea bag for Clara and put it in a mug next to her own, which was already waiting with an Earl Grey bag as well, and poured in the water.

"Whose cadence?" Clara asked, continuing to the piano right next to the tea-kettle cart and playing a little diddy. Again, Mrs. Flannery stopped, surprised, and walked over, drawn to Clara. She listened as Clara finished the tune—the last key off. Mrs. Flannery reached over and moved Clara's finger to the correct key.

"That's the first thing I teach my students. For fun," Mrs. Flannery told Clara, then she turned and touched Clara's hair and face. "Emmeline always got that last note wrong too."

Clara got the chills when she saw Mrs. Flannery's face soften as she ran her hands over Clara's features. "Who?" Clara asked.

"The girl with the step like yours," Mrs. Flannery explained.

"Who is this Emmeline?" Clara asked.

"Emmeline McGuire," Mrs. Flannery said.

Clara gasped, "What?!" She couldn't believe it. There was that name again. "McGuire? Isn't that the same name as the girl that disappeared?"

"Yup. Thirty years ago," Mrs. Flannery confirmed. "When I first heard your step, I was sure it was her." Mrs. Flannery laughed at herself. "The absurdity. Maybe I'm finally getting overly sentimental in my old age. How old are you?"

"Thirty," Clara replied, still shocked and wondering how Mrs. Flannery could remain so jovial with all this tragedy around.

"Well, there you have it," Mrs. Flannery joked. "Emmeline disappeared when you were born."

Clara took a deep, shaky breath.

"I'm sorry," Mrs. Flannery said, kindly. "You need comforting and tea. All this talk isn't helping. Please, tell me what I can do." Mrs. Flannery went back over to the mugs and served the tea at the little table. Clara joined her, surprised by how deftly Mrs. Flannery moved about the place, and they both sat down.

"I keep seeing a ghost. A girl," Clara explained as she sipped her tea.

"Who looks like Emmeline, Billy told me."

"What?"

"With red hair," Mrs. Flannery said. "Emmeline had beautiful, long, curly, red hair and a wonderful laugh."

Clara took this in, trying to grasp what it meant.

"Never mind, dear. Just tell me about the ghost."

"Billy thought you'd know the history of the house. The Dunne house. In case, the ghost is trying to tell me something."

"How do you know it's a ghost?" Mrs. Flannery asked.

"Well, if it's not, I'm just crazy. Or possessed," Clara joked. "I mean, you heard the footsteps."

But Mrs. Flannery didn't laugh now. "It's strange that you'd have a ghost there. No one's ever said anything about a ghost at the Dunne house. And you know how people love a good ghost story. Then again, no one's lived there for at least twenty years. Ghosts usually are only fun when there's drama or scandal," Mrs. Flannery said, finally her humor coming back. She handed Clara a plate of cookies off a tray sitting in the middle of the table.

"Could it be Mrs. Dunne? Seamus's mom?" Clara asked and took a nip of shortbread cookie, "Mmm," and poured a bit of cream in her tea.

"Could it?" Mrs. Flannery asked. "Haven't you seen photos of her? Stella Dunne? Quite a fireball herself that one was."

Yes, Clara had seen photos. The red-haired girl was definitely not Seamus's mother. "It's not her," Clara confirmed.

"Well, what I know is this," Mrs. Flannery went on. "The first owner, the woman whose husband built the house, was pregnant while he was away at war, Vietnam."

"Maybe it's her," Clara said. This was hopeful.

"She had the child just fine though, Clara, so no, I'd say it's not her," Mrs. Flannery went on and reached out for Clara's hand. Clara let her take it and squeeze it and rub it with her thumb, looking at Clara but with blind eyes.

Then, abruptly, Mrs. Flannery let go and went back to her tea, as if she had surprised herself with what she'd sensed. She paused taking in something—something she'd felt in Clara's being, something that gave her a shock—and then, finally, she said, "I always had hope Emmeline would come back. But maybe there's something you don't want to see."

"You say that as if you're sure the girl I saw is Emmeline. That the ghost is Emmeline. Or what are you saying?" Clara demanded, confused and agitated now.

"I'm sure Emmeline is here," Mrs. Flannery said in a low, serious voice. "So, it's just a good, logical guess."

Clara couldn't stand it. No one believed her. Why was this happening? "I'm seeing a ghost!" she cried, unable to hide her anger and frustration, standing up. "Or being possessed by one! This is not funny!"

"I don't sense ghost energy," Mrs. Flannery said, worried. "Please sit back down. I just sense Emmeline." This just made it worse for Clara. "It's strange," Mrs. Flannery continued, staring out with her blind eyes again, "as if lingering from long ago. As if an old and wise soul but full of shame."

Clara clenched her fists, angry, a pit of rage in her stomach, not sure what to do or where to put it—angry at herself for not being able to stop all these feelings, angry at herself for having these visions, hating herself as if it were her own fault when it wasn't—and suddenly, she felt a stabbing on her forehead. "Ow," she cried, grabbing her head.

"Oh, dear," Mrs. Flannery said, "I've gone too far again." She got up and felt her way around the small table to Clara, rubbing Clara's back, comforting her, then pulling her close for a hug. "What does your husband say? Seamus?" Mrs. Flannery asked.

"He thinks I'm overreacting because I haven't let go of the miscarriages. I had three," Clara told her.

"Oh, dear," Mrs. Flannery said, "come here," and she took Clara's arms in her hands, holding her firm as if to look at her and tell her something important. "Listen for what the ghost wants to tell you. Perhaps it's a warning. Or perhaps she wants to help you have your baby. Or teach you something she didn't learn."

Clara nodded, not knowing what to say.

Mrs. Flannery smiled. "It's a blessing, and it's up to you to see it that way. For your baby. This is for your baby. And strange things happen around life. That's where the magic is. And don't try to explain it. Or fix it. Another thing we can't fix. Fate or God—or whatever it is—is driving this show."

Clara let out a little laugh.

"There you go," Mrs. Flannery said, squeezing Clara's arms, then letting go. "I have something for you," she said and walked back out of the studio and over to the dining room table and picked up a book. Clara followed. "Billy was reading it to me," Mrs. Flannery said and handed the book to Clara. "It's about ghosts. Laugh a little.

It'll help. Enjoy your pregnancy. It's such a beautiful time." Clara turned the book over, perusing the cover. "Don't stare at anything too long," Mrs. Flannery added, somehow sensing Clara trying to discern what this book was about. "This is for fun. You need to have fun. Laugh at yourself."

***

Clara felt a sense of relief after leaving Mrs. Flannery. She was worried about Billy, but Mrs. Flannery had given her good advice about herself, even if she didn't quite want to admit it. And she was going to take it. She was going to listen to the girl if she appeared and hear what she had to say. Dr. Goldberg had said the same thing. Clara also was going to lean into the humor. That was one thing that didn't come with sadness, and it seemed to align with everyone she loved. Even the girl was always laughing. When she wasn't angry.

And it worked. Clara managed to keep it light with Seamus at dinner that night and told him about visiting Mrs. Flannery with Billy, who was making inroads in the guesthouse. She told Seamus that they had had tea and that Mrs. Flannery gave her a funny ghost story book. She didn't tell him about Billy's addiction.

Then, later that night, when she and Seamus were reading in bed —thanks to the perfectly polished iron nightlights she'd installed— Clara started in on the book. Seamus glanced over with a teasy look. "Really? You're going there?"

Clara laughed. "She is quite a nut that Mrs. Flannery."

"Just be lucky you didn't take piano from her," Seamus joked. "She's wonderful, but I hated those scales." Which made Clara laugh, and he added, "I'm so happy you're feeling better." And took a swig of a local IPA he had on his nightstand.

Clara hadn't noticed it. *Drinking again*, she thought. This was unsettling. Seamus had brought out an expensive bottle of wine at dinner too. And come to think of it, he'd been drinking every night that he'd been home since the yearbook incident two weeks earlier. Was that why he was so happy and easy going all the time? Not pressuring or doubting her? she wondered.

She told herself not to go there. Not now. They had to keep moving forward for the baby's sake.

"Yeah, it's completely stopped," Clara joked back at Seamus, lying, "the worry and the stupid imaginary kids." She hadn't told Seamus what had happened that day with the three kids and the girl yelling in the bathroom or anything Mrs. Flannery had said about sensing Emmeline McGuire.

Seamus kissed her belly and rubbed it. "Then, we made the right decision."

"And now, we need to make the right decision to let me clear out that studio all the way," Clara told him. "ALL the computers—so that I can work."

"Fine! Fine," Seamus agreed playfully. "Do it. Do what you have to. I trust you. Completely."

And Clara knew he did. At least about clearing out the guesthouse. And it was a good start.

But then, Seamus smiled at her with a sexy look over his reading glasses and tech magazine, and she felt a flash of panic in her stomach—*Trust*, she thought, *but can he trust me? Can I trust him? Can my mind be playing tricks on me, imagining a ghost that looks like Emmeline McGuire?*

25 |

The Girl Full of Rage

The next day, with Seamus's full permission, Clara launched in on clearing out the guesthouse again. She ignored her apprehension about Seamus drowning his pain in alcohol instead of feeling it and carried on. Her head was swimming with ideas for photos, and she couldn't stop taking them. She'd been at it around the neighborhood all morning and, now that it was afternoon, was in the guesthouse on the phone with Erin forcing herself to get to work cleaning. Still, she was completely distracted.

"I'm going to call it Nosey Neighbors In A Small Town," Clara told Erin on the phone while looking out the guesthouse window and taking pictures of neighbor Mrs. Lee, who was peeking into another neighbor's house. "It's just too funny. Or maybe it could be Look-e-loo Lee. Her name is Mrs. Lee. I don't know her first name."

"Wow," Erin said. "Finally, you sound back to normal, girl."

"I'm not, but he's letting me get rid of all this crap. You saw it. He's like a hoarder. So now, I'm on a high," Clara said and turned. There was so much stuff there—computers on top of computers, floppy drives, charts, whiteboards, pens, boxes, chairs. "Actually, how's this for a coffee table book two: Pack Rats, Secrets of the Hardcore Nerd Gamer."

Erin laughed, and Clara snapped a photo of the old, boxy PC desktop computer next to the old typewriter. "Okay, I'm gonna get started here. Actually. I'll call you later when it's done," Clara said, "and I'll text you some before and afters."

"You get 'em, girl," Erin said. "Just don't make me feel bad about our mess—at our house. It's gotten worse. You'll see—when you start popping out those babies. It's endless."

Clara laughed, so grateful for her friend. "Okay, talk soon," she said and hung up and lifted her camera to take a picture of the computer screen of the old HP desktop. Through the lens, she saw the red-haired-girl typing at the typewriter next to it.

Clara gasped and jumped back, bringing the camera down and seeing her own reflection on the computer screen. "Oh my god," Clara sputtered and laughed it off. "Stupid, stupid, so not a thing." She sat down at the computer and tried to turn it on, pressing what seemed like the right button. Maybe she could get a quick game in, even though she'd already beat the whole thing once.

The computer fired up, but a screen appeared that required a password. She had no idea what it could possibly be, so she moved on to the typewriter. "Whatever," Clara said and grabbed a piece of paper from a pile. Dust flew. "Guess I missed a spot," she joked to herself and waved the paper around then brushed it off and put it in the typewriter, rolling it upward so it was ready to be typed on. She remembered using a typewriter as a kid while visiting her grandparents in Michigan, back when her gramps, Nonno, was still alive. He'd had a cool old Oliver Courier and had showed her how to use it.

Clara punched a few keys—definitely not as easy as a computer keyboard. You really had to push down to get the arm to fly up and hit the ribbon. The letters that appeared on the page were faint, but there was still a bit of ink on the ribbon. Clara turned the ribbon and tried again. The letters appeared darker this time. "That's fun," she said and typed "hello" and laughed, not sure why this was so funny.

Suddenly, Clara felt a breeze on her cheek and heard a girl's voice whisper, "R-E-X," and saw a wisp of red hair flash by. Chills came over her. "Go away," Clara said in a low, sharp voice, turning to look: Nothing.

She shook her head and typed "R-E-X" in defiance.

"Rex," Clara heard the girl's voice say and saw the edge of the red-haired ghost right over her shoulder. Clara screamed and ran out, grabbing her phone off the box by the door. "This is not happening!" Clara shouted and hurried into the house through the back kitchen door, slamming it shut, leaning against it, fumbling with her phone, dialing Seamus, then hearing the ghost's voice again. "You can't trust him," the ghost said.

"What do you want?!" Clara yelled out into the kitchen, not sure where the voice was coming from, hanging up. Then, she saw the red-haired girl at the window in the living room, looking out at the backyard, solemn. "It's all your fault," the girl said.

"Look at me!" Clara shouted.

The red-haired girl turned. She was pale and somber, holding her belly under a billowy top—definitely pregnant and with the same white birthmark next to her bellybutton as Clara had. Clara gasped when she saw it and felt sweat beads forming on her forehead, hoping she wouldn't pass out. The girl looked right through Clara, scared, angry, sad and yelling, "It's all your fauuuuuuuuult!!!"—the girl's face turning red with fury and the sound so loud it tore through Clara's head.

Clara fell to her knees and screamed, "Noooooooo!" back at the girl with the same rage and power, the sound waves of her voice annihilating the ghostly girl for a moment, Clara's whole body shaking. Then the girl appeared again with fury, standing above Clara and staring down at her as if disgusted. "You did this," the ghost whispered, then turned her face upward as if to the heavens and exploded in a silent scream. When she stopped, the ghost girl's shoulders slumped, her rage turning to tears and disappointment, and she disappeared.

Please Make Her Leave

Clara stood at the back of the church behind the little stand of candles, shaking, scared, wringing her hands, praying, "Please help me, please help me," over and over, even though she never prayed. It felt as if the candles would protect her, the flames, hot, guarding. Because the red-haired girl was in the second pew down from the back where she was standing—praying and looking equally desperate and terrified. Or maybe more so.

The red-haired girl had appeared in the pew within minutes after Clara had stepped into the church—as soon as Clara felt a moment of peace and protection, even though she wasn't a believer in religion. Sure, God might be there in that church, but religion was a strange bird as far as Clara was concerned. Her parents had taken her to church as a kid, but they'd only done it for her, and they mostly went at Christmas and Easter. Clara liked the traditions but not the idea that there was only one way or one truth. That seemed to minimize the power of a god. God was bigger than that, Clara assumed. Also, religion seemed to be the source of so much pain in the world and made Clara feel like she never wanted anything to do with it.

But today, Clara needed something—some kind of protection, some kind of help—so she had called Derek. And as soon as she'd entered the church and found a smidgeon of peace as she waited for him, the red-haired girl had appeared to ruin it, as if to purposefully torment her. Clara felt angry and afraid and squeezed her eyes shut and prayed harder, "Please, please, please make her go away. And keep her from hurting my baby."

Cold sweat dripped down Clara's clammy face as she heard the door open. She saw the girl turn and glare, and then, the girl whispered to Clara, "You..."

Clara gasped and turned and ran right into Derek, frantic—"There's the ghost. Again. I said it hasn't been happening. But it has. And now, she's right over there. Please tell me you see her. Please."

Clara clutched Derek's vest as he peered around her to look. Derek shook his head—he didn't see the ghost. Clara looked again—the girl was still there, but she faded until she was gone. Clara turned back to Derek. "She shouldn't be here."

Derek pulled Clara close and hugged her. She buried her head in his chest and wept. He stroked her hair, comforting her. "Who said ghosts can't come into churches? Huh?" he joked, trying to get her to calm down.

Clara nodded and pulled back, wiping her tears. "She was at our house. The red-haired girl. And she was pregnant. And angry. And what if she comes back?"

"You've been through a lot, my dear," Derek comforted.

"I'm so afraid Seamus won't understand," Clara cried. "Please help me. Please."

***

Clara clutched the dining room chair as Derek blessed the house in Latin with holy water—"In nomine Patris et Filii et Spiritus Sancti..." Again, beads of cold sweat covered her forehead and upper lip. She was shaking and hoping she wouldn't pass out and hoping this would go quickly and be done before Seamus came home. If he came home. She didn't know. Couldn't remember. Was so confused. And it was getting dark now, candles lighting the house.

Hoping, hoping Seamus wouldn't see.

And most of all hoping that whatever Derek was doing would work and that the girl would disappear forever. At least, Derek was trying something, Clara thought, even though her gut told her this wasn't the answer. But she was desperate, and as Derek walked past the chair doing his blessing, Clara suddenly became nauseous and ran into the kitchen to throw up in the sink. Maybe she should have listened to herself and stayed away from anything religious. But she needed this. She couldn't let this girl hurt her baby. She had to make it stop.

Derek watched Clara, waiting, stopping what he was doing as she grabbed a paper towel, wiped her mouth and returned to the living room, shakier than ever.

"I think you should sit down," Derek told Clara, gesturing to the closest chair at the dining room table.

Clara hesitated, even more confused now.

"Sit down, Clara," Derek told her firmly.

This frightened Clara. Why was he so angry? *Why is everyone so angry?* she wondered and stammered, "Let me, just...," and gestured toward the kitchen, needing water, but then, she just sat down afraid—afraid of continuing, afraid of Derek now, afraid of letting him pray over her again. "What are we doing?" she managed. "I think I need some water."

"Relax, it's okay. I'm here to help," Derek assured her.

And BAM, Clara saw a flash of light, and suddenly, she was under the blue trim of loosely woven dress fabric, struggling to breathe with a young man's voice on the other side of the fabric telling her that she was okay. "This will help," the voice said.

Then, suddenly, a key turned in the door, and Clara snapped back from the blurry vision to the Dunne living room.

It was Seamus at the door. He stepped in, shocked to see them. "What's going on here?" Seamus asked. Clara ran to him sobbing, Derek looking guilty. "What is going on?!" Seamus shouted at Derek.

Derek stuttered, "She...she had..."

Seamus lost all cool. "Don't you know when to back off?!" he shouted. "You're the priest now!"

Clara saw the fear and rage in Seamus's eyes. "No, please," Clara defended, "It's not Derek's fault." She put both hands on Seamus's chest, firm, pushing him back. *This can't happen!* she thought. "He was, it happened again," Clara told Seamus, begging. "Please, leave him alone. I didn't want to tell you."

"The crazy ghost thing?" Seamus cried. "Is that why you called and didn't leave a message? Do you not know how much that scares me? I ran out in the middle of a meeting! I called ten thousand times! There was traffic! An accident! I couldn't get through! What is going on?!"

"She came to the church," Derek tried to explain.

"Oh, that's helpful," Seamus mocked him.

Derek looked down, like a broken child, then back up. "She's trying," he said.

"Leave. Just leave! I understand!" Seamus shouted.

Derek froze.

"Please, Seamus," Clara pleaded. "I asked him to come here and help."

"And you're doing an exorcism?!" Seamus yelled at Derek.

"It's a blessing," Derek said.

"For what?" Seamus continued. "You believe this ghost bullshit too?!"

Pain filled Derek's eyes, and Seamus turned to Clara, angry, wanting an explanation.

"I, I, was cleaning out the cottage. I was on the typewriter. The, the—" she stuttered.

"Ghost?" Seamus mocked.

Clara felt the tears rising. "She told me to type Rex. R-E-X."

Seamus froze in shock. "What?" he whispered.

"Rex. The ghost told me to type Rex," Clara explained.

Seamus had to look away.

"I'm gonna go," Derek said, gathering his things.

Seamus took a deep breath, regrouping, turning back to Clara. "Rex. Your dog's name? As a kid?"

Clara closed her eyes and tried to be still, clenching her fists as if to protect herself somehow. This was too much. All her defenses were broken. "Yes," she whispered, "like my dog, Rex."

Her despair was too much for Seamus. He couldn't stand to see her so upset. "I think we need to leave this place," he told Clara, then turned to Derek and whispered with sheer venom, "So I don't hate you anymore."

Derek lifted his chin and let the anger hit him, as if he deserved it. As if he could take it. As if it was his own doing. Pain everywhere. Then, he turned and left.

As soon as the door shut, Seamus turned to Clara, trying to hold down his rage, his eyes looking for some kind of answer.

"It's not his fault. Or yours," Clara told him. "Can't you please give him a chance?"

"I don't think that's possible," Seamus said.

"I'm going after him. He needs help. More than us," Clara insisted and ran out, leaving Seamus in shock.

Gravestones in the Woods

Clara walked through the woods behind the house looking for Derek, only a sliver of the moon giving some light through the trees. "Derek? Derek?!" she called out, hoping he'd reply. "I know you're out here somewhere! I saw you walk off this way!"

Clara heard nothing from Derek but, after a few minutes, came to a clearing and a tiny cemetery of just two headstones. A sense of déjà vu came over her, like she'd been there before—*Or maybe it's from the dream*, she realized, *oh my god*. It was just like the clearing in her ever-recurring nightmare, the clearing that she couldn't get away from unless she woke up, the one with the headstones and the rat in her hand in the coffin.

Chills came over her.

And then, she saw Derek.

He was sitting on a small concrete bench. Clara went over and sat next to him. And then, she saw the names etched on the simple stones: Caleb and Stella Dunne—Seamus and Derek's parents. Clara hid her surprise. "I'm sorry," she said.

"Don't apologize," Derek told her. "That's our thing, me and Seamus. Jealousy and control. That's as far as we go."

Clara nodded. "And I'm sorry about your parents," she added, still shocked by what she was seeing.

"I know what you're going through," Derek continued. "With these visions. The stress. Losing someone is one of the most difficult things anyone can go through. I lost my parents. The pain is as immense today as it was the moment they left. I can't imagine what your loss is like."

They stared at the graves for a moment before Clara broke through the silence and grief filling the clearing, as if it couldn't escape the tall pine trees holding it in. "You're a good man, Derek," she said. "You and Seamus went through so much. You need to take it easy on yourself."

"Look at you—the devastated leading the traumatized," he joked. "You need to not blame yourself," he added, trying to smile, but his pain was unbearable. And Clara saw it and nodded and stood up and squeezed his shoulder and went home.

Clara wasn't going to tell Seamus, she decided as she walked back through the woods. She'd say she couldn't find Derek and tell Seamus that he was right—maybe just a few weeks more here at the lake and then they should go back to the city after all. The baby seemed to be fine, but Clara could feel herself breaking down—her heart was crumbling. There was just too much sadness and heaviness here. And that awful girl. And even if the baby made it, this environment wouldn't be healthy.

And now that they'd established the connection with Derek, even if tenuous, maybe they could build it slowly from the city. And just sell this Dunne family house once and for all. They could probably make a killing if she finished renovating it. It was so beautiful here.

But then, Clara thought about the graves—knowing that was probably the reason they hadn't sold the house—and she felt a squeezing in her throat and lungs. She stopped walking and paused, breathing in deeply through her nose and reminding herself that she was okay—reminding herself, like Dr. Goldberg had told her, that she *did* have some control in this situation. She had control over herself. She could choose how she responded. And she was going to respond like an adult. If she'd gotten nothing else from being at the house—besides, of course, their beautiful baby and family—it was that she'd grown up. Yes, Clara Aiello Dunne had grown up here at the lake house, and that's something she needed before she could be a good mom. Maybe that's what the baby had been waiting for all along.

28

The Ghost in the Machine

Billy's in good form, Clara thought the next morning as they began boxing up Seamus's old stuff in the guesthouse. *And we're gonna make a huge dent*. Clara was still a bit shaky from the previous day, and Billy was shaky from whatever he was up to, so they were the perfect pair—*No judgment here*, Clara thought.

Cleaning the guesthouse and keeping all scrutiny at bay helped her feel grounded, as did the fact that she had a new tactic: Box everything up and then Seamus could peruse anything "valuable" at his leisure. Then, even when they went back to the city, Clara could either come back out to the lake occasionally and use the space for herself as a darkroom for her photography or she could make it into a fabulous guest space or rental unit and up the value of the property for a sale.

"This one for Good Will," Clara said, pointing to a desk chair with two wheels.

Billy stopped to watch Seamus walk from the house to his car in the driveway as he headed out to the city for work. Clara noticed Seamus too and felt the dark cloud of her own dread moving in. "I don't think we're gonna last long here," Clara told Billy, doing her best to stay in reality and keep it rational, not letting the darkness overtake her like she'd done the day before. *I can do this*, she told herself.

Seamus looked over at them as he reached the car. Clara and Billy waved. Seamus didn't respond and opened his car door, simultaneously getting a call on his phone—the typical morning barrage. Usually, Seamus didn't answer. This time he did. "Hello?' Seamus said into the phone.

Clara and Billy heard him begin the conversation as he sat down in the driver's seat. They watched, somehow unable to look away from the tragedy that was weighing down the man before them.

"He doesn't like me," Billy said. "He's jealous. And rightfully so."

Clara looked at Billy, her brow furrowed.

"I'm kidding," Billy said, even though he wasn't completely. "We gotta lighten it up here."

"At least he cares," Clara said defensively, still watching her husband, trying her best to find anything positive.

"There you go," Billy said and went for a fist bump. Clara pulled it together and gave him a half-assed bump back. "C'mon, let's do this," Billy suggested and started back in, sliding another "FOR SEAMUS" box towards the door. Clara took one more look at Seamus, still on the phone, car door wide open, and told herself under her breath, "Okay, I can handle this. I can handle our life exactly like this. I can handle Seamus exactly like this. For now. For today. Until we leave." Then, she turned and forced a smile at Billy, even though she was completely rattled all over again.

"Just tell me what's next, Boss," Billy said with a grin.

They heard Seamus's car door slam and saw him slowly back out of the driveway.

Clara exhaled in relief and turned back to Billy. "Thank you," she said. "I appreciate you calling me Boss," she teased, finally letting the heaviness go, then looked over at the lineup of computers and gadgets on the huge desk by the wall. "Okay, we got this," Clara said out loud, pumping herself up and pointing to the computer next to the typewriter, the one that she'd been gaming on when she'd heard the cries from the girl in the woods and the fighting. "In the box for Seamus to keep," Clara told Billy. "I'm sure he won't get rid of that one."

Billy sat down on the bright-orange desk chair in front of the computer where Clara had spent hours going from level to level with the knight and dragon game.

"The beaut?" Billy said about the old machine, curious, powering it up. "I just gotta see what it looks like before it goes."

"There's a password," Clara told him. "I tried. Seamus knows it but...you know."

Billy tried it anyway, entering random passwords. Nothing worked. "You didn't ask him what it was?" Billy inquired.

"Yeah, I guess that would've been the thing to do if I'd been thinking clearly," she joked. "If I thought I'd ever want to go back in there."

Which is when Billy noticed the word "REX" typed on the white paper in the typewriter next to the computer. He tried it, typing R-E-X into the password box. "Bingo!" Billy cheered. "It works."

"What?" Clara said in disbelief and went over.

They looked at the screen: "Welcome Emmeline McGuire" was written in small type at the bottom, in blue, almost like an after-thought, but still there.

Clara gasped, "Oh my god. I didn't see that. I must've...he must've...when I played before. I didn't see the screen. Just the game. I was focused on the game." She moved closer, looking, reading, shaking, clutching the top of the orange chair, needing something to hold her up. "Oh my god," she whispered.

"What's wrong?"

Clara was frozen.

"Clara? What's happening?" Billy demanded, getting worried again as he saw her face pale, beads of sweat forming on her forehead, hand trembling.

Clara took a deep breath, her lungs starting to constrict. "I can't believe it," she whispered. "It's her. She's the one. The friend. She's the reason. I have to know," Clara said and ran out—out the door of the guesthouse, across the lawn, noticing Seamus out of the corner of her eye, still in his car, in the middle of the street, still on the phone, car running, engrossed in his conversation. She didn't care. Even when his eyes turned, noticing her, she kept moving—she had to—in the sliding glass door, up the stairs, into Seamus's childhood room and straight to the armoire where Seamus had locked the yearbooks so she couldn't get to them. Because he didn't trust her. *Why? Why? Why?* Clara screamed in her head and pulled at the armoire door, yanking, jerking, yanking. Nothing happened. She shook it with all her might. Still nothing.

Then, Clara ran out, back down the stairs, out the sliding glass door, into the work shed, out with an axe, not acknowledging Billy in the door of the guesthouse watching her, mouth agape, or Seamus, still on the phone in his car, watching her too, also shocked. She just continued on, adrenaline coursing through her veins as she hustled back up the stairs and straight to the armoire. She hacked the door to pieces and pulled it back, then heard Seamus's voice from downstairs. It must've been loud.

"What's going on?" Seamus yelled up.

"Get away from me!" Clara shouted, fury filling every fiber of her being. She pulled out the yearbooks, turning straight to Seamus's freshman class, searching the *M*s. And there she was: Emmeline

McGuire. "Emmeline McGuire," Clara whispered, heart racing—Emmeline was the red-haired girl. Clara gasped.

Seamus ran in, stopped in the door, saw what she was looking at.

"The ghost is Emmeline McGuire," Clara confirmed without looking him. He remained frozen as Clara found the science fair page in his freshman yearbook, and there they were: Emmeline and Seamus winning awards. Clara grabbed Seamus's sophomore yearbook: More of Emmeline and Seamus everywhere, including them winning more awards. "That's why you didn't want me to see," she whispered.

Seamus paled, as if wounded, sliding to the floor, leaning against the doorjamb for support.

Clara turned to him, angry, tears flowing. "This is her! The ghost! And you knew it!" she shouted.

"I didn't know it," Seamus defended, unable to look at Clara, desperate not to feel the pain rising.

"Why didn't you tell me you knew her?! She was your best friend!" Clara continued.

"Because it hurts too much," Seamus whispered, jaw clenching as if the excruciating pain was overtaking him.

"And why won't she leave me alone?!" Clara cried.

Seamus covered his ears as if he were breaking, as if every question were tearing him down more and more and he needed to defend himself from any recollection at all. "Please, please stop this," he said. "You're scaring me. Somehow you've put these pieces together, and it's all coincidence. Rex was your dog's name. It also happened to be the name Emmeline called the horse in the knight and dragon story she wrote that I based my first game on. The one you aced. I wrote the program on that computer after she was gone and used Rex as the password. I said 'Welcome Emmeline,' because I wished she would come home and I could show her." He emitted a small sob, unable to control the emotion anymore.

Clara watched him, her anger pounding but her heart bleeding for him. She wanted to help him, touch him, love him, but she couldn't. Rage. Fear. Grief. Betrayal. Emotions coursing. Her entire being trembling. She grabbed her hand to stop it from shaking. "But why did you pretend you didn't know her?" Clara whispered. *And why did Emmeline have a knight story?* she wondered. *I have a knight story.*

"Because I missed her so much—I told myself she didn't exist," Seamus tried to explain and looked up at Clara with desperate eyes, hoping to God she would understand and believe him.

Her heart pounded. She didn't know what to think. "Was she your girlfriend?" Clara managed.

Seamus recoiled from her words. "No," he replied and steeled himself against a truth that was more painful than all others.

"But what if something happened to her? And she wants you not to give up on her?" Clara wondered, uncertain, afraid of his sudden change.

"No! This is not my fault!" he shouted. "Do not make this my fault! It's hers!" And he stood up, defensive, angry.

"What?" Clara cried, not expecting this.

"She didn't love me because I was too young! And what you're seeing is not a ghost! You're imagining it! We're going back to New York. And getting rid of that crazy shrink!"

"No, no, please. I'm fine. See," Clara pleaded, lifting up her shirt, stroking her belly. "Please. I know I said I wanted to go back, but we can't just leave all this here. Not now. Not anymore. Now that I know what this is about. All your history. With Derek. And this girl. It will come with us if we ignore it now. And we need it to heal. For our baby. We can do it together. And this is the farthest we've come—the farthest we've come where I believe the baby is okay. Five months. Since the first time. Five months! We have to stay!"

Seamus looked at her baby belly, struggling with his demons. "You want us to stay?" he managed.

"Yes, yes, I do," Clara said, pleading, tears filling her eyes.

She took his hand. Squeezed it, tried to meet his gaze. And slowly, tears forced their way through his rage. He tried to shake them off and got on his knees, hugged her belly and wept.

Clara heard light footsteps in the hall and looked, catching a puff of Billy's brown curls as he disappeared down the stairs.

29

Searching for Emmeline McGuire

Seamus remained rattled about Emmeline late into the morning. His feelings of loss were enormous, and Clara assured him that they didn't need to talk about Emmeline or rehash the past, just that maybe he should slowly let himself accept that she was gone so that he could properly grieve and celebrate how he had kept her spirit alive by creating a game based on her story. Clara also reminded Seamus that, together, they would keep his parents' spirit alive by creating a family and bringing their little bean into the world, carrying on the Dunne name and their loving way.

Clara told Seamus that she was there to pick him up if needed and that she was going to bake a peach pie right then, out of the fresh peaches she'd picked at the farm the other day. It was the family orchard that he'd recommended—the one his mom used to take him to when he was a little boy. This was all reassuring to Seamus, and by noon, as the comforting smell of pie baking wafted through the house, Seamus agreed to go to work in the city after all and also agreed that they could stay at the lake house just a little while longer. "I'm sorry," Seamus told Clara. "I overreacted when I said we should leave here right away. It's an old wound, and I appreciate you understanding."

And now that Seamus had just left for work for the day, Clara was on her own in the house and could do all the digging she wanted, because she wasn't going to let this lie. She wasn't going to bring the past up with Seamus again, because clearly that just made him unravel, but she had to find out about Emmeline McGuire, everything about her—her dreams, her joys and if she had loved Seamus as he had loved her and what their relationship had been.

Clara immediately ran upstairs and put on her happy caterpillar dress as soon as Seamus pulled out of the driveway, then ran out the door with one of the pies so that she could make it to Derek's just in time for his free period, the one that she knew he had right after lunch.

Clara got there right on the dot and knocked on Derek's office door, holding the peach pie in one hand and her charmed picnic basket in the other.

Derek opened the door, surprised.

"Surprise!" Clara cheered.

A flash of hesitation crossed his face, but he quickly covered it and replied enthusiastically, "Wow, and what have we here?"

"Peach pie," Clara beamed. "Freshly picked and baked. And I was thinking picnic. On the bench at the start of that beautiful walk we did." She waved the pie around as if to tempt him with the deliciousness. "We're all set. We just need you." She caught herself flirting, and he did too, and his smile was suddenly full of charm.

"You know how to get to a man's heart," Derek said. "And a priest's stomach. Let me just send off an email. I'll be right out."

Clara waited outside his office, pleased. She put the pie in the basket and was ready when Derek returned a moment later. They headed off on their stroll, walking until they came to the bench just off the school grounds and before the walking path into the field—perfect for sitting and talking, Clara's goal.

Clara set everything out and gave Derek a slice of pie and started right in, asking him to tell her about Seamus and Emmeline's relationship. "While we enjoy this deliciousness," she added with a beaming, friendly smile. "I found out they were friends."

Derek tensed for a second but then hid his emotions and took a bite of pie. "Mmm," he said. "And the girl can bake too. Seamus is a lucky man."

Clara was pleased and cut herself a slice of pie as well, taking a bite. It truly was delicious. "Yum!" she said with a mouthful smile, trying to engage Derek so that he would be at ease and open up. "What a little country living won't do for a novice baker," she joked, covering her full mouth as she spoke. She noticed Derek watching her—her hand, her mouth. He seemed charmed and maybe a little more, as if there was some kind of longing in his eyes when he looked at her, something that she couldn't put her finger on.

Derek laughed it off and took another bite of pie, confirming her mad baking skills with a grin, then finishing his bite and wiping his mouth with the happy, summery strawberry napkins she'd found at the local thrift shop. "So, you want to know about my brother and Emmeline," he said matter of factly.

"I do," Clara replied with a sing-songy voice, trying to keep it nonchalant, as if Seamus and Emmeline's relationship was the least important thing they would ever talk about, when it was definitely the most important thing to Clara right now, in her heart, which was racing, hoping Derek would talk.

And he did.

"Well, that's easy," Derek said, scooping another bite of pie onto his fork. "I mean, they were best friends for, oh, three or four years? We saw Emmeline all the time. She ate dinner with us, and dessert, which my mom was the queen of, queen of dessert." A bittersweet memory flashed across his eyes. "And our parents loved Emmeline too. She and Seamus were going to do great things together. She was young like he was. Skipped one grade. And Seamus skipped two." A shadow crossed over his face when he said this. He looked down at the pie on his fork as if remembering something else now. Something that pained him. He shook it off and took the bite, then added cheerfully, "They were happy."

Clara pretended not to notice his discomfort. "So, they weren't going out?" she asked.

Derek shook his head *no*. "Not that I know of. Our parents' death was so hard on him. Especially losing our mom. And he put all the emotion onto Emmeline. She was a breath of fresh air. And whip smart, like him. But maybe she didn't feel the same for him."

"So, what happened?" Clara asked.

"She disappeared," Derek told her.

"Because of the baby?" Clara said.

"Baby?!" Derek exclaimed, as if completely surprised.

"She was pregnant, right?" Clara continued, even though she wasn't sure.

Derek looked at her. His eyes seemed empty. "I don't know," he said, shaking his head, coming back to normal. "I tried to keep an eye on them. I wasn't much of a replacement father. Brother. Father brother." He tried to laugh at his joke but couldn't. "If Emmeline was pregnant, it probably was his, Seamus's. And I'm sorry but I have to get back to work. It was so nice of you to visit." He stood up abruptly.

Clara nodded—"Oh, right, right," she said, completely taken by surprise by his sudden change in attitude. Then, she heard an audio-flash of a guitar playing. *What was that?* she wondered, heart pounding. "I-I, I have to go too," Clara stammered. She forced a smile at Derek as she stood up now too, sweat beads forming on her forehead.

"Are you okay?" Derek asked.

"Oh, yeah, I just, suddenly...pregnant," she declared playfully and smiled as big as possible, trying to cover up how rattled she was by all this, gathering her things.

"I am sorry," Derek told her. "This was so nice. I'd love to take a couple pieces for later." He smiled warmly but there was something strange in his eyes.

Clara's stomach gripped with anxiety and her heart raced. "Of course."

30

Never Let It Go

After meeting Derek, Clara went straight to the police station and asked for a missing person's report on Emmeline McGuire. She told them that she was just trying to get some closure for Seamus and their family. They didn't usually get requests for such reports from local townsfolk, but Officer Peters was there behind the desk and was happy to help her immediately—a definite perk of the small town.

"So, you're back on the case?" Officer Peters teased.

Clara was grateful for the lighthearted humor and help and told Officer Peters that she wanted to verify that Emmeline had been pregnant when she disappeared. The report confirmed that this was the case. And oddly, Emmeline's disappearance in November, now almost thirty-one years earlier, was just nine months before Clara's birth the next August in Paris, where her dad had been stationed at the time. Dr. Alex Madison had verified Emmeline's pregnancy for the police detectives at the time—one of them being Officer Peters as a young man, the junior detective on the force.

Clara wondered if Dr. Alex Madison had been the doctor that she'd heard in Dr. Eve Madison's office. "Excuse me?" Clara asked

Officer Peters, who'd gone back to his mound of admin paperwork. "Do you know if Dr. Alex Madison still lives in town?"

"Sure does," Officer Peters replied. "He and his wife live right over on Third Street. They've lived there forever. He just celebrated his eighty-fifth. All eight kids and their families showed up. The other Dr. Madison too, you may have met her?"

"Yes," Clara replied with a smile.

"They had fireworks," Officer Peters added. "Illegal. We looked the other way."

They laughed, and Clara thanked him and headed over to Third Street with more information than planned.

Dr. Alex Madison—a quite fit eighty-five—was gardening in front of a beautiful Victorian house with a porch and a giant oak as Clara approached. "Excuse me? Dr. Madison?" she called out.

Dr. Madison looked up.

"Hi, I'm Clara Dunne, Seamus Dunne's wife, and I was wondering if I could ask you a few questions about Emmeline McGuire."

"Emmeline McGuire? I haven't heard that name in quite a while," he said, taking off his hat and wiping his brow. "Quite unfortunate. What a lovely girl she was."

Dr. Madison looked so kind, and Clara walked through the little wooden gate and stuck out her hand to shake.

He shook it gladly.

"So, I've heard," Clara said about Emmeline. "I was just...my husband...I'd really just like to find out what happened. For Seamus."

"Why don't you come inside for some lemonade?" a woman called out from one of the front windows. Clearly, she'd been listening all along.

Dr. Madison saw the look of surprise on Clara's face. "That's what happens when you live in a small town and know everyone's business," he joked.

"So, I've noticed," Clara joked back.

And they laughed. And Dr. Madison led Clara inside to introduce her to Mrs. Madison, Maeve, and before Clara knew it, the three of them were out on the porch drinking lemonade and Dr. Madison had confirmed that, in fact, Emmeline had been pregnant when she vanished. "She was about five months along. Just like I imagine you are," he said with a smile.

"Yes," Clara laughed in surprise.

"He always gets it right," Mrs. Madison teased. "He's been at for a while."

"Maeve here was my nurse," Dr. Madison told Clara. "We both knew her well."

"It's a small town. Everyone's close," said Mrs. Madison.

Clara and Dr. Madison burst out laughing.

"Oh, Alex must've told you how much I love to gossip," Mrs. Madison joked, making fun of herself and smiling at her husband. "In a good way. I like everyone."

They're so cute, thought Clara. "Well, thank you for telling me about her pregnancy," Clara said. "Emmeline was close to my husband, and I'm trying to help him through this. It's somehow all surfaced since we've been out here for the summer."

"Yes, they won that science fair, Seamus and Emmeline," Dr. Madison remembered. "She was a smart cookie, that one."

"So, how did she cope with being pregnant?" Clara asked.

"She was terrified," Dr. Madison explained, "of her parents finding out."

"And all the other good Catholics in town," Mrs. Madison joked with smirk of feisty sarcasm.

"But she was the middle of eight children," Dr. Madison continued, "so they didn't even notice."

"That she was pregnant?" Clara asked.

"That's right," Dr. Madison clarified, "and like I said, she was just five months along, so barely starting to show. She could still hide it."

Clara got the chills.

And saw a flash of the scared red-haired girl in the bathroom finding out she was pregnant.

"Are you okay, dear?" asked Mrs. Madison.

"Yes, sorry," Clara said, coming back to. She took a sip of lemonade. "We've had a rough time getting this far. Almost five months. I'm just hoping we can hang on."

"Well, you are glowing like a peach," Mrs. Madison said.

"I agree," Dr. Madison concurred. "And I have a good sense about these things."

"He does," Mrs. Madison told Clara.

A shadow came over his face. "Emmeline was healthy as a horse. And yes, her parents didn't notice. I don't think anyone did. I'm sure she hid it well from everyone. She was quick as a whip that one. As was your husband. Is your husband," Dr Madison corrected, then laughed warmly at his mistake.

"Emmeline was also terrified that if she had a baby she'd be stuck. I remember that too," added Mrs. Madison.

"That girl could've been—" Dr. Madison began.

But Mrs. Madison cut him off, "Don't you say President, Dr. Alex. That is so cliché. That girl would've come out with the iPhone or something."

"Stevena Jobs?" Dr. Madison teased his wife, like this was some kind of inside joke. They both laughed. Clearly, they adored each other.

Mrs. Madison picked up the plate of lemon cookies and offered some to Clara. "I'm sorry, honey, we don't have much more to tell you about Emmeline McGuire than that," she said as Clara took one of the scrumptious scone-like lemon treats and Mrs. Madison offered the plate to her husband who took two.

"That's okay," Clara said. "It's nice to see you both so happy. I can only hope my husband and I are just as happy in another forty years."

"Sixty-two years we've been married," Dr. Madison said and kissed his wife on the cheek, then added, "Alright, my garden awaits. I'd better get back to it. Unless you have more questions?"

Clara hesitated. "Just, did she ever mention having an abortion?"

Dr. Madison grew solemn. "No. And she couldn't talk to me about it. In case it got back to someone. It was such a touchy subject. And I didn't...we didn't do that here. But the truth is—" He looked at his wife as if shaken and remembering.

"We always suspected she went to get an abortion and something happened," Mrs. Madison filled in the rest of the story. They nodded to each other, then turned to Clara with heavy hearts, as if hoping she'd have the answer to what happened to Emmeline—or that she would tell them that Emmeline was waiting down the street and would be there shortly.

Clara scrunched her lips with an understanding and forgiving smile and nod. "I understand," she said.

The Madisons looked at each other sadly, then back to Clara nodding—as if this were cathartic for them.

Clara hesitated, then asked her last question: "And do you know who the father was?"

"She never said," Mrs. Madison told Clara, and Mr. Madison confirmed it, shaking his head *no*.

"Do you think her parents'd know? Who the father was?" Clara asked.

"Honey, like we said," Mrs. Madison reiterated, "They didn't even know she was pregnant."

"But maybe they knew her boyfriend," Clara suggested.

"Well, it can't hurt to ask," Dr. Madison said kindly, even though it was obvious he didn't think she'd get any answers from them.

"You may get some more lemonade though," Mrs. Madison joked.

"And peach pie," Dr. Madison chimed in.

"Oh, yes," Mrs. Madison told Clara. "The McGuires always made the best peach pie. Emmeline made the best peach pie."

"And always brought us one or two a month, I'd say," Dr. Madison added, grinning at the thought.

"Sounds great," Clara told them, again getting a chill. This place was too strange.

"Yes, dear," Mrs. Madison said, "Emmeline McGuire was a very lovely girl. I wish you'd known her. Or would get to know her if you find her. Bright, happy and so, so smart. And funny too. Always laughing with those Dunne boys, your husband and Father Derek. They were her world. Her place to shine instead of being invisible like she was in her own family with so many kids."

"Believe me, we had eight too, and you always lose one or two," Dr. Madison joked. "Or maybe you were one of many?"

Clara shook her head, laughing, "I wish. It was just me."

"An only child!" Mrs. Madison exclaimed, as if this were the biggest rarity, then laughed and took Clara's hand, kindly, studying her. "Emmeline was everything to those boys too when their parents died. They, all three—Seamus, Derek and Emmeline—needed each other. She was a blessing. I wish she'd stayed."

"Or come back," Dr. Madison said.

"I can see why you would want to find out more about Emmeline's story and maybe even find her," Mrs. Madison said to Clara. "It would be such a healing gift for Seamus."

"And Derek," added Dr. Madison. "That boy suffered greatly."

"His parents were going to see him play ball when they had the accident," Mrs. Madison told Clara. "He held his mother's hand as she passed, his father was already gone."

"Seamus was back at the house," Dr. Madison said, exhaling as he remembered. "He never saw his parents again. And Derek blamed himself for it all. Couldn't shake it. I understand. Their death is still a hard one to swallow, even for me after all these years. I was a friend of Caleb's, their father, a good friend. We had a weekly poker night. Solid family." He nodded then looked up, doing his best to smile. "And your Emmeline helped those boys through it."

"My Emmeline?" Clara laughed.

"I think you're going to find her," said Mrs. Madison. "I have a good feeling about it."

"That's because Maeve's the gossip," Dr. Madison teased his wife.

"Oh, stop, Alex, gossip has nothing to do with being clairvoyant," Mrs. Madison joked, and Mr. Madison hugged her, and Clara thanked them, got the McGuire's address and was off to see what she could find out about Emmeline's family.

***

The McGuire house was several blocks away from the Madisons', up on a little hill, two stories. It looked well-lived-in, worn, but seemed to be embraced by love, with cute shutters and flowers in the bed—but also weeds and an old Plymouth on blocks in the driveway.

Clara walked up the stairs from the sidewalk hesitantly. An Elvis song, "That's Alright Mama," blared out from a radio sitting behind the screen in an open window upstairs.

Suddenly, Clara saw a flash of light and heard the red-haired girl's laugh, Emmeline's laugh. Then, a flash of light filled her entire vision, followed by the red-haired girl—Emmeline—running out of the McGuire house, scared. Clara began sweating, and then, everything went black.

31

The McGuires

Clara came to on a couch. An older woman was wiping her brow with a cool cloth, wisps of red hair between the grey. "There, there, dear," the woman said to Clara with a gentle, kind smile.

An older man was standing by with something in his hand. "Just let me do this, Amanda," he said to the woman. "Works every time."

"She's coming to, Will," the woman replied. "Simmer down. We don't need to shock her with smelling salts too."

"Hi, yes," said Clara, coming up onto her elbows. "I'm here. I'm sorry."

"No, dear—no need to apologize," the woman said. "Are you alright? What happened? You knocked. On the front door."

"Yeah, I, uh—" Clara began, trying to get her bearings. "You're Mr. and Mrs. McGuire?"

"Yes, we are," Mrs. McGuire said with a welcoming smile.

Clara's heart warmed. Suddenly, the flash of light filled her eyes and before her stood Mr. and Mrs. McGuire from thirty years ago smiling at her.

Then, another FLASH, and she was back to present day.

Clara blushed and sat up awkwardly, automatically touching her belly. "I'm Clara Dunne," she said.

"Oh, my. Are you pregnant?" Mrs. McGuire asked, looking at her belly.

"No!" Clara yelled out of nowhere as the light flash filled her eyes, and suddenly, the Mr. and Mrs. McGuire from thirty years ago were looking at her, worried. Clara gasped. Then came back to present. "I mean, yes. I am pregnant. I'm, um, my husband is Seamus Dunne."

"Oh, yes," Mr. McGuire said, relieved, "we've known Seamus his whole life." He smiled, welcoming again.

"Congratulations to you both," Mrs. McGuire chimed in. "We've heard about you and Seamus being in town for the summer. Good 'ole neighbors. Everyone knows everyone's business." They all laughed. "And I'm just glad you're okay, especially since you're expecting," Mrs. McGuire added.

"Even with all the new people moving in here, we still know everybody's business," Mr. McGuire joked and shook his head, clearly not into the gossip like his wife was.

"Oh, Will!" Mrs. McGuire scolded playfully, and they shared a laugh.

Clara saw a flash of light and heard a door slam, then saw red-headed Emmeline rush out from the hall and past them, through the living room, trying not to be noticed by Mr. and Mrs. McGuire. She made it to the front door and looked back at Clara with fear and guilt before exiting. Clara looked back at Mr. and Mrs. McGuire—who clearly hadn't seen Emmeline like she had—and laughed nervously, shaking it off. "I'm still a little off, I guess," she told the McGuires. "But I, um, I was just coming by to ask you about..." Clara looked at their warm smiles wondering—*What? What? What to say?* "...the tulips. I love your tulips!" she exclaimed.

"Oh, yes," Mrs. McGuire said. "You must've seen them in the spring."

Clara glanced outside into the front yard, fully visible from where she sat through the giant bay windows—no tulips, only roses. "Yeah, I did," Clara lied with a huge, beaming smile. "And I think I'd better get going." Clara stood up, realizing she could never bring up Emmeline to them. Who knows what kind of vision she would have next if she did, and hearing about Emmeline probably would just bring up unnecessary sorrow for the McGuires, opening that wound again. "But I so appreciate you helping me, and it's so nice to meet you," Clara added.

"Likewise," said Mrs. McGuire. "You know what? Why don't I give you a few of those yellow roses to take home. They're so happy." And she quickly disappeared into the kitchen and came out with garden clippers, a glove, a wet paper towel and a plastic bag. "And you're going to have to be sure to say hello to Seamus from us. It's so nice to have him back."

Clara and Mr. McGuire followed Mrs. McGuire out into the front garden and watched as she cut a bouquet of roses for Clara. "We see Derek regularly at church," Mr. McGuire told her. "I'll bet he's happy to have his brother back too."

"Yes, yeah, he is," Clara agreed, forcing a smile, even though she still had no idea at all about what was going on between the brothers, and this wasn't telling her anything.

Mrs. McGuire deftly flicked the thorns off the rose stems, wrapped the flowers in the wet paper towel and put the stems in the plastic bag. "This should keep them fresh until you get home," she said and handed the bouquet to Clara.

"Beautiful," Clara replied, then, in a FLASH, she saw Mrs. McGuire from thirty years ago handing her a yellow tulip to add to the bunch of tulips in her hand. Clara came back to present. "They will definitely brighten up the space," Clara told Mrs. McGuire and waved awkwardly as she left down the front stairs to the sidewalk. Shaking hands would've just been too much in that moment.

"Come back for more. And tulips in the spring!" Mrs. McGuire called after her.

Clara yelled back, "I will, thank you," then continued onto the sidewalk and started walking, not at all sure where she was going and feeling sad and overwhelmed. Which is when she saw Emmeline up ahead, sitting on the roots of another giant tree, intensely writing in her notebook. *Or a diary,* Clara thought. It had to be a diary. And she knew it with some kind of strange certainty—that weird knowing she got sometimes, like when she met Seamus. Or maybe it was just because Clara had had a diary at some point and had written in it furiously as well. *Probably about nothing,* she mused and wondered where on earth her old diary could be.

Which is when Emmeline spotted Clara and immediately shut the notebook, stood up and starting walking quickly down the sidewalk away from Clara and towards town.

Clara picked up her pace and followed Emmeline through the streets, down the sidewalk, keeping a good distance so as not to frighten her, hoping she wouldn't disappear. But somehow, Emmeline didn't disappear this time. It was the longest that Emmeline had allowed Clara to see her. Maybe Emmeline *wanted* Clara to follow her, Clara thought. Maybe Emmeline was going to finally show Clara what she wanted to show her and this trauma could be done with. "Please, please, show me, Emmeline," Clara whispered as she hurried along after the girl. "I just want to help."

Emmeline continued walking until she came to Mrs. Flannery's house, where she stopped near the stairwell up to the house and studio. Emmeline looked back at Clara and then disappeared around the back of the house.

Clara followed her around, but Emmeline was gone when she got there.

32 |

Hidden Corners

Mrs. Flannery set tea for Clara at the table with a warm smile. "Oh, I'm looking forward to this," she said and pulled out the second chair for herself and joined Clara.

It's amazing, Clara mused, *how she knows every inch of her place and doesn't need to see anything or anyone's reactions to be herself.* It was as if Mrs. Flannery had a different kind of sight. *A heightening of all her senses.* "Yes, thank you," said Clara, taking a bag of Earl Grey and opening it. "It is nice to see you. And I have something to tell you. I mean, I've been poking around, and I'm pretty certain that the ghost, or whatever it is, is definitely your Emmeline. I thought you should know."

"I knew there was something of Emmeline about you," Mrs. Flannery said warmly as she poured the hot water into each of their mugs.

"But she isn't me," Clara insisted. "I don't know why you keep saying that."

"What did she say, that Emmeline?" Mrs. Flannery continued, disregarding Clara's comment, putting the kettle down and dipping her tea bag.

"Nothing," Clara said, dunking her tea bag into the hot water and swirling it around. "She led me here. Maybe to...uh..." Clara hesitated, exhaling, wondering if she should say it, then did, "...to find out about her baby. For me to find out."

Mrs. Flannery stopped mid tea-bag dip.

"She said it was her fault," Clara continued, recounting what Emmeline had told her when she had appeared in the Dunne house and was so enraged. "And she screamed that she couldn't have a baby. She didn't want to be pregnant. She was afraid."

A wave of sadness crossed Mrs. Flannery's face.

"You knew she was pregnant, right?" Clara asked.

Mrs. Flannery didn't respond. Clearly, this was a painful memory for her too.

"I already know," Clara said. "That she was pregnant. From the doctor and the missing person's report. Do you know who the father was?"

Mrs. Flannery took a deep breath and exhaled slowly. "She wouldn't tell me."

"Was it Seamus?" Clara asked.

"I don't know," Mrs. Flannery insisted. "She loved Seamus, and lord knows, he loved her. But they were just kids. And she was older. I don't think they understood each other's feelings. I don't know. Emmeline got very quiet after it happened—the pregnancy."

There was silence as Clara took this in, then said, "I think she wants to tell me something about her disappearance. Or death. She wants help. I just hope she doesn't get angry if I can't figure it out." The thought of the girl screaming with fury was overwhelming and brought back all Clara's worries for her baby's safety.

"I always hoped to meet Emmeline again," Mrs. Flannery admitted. "Maybe that's why it's hard for me to understand the truth. And why I keep sensing her in you and hoping you're her."

"What?" Clara said. *Why does she keep saying this?*

"But the answers will come," Mrs. Flannery continued, ignoring Clara's question again. "They're inside you."

"But what if I'm going crazy?" Clara mused, feeling herself begin to come undone. "Am I losing my mind? I mean, I don't even believe in ghosts. But if she's not a ghost, what's happening to me?" Tears rose in Clara's eyes.

Mrs. Flannery took Clara's hand, sensing her distress, and held it firmly. "My dear, the universe and our very existence is a mystery. A beautiful, natural mystery, Mother Earth holding us in her arms. And it seems that we mere humans can't possibly comprehend how it all works. Especially when I see things that you can't see and you see things that no one else can. No one has the answers. But Emmeline is somehow with you, and we can't ignore that. Her past is speaking to you, whether she's alive and living in Memphis or somewhere with the baby she was carrying, or speaking to you in some other way—from inside you or some other realm."

Clara's breath caught. She hadn't considered this. "Do you think Seamus has a child somewhere?" she asked, suddenly afraid. "And he's not telling me?!"

"Clara," Mrs. Flannery said firmly and took both of Clara's hands in hers, squeezing them tight. "Do not make assumptions, especially out of fear. Trust your heart. Trust me that there is a spirit here that feels like Emmeline—I feel her in *my* heart. She is a beautiful and lovely girl. Do not fear her. Ask her what she wants. Follow your intuition. Look in the hidden corners."

***

Clara spent the rest of the afternoon walking down along the lake boardwalk, watching the ducks and passersby and just letting herself decompress from the day. She hated the word decompress. Her business partner, Greta, used it all the time. But today, she tried it out of desperation—tried to escape from the overwhelming fear she felt after leaving Mrs. Flannery's.

She knew Mrs. Flannery had meant well and wanted to help, but it was like she'd opened up a vault of possibilities, none of them comforting. *What if Seamus has a child out there? What if he knows about the child? What if he doesn't? What if I'm going crazy? Or what if I'm possessed? Or what if Emmeline is an actual ghost?!*

A ghost. That was too much to comprehend or bear. The whole thing was.

Clara took a deep breath and reminded herself that at least Mrs. Flannery didn't think she was crazy and was there for her. That was a start. And it helped.

Then, Clara reminded herself that she was outside in the beautiful, fresh air, in a place that was almost exactly like her safe, peaceful spot—the one she imagined whenever she was meditating with Dr. Goldberg. She tried to feel grateful, and this brought her back to the present moment—feeling her body move, the air filling her lungs, the endorphins coursing through her veins as she sped up her gait. And finally, Clara began to get a few moments of freedom from the story of Emmeline and all her worries about her baby and Seamus.

Her mind became open, and she was able to look at her world with renewed clarity and less fear. She knew she had to face what was before her, and Mrs. Flannery's words had been a reality check again and a comfort too, empowering Clara to move forward and giving her the courage to continue to investigate the past. And that's what she was going to do—but this time, she would go to the source, Emmeline, whatever she was. She would ask her directly. And with Mrs. Flannery's encouragement and support, she'd be ready for whatever came next.

And what came next, Clara wasn't expecting at all. She came home, feet tired, around 7:30 P.M. and found Seamus passed out on the couch, TV blaring, whiskey bottle on the table. She smelled his breath. He was skunk drunk.

"What the hell?" Clara said, waking Seamus.

He covered his eyes from the brightness of the sunlight as if it hurt. It was just streaming in the window as it headed westward, getting lower in the sky.

"What the hell?" Clara repeated.

"I thought we were going out," Seamus slurred. "I came home early to spend the evening with you. Where were you?"

"You went to the city," she replied. "I didn't think you'd be here. I walked at the lake. What—did you, like, get there to work and come right back?"

"Yeah," Seamus said. "Two hours in the office and I was missing you. That's what I did. I drove back. What about you?"

Clara got flustered. She didn't remember making plans with Seamus for this evening. And it felt as if he were probing or suspicious or something. Had they made plans? Or was this something else? Did he suspect she was trying to find out about Emmeline somehow? "I went to see Mrs. Flannery," Clara told Seamus, trying to keep any suspicions at bay.

"Not Billy?" he said with a twinge of sarcasm.

"No," Clara insisted. "In fact, I haven't seen him in a while. A few weeks maybe. Since we finished more of the work in the guesthouse. He went to see friends. And now, he's...." She thought about how worried she'd been about Billy. He'd been out of it the last time she stopped by the market, and she knew he was back to shooting up. "He's probably working at the market. I saw him two days ago," she said.

Seamus jumped on that, "You just said you haven't seen him in weeks!"

"I mean...hanging out...as friends," Clara stammered. "I was shopping. He's a mess. I'm worried, so stop accusing me!"

"I'm sorry," Seamus said, immediately backing down. "I just, I'm sorry too. It's okay. Come here." He put his arms out for her to sit next to him while he was still lying there.

Clara hesitated then sat on the edge of the couch. He reeked up close which made Clara more tense. She tried to let it go, brushing the hair out of his eyes, but she couldn't.

Seamus sensed it. "Are we back on Emmeline? Because I can't handle that. You told me this morning we didn't have to talk about her."

Why is he being so mean? Clara wondered. "No. No. I decided to take piano again," she lied defensively. "That's why I was at Mrs. Flannery's. To distract myself," she added and smiled reassuringly.

Seamus seemed to believe her and relaxed a little and hugged her belly.

Which is when Clara felt the tickle of a kick inside. "Oh! Little Bean kicked!"

"Just now?" Seamus asked and brightened.

"Yes!" Clara exclaimed and put his hand on her belly.

The baby kicked again, and he felt it too this time. "Yes, there it is!" he cheered.

Clara watched Seamus laugh, wishing this moment had happened some other time—without all the fear and distrust between them and without him being drunk. It would've been perfect if he weren't drunk. And if she didn't know that he was sinking inside himself here at the lake house that she was beginning to love.

"Little bean," Seamus said, melting, and brought his hand down and smiled at Clara lovingly.

She watched his eyes grow heavy as he drifted back into sleep. Her heart grew dark and her gut filled with anxiety and she whispered to herself, "And *I* can't do this anymore either."

33

Come Out, Emmeline McGuire

It was the day after the Emmeline sighting and Clara's visit to Mrs. Flannery and Seamus getting smashed. Seamus had left early with a raging hangover. Clara had made her super-duper remedy of raw eggs and Tabasco sauce followed by a glass of fresh-squeezed orange juice. Seamus had been grateful and apologetic and took the cold purple grapes Clara sent along with him because cold grapes always made Clara feel better when she was nauseous. Hopefully, it would work for him too.

The new day gave Clara hope, but still, she was worried about Seamus and knew she had to get to the bottom of Emmeline's past soon. She had felt Seamus's rage simmering beneath the surface, even that morning at breakfast. And as soon as Seamus pulled out of the driveway, Clara sat down on the sofa in the living room and got quiet, determined to wait for Emmeline until she arrived with answers.

"I'm here, ready to hear you," Clara called out into the room, mustering all her courage. She quickly felt afraid and hoped this was the right thing to do, fear gripping her heart more and more with every passing moment. She hesitated then called out again, "Emmeline?"

A chill came through the room. Clara saw Emmeline and the dark-haired boy run past the window over the grass towards the boathouse and lake.

Clara saw a light FLASH and heard music and the springs of a bed. She also heard laughter.

Emmeline and the boy ran back from the lake, dripping wet in their bathing suits, and disappeared into the guesthouse.

Clara felt a chill of fear course through her again, knowing this was it—she was going to the source and would find out the truth. Her stomach clenched, and she rubbed her pregnant belly, whispering to the universe, "Please, let us be okay." Then, she stood up and slowly went out the sliding glass door onto the back porch and down the stairs onto the grass.

The grass felt cold on her bare feet and slightly damp as she slowly approached the guesthouse—the laughter, the music, and the springs of the bed getting louder and louder the closer she got. Her heart began racing as she stepped up to the door.

Clara stood before it listening, gathering courage, telling herself she had to do this—*Go in!* she yelled in her head. "This has to happen," she said out loud. "For you. Little bean." She looked down at her belly, took a deep breath and opened the door.

The laughter, music and jumping stopped immediately. Complete silence. No one was there. It was the guesthouse as she'd left it last—normal, the daybed in the corner, the space mostly clean now. The only difference was the air—it felt colder than usual, and there was a moldy smell, a dampness, as if it were a cave.

Clara slowly went in, step by step, looking around, afraid but forcing herself forward. She sat down at the computer, about to enter the password, when suddenly the music blasted behind her.

She screamed. The jumping, bed springs and laughing sounded too. Clara saw Emmeline's reflection on the computer screen—as if it were Emmeline's ghost jumping on the bed, which was actually the daybed with her beautiful, new, scarlet, cotton cover.

Clara turned, and there was Emmeline, clear as day, jumping on the daybed, laughing, waving the blue fabric around, so happy. It was the exact image that she had seen in her hypnosis with Dr. Goldberg. And the fabric was her new beloved sun-faded scarf that she'd found in there. And there was a smell. Was it alcohol? she wondered. It sure seemed like it was. Yes, the girl's eyes looked glassy, Clara thought, as if she'd been drinking, but her eyes were joyful too, as if Emmeline were in the moment, not a care in the world, laughing. And as Emmeline turned, oblivious to Clara, Clara got another whiff and knew the smell was whiskey and lemonade, exactly what Seamus had been drinking the night before. *Strange*, she thought, getting another chill, wondering what the connection was.

And then, she saw angry eyes in the window—Seamus's eyes.

And Clara's heart pounded out of her chest. She screamed at both the girl and the boy outside, "Tell me what you want! This has to stop! You have to leave us alone!"

But they didn't hear. Or respond. Instead, the girl's laughter got louder and louder, and the boy outside screamed with rage.

And terror overtook Clara. She burst up out of the bright-orange desk chair without looking at the girl and out the guesthouse door, across the lawn. She ran inside the main house and shut the sliding glass door behind her, locking it. *As if that would help*, she thought, knowing it wouldn't but doing it anyway—anything to put distance between herself and the girl and the boy outside with Seamus's eyes, anything to keep her baby safe, wondering what on earth she'd been thinking trying to conjure up Emmeline. Mrs. Flannery was crazy to tell her not to be afraid.

Clara frantically scoured the room for her phone. "Kitchen," she remembered and ran in. There it was—on the table, next to the empty glass of hangover remedy. She grabbed her phone, fingers trembling, and dialed Dr. Goldberg. She sat down, drenched in a cold sweat, praying for help until Dr. Goldberg answered, and Clara told Dr. Goldberg everything.

Dr. Goldberg was calm at first. "So, it was just like that day when you were here—the first hypnosis," Dr. Goldberg said when Clara had finished.

"It was," Clara confirmed, her voice distressed. "It's exactly what I saw in the hypnosis. And I want to do it again. I need you to see me today. Something bad happened in that guesthouse. And I think it was Seamus that did it. He was so angry. And he's still angry."

"Honey, it's not safe for you to drive like this," Dr. Goldberg told Clara.

"I'm fine!" Clara insisted. "Why can't I drive? Or I can drive part way and take the train!"

"Because you're upset and you're under too much stress."

Clara heard the concern in Dr. Goldberg's voice this time. "I'll get a ride," Clara said, toning it down, pleading. "It'll be fine. I need your help. I need this to stop. I need to know what happened. And the girl won't tell me."

"It's not safe for your baby to go under hypnosis at this time. Or for you," Dr. Goldberg said firmly. "You need to be there for your baby."

Clara felt as if the walls were crumbling in on her. "I need to know! To save my baby! I need you to hypnotize me!" she shouted.

"I'm sorry, Clara, I can't do that," Dr. Goldberg insisted.

Clara stared at the phone, heart pounding, trying to decide what to do.

"Clara?" Dr. Goldberg said calmly.

Clara didn't respond, realizing Dr. Goldberg would never do it.

"Clara?!" Dr. Goldberg shouted when she didn't respond.

And Clara hung up, grabbed her bag and ran out the front door.

34

Under Hypnosis with Billy

Clara ran up to The Corner Market, still drenched in sweat, heart racing, anxious and determined to get Billy's help. She threw open the door and entered, bells ringing as the door shut behind her.

Billy sat behind the counter at the register. He looked up. She stared. Both of them looking gaunt and afraid.

"Clara, here, sit down," Billy said and got up and brought a chair around for her.

She saw his hands trembling—just like hers were. "I need you to do me a favor," Clara said, not sitting, distressed, like she needed a fix as bad as he did. Only a different kind of fix.

"Whatever you need," Billy said, understandingly.

"I need you to hypnotize me," Clara told him.

Billy laughed.

"No, I'm serious," Clara insisted. "My doctor refused. And I have to know what happened to Emmeline. If I don't find out the truth, I'm afraid she's going to kill me. And my baby. Emmeline will." Clara's eyes filled with tears.

Billy hesitated, afraid but wanting to help her. "I just, if your doctor...," he stammered.

"I'll pay you. A lot," Clara said.

Their eyes met. Billy took this in. The thought of getting money, getting a fix thanks to that money, was tempting. And Clara knew exactly that that's what Billy was thinking, and she knew he'd help her.

***

A bag of heroine sat on the side table of Billy's bed. It was later that afternoon. Clara had never been in his room before or seen the stairs inside Mrs. Flannery's, just off the kitchen, leading down to his studio. It covered the size of the whole house and was tastefully full of souvenirs from his travels—lots of souvenirs and a twin bed, side table, small kitchenette and a cute country table where they were sitting.

Billy was no longer shaking as he read from a script prepared for him by Clara. It contained everything she remembered from the hypnosis with Dr. Goldberg, plus some things she'd found online. Clara went under easily, and her eyes were closed, and she was relaxed as Billy began to take her back to the past and Emmeline. "You're in your safe, peaceful place," Billy read.

"Yes, I am here," Clara replied. Like with Dr. Goldberg, Clara imagined herself sitting on a boulder overlooking a pine-tree-filled valley and a crystal-blue lake.

"Alright, now we're going to go back to your first miscarriage," Billy continued.

Clara saw herself. She was devastated. Seamus was comforting her. She couldn't look at him though. She felt so bad. Like the miscarriage was her fault. And she didn't want to hurt Seamus or let him down because she loved him so much. She couldn't look into his loving eyes at that moment though, because when she told him about the miscarriage, behind his love, she saw his pain, almost as if it were driving his love for her. As if he could only love her because of the pain. She hadn't understood it at the time and it didn't under-stand it now. "We're sad," Clara said out loud. "Seamus has pain I don't understand it. But maybe he loves me in spite of the pain. Or because of it."

Next, Clara focused on what she had felt in the moment right after her OB had performed the procedure for her first miscarriage. She was nauseous and felt the cutting sharpness as the doctor took out the remains of her baby after its heart had stopped. It hurt so badly, both physically and in her soul. Clara remembered feeling like a failure in that moment and for days after, as if it were all her fault. "Guilt," Clara said out loud to Billy. "I feel guilt."

"Why guilty?" Billy asked, looking at her with worry. "I mean, you told me to ask." He was hesitant, not wanting to hurt her or the baby, but he kept following her instructions because he wanted to respect her—because it's what she wanted. And he didn't want to judge her choices because she didn't judge his. And she saw through his pain to his loving soul.

Clara, under hypnosis, became flushed and anxious. "I don't know why I feel guilty."

Billy nodded to himself and took a deep breath to give himself courage and continued: "Now, to Emmeline. Jumping on the bed."

Clara saw a flash of light, and suddenly, she *was* Emmeline—jumping on the daybed in the guesthouse, laughing, music, the blue scarf waving around. Then, she mis-stepped and fell—BAM. She hit her forehead. "Ow," Clara said, grabbing her forehead, blood trickling down.

Billy gasped. "Oh, shit." He tried to pull it together. "Okay, I'm going to keep going, like you said, but I don't like it. What happened next, Clara?"

Clara was in the guesthouse. She was Emmeline and saw a flash of light. From the bed, she clutched her head and saw the sandy-haired boy look in the window at her lying there squeezing her forehead, hoping it'd stop, feeling drunk and woozy, everything blurry. He had hurt eyes—Seamus's eyes, definitely Seamus's.

Clara gasped. Another FLASH of light, and suddenly, she was at the lake—as Emmeline with a 17-year-old Derek. He was the dark-haired boy, and he was playing with Emmeline at the pier, looking at her with loving eyes—flirtation. She felt so happy, giddy. He handed her a flask. She drank—whiskey with lemonade, her head spinning.

Then, Clara heard Emmeline's voice in her head, whispering: "It's all my fault."

A flash of light. Clara saw Seamus's scary eyes.

A flash of light. Her sight became blurry through blood streaming down her face and the blue scarf. She was on the daybed. There was a boy on the other side, caressing her face, telling her, "It's okay. It's okay." Clara couldn't tell who he was. She was confused, her vision blurry. But she could tell that he was kissing her lovingly, touching her thigh, bringing his hand up.

Clara felt his hand, shook her head *no*, terrified. A FLASH. Seamus's eyes looking at her lovingly.

Another FLASH. Clara was suddenly outside the door of the guesthouse—the girl, Emmeline, was crying inside. Clara heard her say, "It's all my fault."

"I love you, Emmeline," Clara heard the boy say.

A FLASH. And Clara was back in Emmeline's body lying on the bed, looking through the scarf at the eyes of the boy. He was desperate, like he needed her so badly to love him. But who was he? "I can't," Emmeline whispered to the boy. "We should...it's just..."

"Shhh," the boy said and pressed on.

Emmeline started hyperventilating, panicking—she couldn't breathe.

Clara felt her throat tighten and started gasping for air. But she understood what was happening finally—this is when Emmeline got pregnant and she didn't want to have sex.

"I don't want to," Emmeline managed, barely audible. "But I...later...this isn't your fault...just please stop...it's mine...,"she said to the boy, feeling so much shame.

And then, she saw flashes of Seamus's eyes close up—loving, desperate, longing. And behind the images, she heard him roar with rage.

And suddenly, Clara couldn't get any air.

"Clara? I'm scared," Billy told her.

Clara saw the flash of light again. And suddenly, she was in a coffin next to a corpse.

Clara screamed. Billy jumped up and started to shake her.

Clara saw the flash of light, and suddenly, she was Emmeline in the coffin—no air, suffocating, crying. "Please help me," she whispered.

"Wake up!" Billy screamed and shook Clara awake. "Where's your inhaler?"

Clara pointed to her bag. Billy tore through it and found the inhaler, shoving it at Clara. Clara grabbed it, pressing down, sucking in—the cool air finally reaching her lungs. "She was inside of me," Clara managed. "Or I was inside of her, inside of Emmeline." She looked at Billy who was waiting, scared. "I think someone killed her. Like she was buried alive. And Seamus and Derek. Seamus was so angry. And someone raped her. Date raped. Or she couldn't say no. Or he didn't hear." Clara saw pain in Billy's eyes, both of them feeling so distressed and small. She felt small, shaking her head, feeling Emmeline's shame. "And she, he loved her, like he didn't know. Like he didn't hear her. And she knows she didn't stop him. And he needed her. And somehow, she needed him, but she didn't know why. And didn't want it. She didn't want him to do it and didn't know how to not hurt him because she loved him and wanted to help him make his pain disappear because he helped her be seen."

35

The Monster In Seamus

After the hypnosis, Clara knew she had to leave—go back to the city. Now. She wasn't sure where she'd go, probably Erin's, but she was terrified and frantically packing. Luckily, Billy was willing to help. Clara was worried about Billy and hoping he didn't shoot up again before they left. But she almost didn't care as long as he could drive. If she had to, she'd just call a cab. She didn't care how much it cost because she was so worried for her own safety. And her baby's. She had to protect them. "We're going to be okay," Clara whispered to her baby as she zipped her duffel bag and grabbed a second for some things in the nursery.

That's when she heard a car door slam in the driveway. She looked out. It was Seamus. Seamus saw her and waved with a smile.

"Crap," Clara said and hurried out into the nursery.

"Hello!" Seamus shouted as he entered the house.

"Hi!" Clara called down, trying to sound normal, racing, throwing the beautiful Beatrix Potter art into her bag.

"Hey!" Seamus said, suddenly in the door.

Clara gasped and jumped.

"What the hell are you doing?" he demanded, then glared at Billy. "And what are you doing here?!"

Clara couldn't hide her fear and tears rose, giving her away. "I need to leave," she said. "Billy's gonna take me to Erin's." Clara grabbed the handles of the duffel bag and started towards the door.

Seamus blocked it. "What? No! The city? What's going on? You told me you wanted to stay. Begged me to stay. For us!"

Clara walked up to Seamus and got in his face and whispered low, angry and with all the force she could manage, "I know what happened to Emmeline."

"What do you mean?" Seamus demanded, panic growing as he saw the mistrust in Clara's eyes. "No one knows what happened to Emmeline."

"Stop lying!" Clara shouted. "She was buried alive! I saw! Next to a corpse!"

"Oh my god. Oh my god," Seamus cried. "What did you do?"

"I went back! And Emmeline showed me! And you were there! And she was raped," Clara shouted. The tears flowed.

"No," Seamus insisted and reached out to touch her.

"Get away from me!" she shouted and pushed him back. "You did it. Didn't you?"

"No, no, please stop," Seamus said. "Please. Please sit down. The baby."

"You are a monster," Clara hissed.

"It's symbolic! You have to remember that! What Dr. Goldberg said. Whatever you're experiencing is symbolic! I'm sorry about the miscarriages. We're going to be okay. We'll go back to the city."

"This isn't about that! It's about you raping and killing an innocent girl!"

"Please. Please. I would never hurt you. Or her. You know I love you. I love you, Emmeline."

A FLASH of light. Clara saw Seamus's angry eyes in the window as a teen boy.

Then, Clara was back. Lungs tightening. She couldn't breathe. She bolted. Crazy eyes. Running. Seamus chased her. Caught her. Held her. She struggled. Crazy. Crazy. Nothing made sense. *Please don't let him hurt us*, Clara pleaded to anything that would listen. And then, everything went BLACK.

***

Clara woke up in a hospital bed. Dr. Goldberg was holding her hand, Derek and Seamus standing nearby.

"The baby—" Clara whispered.

"The baby is fine. And so are you," Dr. Goldberg assured Clara warmly with a kind, understanding smile.

Clara looked at Seamus. He looked like hell. "I don't want him here," Clara told Dr. Goldberg.

"Honey, it's okay," Dr. Goldberg insisted, squeezing Clara's hand, trying to comfort her, still smiling. "You're safe. Your baby is safe. And healthy. It *is* okay."

Clara turned away. She looked out the window—at the sky, the tips of pine trees peeking out. "No, it's not," Clara said, trying to remember her safe place on the rock that was out there somewhere. "It's not okay," she repeated. Clara didn't have strength for more but saw Seamus in the reflection of the window. He nodded to Dr. Goldberg and exited the room. Then, she saw Derek gesture for Dr. Goldberg to leave too. She did.

Clara turned to look at Derek. His smile was warm. "He hurt Emmeline," Clara told him, voice barely audible. "Seamus hurt her," she repeated. She felt so weak.

"No. He didn't," Derek said.

"She was raped," Clara continued. "You have to know that. Do something. Someone has to do something. Maybe it was unclear to Seamus, but she didn't want it, the baby or to sleep with him. And I think he did something bad to her. Something else. I think he hurt her."

"Hmm," Derek said, taking this in.

"I know you don't believe me. Or don't want to. And neither do I, but I think Seamus might have killed Emmeline," Clara whispered.

Derek's brow furrowed. He took this in. And nodded. Not like he thought Seamus killed Emmeline but like he could tell Clara was coming undone, just like he'd seen so many times before as a priest, people losing their way. He looked up at Clara like he felt sorry for her. "Clara," he said in a low, steady voice. "I knew Emmeline very well. I didn't want to tell you everything. But I see that was a mistake. She was pregnant. She wouldn't tell anyone who the father was. Even though I suspected Seamus. And I don't know about a rape. But Emmeline wanted to have an abortion. I think something happened when she went to do that. Or she was too ashamed to come back. For all we know, she's out there somewhere. But I do know Emmeline loved Seamus. And maybe you're sensing some kind of jealousy."

"Jealously?" Clara said in surprise. "Emmeline wasn't jealous."

Derek paused for a moment as if trying to decide how to continue. He treaded carefully, "Emmeline would've been jealous of you. She was such a joyful spirit and beautiful, just like you. You are so much like her. Maybe Seamus can't let go of her magical spirit and her. Maybe he feels lingering guilt for moving on to you, and guilt for the jealousy, the jealousy Emmeline would have felt towards you. And that jealousy is somehow appearing now, like an apparition, doing everything to stop you from having what she would've wanted with Seamus. In a different circumstance, of course. Not when she was sixteen. She's jealous that she's not you here and now."

Clara shook her head—this was a lot to take in, an overwhelming, frightening thought. What if she had been right—what if Emmeline could actually hurt her baby? What if Emmeline could somehow stop her from having Seamus's child? Clara's heart began to race. And then, she remembered the guesthouse and what she'd seen there under the hypnosis. And that seemed more real than anything. "But I saw him," Clara insisted. "I saw Seamus. With Emmeline. In the guesthouse. When she hurt her head. And got pregnant. He was there. And maybe *he* was jealous, because she only ever seems angry. At herself."

Derek's jaw clenched, as if frustrated that Clara wasn't getting it—that she wasn't getting the reality here. He looked away for a moment, then returned with a calm intensity. "Please don't blame Seamus," Derek said firmly. "He's your husband and my brother, and he's not responsible for anything Emmeline did."

Clara saw Derek's pain again.

"Seamus loved Emmeline," Derek continued, "almost too much. Because he was afraid of losing her. Even before she disappeared. I loved her too. But Emmeline loved Seamus." Derek stopped when he said this. He looked down at his hands squeezing the hospital bed rail, then took a deep breath to regroup and continued, "And it was too much. Seamus didn't know how to handle all that emotion. Neither did I." He nodded and looked down again, clearly struggling.

Clara felt the hairs on her arms prick up with the sudden chill in the room.

"But Seamus loves you," Derek said. "He never would hurt either of you. I beg you to go back home to the city. Cut all ties with this ghost. Or this memory or whatever it is. Love Seamus. And save your family."

Clara nodded, taking it in. "I'll try. I'm still not sure about what I saw or if it's all just a figment of my imagination, but I'll try," she assured him.

"Thank you," Derek said. "And just so I know how to talk with my parishioners about this, does anyone else know about what happened? This idea that Emmeline was murdered? It could cause some distress."

"Just Billy," Clara told Derek. "He helped me. And probably Mrs. Flannery. Billy needs help. Please help him."

Derek took Clara's hand. "I will," he said with a comforting priest smile, which seemed so distant and insincere after all the emotion that had just passed between them. He squeezed Clara's hand. "And now, I'd better get back. You let me know how you are." He nodded again as he let go.

A shiver came over her and she wondered what this sudden formality meant. Was Derek telling the truth about Seamus? Or was he covering for him?

"I'll do my best," Clara assured Derek, but she wasn't convinced or convincing.

Derek gave her a forced smile, then turned to go.

Clara watched him walk to the door with a slight stoop, like he had weight on his shoulders. But then, he stopped. "You should know too that I'm sorry for whatever you're experiencing," Derek said. "God works in strange ways sometimes, and it doesn't make sense. Like this ghost that surely can't possibly be a ghost. But you must be tuning into Seamus's memories about his relationship with Emmeline. He must've talked about all those moments in his sleep or something. Otherwise, it's impossible."

"No, no, but I don't remember that," Clara insisted. "He never talks in his sleep. I mean, maybe sometimes."

"While *you* were asleep, or half asleep, so you don't remember," Derek persisted. "But your unconscious remembers, like a dream. Honestly, I don't believe in ghosts or possession, but I have seen things like this before—where one loved one is so in tune with their spouse or child or parent that they take on all the feelings of the other. Think of it like a unique form of empathy. A gift, in fact. You have a gift. And when Seamus talked in his sleep or told you about his past when you first met and you were both high—I know you two got high a lot—and you don't remember, your unconscious remembered. And it's okay about the drugs. No judgment. But you have to stop judging Seamus and leave this tragedy with Emmeline and our parents behind, and you have to leave this place. This town. And the house. It's all surfacing here again, and it's your responsibility to put it away. Now that you've shone a light on it, it can heal. But only if you stop looking at it. That's how life works. And as much as I hate to say it, Seamus was right to stay away."

"But what about the coffin?" Clara pleaded. "I saw Emmeline in a coffin. Surely, Seamus wouldn't know about that if it's true—unless he did it."

"It's probably Seamus's dream about losing our parents," Derek said softly. "He was traumatized. You have to accept it. Please let it go, Clara, and help him. This is all about Seamus, and Seamus needs you. I'll come to the city to see you two. But this place is not a good place. You have to leave. Do not come back. And then, I assure you, everyone will be safe. I'll keep an eye on Billy for you, and Mrs. Flannery. And try to get Billy help at a rehab in the city. I'll pull some strings. And if you stay away, I guarantee they will be okay too. Your friends here. And most importantly, your baby. Just stay away. Trust me, as a priest, with all my experience, and as your brother-in-law who loves you and Seamus." He nodded with his most persuasively charming smile. And then, he left.

***

Clara only had a few minutes to ponder what Derek had said before Seamus peeked in. She had to look away, turning to the window. She wasn't ready to see him. But she knew she had to try.

Seamus came over to her bedside. Clara nodded without looking at him as if acknowledging that he could stay. He touched her hand, which was lying limply on the bed beside her. Clara let Seamus hold it but still couldn't look at him or move her hand to show affection in any way. She felt heat coming from his hand to hers. It was powerful. But the fear she had took over instead. "I'm scared," Clara whispered, still looking out the window, still afraid to see his eyes, "but I love you."

"Thank you," Seamus replied and dropped his head onto her hand.

Clara finally turned to look at him and lifted her hand to caress his head, run her fingers through his sandy-blond hair, let him know she loved him—but she couldn't. Her hand stopped a few inches above Seamus's wavy hair, and she quickly brought it back and down onto her baby belly. She felt the fear course through her body, because she knew her next step was to move back to their home in Brooklyn with Seamus and their baby in her belly and to trust that the past would go away. Trust that Derek was right. Trust that he wasn't covering for some horrendous act that Seamus had done. Trust that Emmeline had run away and something had befallen her on her escape or she was living, hiding in some small town, too ashamed to return. Or happy and living a fulfilling life without them, sacrificing her love for Seamus so that Clara could experience it, finding new love with someone else. There was enough love to go around for everyone after all—*Right?* Clara thought.

But Clara couldn't trust any of that. Something inside her said that Emmeline needed help and that it was only time before her ghost came knocking again. And Clara would have to acquiesce to Emmeline's needs in order to save her baby's life.

36

A Visit from Emmeline in Brooklyn

Clara was surprisingly relieved when they moved back into their Brooklyn walk up. She loved fall in the city and got busy right away, redoing the plants in the bay window and outside it, visiting with Erin, having lunch with Greta, going to museums, breakfasting by herself at her favorite spot, Balthazar on Spring Street in SoHo, and forgetting about Emmeline. It was surprisingly easy. Maybe Derek had been right after all about leaving the trauma behind at the lake house and in the past where it belonged. Maybe all her visions had truly been manifestations of Seamus's dreams, his own unconscious needing to shine that light on his sorrow and move on, her own empathy and deep love for him allowing her to see what was in his past. And now that they were back in Brooklyn, their true home, Clara could see the hope clearly again and start to forget everything that had happened at the lake house.

Seamus was content to be back as well. Their baby was now six months along, and Clara was slowly letting Seamus get closer to her again, at least when he touched her baby belly. Clara still was hesitant, and the fear of Seamus reared its monstrous head occasionally, but time was doing its job and the anxious nudging was dulling and being replaced by a calm sense of warmth and grounding.

Clara had also called Derek to let him know that things were going well for them in the city. He seemed relieved and told Clara that he was looking out for Billy. Billy was still a mess but had agreed to consider rehab. Derek said he'd keep working on Billy. And Mrs. Flannery seemed fine as well. Derek had told both Billy and Mrs. Flannery that Clara would be in touch as soon as the baby was born and that, until then, she was lying low.

This was a relief to Clara. She didn't have to feel guilty that she and Seamus had left so quickly without saying goodbye. No worries.

And today, Clara was even venturing back into the nursery, attempting to get back into her element there too, making everything beautiful with her special touch and bringing the charming room to life like a proper nursery—the lynchpin being the Beatrix Potter character art.

Clara had just put the various pieces back up on the hooks, which still remained on the wall above the crib from before. She stood back and looked at them—*Better than the first time*, she told herself cheerfully. "Maybe there is a silver lining here for us," she said out loud to her baby. Then, Clara mosied over to the rocking chair and picked up the cute pillow she'd found thrifting. It was adorned with a needlepoint Mrs. Tiggy-Winkle, her favorite Beatrix Potter character. She put the pillow in the crib and positioned it just so, feeling a rush of joy and pride.

Maybe she would be a good mom after all, Clara mused. And then, Emmeline entered her thoughts. She imagined that Emmeline McGuire might've liked the Beatrix Potter art as well and would've appreciated having the nursery just so, with magical characters like her dragon and knight. Clara felt sadness thinking about Emmeline. Maybe she was just being nostalgic for a past that didn't belong to her. Maybe Clara herself would be jealous of Seamus's relationship with Emmeline if she really knew how special it was. But she didn't. And none of that was real, she told herself, laughing at this absurdity.

But then, Derek's words surfaced—*Emmeline would be so jealous of your life with Seamus and your baby.* And the fear filled Clara's belly. She felt a cramp. "No, no," she gasped. "No cramps. We're fine. We're home. We're healthy. That is not happening. There's nothing we can do to help Emmeline. And nothing she can do to hurt us. It's a sad story, but it's not ours. And we can still honor her with our love for Seamus. And I can honor her with my love for you, Little Bean."

Then, suddenly—a FLASH. Emmeline appeared next to Clara looking in the crib, hands on the rail, trying to breathe, suffocating, wheezing for air, turning blue. Emmeline tilted her head and looked directly into Clara's eyes—but as if looking through Clara with hatred and shame. "This is all your fault," Emmeline said at Clara.

Clara felt the sound waves of Emmeline's voice pulse through her, and she shuddered, all sense of strength leaving her.

"You hurt everyone with your love," Emmeline continued, fury spewing from her lips. "You don't deserve him." Then, she walked right into Clara as if possessing her.

Clara began to suffocate.

Another FLASH, and Clara was in the coffin, pushing up on the lid, trying to get it off, to open it, to get air. And this time, Clara was herself, and she was lying on a skeleton. But Emmeline's voice spoke from somewhere inside her: "Please let me out!" Clara's lips didn't move but Emmeline's desperation was palpable. "I won't tell anyone! I'll throw away the diary! I'll have the baby! Please, Seamus, please. I'm so sorry. I don't know why I was so nice to him," Emmeline cried and began sobbing inside Clara's being, and Clara's lungs tightened. "Seamus...!!!" Emmeline screamed.

Suddenly, a phone rang, and Clara came to, gasping for air. Her cell phone was ringing from the dresser. She grabbed it and wheezed, "Hello?"—heading out to find her purse and inhaler. *The kitchen,* she told herself.

"Clara?" Seamus's voice rang out from the phone. "What's going on?"

Clara gasped for air.

Seamus panicked. "Clara! I'm coming home!"

Clara hung up on him and yanked her inhaler from her bag. She pumped it and inhaled the relieving drops, finally getting air, then dialed Dr. Goldberg. No answer. Her outgoing message began immediately: "You've reached the voicemail of Dr. Goldberg. Please leave a message with your name and number. Thank you. If this is a medical emergency, please dial 911."

"Dr. Goldberg, it's Clara," Clara began, trying to hide her desperation. "I have to do another hypnosis. If I don't find Emmeline's diary, something bad is going to happen to the baby. I know it. I'm going back to the lake." She hung up, found her keys, started out, then stopped. *Derek!* she thought and dialed his number.

Derek was in his office smoking a cigar and working on admin for the high school when the phone rang. He saw Clara's New York City number flash on the screen and let it go to his old-school answering machine, sitting back and listening as his voice rang out on the outgoing message: "You've reached Father Derek. Please leave a message."

Clara couldn't believe he wasn't answering. He had to be there! Where was everyone? She waited for the beep then croaked, "Derek, it's me. You were wrong. Seamus did something to Emmeline, and

I'm going to find out. I'm coming back. I'm going to Billy's and to find the diary."

Derek grabbed the phone. "Hello? Clara? You need to wait. I'm going to come get you. You shouldn't drive."

"I'm fine," Clara told him. "I promise."

"You don't sound fine, Clara. You're overreacting," Derek insisted. "It's irresponsible to drive like this. You don't want to put anyone in danger, especially yourself and your baby."

"No. Please. Do not come here," Clara said. "There's no time. Just meet me at Billy's." And she hung up and ran out of the house to her car and began her drive upstate.

***

Minutes later, Dr. Goldberg came back to her office and heard Clara's frantic message. She called Seamus.

"Dr. Goldberg?" Seamus answered as he raced home from his office in his car.

"Clara's had another episode," Dr. Goldberg launched in. "She left a message. Something about a hypnosis. And a diary. She's going back to the town to look for it. I'm assuming it's this apparition of this girl, Emmeline."

"Oh my god. What should I do?" Seamus said.

"If there's any way you can stop her or find that diary, do it. If not, just—pray," Dr. Goldberg said, unsure why she would ever say such a thing—*Just pray*, she mocked herself in her head. *What is that about?*

Even Seamus was surprised. "Pray?"

A laugh escaped under Dr. Goldberg's breath. "Well, it's not my usual modus operandi, but right now, that's all I have left to offer. Sometimes we have to walk away from the known to find answers.

And this may be one of those times. There is no other rational explanation besides the unknown or perhaps mystical for what has been happening to Clara. So, to make it easy, we can call it God. Or higher power. Or magic. And pray."

***

Seamus hung up after the call with Dr. Goldberg and immediately called Clara, speeding up as he headed home to Brooklyn.

But Clara wasn't home, she was already driving north on the highway—no music, no sounds, no phone ringing—just speeding and hoping she didn't throw up out of fear and that her mind would stay clear until she got back to the lake town. 'We're going to be fine," she whispered to her baby over and over.

***

Seamus raced from his car to the door as soon as he made it home and burst in. "Clara?!" he shouted. Her phone was on the kitchen island, but Clara didn't respond. He ran through the house—nothing. He came back to the kitchen and picked up her phone. The last call was to Derek. He screamed and raced out with the phone, hopped in his car and began driving north, heart racing, knowing Dr. Goldberg must be right.

37

Diary Under the Porch

Clara raced out of the off-ramp toward the lake town, feeling the pull of the steering wheel too hard, slowing down. "Come on, come on," she yelled at the light impatiently then looked for her phone. She rifled through her purse. The light turned green. "Crap," she swore, slamming the steering wheel, realizing she'd forgotten her phone. The car behind her honked. "Yeah, yeah, shut the eff up," she yelled as she hit the gas. "I'm doing my best!"

Clara peeled out and drove farther and farther away from the highway and into the countryside, through the fields and rolling hills and towards the lake, until she finally reached town and drove towards Mrs. Flannery and Billy's house—just as an ambulance sped by and Clara spotted a fire truck and police car at The Country Market. People were gathered round, and Mrs. Flannery was standing outside on the sidewalk next to a fire fighter who was leading her to the police car.

Clara pulled up to the curb in front of the market and jumped out. She ran over and up to Mrs. Flannery. "Mrs. Flannery. It's Clara," she said, squeezing her beloved old friend's arm.

Mrs. Flannery looked frightened and worried for the first time since Clara had known her. "Oh, honey, he did it again," Mrs. Flannery cried. "My poor dear, Billy. He is just in so much pain." She was clutching a photo and handed it to Clara. "He was holding this."

It was a photo of Clara on the day of the BBQ.

Which is when Clara realized—"Oh my god, this is all my fault."

"No!" Mrs. Flannery exclaimed. "Why would it be your fault? It's never your fault when someone else hurts themselves."

"Because I...I was too friendly with him," Clara insisted. "He thought...maybe he thought it was more."

"I don't understand. In a romantic way?" Mrs. Flannery asked. "He knows you're married. He never seemed upset."

"Yes, no...in a deeper way," Clara cried, not understanding fully herself. "We have a special connection. C'mon, let's go to the hospital. We have to go to the hospital."

"Yes, this nice officer, Officer DiPaola, Berniece—I used to teach her piano—was going to take me," Mrs. Flannery told Clara.

Officer DiPaola laughed, overhearing. "Yes, I can give Mrs. Flannery a ride," she said. "You can come with us."

"No, no, I want to have my car," Clara insisted, feeling overwhelmed by all the commotion.

"Are you sure you're okay?" asked Officer DiPaola.

"I'm fine," Clara assured them—as Officer DiPaola got a text. "Oh, this is good news. Mrs. Flannery, your grandson, is going to be okay. Bruce just texted me. It's not protocol, so keep it on the downlow, but they're pretty certain Billy will recover just fine. And we're all rooting for him, you know that."

"Oh, thank god," Clara blurted out.

"Yes, wonderful, dear," Mrs. Flannery told Officer DiPaola and squeezed her hand, the relief showing on her beautifully wrinkled face. "I have a lesson at three, but I'd love to pop by the hospital."

Officer DiPaola was amused by Mrs. Flannery's spunk—wanting to teach piano even in the midst of a crisis. "Then, let's go," Officer DiPaola cheered. "Now that I know how you stay so young and frisky—no worrying when it's not needed."

"That is my motto," Mrs. Flannery confirmed. "And the piano lessons are what keep me going. Wouldn't want to disappoint a young student now, would we?"

Officer DiPaola laughed, but fear and anxiety overwhelmed Clara again in spite of the good news and Mrs. Flannery's optimism. "I'll see you there," Clara said, barely acknowledging them, as she headed back to her car in a flurry. She had such a bad feeling about everything. "I'll meet you there," Clara called back when she saw Officer DiPaolo kindly helping Mrs. Flannery into her squad car. Clara knew she had to relax and get centered so her mind could stay clear and she could focus properly on the tasks at hand.

Officer DiPaola put on the siren and pulled an illegal U-turn. Clara saw Mrs. Flannery laugh like a little girl, which made her so happy for a moment. But then, Clara thought about Billy and her tears began to flow. Now that she was alone and Mrs. Flannery couldn't sense her grief, Clara let herself go.

She followed the patrol car with a U-turn, racing after it and not noticing Seamus pass on the other side of the road and pull up to Mrs. Flannery and Billy's house.

Seamus parked just past the house and went around the side. He made sure no one was looking, then searched the floorboards of the porch in back, counting from the edge and pulling up the fifth board. And there, he found it—Emmeline's diary.

Seamus gasped, his heart racing. He was moved to tears by what he saw as he opened the cover. There, inside, were doodles of the dragon in his game and the knight. And there was a comic doodle of a kid that looked just like him with a funny helmet. Seamus rubbed the drawing gently with his fingers, remembering Emmeline and the way she used to smirk when she drew and her laugh of gold whenever he peeked to see what she'd made. And then, she'd tease him and say, "Stop looking!"

Seamus laughed through bittersweet tears, and his heart ached more than he knew it could.

Then, slowly, he turned the page, opening the diary to her first entry. His hands began shaking, terrified by what he might find inside—terrified that he might fall apart and not be able to get back up. Terrified of his love for Emmeline and the sadness that came with it—the loss. And the fire roaring up inside of him—a fire of rage at her and himself. A fire fueled by betrayal. And his inability to stop it.

"I just...," he stuttered, as if he could talk to Emmeline, wishing with all his heart that she were there to listen. Listen to him ask her for her forgiveness—for all his fury. And listen to him ask her to help him forgive himself.

Seamus shook it off and stood up on the porch. And suddenly, an image of his mother appeared. His mother hugged him so tightly, and he stood there and wept. "I love you, my son. I'm here for you," Seamus's mother told him and kissed his head and disappeared.

And she was gone. *Gone!* Seamus shouted in his mind, feeling himself crumble inside, the momentary relief vanishing.

And the space around him flooded with despair. And then, rage entered his heart again as he squeezed the diary and hurried back to his car.

38

Blood on the Tracks

Clara pulled into the guest parking of the hospital in the next town over, honking at Officer DiPaola as she parked right in front to let Mrs. Flannery out. Officer DiPaola waved back. *What a difference a small town makes*, Clara thought. It was nice, even if she preferred the hustle and bustle of the city, even if everyone led with brashness there before revealing their humanity beneath.

Clara caught up to Officer DiPaola and Mrs. Flannery in the ER and took Mrs. Flannery's hand as Officer DiPaola nodded at the nurse to let them in. The nurse smiled and waved them through as if they were royalty or celebs with backstage ER access.

Behind the curtains surrounding the second ER bed in, they found Billy—out cold. Clara and Mrs. Flannery stepped in, while Officer DiPaola stayed outside the curtains to give them privacy. "His eyes are closed. But he looks okay, like he's breathing calmly," Clara informed Mrs. Flannery.

"I can hear that," Mrs. Flannery replied and stepped forward to touch the hospital bed to get her bearings. She found Billy's hand and took it in hers, turning her face in the direction of her grandson but speaking towards the space just above his head. "My dear boy,

I'm so glad you are going to be okay," Mrs. Flannery declared with so much love, hoping with every fiber of her being that she was right.

Mrs. Flannery squeezed Billy's right hand, which is when Clara noticed the fresh marks on his left arm. "That's the wrong arm," Clara said. "He shoots up on the other arm."

"I'm sorry?" Mrs. Flannery said.

"You're holding his right arm, where he usually shoots up. He's left-handed. The new marks are on his left arm. Someone did this to him." Clara felt her lungs tighten and her airways begin to close. No air. She began to wheeze.

"Honey?" Mrs. Flannery called out, sensing that something was terribly wrong.

Clara rifled through her bag, grabbed her inhaler and pressed the mist into her throat, sucking it in—until she got relief. She breathed deep and hard until she could talk again. "I need to find her diary," Clara told Mrs. Flannery. "Do you know where Emmeline kept her diary?"

Mrs. Flannery paled.

"What? What happened?" Clara panicked.

Mrs. Flannery took a deep breath through her nose and exhaled slowly through slightly parted lips, realizing her possible mistake, trying to remain calm. "She buried it behind our house. Under the planks of the back porch. But you may be too late. Seamus called, and I told him the same thing."

Clara gasped. "No, no, why did you do that? I know it's him. He's the one that hurt Emmeline. And the one who did this to Billy. I'm sure. Why did you tell him?" Clara cried.

"Please, just stop for a moment," Mrs. Flannery said calmly and turned toward Clara, reaching out for her.

Clara looked at Mrs. Flannery and a blast of fear and adrenaline hit. She knew what she had to do. She had to stop Seamus no matter what. To save her baby. And she knew where to go at the Dunne house to find exactly what she needed to do just that. "No, no, I have to go," Clara insisted to Mrs. Flannery, her voice full of urgency and desperation. She turned and blasted out, running smack into Officer DiPaola, who was waiting on the other side of the curtain surrounding Billy's ER bed. Clara gasped, as if caught—knowing what her next move was, knowing what she was ready to do to protect her baby and herself. Her heart pounded. She hoped no one could hear it.

"Are you okay?" Officer DiPaola asked Clara.

"I am, yes," Clara smiled, pulling herself together, pretending she was fifteen years old in some embassy in Europe meeting her dad's important colleagues, knowing her appearance and calm was of utmost importance. "I, actually, I remembered something, for work," Clara lied. "Can you...? Would you mind giving Mrs. Flannery a ride back home again? So she can teach her next lesson?"

Mrs. Flannery pushed the curtain away and came out. "I can call an Uber," she joked.

"No, no, of course, I don't mind," Officer DiPaola told Clara, then turned to Mrs. Flannery. "I don't get to play that siren often enough, and you are worth it, so you are driving with me. I insist."

"Thank you, dear," said Mrs. Flannery, then turned to Clara who was doing her best to hold it together even though her heart was still pounding like a drum. Mrs. Flannery's smiling eyes turned sad. "Please take a moment before you act, Emmeline," she told Clara. "I know you are frightened, but we all love you, and you will be fine whatever you choose, if it's a choice not out of fear. Never choose out of fear. Only love."

Clara shuddered. Mrs. Flannery had just called her Emmeline again. But Clara shoved that away and took Mrs. Flannery's hands to assure her. "Of course, I will be careful," Clara said with a smile.

She saw Mrs. Flannery didn't believe her and squeezed the old lady's hands. "I'll see you back at your house in a bit," Clara added and bolted out of there.

39

Revolver in the House

Clara raced to her car in the hospital parking lot and headed straight to the lake house. She ran in and barreled upstairs and to the master bedroom. She opened the bottom drawer, shuffled through her sweats that she'd left behind in case she and Seamus ever returned to the house and pulled out a .22 revolver and the bullets left behind by Seamus's mom.

Clara turned the weapon over in her hand. How strange it was that she was ready to use it on Seamus if it came to it. And how his mother was the one that kept this firearm for protection. What would Stella Dunne think if she knew Clara was about to use it on her son? She'd feel the pain of motherly love for her son and a great loss. The tears welled in Clara's eyes—she too could feel that mix of motherly love for her lost babies and her own love for Seamus and his baby in her belly. *Why is this happening?* Clara wondered. *I love him. I love Seamus. Why?*

Clara sat down on the bed, the heaviness and fear taking over. She put her head on the pillow and curled up on her side, pulling her feet in, *just for a moment*, she told herself, curling into a ball, and just weeping.

****

Meanwhile, Officer DiPaola raced through town, siren blaring, with Mrs. Flannery laughing shotgun. "We're going to frighten the townsfolk," Mrs. Flannery said. "I wish I could see their faces."

"Yup, they are looking," Officer DiPaola told her. "Always happens when there's not much else to do here. It's good to get a little excitement."

Mrs. Flannery agreed. "I think when my Billy heals again, I'll suggest he go back to the city. I keep wanting to protect him here, but he needs to find his way in the world where he can find some excitement too. He's too big for this town. Not physically, of course," Mrs. Flannery joked.

"But I know what you mean," Officer DiPaola assured her.

"Thank you, dear. It helps to have an understanding ear."

"I think it's a good idea," Officer DiPaola added. "As long as he stays connected to you. And it seems he has a good friend in Clara. Maybe she'll be a touchstone for him too in the city."

Mrs. Flannery reached out and touched Officer DiPaola's shoulder gently and squeezed it. "I'm sorry I made you play Bach when you hated it so much," she teased.

Officer DiPaola laughed. "Well, I'll have you know, I recently bought sheet music for Shostakovich Waltz 2, and I've been practicing."

"Oh, that was your favorite," Mrs. Flannery remembered fondly.

"I'm learning," Officer DiPaola told her.

"Well, good. I was going to let you try it after Bach. But then you quit," Mrs. Flannery teased with a smirk, then said gently and genuinely, "I'm sorry."

Officer DiPaola laughed again. "I forgive you, Mrs. Flannery. That was a long time ago. And it didn't hurt that much. In fact, I still loved you. And was happy I didn't have to practice anymore. So, you know, it was a hidden blessing."

Mrs. Flannery was pleased. "And I forgive you for quitting and butchering that sonata. Poor Bach."

"Thank you," said Officer DiPaola as she pulled up in front of Mrs. Flannery's house just as Seamus drove away, heading over to the parish high school.

Seamus was angry, his eyes red from crying. He parked several blocks away from the school and snuck up, peeking into Derek's office. The lights were off—everything was dark. Seamus broke in. He spotted the old answering machine and hit play and heard Clara's desperate call and the whole conversation.

40

Body in the Closet

Clara woke up in the Dunne house master bedroom in a start, heart racing. Mind blank. She looked around. Saw the gun. Felt the fear and tears rising again, heart pounding louder than ever, panic in her stomach. Was this real? It was!

"C'mon," she told herself, sitting up. "We have to go." Even though Clara had no idea what to expect and what she would do if she found Seamus, she had to try to stop him. That's all there was. Emmeline hadn't appeared at all since Clara had been back in town, but Clara knew she would, and right now, Clara was afraid of everyone and ready to take them all down if she had to. Mama bear was on.

Clara hurried down the stairs, remembering what Mrs. Flannery had said—to take her time. But she had already done that. She'd gotten the gun, and she'd cried. And Clara still knew that she had to find Emmeline's diary no matter what. And now, she had a weapon to help.

And Mrs. Flannery called me Emmeline again, Clara remembered.

But she couldn't go there now. It was too much to handle. So, she shoved the memory out of her mind and got in her car and hurried over to Mrs. Flannery's house, passing it and parking a few blocks away.

Clara made sure no one was watching as she approached the house and then ducked around the side. She hurried to the back porch and found the one porch board moved. No diary. Seamus had been there. He'd beaten her to it. But where was he now? And why hadn't he gone back to the house to find her? Or at least look? Clara knew she was lucky that he hadn't found her asleep.

Clara shook it off and entered the back door into Billy's studio. Everything was torn apart, drawers out, bed moved, bedding rifled through, dishes and silverware all over the kitchen floor, bookshelves empty, books strewn everywhere. "Oh my god," Clara whispered under her breath then stealthily made her way up the stairs into Mrs. Flannery's part of the house—everything there was torn apart as well.

Seamus must've done this when he was looking for the diary, Clara thought.

She started looking around. "Emmeline. Please, help me," Clara whispered and suddenly the scar on her forehead began to bleed. Then, Clara saw Emmeline just standing in front of her, pale. Emmeline turned to the window and stared out, then pointed. Clara walked over and looked out and saw Seamus drive up.

"Hide," said Emmeline. "You have to hide."

Clara ducked to hide and peeked up and out the window to make sure this was real. It was. Seamus got out of the car and looked up at the window. He saw her and headed into the house. Clara heard the door open downstairs.

"Clara?!" Seamus shouted.

Clara ran and hid in a closet. She heard Seamus come up the stairs from Billy's studio to Mrs. Flannery's, then felt a leg. She tried not to scream—then saw the outline of a body, propped against the back of the closet. Clara gasped silently, terrified, body shaking out of control. *Please, please, please, help us*, Clara thought out to the universe.

Then, the head of the body shook—alive! And Clara realized it was Mrs. Flannery, tied up and gagged.

Clara heard Seamus's footsteps heading back downstairs and quickly untied and ungagged Mrs. Flannery, who immediately whispered, "Run girl. He's still here. It's Derek."

They heard the door open downstairs into Billy's studio. They heard footsteps entering. The door slammed shut. Mrs. Flannery recognized the gait. "It's Derek," Mrs. Flannery whispered again.

"Where is it?" Derek bellowed out in a deep, frighteningly calm voice.

"Bastard," Seamus called out and ran at Derek and pummeled him. Derek stumbled back then recovered and came at Seamus, punches flying, wrestling, yelling.

Clara ran out of the closet and down the stairs, pulling out the revolver. "Seamus!" she screamed

Derek turned towards her voice. Seamus slammed him to the floor and knocked him out cold. Clara gasped and looked at Seamus, still afraid of him, unsure, pointing the weapon.

Seamus pulled the diary out of his jacket, shaking, and read Emmeline's words: "I'm only four months pregnant, but I can tell the difference. My birthmark looks a bit bigger. If I push my stomach out, it looks like a bear. If I get any fatter, it'll probably look like a walrus." Seamus turned pale.

Clara gasped. Her arm dropped to her side. The gun fell to the floor. It bounced on the hardwood. What could this possibly mean?

she wondered. "How could...? She can't. It can't be possible," Clara uttered and shook her head, unable to grasp what was happening, her mind flying through all the possibilities.

"It can't be real," Clara insisted finally and grabbed the diary. "Someone did this! Someone wrote this as a trick!" Clara cried, but as soon as she squeezed the diary in both hands and took in the sketches of the knight and the other doodles of Seamus and the dragon, it hit her, and she saw everything:

First, a light FLASH. Then, Clara was back in the guesthouse watching teenage Emmeline jumping on the bed. Emmeline fell off. Hit her head. Was completely out of it from drinking the whiskey and lemonade. "Ow," Emmeline said but was still laughing, drunk. She draped the blue scarf over her head, playfully, looking through the gauzy fabric, enjoying the blur of bright blue and purple colors.

Teenage Derek came over and kissed Emmeline, climbing on top of her.

"No, no," Emmeline said, "Ow." She was drowsy. Everything looked blurry.

Then, teenage Seamus appeared in the window of the guesthouse, looking in, seeing Emmeline and Derek on the bed. Emmeline spied his angry, hurt, jealous eyes. She tried to push Derek off, "Seamus, no."

"Your head," Derek said sweetly and kissed her, touching her thigh, bringing his hand up. "It's okay.

"I'm, no, not now," Emmeline insisted.

"It's okay, no one's here," Derek assured her.

"Please, no," Emmeline repeated, but the words barely come out, and Derek pulled down her lavender cotton underwear, not at all sexy or like she was planning for this. "I love you, Emmeline," Derek told her. "It's okay. We had so much fun today. I love that you listen to me playing."

But Emmeline couldn't hear Derek's words. All she could see was Seamus still looking in through the window, watching her, hurt and angry. And then, Clara's eyes met Seamus's, and he ran off.

"Seamus, no...," Emmeline called out.

Then, there was another light FLASH. And suddenly, Clara was back to reality in Billy's studio. She looked at Derek knocked out on the floor. She felt sick. She wanted to say it was a rape. But was it a rape? Or did Emmeline love Derek too?

"He did this to her! To Emmeline!" Seamus shouted in fury, pointing at Derek on the floor. "Do you understand, Clara?! Emmeline didn't want him to. That's what it says in there. In the diary. On the last page." Seamus's fists clenched. He looked like he was going to explode, looking down at his knocked-out brother and screaming with rage, "Motherfucker!" He spit on him in disgust.

Clara gasped then turned to the last page in the diary and read Emmeline's words. Seamus was right. "You're right," she said. "Emmeline didn't want him to. And she was terrified. But that's where it stops."

"That's called rape," Seamus seethed then turned to Derek and kicked him and screamed, "Motherfucker!" again.

"We still don't know what happened," Clara said. "Please, wait."

"I saw them fight at our parents' graves," Seamus admitted. "Emmeline wanted to run away. I didn't stop her. I thought she loved him. I was so jealous. It was my fault."

"Only you can know what happened after that, Emmeline," Mrs. Flannery called out from the bottom of the stairs where she'd been watching silently.

Clara got chills and turned to Mrs. Flannery. The elder woman's face was solemn and certain, and Clara knew she had to press on. She bent down slowly and touched Derek with her broken finger and, in a flash, saw what happened:

Emmeline and Derek were at the headstones in the clearing in the woods. They were fighting, just like when Clara had heard them that one evening from the guesthouse. "I'm going," Emmeline whisper yelled. "I can't have this baby. I found a doctor that'll do it."

"Please, no. I love you," Derek pleaded. "Please don't hurt our baby. We can be a family."

Emmeline tensed. She couldn't look at him and covered her eyes, shaking her head. A twig snapped. It was Seamus, watching them, hiding between the trees. Emmeline's eyes met his. He ran. "Seamus, wait!" Emmeline called out and started after him.

Derek pulled her back, pulled her close.

"Let go of me, you monster," Emmeline raged with all the venom she could muster and tried to pull away.

Derek clutched Emmeline's hand tighter.

"Ow!" she cried.

"I'm not a monster," he pleaded desperately. "I just love you."

Emmeline jerked her hand back and her pinky finger snapped— broken. The snap was loud. Derek lost his hold. Emmeline fell back and hit her head on the headstone. She was out cold, blood pouring from the wound on the side of her head.

"Emmeline. No. No!" Derek cried out, trying to revive her. "Please, please!" he begged Emmeline and then God and the universe or anyone or anything that could help. But Emmeline was limp. And there was nothing he could do. "Noooo!" Derek wailed.

Clara saw another light FLASH.

And then, she came back to Seamus in the present in Billy's studio. Her heart was racing. She took her hand off Derek and stood up, panicked. Mrs. Flannery was heading towards her. "Honey, why don't you sit down?" the old lady said firmly.

Clara refused. Mrs. Flannery grabbed Clara's arm as if to try to keep her in the present, worried about what would happen if she went back.

Somehow, she knows what happened, Clara realized about Mrs. Flannery.

Clara pulled away and bent back down, placing her hand on Derek's arm. Again, she saw a light FLASH. And then, she was back to the clearing by the graves. It was a bit later. The moon was higher and a panicked teenage Derek was digging and opening his mother's coffin. Derek put Emmeline's limp body inside, closed the coffin and shoveled the dirt back on. "Seamus can't know," Derek insisted to himself desperately. "He can't know! I have to take care of him."

Derek looked at his mother's tombstone. "I'll take care of him, Mommy. I promise. I'm so sorry. Seamus won't ever know I did this. I didn't mean to do this." Derek began to weep and crumble. "Emmeline, beautiful, Emmeline. I'm so sorry. I love you, Mommy."

Clara saw another light FLASH, and then, suddenly, she was in the coffin, like in her dream. She saw Emmeline come to in the coffin. Then, Clara was out in the clearing looking at the headstones. It was completely dark outside now, only a sliver of moonlight coming in. Then, Clara was back in the coffin and could see Emmeline lying on top of the skeleton of Seamus and Derek's mother. Emmeline screamed and started to lose air. "Wha..? No! Help!" Emmeline cried out, her voice filled with terror. "Seamus! Help! Please stop! Help me...!" Emmeline pounded and pushed on the inside of the lid of the coffin, trying to get out, but it was no use. The lid wouldn't budge, and no one was there to hear her or help. Seamus was long gone. Derek had left. And Clara watched Emmeline turn blue and suffocate to death.

Clara came back to reality in Billy's studio. She was sitting in a chair, trembling like a leaf, cold, clammy, beads of sweat covering her forehead. She didn't remember sitting down, but Mrs. Flannery was in the chair next to her, clutching her hand. "We have to go to the grave," Clara told Mrs. Flannery, pleading, unable to look at Seamus—afraid of what this would do to him.

"Whose grave?" Mrs. Flannery asked.

"Seamus's mother," Clara whispered, feeling her lungs tighten, feeling her baby kick, as if distressed. "Now. We have to go now," Clara insisted and rubbed her belly and saw Seamus gasp at the anguish in her eyes.

Mrs. Flannery gave Clara's hand two squeezes. "I understand, Emmeline. We're here to help."

Seamus's eyes filled with fear. This was just too much for him, just like Clara suspected. He turned away. "I'll call the police," Seamus said, looking at Derek, who was starting to come to.

"No," Clara insisted, standing up, grabbing Seamus's phone so he couldn't call, getting a cramp. "Ow." Grabbing her belly.

"Clara," Seamus cried.

"Drive us, now," Clara told him and started toward the door, clutching his phone. This was more important than dealing with Derek. They had to go to the grave if Emmeline was going to let their baby survive. "Mrs. Flannery, please come with us."

"I'm coming, Emmeline," Mrs. Flannery told Clara as she made her way to the door, stopping and reaching out towards Seamus. "C'mon, Seamus dear, I need your help."

Seamus was shaken, tears streaming down his face. He took Mrs. Flannery's arm, supporting her and letting her support him.

41

Mama in the Coffin

The moonlight lit the clearing in the woods where Clara, Seamus and Mrs. Flannery watched two policemen shovel the ground and dirt off of the lid of the decaying coffin in Mrs. Dunne's grave. Seamus's body began to sway back and forth slightly in distress. Mrs. Flannery took a slight step back so she was almost behind Seamus and put her hand firmly on his back to support him. Seamus nodded, acknowledging her kindness and strength and doing everything not to let his tears escape. He was like a child again who'd just lost his parents.

Clara's entire body was shaking. She held her breath as the police officers began to pull the lid off the coffin. And there it was—Clara gasped—the second skeleton, Emmeline's skeleton on top of Seamus's mother's skeleton, the bones of Emmeline's arm up by her head where she had tried to push the lid off, her pinky finger broken and her hand holding a rat's nest. "Oh, no," Clara cried when she saw the nest.

Then, Clara's eyes moved down Emmeline's skeleton and saw the tiny skeletal frame of a baby, thumb to its mouth as if lying on its mother's belly. Clara collapsed to the ground weeping. "It wasn't my fault; it wasn't my fault," Clara cried.

"No, it wasn't, dear," said Mrs. Flannery, gesturing for Seamus to lead her over to Clara. Mrs. Flannery reached down and found Clara's head and stroked her hair. "My dear, Emmeline, be free."

Clara reached up and squeezed Mrs. Flannery's hand, pulling it close as she wept until she couldn't any more.

Mrs. Flannery stroked Clara's hair again gently as Clara lifted her head. There were two detectives there now as well, and Clara overheard one of them whisper to Seamus, "He wasn't at the studio when we arrived. We're looking at the church and will be searching the area if he's not there."

"Thank you, detective," Seamus said then turned to Clara, who was still on the ground, sitting back on her heels.

Clara rubbed her belly. "I think I need to be alone for a minute," she told Seamus. "Can I have the car keys please?" She stood up.

"Sure, sure," Seamus said, flustered, and dug the keys out of his pocket. He gave them to Clara. "I'll go with you," he said gently and gestured toward the car.

"No, you need to stay here," Clara told him. "Mrs. Flannery, please stay with Seamus. So he can be here with his mother. To respect his mother. And Emmeline." Clara looked at Seamus. He was pale. "You have to stay here," she reiterated. "I want to give you that space and time with Emmeline alone—for us." Clara wasn't going to back down and turned and started off through the woods.

Seamus chased her down. "Clara!" he called out. Clara stopped. "Please don't leave me," he pleaded.

"I know where he is," Clara said. "Please don't ask me how. And I have to do this alone. And you have to stay here with Emmeline so she can let go. And be free." Clara turned and continued to the car.

Seamus watched her go, more afraid than ever, paralyzed and unable to move or follow. He was broken inside.

But Clara didn't look back. She didn't think. She was going on pure instinct. There was no way she could know where Derek was, but yet, she did. And she wasn't afraid. She felt like a warrior. A protector. A warrior who could already see victory. Fighting for someone she loved. Someone inside her. Someone she knew but didn't know: Emmeline McGuire.

42

This Is for Her

Clara passed the church and high school, police vehicles all around, and kept driving until she reached the beginning of the path where she and Derek had walked that day when she had needed a friend and wanted to find out about Emmeline. They had walked through the fields and into the woods, talking about philosophy and life and only a little about the past.

Clara parked off the road so her car was hidden from the detectives and got out and walked down the dirt path. Luckily, the moonlight was strong so it lit the way.

As Clara got closer to Derek's favorite spot, where they'd sat and talked and watched the robins and hawks, she slowed down and tried to be silent with her footsteps.

Then, as she rounded the bend, she saw Derek. He was sitting on his favorite rock, bending forward, elbows on his knees, contemplating whatever he was holding in his hand. She let her eyes focus. It was the revolver—the revolver that she'd brought from his mother's drawer to Mrs. Flannery's house. *How ironic*, Clara thought—here she'd been worried about using it to stop Seamus and now Stella Dunne's gun was waiting to take down her older son.

Clara remembered dropping the gun on the hardwood floor at Mrs. Flannery's house and the sound of it crashing down.

Derek moved the revolver back and forth, turning it in his hands, the moonlight reflecting off the silver metal.

No, Clara thought from somewhere deep inside her, that instinct. *He can't do this. This can't end here.* "No!" Clara shouted and started towards Derek on the rock.

Derek jumped up and saw Clara. "Stop! Clara!" he screamed.

Clara broke into a sprint as she came at him.

Derek cocked the gun and pointed it at her. "Stop!" he cried.

Clara didn't waver and kept racing forward, pumping her arms. Derek's breath quickening. Clara came straight at him. Derek was paralyzed. Clara grabbed the gun as she barreled into him. Derek gasped. The revolver went off as Clara wrestled it away and pointed it at him, stepping back, aiming the weapon straight at Derek's heart, shaking, fury raging within her until the tears came. "You did that to her! You killed her!" Clara shouted. "You killed Emmeline McGuire! And you didn't know! You didn't hear her!" The pain and tears gushed out. "And she loved you," Clara cried in a whisper. "You were like her brother. Why couldn't you hear her?"

Clara could barely see Derek through her tears. She tried to focus, hands shaking, looking over the top of the barrel at his eyes drowning in sorrow.

He was silent

Which enraged Clara more. "You didn't hear her!" Clara screamed, "Like she heard you!" Tears flowed down Clara's cheeks as she shuddered under the weight and sadness of it all. "Why couldn't you have just heard her say no?!"

"Just kill me, please," Derek said.

"No," Clara replied.

"Why?" Derek pleaded.

Clara stared at him, unsure. Finally, the answer came. "Emmeline isn't done with you," she told him and shuddered as she said it, then whispered, "And neither is Seamus."

Which is when Derek broke down and wept, buckling to the ground. Clara's heart squeezed with sorrow. She tried to yell but it came out broken and hoarse: "Get up. Please just fucking get up."

Derek pulled himself together, standing back up. He nodded, unable to look at Clara, then started walking towards her along the path. She backed up, keeping the gun pointed at him, letting him walk around her, seeing the tears stream down his face as he passed.

43

Restless Soul Raging

Clara didn't know what to do or think or feel after that night had passed—the night Derek led her back to the rectory and the police detectives took him in. Derek told them everything he knew. He confessed to sleeping with Emmeline and that they had been drinking and that he hadn't realized Emmeline was unwilling to sleep with him at the time. Derek told them that he had probably been too drunk to hear what Emmeline was saying in the moment but that Emmeline had expressed her anger to him afterwards. They also had Emmeline's diary as evidence that Derek was the father of her child and that Emmeline hadn't wanted to have sex with him or to be pregnant.

Derek confessed that he and Emmeline had fought at the clearing where his parents were laid to rest, and as Emmeline had pulled away, she'd fallen back and hit her head on their mother's gravestone. Derek confided that he had panicked and buried her in the coffin. Derek didn't try to defend himself in any way in his statement and didn't mention that Emmeline had wanted to run away and that the fighting was because he had wanted her to stay and loved her and had wanted them to be a family with their baby. But their disagreement about the baby was in the diary—where it said that Emmeline had wanted to get rid of this problem and didn't know where to go.

The forensics report confirmed that Emmeline had died from a blunt hit to the head from the headstone, and Derek's story made sense. No one knew that Emmeline wasn't dead when Derek put her in the coffin, including Derek, and that she had suffocated to death in Stella Dunne's coffin. Emmeline hadn't needed to die.

If only there hadn't been so much fear, Clara thought as she heard Derek's statement. *Everything would've been different.* Clara didn't mention that Emmeline had suffocated to death and hadn't died from hitting her head. She didn't mention how she knew so much about Emmeline. She also didn't mention that the rape was a blurry confusion and that she was almost certain that Derek had heard Emmeline tell him to stop. Seamus testified to the fight at the grave, and the DA prosecuted Derek for involuntary manslaughter of Emmeline McGuire and date rape, and he was found guilty and sent to prison.

After that night at the grave and the confession and conviction, Clara thought Emmeline was free. Her truth had come out—how she had died and who had killed her. Justice had been served, and Derek had expressed remorse. But Emmeline was not free and continued to appear to Clara. After that night at the grave, whenever Emmeline appeared, she was mostly sullen and quiet. She didn't threaten Clara or her baby or show anger towards Seamus. She simply sat with her head down and cried.

Then, every once in a while, Emmeline would rage in front of Clara with a guttural scream at the heavens or anyone in the ether that was listening. It seemed to Clara to be a cry of frustration, a fury that, once again, only Clara could hear and feel. It was as if there was something Emmeline couldn't fix or change, and that enraged her, like Clara had felt before with the miscarriages and the asthma that had now disappeared.

Why hadn't those feelings subsided for Emmeline? Clara wondered.

Clara spoke to Dr. Goldberg after that night at the grave and over the next few months, but only on the phone. She couldn't bring herself to go to Dr. Goldberg's office. Clara mentioned to Dr. Goldberg that Emmeline was lingering and expressing mostly sadness—no threats, only intermittent internal rage, like it was coming from the core of her being. Clara told Dr. Goldberg that she just couldn't make sense of it. "Emmeline should be happy," Clara insisted. "I gave her what she wanted. Justice is served. Why is she doing this?"

Dr. Goldberg told Clara what Clara didn't want to hear: that there was likely more beneath the proverbial surface to uncover.

"I don't want to hear it," Clara confirmed to Dr. Goldberg. "I just want Emmeline to go away and leave me alone. Why is she doing this to me?"

"Because she is deeply connected to you," Dr. Goldberg said.

Clara hated this.

Dr. Goldberg sensed it but continued, "You have to accept it, and like any story or reality, there are many sides. What is Emmeline's story? Why was she with Derek? Did she love him? And why? Or did she love Seamus? What is her anger about? What is her sadness? You don't know anything about Emmeline—only about what happened to her."

"So, why didn't she tell me?" Clara demanded, as if Dr. Goldberg had an answer. "Why didn't she write *that* in the diary?"

"Maybe she did," Dr. Goldberg suggested. "In another diary. Is there a diary that came before?"

"I don't know!" Clara snapped, feeling so frustrated again.

"Maybe someday we'll know," Dr. Goldberg said. "But it's likely Emmeline didn't write it in the diary you found because that was about her pregnancy. And she probably didn't tell you because she was traumatized by the pregnancy and her death. And when traumatized, all you can see is the trauma, until it's addressed."

"She's a ghost!" Clara cried.

"Or more," Dr. Goldberg insisted.

Clara backed down when she heard this. She knew there could still be something else going on with her own reality and forced herself to continue calmly. She needed Dr. Goldberg to back off. "It's dealt with," Clara stated in a clear, diplomatic tone. "Justice. Emmeline got justice, and she should just tell me then what it is. It's not fair."

"Maybe this story is harder to tell," Dr. Goldberg argued. "It's easy to be angry at others, but if there's sorrow beneath the anger, that's more complicated. And perhaps, Emmeline at sixteen didn't even really know what was happening or her reason for spending time with Derek, perhaps loving him, when she also loved Seamus."

"You don't know this!" Clara shouted again, losing all composure. "You don't know anything! You're just spit-balling!"

"Yes, I am," Dr. Goldberg confirmed this painful truth—which was almost worse for both of them because it meant Dr. Goldberg didn't have the answers either.

"I can't do this," Clara said. "It's too much. Emmeline is asking too much of me. And I have to go. I'm sorry. Thank you for your help." Clara was unable to finish the conversation and hung up. She decided that she would stick to that—calmly saying, *No, thank you*, whenever Emmeline appeared. And she continued to ignore Emmeline as her baby grew inside her.

After that last phone conversation, Dr. Goldberg sent Clara a note telling her that when Clara was ready, the door was always open. *You've dealt with Seamus and Derek's pain but not Emmeline's,* Dr. Goldberg wrote. *When you're ready, I trust you will be able to truly set her free, completely, and be done.*

This isn't my pain to deal with! Clara wrote back.

Dr. Goldberg replied: *But maybe you're here to help Emmeline. Maybe that's your path at this moment in time.*

Clara wrote: *I'm not going there! It's not my responsibility. It's hers.*

Dr. Goldberg replied: *And if you are her?*

Clara wrote: *I'm done. Thank you for everything.*

Clara assumed Dr. Goldberg was going off the deep end. Maybe that was the nature of being an analyst—always finding more to uncover, more to heal, more work to do—but for Clara, the searching was over. Seamus was happy. They were both back into their life in the city. Clara was even going in to work at Frock three days a week, even though she was as big as a house. And the baby was thriving inside her.

And then, the baby was born—a girl. They named her Lucia—bringer of light. And Lucia *was* the light, beautiful, happy, healthy, perfect, and Clara felt a love she'd never felt before. And Seamus wept with joy.

And Emmeline sat in the corner in the hospital room and wept with sadness when Lucia was born and raged at the heavens. And Clara felt it to the core of her being.

44

Going to the Source

Baby Lucia brought love and light to the Dunne home in the city. Everyone was overjoyed. Clara's parents visited. Clara and Seamus visited them with the baby in Brussels.

It was everything Clara had dreamed of—except for the fact that Emmeline McGuire was still around, not talking, sinking deeper into despair, the rages disappearing, no fire at all, like she was giving up, and under the surface, Clara was sinking too.

Clara hid her sadness well—all that learned diplomacy paying off. Billy was the only one who noticed what was under Clara's surface. He'd moved into a studio in the Village, was finishing up a couple of classes at the junior college and heading to NYU for grad school in the fall. He was clean, and he and Clara went for long walks through the city weekly, which is when Billy felt Clara's hidden sadness even though she didn't tell him about Emmeline still being around.

Dr. Goldberg was the only one who knew about Emmeline's continued presence, and Clara had made Dr. Goldberg swear not to tell anyone, especially Seamus. Clara was sure Mrs. Flannery would've felt the sadness too had she seen Clara—or been in her vicinity. Mrs. Flannery had such a good second sense, but Clara wasn't ready for that and kept promising Mrs. Flannery on the phone that she'd bring baby Lucia out to see her in the country.

"No, no, you wait," Mrs. Flannery would reply. "Billy's going to come bring me to the city."

So, Clara and Mrs. Flannery made a plan for the end of the coming summer when Billy would be done with his classes and the baby would be bigger. Clara suspected that Mrs. Flannery knew somehow about Emmeline. Clara didn't know why she had that suspicion, but maybe it was enough to understand that Mrs. Flannery was just like that—with her special gift of knowing.

Then, summer rolled around, and everything became so bright again in the world, and Clara couldn't bear Emmeline's suffering any longer, so she made an appointment with Dr. Goldberg. Clara had also decided to tell Erin about Emmeline being there in the city. She figured Erin would understand somehow or pretend to and make jokes—which is exactly what happened. Erin agreed to babysit Lucia while Clara went under hypnosis again.

Erin was worried when the day came—but in a kind of Erin-respectful-devil's-advocate kind of way, like she'd go with Clara's choice and do her best to be there for Clara no matter what, but still asked: "Are you sure you want to do this?"

"No," admitted Clara. "I don't want to do this at all, but I'm sinking."

'What if it never stops?" Erin added, joking. "What if you go there and it never stops? It keeps going? Further? More issues? Emmeline's past lives?" Erin grinned.

"That's exactly what I was thinking," Clara confided, and it made her laugh. Hearing it out of Erin's lips made the thought bearable though, made it smaller, and funny. Erin truly was a relief. Because Emmeline's ongoing presence was absurd, and Clara had to become untrapped and unafraid of the absurdity. "I mean, *exactly*," Clara repeated and joked, "What if I have to deal with Emmeline's past lives and Seamus's in addition to my own?" They both thought this was hilarious, even though there was more truth there than either of them wanted to admit, and Clara smiled at her friend, forever grateful for her humor, the only thing that ever helped. Clara hugged Erin, this time squashing baby Lucia between them, not Henry, who was now ambling about. Lucia squealed with delight.

Erin grinned again, "Okay, fine, maybe you will be okay, in spite of this mumbo jumbo."

Clara agreed, and Erin drove her to Dr. Goldberg's and took the kids to Central Park. But not before she told Dr. Goldberg, "I'll have my phone on stand-by if you need me," and wrote her number in giant Sharpee on a Post-It note that she stuck on Dr. Goldberg's desk.

"Thank you," said Dr. Goldberg. "I think we'll be fine. I've done much research on the topic of past life regression in the past few months."

"Ohhhh, nooo!" Erin teased.

"And I'm convinced," Dr. Goldberg continued without skipping a beat, "that hypnosis and going to the source in the past is where the healing lies for Clara. And Emmeline. Together with forgiveness," she added and looked directly at Clara for emphasis.

Clara got chills and suddenly felt nauseous.

"Are you okay?" Dr. Goldberg asked.

"Yes, I just need a sip of water," Clara told her, opening her bottle and taking a small sip. Erin felt uncertain. Clara could tell but told her to leave, "I have to do this, Erin, or it's going to take me down. You have a nice time at the park."

"And there you have the golden rule of moms," Erin chirped. "Lead by example. And that means take care of yourself and get your own life in a good place first, because you can't give what you don't have." Erin laughed and added, "As if I know," taking the piss out of herself. And then, she left.

45

The Uncovering of Emmeline McGuire

The hypnosis session began as it always did. Dr. Goldberg led Clara to her safe and peaceful spot, and Clara declared, "Okay, I'm here," when she found herself back on the rock overlooking the clear-blue lake and pine-filled valley.

But this time was going to be different Dr. Goldberg informed Clara. She was going to take Clara back farther—back to before she was born to see what was there. To see if they could find Emmeline. To see if Clara and Emmeline were truly connected, whether in spirit or through Seamus or a continuation of lives.

Before the session, Clara had told Dr. Goldberg everything that had happened with Emmeline and had given her the diary so Dr. Goldberg knew as much about Emmeline as Clara did and was prepared to delve into Emmeline's past and find the source of her sadness and pain. "Okay, Clara, now today, we are going to go slowly into the safe space of when you were born, right after your birth," Dr. Goldberg began, "into your parents' arms. Imagine what that feels like and know that I'm here holding you safe to come back to your rock at any time. Your rock is here for you, supporting and protecting you. Okay?"

Clara nodded and took a deep breath and slowly let herself drift into her past with her whole, relaxed being. It was dark for a moment with specks of light, like a tunnel, and then, there was just a vast plane of black with light on what seemed to be a horizon. Then, a FLASH, a BAM. And Clara saw her parents' faces, both smiling down at her, and she felt her mother's warm arms holding her tight. It was blurry. She felt safe.

"Okay, I think you are there," Dr. Goldberg said. "Are you there at your birth, Clara?"

Clara had no words. Instead, she made gurgling sounds. Her mind was aware as adult Clara, but her voice had embodied herself as a baby. This was different from the last hypnosis when she had started as an observer then went in and out of observing and being her younger self or the girl, Emmeline, jumping on the bed. Today, Clara went straight to *being* her younger self.

"Yes, Clara, I think you are there at your birth," Dr. Goldberg continued. "I see joy and peace. That is nice, Clara. Your parents love you, Clara."

Clara made another sound, feeling the joy, aware enough to confirm what Dr. Goldberg was saying.

"And now, we are going to go to what happened before," Dr. Goldberg went on. "Let's go to the last happy moment before your birth—when you felt this happy and safe and loved. Let's go there."

Clara saw another light FLASH and heard a BAM, whooshing, white, love, perfect love, tunnel, light, sounds. Were they voices? Clara wondered. Yes. Voices. Watching. Understanding. Knowing. Being. Love. Perfection.

Dr. Goldberg saw Clara's face completely relax. Clara seemed to have an aura of light about her and exuded something like bliss. "I see you made it," Dr. Goldberg said. "You are in happiness, safe. You are loved."

Clara didn't move or react. Dr. Goldberg was in awe. It was as if she could feel the bliss radiating off of Clara. Dr. Goldberg wanted to stay there in that moment and observe—it was so otherworldly, confirming everything she'd been reading in her research about past lives and the time in between. But Dr. Goldberg was still just hoping, not yet believing, and she knew she couldn't just leave Clara there in the in-between. So, she continued, "Okay, now, Clara, let's go back in human time to when you last felt happy and safe and loved."

Then, another FLASH, a BAM, and Clara was a girl, riding a bike. Laughing. Wind in her face. Riding with her friend, a sandy-haired boy. They were about twelve. Clara narrated for Dr. Goldberg, saying that she knew the boy's name was Seamus. They were laughing. Riding through town. Wind in her hair, hair flying back and in her face, red hair. And there was another boy speeding up past them, racing them. "His name is Derek," Clara told Dr. Goldberg, now speaking in the girl's voice as if she was the girl, experiencing everything the girl was experiencing.

The girl continued narrating for Dr. Goldberg. Derek was older, she said. She and Seamus fell behind him on their bikes but raced on. The girl beat Seamus, but it was funny to both of them, and they continued on the road for a while then veered off into the woods along a mossy path and rode down a hill.

"Okay," Dr. Goldberg said to Clara as the girl. "It looks like you are happy. Here. And where you were before."

"Before?" Clara asked in the girl's voice.

Dr. Goldberg hesitated. She wanted to find out more about the transition between the lives and to see if the girl remembered the in-between and how the girl related to it. But as soon as Dr. Goldberg saw the girl's confusion, she realized that this discussion had to wait. It could be a bad choice. So, she changed tactics. "I mean, *now*—you look happy on your bike with Seamus now," Dr. Goldberg reflected back.

"Yes," the girl confirmed, beaming with laughter. "I am happy."

"Where are you?" Dr. Goldberg asked.

"I'm on my bike," the girl replied.

"What's your name?" Dr. Goldberg continued.

"Emmeline McGuire," she said.

"How old are you?" Dr. Goldberg asked.

"Twelve."

"Who are you with?"

"My best friend."

"Who's that?" Dr. Goldberg asked.

"Seamus Dunne," the girl told her.

"How old is he?"

"Eleven," the girl said. "I'm a year older."

"So, why do you like Seamus? Why is he your friend?" Dr. Goldberg went on.

"We're building a game," the girl explained. "Me and Seamus. And he's so happy. I love going to his house."

"Why?" Dr. Goldberg asked.

"At my house, there are so many kids, all my brothers and sisters," the girl replied. "I just work on homework and chores. No one cares about me. Or gets me. I mean, they love me, but they think I'm weird because I like to think so much."

"How is it different at Seamus's house?" Dr. Goldberg pressed.

"His parents are so nice!" the girl exclaimed. "And his brother too. And we have dinner and play games and laugh. I get to stay late. His mom makes us hot cocoa or lemonade in the summer and always some special dessert. Like homemade ice cream. Or peach pie. I get to help make the ice cream. We put it on the pie. I also like Mrs. Dunne's brownies."

"That's nice," Dr. Goldberg said.

"Yeah," agreed the girl, and she smiled at Dr. Goldberg, even though Clara's eyes were closed.

"What do you talk about with Seamus?" Dr. Goldberg continued.

"Uh, I don't know, the dragon? And how he's going to get to the end of the game?" the girl shrugged.

"What kind of game?" Dr. Goldberg asked.

"On the computer," she explained.

"Tell me about the dragon," Dr. Goldberg went on.

"Well, he's the hero in the game," the girl continued. "But not like a regular hero, you know. Because usually, the knight is trying to slay the dragon. But this is a gentle dragon. People only think he's a monster because they don't understand him. So, they're afraid of him. I like that."

"That he's a monster?" Dr. Goldberg asked.

"That he's gentle and kind and funny," the girl said with a smile.

"So, is there a knight in the game?" Dr. Goldberg asked.

"Yeah, he's funny too," the girl continued. "And more of a brainy knight than a warrior. And he loves this girl. Her name is Anna-Devana. She's named after a character in a book I love, that's Russian, Anna Karenina, and a Slavic goddess, Devana. One day, I'm gonna learn Russian and go there. Somehow, I just know I'll be good at it and love it there. Anyway, the knight's love, this girl Anna-Devana, is even more of a warrior and hunter than he is. She's like the Slavic Artemis, goddess of the hunt and animals and nature. So, when the knight is sent out to kill the dragon, Anna-Devana sneaks out and goes with him."

"Wow, this is amazing," Dr. Goldberg complimented.

"Yeah, I think it's gonna be good. Seamus's writing the code. And I'm making the story," the girl explained, full of confidence and joy.

"It's some story," Dr. Goldberg praised, noting that the girl loved *Anna Karenina* just like Clara did.

"Well, then, you have to hear the end," the girl continued, "because what happens is that Anna-Devana is very curious and finds out that the dragon had to raise himself, like most dragons do, and all he ever wanted was love and a family. But when the dragon tries to make friends, he breathes fire. So, people think he's trying to kill them. But really, he's like Frankenstein—he's just so nice. And misunderstood. And the girl warrior has to convince the knight not to be afraid. And that's how you win the game: When you aren't afraid, there's no more monster dragon to worry about, as if you're wearing new glasses and can see everything clearly. So, the dragon becomes nice, and he's your friend and you can fly to the castle with him and everyone in the land sees that they don't need to be afraid because there's no monster."

"Wow!" Dr. Goldberg exclaimed. "Did you think that up?"
"Yeah, sort of," the girl replied. "I mean, I didn't really think about it too hard. It was more like the story and the characters just popped into my head."

Clara laughed in her own voice for a moment, like she'd been pulled back to observe the girl from the present and was pleased about the story and hearing the origin of the game.

"I see," said Dr. Goldberg, unsure how to react.

Then, Clara popped back to the past and continued as Emmeline, "And Seamus wrote the game. The way it works is that the person that's playing the knight in the game has to find treasure chests. And in the treasure chests are clues that tell you the story and make you not afraid of the dragon. So, it's quite simple and fun too. And then, there's the bad guy, who's kind of like a mayor or someone that runs the kingdom for the king, but he's kind of sneaky. So, if you're the bad guy in the game, you don't want the knight and warrior girl to get the treasure chests, so you try to stop them. Because if the knight never finds out that the dragon isn't a monster and doesn't tell the people how nice the dragon is, you can rule the land. Because as long as the people think the dragon is bad and that he's going to burn them to the ground with his fire breath, they're afraid of him, and they'll pay you tons of money to protect them from the not-mean dragon. And then, you win. And all the nice people lose."

"That is a wonderful, wise and complicated story," Dr. Goldberg declared with an admiring laugh.

"Like I said," the girl continued, "the actual game isn't that complicated, but then, you get to find the little secret story truth-bombs when you find each bit of treasure."

"So, how did you come up with that game?" Dr. Goldberg asked. "You said you came up with the story without thinking?"

"Yeah. I don't know. It was just there in my head, like I said," the girl reiterated. "Both the story and the way the game should go."

"And you're just twelve and eleven—you and Seamus?"

"Yes," she confirmed.

"I see," said Dr. Goldberg, astonished by how odd and bright this girl Emmeline was. She could see how Seamus would be an oasis for her. "Thank you so much for telling me all about your game, Emmeline," Dr. Goldberg said.

"Of course! It's fun to talk about," the girl chimed, not blinking at being called Emmeline.

"Okay, then," Dr. Goldberg continued, taking note that Clara was definitely Emmeline right now. "Now, let's see if we can find something else fun to talk about. Like how about if we go forward to when you're fourteen, Emmeline. Do you still have dinner with Seamus and his family?"

"Yes!" Clara exclaimed in Emmeline's fourteen-year-old voice. The transition forward through time was seamless. She sat up taller with an older demeanor and lit up with a bright smile on her face.

"Oh, good," replied Dr. Goldberg, taking note of the joy Clara exuded, even though her eyes were still shut. "That's so nice for you."

Fourteen-year-old Emmeline nodded her head.

"Anything else?" continued Dr. Goldberg. "How's the game going?"

"Good!" Emmeline exclaimed. "Seamus's got it going with the code, and I'm helping by doing the designs."

"Drawing?"

"A little," Emmeline explained. "I'm not that good, but I can sketch and doodle, and then, we're going to get someone to make the art better."

"And tell me more about the fun dinners with the Dunnes," Dr. Goldberg went on, "and what you like about them. You said they're nice. Can you elaborate?"

"Well, I guess it's super nice that they encourage me," Emmeline told Dr. Goldberg. "Mr. Dunne spoke to the principal when I was in sixth grade, and the school let me skip a grade. Like Seamus. He skipped two actually. Which is funny because I can tease him about it, and so, I always call him pipsqueak, even though we're both pipsqueaks at school, relatively. And Mr. Dunne always pays for me and Seamus to go to science camp. He's done it every summer since we were in seventh grade together. Actually, when we were little too. He helped my mom and dad pay for stuff. Even in elementary. My parents didn't really get how important it was to me to go to camp. Or that it mattered. And they didn't have the money anyways."

"Do you still go to science camp?" Dr. Goldberg asked, pressing further.

"It's more coding camp now, for the last two years, since we started the game," Emmeline explained. "Seamus's really into coding."

"You too?" Dr. Goldberg asked.

"Yeah. It's fun. I like coming up with the stories mostly though. And making up the characters. Like I told you."

"Well, that's really cool of Mr. Dunne," Dr. Goldberg said.

"Yeah," agreed Emmeline. "And he took me and Seamus to DC when we won the state championship science fair." She beamed proudly.

"This year?" Dr. Goldberg asked.

"The past three years," Emmeline told her with a shy giggle. "And we went to nationals. Mr. Dunne thinks I'm going to be some kind of genius scientist. And he teases Seamus that he'll be my assistant."

"And Seamus is okay with that?" Dr. Goldberg wondered.

"Yeah. He's pretty chill. And he gets it because it might be true." Emmeline joked. "I'm joking. That's how we roll, and it's good. Like I'm free. I'm totally free there at Seamus's house."

"Free from what?" Dr. Goldberg asked.

"Just, I don't know, not being able to do stuff. People not getting me or something." Emmeline looked uncomfortable.

"Who doesn't get you?" Dr. Goldberg asked.

"My family. Teachers. Anybody. No one gets me," Emmeline explained.

"So, you're smart?" Dr. Goldberg asked with a bit of playfulness.

Clara's cheeks turned red as Emmeline blushed.

"What do they not get?" Dr. Goldberg pressed.

"Everything," Emmeline told her. "I mean, not in a mean way, just in general."

"So, is Seamus your boyfriend?" Dr. Goldberg asked as nonchalantly as possible.

Emmeline got quiet and the blood rushed to Clara's cheeks again—this time they turned bright red. "No," Emmeline declared. "We're best friends. I love Seamus though. I don't know what that means either. Except that I'm most happy when I'm with him and especially when we're with his family."

"And what about Derek, when you play games at dinner? What's he like?" Dr. Goldberg tested cautiously.

Clara blushed again. "He always tells me I look pretty."

"Derek does? Do you like that?" Dr. Goldberg asked.

"Yes," Emmeline said, and there was more blushing and embarrassed laughter. "Though, I guess it's superficial and stupid. But Derek's super popular, and so coming from him, it's nice. Especially me being such a nerd and always getting teased. It's like Derek protects me from the jerks at school. And he protects Seamus too. Though, Seamus usually just ignores the assholes. He's really into his games and doesn't care and just thinks the other stupid people at school are a stupid distraction."

"So, is Derek your boyfriend?" Dr. Goldberg asked.

Emmeline became silent—then shook her head *no* and let out a nervous giggle.

"Do you *want* Derek to be?" Dr. Goldberg pressed.

Emmeline looked down at her hands in her lap as if embarrassed. "I don't think that's a thing," she said and smirked. "That's okay, I guess."

"But you like him? Derek? At least the way you like Seamus?" Dr. Goldberg inquired.

"Yeah, I mean. I totally like him," Emmeline admitted. "It's different from Seamus though. I'm a little more...awkward. With Seamus that's never a thing. I'm comfortable with Seamus. Like, just myself."

"So, what do you like about Derek? I mean, like a brother, like Seamus."

Emmeline lit up. "He's so much fun. He's really good at sports, and he takes me and Seamus out on the lake all the time."

"Is Derek jealous of you and Seamus?"

"No!" Emmeline declared.

"Why not?" Dr. Goldberg asked.

"Because he's super into sports and not into computers and that kind of science-y stuff. And you know, that's not a thing in their family anyways—I mean being jealous. My family is jealous some-times. Like everyone—I mean, my brothers and sisters—they get jealous if someone gets something and another person doesn't."

"Are they jealous of you?" Dr. Goldberg pressed. "Your brothers and sisters?"

Emmeline stopped to think for a moment before answering. "Maybe. I can't tell though. It's more like they always just make fun of me for being so into science. I guess they could be jealous, but I'm not sure why they would be or if that makes sense."

"It might," Dr. Goldberg agreed. "I guess we'd have to ask them, right?"

"Yeah," Emmeline said, softening, letting herself be vulnerable, as if she felt safe with Dr. Goldberg, like she was being heard. "It's a little sad that I don't even know how my own family thinks."

"You're not alone. A lot of families are like that. But you seem certain that Derek isn't jealous of you and Seamus being so tight and doing so much cool stuff with the game and science competitions. Would you care to guess why Derek isn't jealous?"

"Maybe because their parents are so nice and totally encourage Derek too?" Emmeline suggested. "And he's so talented. In a differ-ent way from Seamus. He wants to be a musician or an actor or football player."

"Do you think he's good enough?"

"Yeah," Emmeline admitted. "And his parents tell him that too. Which is great."

"They're not just saying that?" Dr. Goldberg asked. "Because they're his parents?"

"No," Emmeline confirmed. "They're pretty real and everything." She seemed to be getting more certain and confident talking about the Dunnes the more she considered it and the more Dr. Goldberg listened.

"So, they're happy," Dr. Goldberg asserted.

"Yes," Emmeline assured her.

"And that makes you happy, Emmeline?"

Emmeline beamed. "I'm so happy."

"You feel loved, I see."

"Yes. Yes, I feel loved," Emmeline confirmed.

"By the whole Dunne family," Dr. Goldberg stated.

"Yes!" Emmeline declared, no doubt in her voice.

"And your parents are okay that you spend so much time there?"

"Yeah, they like the Dunnes," Emmeline explained. "And maybe they're relieved. They don't know what to do with me. And they're grateful to Mr. Dunne for helping and supporting me." Emmeline looked down at her hands, as if embarrassed again.

"That doesn't make you uncomfortable?" Dr. Goldberg pressed.

"A super tiny bit, like how come they're so nice to me? But not that much. Mostly, I feel a little sad," Emmeline replied. "Like I wish my parents could enjoy it too, the science stuff and the video games, and my brothers and sisters also, but that's not a thing. My mom says that people are different. That's what makes the world go round. And somehow, I got the smart gene like Seamus. And they're grateful for that blessing and thank God that I got to know him.

And she and my dad have the love gene to love me no matter what. That's what my mom always says too."

"Do you think they love you, Emmeline? Your parents?" Dr. Goldberg asked.

"Yes," Emmeline declared, and it seemed to make her happy. Clara's cheeks turned pink. "My parents love me," she said and laughed. "That sounds so dumb."

"No, it's not. It's a blessing, like you said," Dr. Goldberg assured her, seeing that Emmeline was every bit as happy as she claimed to be. "I'm so happy that people hear you. And I'm hoping now that we can do some more talking. But first, I'd like you to imagine looking out at the lake from a high rock and seeing the trees in the valley there, just for fun. Do you see it, Emmeline?"

Emmeline nodded.

"Okay, good," Dr. Goldberg said, checking the connection to Clara before continuing. "And now, we're going to do that thing where we go forward again to when you're about a year and a half older, fifteen, right before the start of summer between your junior and senior year. Let's say early May, so end of junior year."

Emmeline nodded. "I'm fifteen and about to be sixteen, in June," she said and then the smile on her face faded.

Heartbreak

"You're fifteen now, Emmeline?" Dr. Goldberg inquired—as Clara transitioned seamlessly in the hypnosis to being Emmeline at the end of her junior year, a few months after the Dunnes' tragic car accident.

Emmeline nodded, her mood suddenly somber.

"You look sad. Are you sad?" Dr. Goldberg asked.

Emmeline's head dropped as if she were looking down at her hands in her lap, even though Clara's eyes were still closed. Her fingers fidgeted with the red tie on the peach-colored skirt of Clara's wrap dress.

"Why are you so sad, Emmeline?" Dr. Goldberg pressed.

Emmeline shook her head as if she were too heartbroken to speak.

"It's okay," Dr. Goldberg assured her. "You can tell me, and always, you have the lake and the valley and your rock to keep you safe so you won't disappear into the sadness. Is something in your family making you sad, Emmeline?"

Emmeline shook her head *no*.

"At school?" Dr. Goldberg asked.

Emmeline shook her head *no* again.

"With your friends, Seamus and Derek? And Mr. and Mrs. Dunne?"

Emmeline's fingers tensed as she began pulling at Clara's red dress tie now, snapping it taught over and over again nervously.

"Did something happen?" Dr. Goldberg pressed.

Emmeline slowly nodded *yes*, then managed in a whisper, "They died."

"Who died, Emmeline?"

"Mr. and Mrs. Dunne," Emmeline confirmed, her face scrunching and the emotion overwhelming her.

"Oh, I'm so sorry, honey. That is tragic," Dr. Goldberg tried to comfort her.

Emmeline nodded and broke down and cried. Dr. Goldberg was unsure what to do. She started to get up to hug Clara but then backed away and sat back down, not wanting to interrupt Emmeline's natural flow of emotion. The whole thing seemed so real. But it was a hypnosis, Dr. Goldberg reminded herself, and it was working. So, instead of intervening to comfort Emmeline physically, she pressed on to see how Emmeline dealt with the loss at that time in her life. To see if fifteen-year-old Emmeline had anyone to help her with this tragedy. "Did you tell anyone how you feel, Emmeline? How sad you feel?" Dr. Goldberg asked.

Emmeline shook her head *no*. "I don't know what you mean actually. Everyone knows they died."

"But did you talk to anyone about it?" Dr. Goldberg pressed. "Like, did any teachers or your parents or the priest ask you how you feel, Emmeline?"

Emmeline shook her head *no*, and her face bunched up in pain with more tears, and she pushed her fingers on her eyelids and pounded them, trying to get the tears to abate. "I'm sorry," she said.

"It's okay to cry, Emmeline," Dr. Goldberg comforted.

"No, no, it's not," Emmeline insisted, trying desperately to hide her feelings. "But I'm okay," she said, trying to be brave, and wiped her tears and took a deep breath.

"Were your parents sad too, Emmeline?" Dr. Goldberg asked.

Emmeline's face scrunched up again. Then, she let out a groan as if trying to purge the discomfort. "They, they....," she stammered. "My parents, they were, everyone was so sad."

"But not as sad as you," Dr. Goldberg said knowingly, realizing how incredibly alone Emmeline must've felt without Seamus's parents there to understand her and include her in their family.

Emmeline shook her head *no* and whispered, "Not as sad as me."

"What did your parents say, Emmeline? About the Dunnes passing?" Dr. Goldberg pressed.

"That they're in heaven."

"I see," Dr. Goldberg said. "Did you cry at home? Did they see you cry—your parents, Emmeline?"

This made Emmeline tear up again. "Yes. At night," she said. "My mom hugged me. But she didn't know how sad I was."

"What about Seamus and Derek?" Dr. Goldberg asked.

Emmeline's head dropped down. She was still. Dr. Goldberg thought maybe she'd lost her. Then, Clara made a weird, low, motor-like groan and took a breath. "They were...they were...more sad than me," Emmeline said, then wailed out into Clara's chest, head still hanging.

Dr. Goldberg's breath caught as she witnessed such intense grief in Emmeline at the loss of her friend—Seamus and Derek—to their own grief at the loss of their parents. Dr. Goldberg understood now. And she was grateful that she had her thick glasses in that moment, even though Clara's eyes were closed. And she was grateful that she had been trained at maintaining her professionalism even when one of her patients' emotions penetrated her armor. "I understand,"

Dr. Goldberg told Emmeline, sustaining composure in her voice. "It feels so sad. You feel so sad about the loss too, *for* them, for Seamus and Derek's loss. I see that clearly." *That was good*, Dr. Goldberg told herself. *Just narrate what you see.*

Emmeline nodded. And came back up from the depths of sorrow —as if being seen by Dr. Goldberg helped.

"And do you feel anything besides sadness? For yourself and your friends?" Dr. Goldberg asked and told herself to keep asking questions—questions were another great tool she had as an analyst, in addition to reflecting back what she saw.

"I don't know," Emmeline replied.

"Do you feel angry, Emmeline?" Dr. Goldberg pressed. "That this happened?"

"I feel angry that they're so sad," Emmeline said.

"Oh, wow," said Dr. Goldberg.

Then, Emmeline broke down again, shaking her head. Then, she screamed out in rage. Then stopped. "No, no, it's too sad," Emmeline cried. She was shaking, completely vulnerable.

"Do you feel afraid, Emmeline?" Dr. Goldberg asked, trying to bring her back to center.

Emmeline nodded *yes*.

"What are you afraid of?"

"That now...I can't...," she stammered, "that we can't...he can't be happy. I can't be happy. It hurts so bad."

"Who can't be happy, Emmeline?"

"Me."

"And who else?"

"Derek."

"Derek is sad," Dr. Goldberg reflected back.

"He's so sad. Please help him. Can you help him?" Emmeline asked and lifted her head as if waiting for a response.

"Do you think I can help him?" Dr. Goldberg asked.

"I don't know," Emmeline said and her brow furrowed and the anger seemed to bubble again.

"You look angry, Emmeline. Are you angry again? At someone?"

"You!" Emmeline shouted. "No one cares. No one loves them. Their mom and dad loved them. And now, no one."

"Both Seamus and Derek?"

Emmeline stopped—she had to think about this. And couldn't seem to understand.

"No one loves Derek and Seamus?" Dr. Goldberg rephrased the question.

"No!" Emmeline shouted. "They're so sad. Derek is so sad. Please help him."

"Do you want to help them? Him? Emmeline?"

Emmeline nodded and started to fight tears. "I want to help him. I want to make him not so sad. Why is he so sad?!" Then, she screamed from deep within her heart. "Stop being so sad, Derek!" she cried out.

"Why isn't Seamus so sad?" Dr. Goldberg asked.

"I don't know!" Emmeline shouted. "He's not sad! Like Derek! He's not sad." Emmeline dropped her chin.

"When did they die—Mr. and Mrs. Dunne? Can you fill me in, Emmeline?"

"Two months ago," she said. "In March."

"Where are Seamus and Derek now?" Dr. Goldberg inquired.

"At home."

"By themselves?"

"They went to their aunt and uncle's for a week, but now, Derek's taking care of Seamus. Seamus doesn't need it though. He doesn't need to be taken care of." Emmeline sat up taller, as if trying to be brave for Seamus, trying to assure Dr. Goldberg that Seamus was a grown-up. "I mean, Seamus doesn't need help," she reiterated with a faux confidence, but then, the tears broke through her fragile courage and her shoulders dropped.

"Okay, Emmeline, can you go back to your rock above the lake and let your heart feel better?"

Emmeline nodded.

"Okay, now, you can stay on your rock or come back again whenever you want, okay?"

Emmeline nodded again.

"Good, good girl, you are such a strong girl," Dr. Goldberg told her with all the strength she could muster.

"Thank you," Emmeline said.

"You're welcome. I'm happy to listen. And when you're ready, you can tell me more."

"Okay, I think I'm ready," Emmeline stated.

"Great," Dr. Goldberg said. "Then, how about if we jump forward to summer? The summer after junior year. You're sixteen now, right? It's early June, and you're hanging out with Derek. What's that like?"

Emmeline looked down at her hands and smiled to herself like she had a special secret. And Clara's cheeks turned bright red.

47

Behind Seamus's Back

Emmeline felt her cheeks get hot. Dr. Goldberg had just asked her about Derek and what it was like hanging out with him. She'd just turned sixteen, and even though everything had been so dreadful since Seamus and Derek's parents had passed away, now that it was summer and junior year was over, things were becoming a little bit bright again.

"It's summer? Emmeline?" Dr. Goldberg asked.

Emmeline nodded and smiled with a quiet laugh, like she had a secret and was thinking about something mischievous and fun. "Yes," she replied.

"And you're hanging out with Derek?"

"Yes."

"Is he still sad, Emmeline? About his parents?" Dr. Goldberg inquired.

Emmeline reflected, then replied, "He's sad inside still. But happier. And he doesn't show his sadness anymore, except in his eyes. He's relaxed again too and tries to make us feel better, me and Seamus. We have fun again, and he's being funny like normal."

"And do you like to be with Derek, Emmeline?" Dr. Goldberg continued.

"Yes. It's fun," she confirmed. "Like I just said."

"The same as before? Before his parents passed away?" Dr. Goldberg asked carefully.

Emmeline's brow furrowed. "No, of course not. But he's always good at making everyone happy and making sure everyone's having fun, so he's like that again, like he used to be at dinner and school."

"I'm sorry, Emmeline, you're right," Dr. Goldberg admitted. "Of course, it's not the same as before. I shouldn't have said that. But there is joy too. I see it. I see joy about you. Is that true?"

Emmeline nodded.

"And is Derek your boyfriend now, Emmeline?" Dr. Goldberg pressed.

Emmeline shook her head *no*.

"Oh, I just thought..."

"No, he's not," Emmeline insisted.

"Is someone else your boyfriend, Emmeline?" Dr. Goldberg inquired.

Emmeline blushed and shook her head. As if guilty. As if suddenly, she wasn't proud of her secret anymore.

"What are you feeling, Emmeline? You can tell me."

"I...no," Emmeline stammered.

"Where is Seamus?" Dr. Goldberg asked.

Emmeline's chin dropped. "He's still my friend. He's my best friend." Her eyes teared up.

"But that's a good thing," Dr. Goldberg insisted. "Right?"

Emmeline sat up straight. "Yes! It is!" she exclaimed, as if trying to convince herself. Then, her shoulders drooped. "He's sad too. That I flirt with Derek," she admitted.

"But you want to flirt with Derek, right?" Dr. Goldberg pressed.

Emmeline nodded.

"Do you want Derek to be your boyfriend, Emmeline?"

"I don't know," she stated.

"Okay, that makes sense," Dr. Goldberg told her. "It sounds like you love both of them in different ways. Both Seamus and Derek. Does that make sense to you?"

Emmeline hesitated then nodded. "It doesn't feel very good though."

"No, it doesn't, but it's okay and normal," Dr. Goldberg explained, then asked, "So, they both make you feel happy?"

Emmeline was silent, thinking.

"When are you happiest, Emmeline?" Dr. Goldberg pressed.

Emmeline pondered this some more. Then, smiled. "When Seamus and I are building our game," she declared, beaming brightly.

"That's going well?" Dr. Goldberg asked.

"Yes, I think it could be a real game," Emmeline reported cheerfully. "Seamus's working super fast now."

"And then, what makes you happy with Derek?" Dr. Goldberg fished.

Emmeline took a moment to decide. "That he's happy," she said. "It makes me happy when he's happy. And more importantly, it makes Seamus happy too."

"It's important to you that Seamus is happy?"

"Yes."

"And when Derek is happy, it makes Seamus happy?"

"Yes. And Derek loves me maybe. And I feel butterflies when I see him and think about him, and I feel silly and like my whole body feels so good and like I just want more and to be with him more."

"So, why isn't that your happiest?" Dr. Goldberg pressed.

Again, Emmeline pondered the question. "Because it goes away. The happiness I feel with Derek goes away. And then, like when you asked before—I always feel happy with Seamus. Or about Seamus. And that doesn't go away. I think about laughing with him. And I know he'll always be there with me. And he is so chill. He's still sad about his parents too but not so much. Not as much as Derek. And I know he'll be okay too."

"But not Derek?"

Emmeline shook her head and felt her chest tighten. She started to gasp for air—but then her lungs managed to pull some in.

"Are you okay, Emmeline?" Dr. Goldberg asked.

"It's like Derek wants all my air," she stated. "All of me. Like he needs me to be okay so that he'll be okay."

"But you're not okay?"

"I'm very sad still," she admitted.

"That is a lot of responsibility for you. Making sure everyone's happy. Do you think you can help Derek be okay, Emmeline?"

Emmeline's chest started to tighten again. She took a deep breath in and exhaled slowly and steeled herself. "I have to. I have to make it okay for him."

"But it doesn't sound like that's good for *you*, Emmeline," Dr. Goldberg insisted.

"It will be. I'll be okay again when Derek feels better. And he can be there for Seamus, which is really important to both of them. And then, Seamus will always be okay, and we can build our game and story."

Dr. Goldberg nodded, understanding. "You really want to help him. Both of them. And that means helping Derek because he's not as strong as Seamus."

"Yes, I want to give him all the love he needs," she admitted, and then, the tears welled.

Dr. Goldberg understood more, remaining silent for a moment, watching Emmeline feel her desperate sadness. Finally, Dr. Goldberg said, "You don't think Derek can do it on his own? Or with a grownup helping?"

Emmeline shook her head *no*. "Unless you can. But he doesn't know you."

"What about Seamus? And your game?" Dr. Goldberg asked. "How can you help Derek and do that at the same time?"

"I can do both," Emmeline assured her.

"What if you can't? And you have to give up something you love —like the game you're making with Seamus—to help Derek?"

Worry crossed Emmeline's face. "No, yes, it's the only way I think," Emmeline said. "Seamus will pull through, and more than anything, I want him to make his game. And if he doesn't have to worry about Derek being so sad, he'll manage."

"It's all very complicated, isn't it?"

"Yes," Emmeline admitted.

"I want to ask you a personal question, Emmeline. Can I ask you a personal question?" Dr. Goldberg inquired gently.

"I don't know."

"You don't have to answer, but have you had sex with Derek, Emmeline?"

Emmeline shook her head *no*.

Dr. Goldberg pressed, "Do you want to?"

Emmeline's chin dropped as if looking down, vulnerable now, maybe ashamed. "I don't know," Emmeline said.

"Has he asked?"

"No, but we kissed, and he touched my leg. I think that's what he wants."

"How did it feel? When he touched your leg? And you kissed?"

"Good," Emmeline said. "Sorry, that's embarrassing."

"So, do you think you will have sex with Derek?" Dr. Goldberg asked.

Emmeline shook her head *no*.

"Why?" Dr. Goldberg pressed.

"I'd be afraid," Emmeline admitted.

"Of what?"

"I don't know. I don't want to talk about it," Emmeline insisted.

"Okay. I get it. If I had to guess, you'd probably worry about getting pregnant. Or just not being ready. Or wanting to be sure," Dr. Goldberg suggested. "Or you'd be worried that Seamus would find out."

Emmeline's breath caught. She nodded. "I feel sick in my stomach talking about this," she said.

"Okay, I understand," Dr. Goldberg assured her in her most comforting voice. Because she did. Dr. Goldberg now understood that Emmeline slept with Derek and didn't say no forcefully because she didn't want to hurt him more than he was already hurting. Emmeline had put Derek's feelings and heart over her own. And she had thought it would help Seamus in the long run. That was most important. But it was also clear that Emmeline felt shame about what she was doing to herself. About not being herself. Forcing herself to go along with things that made her uncomfortable. Keeping herself from freely being with Seamus. Betraying Seamus by not being herself. While also loving him and wanting to help.

Ah, the complicated mind, gripped by fear instead of love, Dr. Goldberg reflected. And she realized that Emmeline's betrayal of self was the reason Emmeline felt so guilty when Seamus saw her in the guesthouse with Derek. And why Seamus's disappointment hurt so bad. And why Emmeline was disappointed with herself.

It was also the reason Emmeline blamed herself for Derek's pain and for Derek hurting her and not hearing her.

Dr. Goldberg also understood that Emmeline had to forgive herself so that her soul could be at peace. So that Clara could live her own life again. So that Clara could move past her previous life as Emmeline.

Dr. Goldberg didn't even fully believe in this idea of reincarnation, but she couldn't deny this girl that was sitting before her.

"Why don't we now go back to the rock, Emmeline? Okay?" Dr. Goldberg pressed on.

Emmeline agreed.

"And then, we're going to go forward," Dr. Goldberg said. She knew it was time for Clara to come back to the present. "But I want you to focus very hard. Okay?" Dr. Goldberg added, knowing that they had to move past the coffin as quickly as possible.

"Yes," said Emmeline.

"Are you on your rock?"

"Yes," confirmed Emmeline.

"Take a moment of calm. And tell me when you're ready."

Clara's body relaxed as Emmeline breathed in and out slowly for a few minutes, her furrowed brow finally relaxing as well, her hands softening as they rested on the skirt of Clara's peach dress with the red tie. "Okay, I'm ready," Emmeline said.

And Dr. Goldberg began their trek to the time and space that existed in between Emmeline and Clara's lives, an experience neither one of them would ever forget.

48

The Voice In Between Where the Colors Come Together

"Okay, now, Emmeline," Dr. Goldberg told sixteen-year-old Emmeline who was sitting on her meditation rock in Clara's mind. "You're nice and calm on your safe rock overlooking the lake and pines. You can always come back here when you need to. Okay?"

Emmeline nodded.

"And now, we're going to go forward to five months later. To November. You're still sixteen and have started senior year. You're pregnant. You got pregnant mid-June. And you just had a huge fight with Derek in the woods, right at his parents' gravestones. You hit your head, and it's about thirty minutes later, thirty minutes after you hit your head."

"Okay," Emmeline said, her voice fragile. Then FLASH, BAM. She was in the coffin and started gasping for air.

Dr. Goldberg panicked, "Go forward, forward. After the coffin."

Emmeline gasped.

"After the darkness!" Dr. Goldberg shouted.

More gasping.

"After you stop breathing!" Dr. Goldberg grabbed the inhaler, ready to go. "More!" she insisted.

One last gasp, and suddenly, Emmeline was able to take a long, deep breath. Sweat beads appeared on Clara's forehead. Then, suddenly, her whole body relaxed and peace came across her being. It filled the room, like at the beginning of the hypnosis.

Dr. Goldberg didn't know what to do. "Uh, Clara?"

Clara didn't respond. Dr. Goldberg started to worry again. "Where are you, Emmeline?"

Again, no response.

"It's okay," Dr. Goldberg said, unsure, waiting for a moment to see if anything would happen. It felt safe for Clara, but Dr. Goldberg was afraid again about going into uncharted territory, and she decided to move on. After all, today's hypnosis was beyond incredible already. She had what she needed to help Emmeline and Clara be at peace. "Okay, then," Dr. Goldberg continued. "Now, we are going to move forward back to Clara's birth. Is that what comes next? Where are you, Clara?"

A different, strange, husky voice came out of Clara. "The soul is in review," the voice said.

Dr. Goldberg's breath caught. "Of Emmeline?" she managed. Her heart began to race. "The soul of Emmeline is in review?"

"Yes," the voice confirmed.

Dr. Goldberg gasped. What was this? Who was this? Were they safe? She didn't know, but Clara looked peaceful and she'd read about past life regressions that went through this phase—a phase where they met other beings. And learned. About life. Here and beyond. And the crossing of times. And Dr. Goldberg was mesmerized and astonished, so she continued, "Can you tell me what it is that happened to Emmeline that she can't let go of, so we can help? So I can understand and help Emmeline? And Clara?"

"The soul can do it," the husky voice said.

"Help?" Dr. Goldberg croaked. "The soul can help?"

"Yes," the voice replied.

"How can it help?" Dr. Goldberg asked. "Or how can I help?"

Silence.

"Who are you?" Dr. Goldberg continued.

"Us. Everything," the husky voice explained through Clara.

"What can I do to help Emmeline? And Clara?" Dr. Goldberg repeated.

"Emmeline has no faith that there is still love. That the dark-haired boy..."

"Derek?" Dr. Goldberg interjected.

"Yes. She has no faith that Derek can love. That love continues. She did not believe or understand that continuum of love."

"And the sandy-haired boy?" Dr. Goldberg asked.

"He holds the love," the voice confirmed.

"Why?" Dr. Goldberg asked and watched Clara chuckle subtly, as if the being or the Everything had a sense of humor.

"You ask many questions," the voice said.

Dr. Goldberg blushed.

"He is wise," the voice continued on to her question, "the sandy-haired boy. Seamus he is called. His science told him the universe is love. Humans cannot explain it or understand. But he understands in his heart, so he is not afraid to love. And his pain doesn't take him away from love. His pain grieves and allows space for healing. More so than the other boy and girl."

"The other girl, being Emmeline?"

"She could not believe in the love," the voice repeated. "And in its continuation for the dark-haired boy and the elders, the parents, as you say. She became overwhelmed by the dark-haired boy's sadness. She was sad because she loved him. And he made her feel loved before the parents died. She suffered from the loss of joy she experienced upon the parents' death and did not recover."

"So, Emmeline's love for Derek was different from her love for the sandy-haired boy?" Dr. Goldberg repeated, trying to get a grip on this.

"Not different love but different sadness. As Emmeline, she did not need to grieve the sandy-haired boy. He was love. And she loved him. She wanted to take the sadness away from the dark-haired boy because he couldn't do it on his own, and she caused herself more pain. She is bound by the pain, his pain, and cannot fly. She binds herself because she doesn't want to leave him behind. She believes that if she flies with joy, she will leave him behind."

"Now? Today? Still bound? Emmeline is still bound? And so is Clara?"

"Yes," the voice confirmed.

Dr. Goldberg felt this to her core. She felt the edges of her boundaries shattering, breaking down, as if she were feeling Emmeline's sadness now too. "I'm sorry, I'm sorry," she said, tears welling, unable to hold them back. "Please help me," Dr. Goldberg cried, losing all composure. "I don't know why this is affecting me like this."

"Because of your son," the husky voice said.

"I don't have a son," Dr. Goldberg insisted and the tears hit hard.

"Jeremy," the voice said.

Dr. Goldberg's breath caught.

"He died when he was three," the husky voice said. "And you don't let yourself live. You are bound too, like Emmeline. You don't believe in the continuation of the love you have with your son. You bind yourself, your wings, like Emmeline. Like a trapped animal. You don't want to let yourself live and leave your son behind. That is your fear. That is your tie that binds you."

Dr. Goldberg had to look away. Breathing, in, out. Pain. Heart clenching. She shook her head, trying to understand, then finally looked back up at Clara. Her eyes were still closed, but she was emanating the energy of some kind of otherworldly brilliance. "How do you know this?" Dr. Goldberg managed. "Clara doesn't...nobody here knows that. About my son."

"He wants you to fly," the voice told her. "Your son wants you to love his sister. He wants you all to fly. So that he can move on too. That part of him—holding tightly to your pain—still exists as it moves through your human time. It exists until you fly."

Dr. Goldberg couldn't comprehend. But there was Clara in her blissful state, eyes closed.

"Shine a light on the pain. Unbind your wings. And fly, Maxine," the voice told her. "And the love will continue. It always does. Forever connecting you to your son," and then, the voice went silent. Clara's chin dropped to her chest.

Dr. Goldberg panicked, "Okay, okay," she said, pulling herself together. "Clara? Okay, Clara, now, come back. Come back to Clara, just born, in your mom and dad's arms. When you were so happy." Dr. Goldberg struggled to keep it together, tears streaming down her face, so happy that Clara's eyes were closed. She had to pull it together before Clara came back to the present. And she had to make sure Clara came back.

49

Love That Binds

Clara was floating in the womb, back and forth as if in space and attached to a rubber band that was pulling her between the farthest stars on each corner of the vastness—back, forth, back, forth, peaceful but monotonous and confining. And then, Clara was pulled back and suddenly into her mom and dad's arms as a baby. And then, finally, Clara was back to her peaceful, happy place on the rock overlooking the clear-blue lake and the pine-filled valley. "Okay, I'm here," Clara stated.

"Excellent," Dr. Goldberg agreed, unable to hide the relief in her voice as she brought Clara back into the room in New York City in present time.

Clara had been able to follow everything during the hypnosis but was unsure about what had happened between the two lives. There were beings. Love. A guide helping Emmeline, but she had been Emmeline too and not Emmeline, just a soul or an angel. Whatever it was it was conscious and felt full of love and light and understanding. And peace. But it was hard now to understand and make sense of the details, as if already everything about Emmeline's life was becoming blurry again. The only thing Clara knew for certain was that there was a sense of calm in the in-between, preceded and followed by a flash of light and a loud static BAM, like electrical wires exploding.

After Clara and Dr. Goldberg drank some water and Clara explained her in-between experience, Dr. Goldberg explained what she'd learned in the past months about past-life regression and the time in between lives with guides that spoke through the hypnotized. "There is much data and studies from scientists, researchers, professors, other psychiatrists and authors in a variety of disciplines," Dr. Goldberg informed Clara—as if trying to convince herself as well that what they'd just experienced was real.

Then, Dr. Goldberg replayed the recording of the session for Clara, and both of them were silent, looking at each other with a strange knowing that required no words.

Finally, Clara broke the silence. "I'm sorry that happened to you. To your son. And your family."

"I don't know how you could've known," Dr. Goldberg whispered, shaken all over again. "That was why we moved from Chicago. Afterwards. After he died. We never talk about it. Except with our daughter and family or friends who bring it up. It was too painful there, in Chicago, so we came to New York. Did you know? Had you heard? Seamus...?"

"I didn't. No," Clara confirmed. Clara didn't know anything about Dr. Goldberg's personal life besides the photos and diplomas on the walls.

Clara and Dr. Goldberg were astonished, realizing the magnitude of what this meant—that there was a continuum to life, to the soul, to the love between souls. And that all this suffering we humans cause ourselves is for naught—the feeling of loss, the longing, the holding onto moments we want to bring back, our loved ones, past joys—because it's all still there and continues to be, somehow, even if it's invisible to the naked eye, even if it's incomprehensible to the human mind. It's hiding all around us like a cosmic secret that only our hearts can experience.

Clara and Dr. Goldberg paused and took this all in, realizing also that there had to be an all-knowing, loving force ready to help us if we let it, if we simply could shine a light on our truths instead of making monsters out of them. All of them. No judgment. No monsters.

Dr. Goldberg finally put down her thoughts, reigning in her emotions. She wasn't doing it very well, but it was a start. "How do you feel, Clara?" she asked. "I'm sorry. I wasn't expecting that—that I would be so impacted and get so emotional. It's unprofessional."

"I don't think you could help it," Clara smiled. Dr. Goldberg's eyes filled with gratitude. "I mean, whoever that was, the Everyone, didn't exactly seem worried about any sort of decorum or manners," Clara said and let out a small laugh.

Which made Dr. Goldberg laugh too. Relief. Finally. Able to breathe.

Clara beamed—once again, the elixir of humor was there.

"Okay, okay, yes," said Dr. Goldberg. "I'm human too. Thank you. And you're too hard on yourself. Give yourself a break to be human as well."

And as Dr. Goldberg's words reached Clara, Clara felt her heart clutch and the sadness of Emmeline wash over her again. Tears filled her eyes. "She's the one that doesn't know how to be human—Emmeline," Clara said to Dr. Goldberg. "She feels like she's a monster. Unseen. Unheard for what she truly is. Unable to recover herself. And she feels shame. For keeping herself bound. For hurting herself. For not speaking her truth. Because if she does and she flies again, he will be hurt and alone and left behind in the dust."

"Derek?"

"Yes. Just like you do for your son."

Dr. Goldberg stopped. Pain. Sadness. She tried to hide it. But this time, Clara saw through the glasses with the thick, black frames. And Clara got up without thinking and gave Dr. Goldberg a hug. And Dr. Goldberg let her. And while she held Dr. Goldberg tight, Clara said, "Do you think you can unbind your wings, Dr. Goldberg? And let yourself fly?"

Dr. Goldberg pulled back and looked at Clara. "I don't know," she admitted.

"That's okay," Clara told her, just like Dr. Goldberg had told Emmeline. "It's a start."

"Yes, it is," agreed Dr. Goldberg. "No more monsters."

Clara nodded, feeling Emmeline tugging at her heart.

"And do you think you can unbind your wings, Emmeline?" Dr. Goldberg asked.

"I don't know," Clara said.

"Clara?" Dr. Goldberg wondered.

"Yes, it's me. And I just want Emmeline to be free."

50

The Unbinding

Clara waited for the prison officer at the desk to call her name. It seemed to be taking forever. At least ten other people had been called before her, some with families and children in tow. She didn't know what she was going to say to Derek, but she knew Emmeline's freedom depended on it, depended on shining a light on her truth and letting her voice be heard.

Finally, the guard shouted, "Derek Dunne guest."

That was her. She stood up and followed another guard into the meeting area of the prison where she could talk to Derek. She sat in a hard chair. He approached on the other side of the glass and sat down. He smiled but his eyes showed what was in his heart: a wounded, hopeless young man who had lost his parents and youth too early. And that's all Clara could see.

They made small talk about baby Lucia, and Clara laughed and blushed, but it was as if Derek were hollow. The emptiness pulled on Clara's heart like an anchor, an anchor strapped to the tie binding the wings of Emmeline's soul. And as the anchor sank further under the weight of Derek's sorrow, it squeezed the binding tighter and tighter. Clara let herself experience it until it began to take her breath away.

Then, she began what she came for: "Okay, Derek, enough small talk. I didn't come here for me," she said. "I came here for Emmeline McGuire."

Derek froze.

"Don't ask me how I know this," Clara continued. "Please, just listen. Okay?"

Pain crossed Derek's face. He steeled himself. And nodded.

"Emmeline McGuire loved Derek Dunne. Like a brother," Clara told him and felt the binding pull taught. "But she did love you," Clara went on. "And your family. And Seamus...she loved him most of all. A true, deep love with many beautiful angles. But she wasn't ready. She was too young to understand." Clara felt a chill and saw Emmeline walk up beside her and come into her. She felt what Emmeline was feeling as if they were one but kept talking with her own voice, Clara's voice, as if she were holding Emmeline tight and giving her courage to do what she was afraid of. "She didn't know how to handle it," Clara told Derek. "Your parents' death. And your sorrow."

Derek felt heat rising inside himself—the self-hatred that had become a part of his being. He held it down with all his might. "Continue," he said.

"You were the lifeblood of that family, the joy. And you and your family were Emmeline's joy too. Emmeline McGuire was seen in your family, and you all gave her a gift—of loving her, hearing her, supporting her—and that gave her freedom and life. And when your parents passed, that was lost. And she was devastated."

Derek nodded. The truth burning. The steel in his armor cracking.

"But worse for Emmeline was your pain," Clara continued.

Derek's jaw clenched.

"She knew you gave up."

He felt a stab to his heart.

"That you were desperate."

The knife twisted.

"That you thought she could help. That she could fill that hole. Because you couldn't take it that your parents were gone and you couldn't believe that there was hope beyond." Clara felt Emmeline's anger and frustration rise inside her.

While Derek's armor crumbled, the fury flaring around the edges, singeing every part of his being.

"Emmeline bound her own wings so you could fly," Clara continued. "But when you didn't, she panicked. She flirted with you because she saw your joy, your heart open when you were together. She was still alive when she hit her head. And you didn't hear her. Her breath. Her heart."

Derek's self-hatred broke through. He cried out in rage.

"She called you a monster because she was afraid. Of you. Of herself. Of what she was doing to herself. Binding herself. Not being herself. Even though she loved you. And only wants your pain to stop. But she needs you to fly. On your own. And you buried her alive."

Derek grabbed his ears. He couldn't bear any more. The self-hatred and shame were too much.

Clara felt Emmeline rise inside her, and Emmeline shouted through Clara's lips, "You didn't hear me! And you buried me alive!"

"I'm sorry, I'm sorry," Derek pleaded.

A guard looked over but didn't say anything.

"And you couldn't handle the pain," Emmeline's voice seethed, whispering from Clara's lips, choked with tears, "You..." She shook her head. "I wanted you to stop. To come back. For you to come back and find me in that coffin. In the world. I wanted to live. I wanted you to live. And not give up. And not be so afraid that there was nothing good in the world. You gave up on Seamus. And me. And your parents. And love. Love that binds us all together. Forever."

"No!" Derek shouted, slamming his hands on the table before him, standing up as if he were going to jump through the glass. "I didn't mean it!"

"And you gave up on yourself!" Emmeline shouted back, full of fury, standing too. Their eyes meeting. "And that's why you couldn't hear me. You were so afraid of yourself and hated yourself so much for hurting your parents that you couldn't hear what was right in front of you." Tears crashed through Emmeline's anger and ran down her face. She sat back down. Trembling.

Derek watched her, breaking inside. He sat back down.

And then, Emmeline said, "And I forgive you."

The air was sucked out of the room.

And Emmeline's voice became very small: "And now, I have to forgive myself."

Clara felt Emmeline sink down inside herself and weep. Then, Clara looked up and saw her own reflection in the glass pane in front of her, the glass between herself and Derek. And the person she saw staring back was Emmeline. Clara was Emmeline. And she had wings, attached at her shoulder blades and bound by rope above her head—giant, powerful, strong. As if she were an imprisoned dragonfly. Clara hadn't been able to see them before, but now, she could. Now that she knew about them, it was obvious. Emmeline looked vulnerable and ashamed and like she was the one in prison.

Clara looked past the reflection at Derek and heard him say, "Thank you."

And in that moment, for the first time, Clara owned every bit of Emmeline's feelings, and they rose into her throat, and she whispered again to Derek, "I forgive you." Then, she felt the tie on her heart loosening, like it had been cut. And the tie on Derek's heart fell away too.

And the anchor of pain crashed to the floor.

And Clara whispered to Emmeline in the reflection, "Emmeline McGuire, please fly," voice cracking, filled with emotion, fragile. "Please go and be your beautiful self. No monstrous dragon to fear. Warrior girl doing her thing."

Emmeline stood up next to Clara, and the ties on her wings fell to the ground. They spread out, now wings like an angel. Powerful. Enormous.

Clara gasped as if breathing for the first time. And Clara saw Emmeline laugh with joy and fade away.

Clara got up and started to go, then stopped. She turned back to Derek for a moment. "Emmeline had the same birthmark as I do, didn't she?" Clara asked.

Derek nodded. And they both knew.

And Clara walked out without looking back, her warrior wings of power carrying her forward.

51

Flight

Clara left the prison and got in her car and drove all the way out to the Dunne house next to the lake. She found the key in the little pocket in her bag and went in. The space was a bit musty but nothing a little airing out couldn't fix. Maybe this place could be full of life and love again, she thought. *We'll see*, she told herself and dug through her bag and pulled out a pregnancy test.

Clara was nervous and exhaled, trying to blow out the jitters. She went into the downstairs bathroom with the cute green curtains, pulled the wand out of the box and sat on the toilet.

"Here we go, Emmeline," she said, toying with herself as she let some of the pee out before sticking the wand under the flow. After eight seconds of dousing, she pulled the wand back out, finished peeing, wiped, rinsed off her hand and waited, heart racing, wondering what Emmeline would do.

"Okay, let's do this," Clara finally said out loud and picked up the wand. There it was: two lines. She was pregnant. "Oh my god," Clara whispered and laughed with joy, then looked around, waiting. Waiting for Emmeline. But nothing happened. She didn't appear. "Wow," Clara said, realizing that maybe Emmeline was actually gone.

She laughed. This was so strange. Then, she looked at herself in the mirror. She took in her light-brown skin, more golden now from the sun. She looked at her wild, curly, black hair. And she felt beautiful. And she laughed again, and said, "Emmeline, if this is a girl, let's call her Anna, after your warrior girl, because I know she's going to be feisty, smart as a whip and clever too. And she's going to fly like you. And so am I."

And for a second, Clara saw her face morph into Emmeline's, a shimmering spirit. Emmeline laughed. And then her spirit moved to the side so she was next to Clara, their shoulders overlapping. Emmeline smiled. And Clara knew that Emmeline was actually free. She looked like the girl on the bike again, so joyful. "Thank you, our warrior girl, with a clever sense of humor," Clara told Emmeline. And Emmeline replied with a smile so warm Clara could feel the heat. "I will keep your characters alive," Clara told her. "In a new game and on a dress. And there will be peace and joy in the land."

And Emmeline with her smile slowly faded away.

Clara laughed, knowing this was absurd. And she took her pregnancy wand and went out into the guesthouse and sat in the bright-orange chair and turned on Seamus's beloved old computer. As it booted up, Clara perused the photos that she'd developed in her dark room—the ones that she'd taken of Emmeline. Of course, Emmeline was nowhere to be found in the images. It made her laugh.

Then, she looked at the photos she'd taken of Mrs. Lee, the lookie-loo neighbor being a lookie-loo, peeking out her window, peeking in a neighbor's car and over the fence. They were hilarious, and Clara knew they'd make a great coffee table book.

When the first screen appeared on the old computer, she typed in "REX" and perused the dragon game. She stopped when she found a rudimentary image of the dragon, the warrior girl and the knight and took a photo with her phone. "We're gonna make a new and bigger version of this game, Emmeline. Your light is gonna shine. And it's gonna be fun. And everyone will know that the monster is only a monster if you're afraid of it. Because really, all the monster ever wants is love too." Clara beamed with excitement and texted the photos to Seamus: *We're doing this! New version. Dragon hero and warrior girl, breathing the fire of love. And she will have a birthmark—a wound from an elk's antler, an elk who was afraid of her, protecting himself from her because he thought she was a monster. So, he gouged her belly before she proved with love that she was just a warrior. All souls that come from her have this beautiful reminder that love beats time. Like mine! Like KAPOW! And...baby two is on the way. Also, what do you think if we took a trip to St. Petersburg? I know that sounds out of the blue, but I've always wanted to go to Russia. Also, note the subtle Slavic style in Emmeline's drawings. We're going with that too.*

Next, Clara texted Greta the photo of Emmeline's characters and told her: *I have an idea for a new line of dresses! These three characters plus some neo-trad Ruskie, Slavskie, funskie goddesses and bobbly things. Stay tuned. I'm back! :) xox*

Then, Clara walked out of the guesthouse with new joy in her being and a smile on her face, totally self-amused, door slamming behind her, feeling like herself again, finally. She looked at the gazebo and the lake and boathouse and the tree-filled valley and imagined her whole family having a lazy BBQ on the grass—two girls running around chasing Seamus, a newborn in her arms, Billy, Mrs. Flannery, Greta and Hank, Erin and family playing badminton, and her own laughter filling the air. And the sound of giant wings, invisible but definitely there.

It was a joyful day full of love.

And Clara knew that one day it would be hers.

Just like she knew that all days of the past were hers too.
And so was now. It was all love.

Many, many thanks to:

The friends who throw magnificent cheerleading lightning bolts and love to talk about life, spirit, love and the universe, in no particular lightning-bolt order: Jessica Herbert, Jenny Zepp, Monica Johnson, Kathy Nolan, Kristy DiPaola, Velvet Phillips Sullivan, and Zvezdana Popovic.

Toni Eyeler for the ongoing cheerleading lightning bolts and for loving this story and encouraging me to put it out there. You really make a difference that keeps me going!

My fabulous manager Seth Nagel at 5X Media.

Everyone at Earnest Parc Press.

Nicole Schubert is an award-winning author and screenwriter with a soft spot for comedy and romance. Her debut novel, Blues Harp Green, delved into coming-of-age and family issues and received Independent Publisher and Readers' Favorite Award nods. Her second novel, Saoirse Berger's Bookish Lens in La La Land, a romcom about a teen in a film industry family, also won a Readers' Favorite Award. Nicole occasionally dabbles in other behind-the-scenes activities, like acting in the Orson Wells' A Christmas Carol radio play with the Gypsy Theatre Guild or producing Improv Diary Show at Santa Monica's Westside Comedy Theater. She produced a music awards TV show and European-wide photo exhibition out of Brussels and enjoyed another side of storytelling working in the editing rooms of numerous Hollywood feature films. Nicole lives with her family —including The Kid—in Montana and Los Angeles, by way of Brussels and New Orleans, where she was born during a hurricane. Visit her at **nicoleschubertwrites.com**.